PRAISE FOR DIANE KELLY'S
PAW ENFORCEMENT SERIES

"Funny and acerbic, the perfect read for lovers of Janet Evanovich."   —*Librarian and Reviewer*

"Humor, romance, and surprising LOL moments. What more can you ask for?"   —*Romance and Beyond*

"Fabulously fun and funny!"   —*Book Babe*

"An engaging read that I could not put down. I look forward to the next adventure of Megan and Brigit!"
                    —*SOS Aloha* on *Paw Enforcement*

"Sparkling with surprises. Just like a tequila sunrise. You never know which way is up or out!"
                    —*Romance Junkies* on *Paw and Order*

P9-DNE-327

LAYING DOWN THE PAW

Diane Kelly

St. Martin's Paperbacks

This is a work of fiction. All of the characters, organizations, and events portrayed in this novel are either products of the author's imagination or are used fictitiously.

LAYING DOWN THE PAW

Copyright © 2015 by Diane Kelly.

All rights reserved.

For information address St. Martin's Press, 175 Fifth Avenue, New York, NY 10010.

ISBN: 978-1-250-04836-3

Printed in the United States of America

St. Martin's Paperbacks edition / August 2015

St. Martin's Paperbacks are published by St. Martin's Press, 175 Fifth Avenue, New York, NY 10010.

10 9 8 7 6 5 4 3 2 1

To Sandra Castro, a good friend whose dogs are much *better behaved than mine.*

ACKNOWLEDGMENTS

First off, many, many thanks to my brilliant editor, Holly Ingraham, for your smart and insightful suggestions. Working with you is always a pleasure! Thanks also to Eileen Rothschild for your help in wrapping up the work on this book!

Thanks to Sarah Melnyck, Paul Hochman, and the rest of the team at St. Martin's who worked to put this book into readers' hands. You're fantastic!

Thanks to Danielle Fiorella and Jennifer Taylor for creating such fun book covers!

Thanks to my agent, Helen Breitwieser, for all of your work in furthering my writing career!

Thanks to fellow authors Hadley Holt, Celya Bowers, Kennedy Shaw, Sherrel Lee, Angela Harris, and Trinity Blake. You ladies are a wonderful support system!

Thanks to Liz Bemis-Hittinger of Bemis Promotions for my great Web site and newsletters. You're the best!

Thanks to my fellow members of Romance Writers of America and the dedicated, hardworking national office staff. A writer couldn't ask for a better organization to put her on the track to success!

And finally, thanks to my readers. I love connecting with you through the books, and I hope you'll enjoy this latest adventure with Megan and Brigit!

ONE
NO DOGS ALLOWED

Fort Worth Police Officer Megan Luz

At nine thirty on Sunday morning, I sat at the card table in the kitchen in my tiny studio apartment with a pen in my hand, circling or drawing an X over each ad in the *Fort Worth Star-Telegram* rental real estate section. My partner/roommate/BFF, Brigit, lay at my feet, her pointy teeth making short work of the chew treat she held between her two front paws.

The enormous German shepherd mix was the reason I'd jogged over to the 7-Eleven for a copy of the newspaper this morning. The hundred-pound beast needed more space than our current home provided, as well as a yard to run and poop in. The energetic dog had chewed up at least a dozen pairs of my shoes while we'd lived here. Did I mention that in addition to being my partner, roommate, and best friend, she was also at times a pain in the butt? I could never stay angry at her, though. Not when she'd look up at me with those big, brown eyes and wag her tail.

Blurgh.

I'm such a sucker.

While Brigit happily gnawed her treat below me, overhead my upstairs neighbor flushed his toilet for the third time this morning. *Flushhh.* Were there no drugs for a bad prostate? Still, I'd take his repeated flushing over the *bam-bam-bam* that came through my floor on occasion, courtesy of the Congolese immigrant who lived below me. At the slightest noise, he'd whip out his broom and bang the handle against the ceiling. Never mind that I was rarely the offender. Okay, so maybe Brigit needing more space wasn't the only reason for relocating. I could use some more space, too. Or at least space that didn't involve sharing walls, floors, and ceilings.

I'd made appointments to see one place at three o'clock, another at four thirty, and a third at six o'clock today, but it was possible none of those would work out. My gaze continued down the listings. Given that the newspaper charged by the character for their ads, landlords tended to use abbreviations. Some of the abbreviations, such as *bd* for bedroom and *ba* for bath, were easily decipherable. Others, like *g/a* and *frog* and *prq*, not so much. Did Brigit and I want a place with a *g/a* or *frog* or *prq*? I had no idea.

Here's an ad that looked promising.

3 bd 1.5 ba big yd S Hulen. $975/mo.

But, alas, the next sentence earned the ad a big X.

No pets.

Damn.

Though we shared an apartment, a bed, and an occasional bowl of popcorn, technically Brigit wasn't my pet. She was a full-fledged officer of the Fort Worth Police Department, just like me. Heck, the dog outranked me.

But, while she was well trained and behaved impeccably on the job, she was still a dog. Despite their extensive training, police K-9s didn't become some type of robot any more than trained human officers did. The K-9 cops still did normal dog things, like dig holes and scratch doors and hork up yucky things on the carpet. Better to have a landlord who was tolerant of animals.

Below me, Brigit lifted her head, her ears pricked. She turned to face the door and stood, her tail whipping side to side with glee as she trotted over to look out the window. *Woof! Woof-woof!* No need to wait for Seth's knock with Brigit announcing their arrival.

I glanced at the clock on my microwave. They were a half hour early. That could only mean one thing. Seth was anxious to see me. *Good.* I was anxious to see him, too. If I had a tail, it would be whipping side to side just like Brigit's.

I walked over to the door and opened it as Seth and Blast stepped onto the landing outside. Seth wore tennis shoes, jeans, and a green Henley that brought out the color of his eyes and was fitted just enough to accentuate his shoulders. An avid swimmer whose best stroke was the butterfly, Seth sported shoulders as broad as they were strong. Blast, his Labrador retriever, wore a black collar imprinted with red fire hydrants. Both man and dog had short blond hair, square jaws, and muscular builds, looking as alike as a man and his dog could given that they were different species. But while Blast's chin sported only whiskers, Seth's had a subtle, sexy dimple, à la Ben Affleck.

Though it was early in February, the day was unseasonably bright, cool but comfortable. A light breeze blew past, carrying the scents of motor oil, dust, and garbage up from the parking lot. *Ew.* Still, the temperature was pleasant. The weather in the Lone Star State could change on a dime, though, going from calm and temperate to violently stormy in an instant. We had a say-ing here in Texas—*if you don't like the weather, just wait ten minutes.*

Brigit bolted out the door as soon as the space was wide enough for her to squeeze through. She ran up to Blast, her back half wriggling from side to side so rapidly and with such force she threatened to snap in two. Shameless, yet a part of me envied her for being a species that wasn't afraid to show its feelings. Humans could be so wary and guarded.

Especially humans like Seth and me.

My brown eyes met his green ones and held for a long moment, as if each of us was trying to mentally feel the other out. Last night, he'd asked if he could come by this morning so we could "sort things out."

What "things" needed "sorting out?" Long story short, last autumn, after we'd dated loosely for several weeks and I'd begun to fall—*hard*—for Seth, he had suddenly ended things for no apparent reason, leaving me confused, lonely, and heartsick. I hadn't seen him again until New Year's Eve when, as a member of the Fort Worth Fire Department's bomb squad, he'd rescued me after a nut job tied me to a carousel horse at the Shoppes at Chisholm Trail mall with a ticking time bomb strapped to my chest. What a way to bring in the new year, huh?

After saving my life, Seth said he wanted to see me again. I'd agreed—*how could I not?*—but on the condi-tion that we could see other people, too. I hadn't been ready to put all my eggs in one basket. Smart move on my part, because it left me free to have some fun with Clint McCutcheon, a good-looking bronc-buster/deputy sheriff who, like me, had been assigned to work the stock show and rodeo. My relationship with the deputy had not set well with Seth, which I took to mean the guy was more emotionally invested in me than I'd realized. If

I had to hazard a guess, Seth had reached the same conclusion. After winning the bronc-riding championship last night, Clint informed me he planned to resign from law enforcement and head out on the rodeo circuit. Though we'd had some fun, it was clear the deputy and I were not soul mates. We parted with no hard feelings.

So here were Seth and I, preparing to "sort things out."

"'Mornin', Megan," Seth said in greeting, his deep voice, as always, causing a little spark inside me.

I tilted my head. "You're a half hour early."

He quirked his brows, a mischievous grin spreading across his face. "I was hoping to catch you coming out of the shower."

"Too late for that." I was dry and fully dressed, though I had left my long, dark hair hanging free and loose, the way Seth liked it.

He reached out a hand, took a lock between his fingers, and tentatively toyed with it, eyeing me all the while, assessing my reaction. He held it to his nose. "Mmm. Peaches."

The fruity scent was courtesy of Brigit's flea shampoo, which I'd discovered left my hair soft, shiny, and—yes—pest free. But let's keep this little secret between us, shall we?

When he finally released my hair, I patted my leg and called the dogs, who ran into and around my apartment, barking up a storm. *Ruff! Ruff-ruff! Ruff!*

Bam-bam-bam!

Seriously, did my downstairs neighbor stand in the middle of his place all day with his broom in his hand?

Ignoring the banging from below, I closed the door behind us and turned back to Seth. "Want some coffee?"

"There's only one thing I want." He stepped toward me, a gleam in his eyes. *"You."*

Instinctively, I stepped backward, looking up at Seth. My breaths came fast as my butt hit the door. I could go no further, but Seth kept right on coming. He wrapped a warm hand behind my neck and captured my mouth with his, not just kissing me, but *claiming* me.

And damn if I didn't like it.

Seth hadn't exactly been the perfect boyfriend. It's not that he cheated on me or lied to me or that I'd caught him dressing up in my high heels and lace underwear. He'd simply been closed, keeping me at arm's length emotionally, which caused me no end of frustration. But he hadn't been an ass on purpose. As I'd recently learned, Seth had been abandoned by his mother as a child and left to be raised by his grandparents. His grandmother, who'd been the one saving grace in his life, the one person he could count on, had died when Seth was a teenager, leaving him alone with a grandfather who was cold and aloof. Seth had never had a relationship with his father, didn't even know who the man was. Add in several tours of duty in Afghanistan as an army explosive ordnance disposal specialist, and the guy had seen more than his share of heartache and loss.

Given his history, it was no wonder Seth suffered attachment issues and wasn't the best at relationships. I couldn't fault him too much. Besides, I wasn't exactly the poster child for emotional stability myself. I was short-tempered and overly self-reliant, priding myself—*perhaps too much*—on my ability to survive on my own.

But everyone can change, right?

When we came up for air, Seth pressed his forehead to mine. "I want you all to myself. No more deputies. No one else, either. Deal?"

Despite the fact that he looked like a one-eyed Cyclops up close like this, he was nonetheless sexy as hell. And he was finally being honest and open about his feelings. I knew that must have been difficult for him. Unable to resist, I found myself saying, "Okay."

He took a small step back and gazed down at me, the look in his eyes softening. "I'm not real good at these things," he said. "But I want to be what you need, Megan."

Before I could stop it, an airy half snort, half laugh escaped me. "That's really sweet, Seth. But I don't *need* anyone." Hey, I only said people *can* change. I didn't say I'd necessarily change immediately. Old habits die hard, after all.

The hurt look that flickered across Seth's face caused a pang of guilt to slice through me. He had probably thought long and hard about what to say to me this morning. I shouldn't have shot him down so quickly. It was the knee-jerk reaction of a long-term loner, of the now-grown woman who, as a young girl, had suffered a horrible stutter that caused her to be a pitied outcast and who'd learned, as a result, to be self-sufficient and independent.

"Everyone needs someone for something," Seth said, surprising me again by his candor. The guy must have done some serious soul-searching over the past month.

"What do *you* need?" I asked. When he didn't respond right away, I looked up into his face, searching for answers.

His green eyes narrowed as if he were thinking, trying to figure out himself what he needed from me. Apparently, his soul-searching had only gone so far. "I don't know exactly," he said finally. "I only know that, whatever it is, you seem to have it."

"Oh, Seth!" I spurted out a satisfied sigh, blinking back happy tears. "That's so . . . sweet."

He stepped back, his face flushing slightly as if he were embarrassed to have bared himself. "Can we be done for now? All this lovey-dovey stuff is making my testicles shrivel."

"You're such a romantic." I rolled my eyes, though secretly I was thrilled he'd gone as far as he had.

Brigit ran between us, Blast chasing after her, putting an end to our intimate interlude.

"Why don't we take them to the dog park?" Seth suggested. "Let them burn off some of that energy."

"Good idea." I grabbed the newspaper and my purse and retrieved Brigit's leash, calling her over and clipping it to her collar.

After locking up my apartment, I squeezed past one of my neighbors, a black man who'd decided to enjoy the brief respite from winter to sit on the steps in his boxer shorts and smoke a cigarette. The residents of Eastside Arms didn't stand on formalities. Most had long rap sheets, low credit scores, and sketchy employment histories. As a college graduate with good credit, I was an anomaly. I'd moved into the place hoping the low rent would enable me to pay off my student loans quickly. So much for that plan, huh?

I followed Seth across the lot to his car, a seventies-era blue Nova with orange flames pointed down the side and license plates that read KABOOM. The car was simultaneously ridiculous and badass. It had a vinyl bench seat in front, which was held together with several strips of duct tape. Ditto for the dashboard, which had long since cracked in the relentless Texas summer heat.

He held the back door open while the dogs jumped in, then opened the passenger door for me. He lifted his chin to indicate the newspaper in my hands. "What's with the paper?"

I slid into the seat. "I'm looking for a place to rent. A house with a yard. Brigit would be happier in a bigger place." So would I. My efficiency apartment might be affordable, but the place lacked charm. And hot water. And insulation. My heating bills had been astronomical this winter.

Seth closed the door, circled around the front of the car, and climbed in the driver's side, picking up the conversation where we'd left off. "Where are you planning to look? Around here?"

Though I'd like to live close to work and avoid commuter traffic, my options for rentals that allowed pets were limited. I'd have to take what I could get, where I could get it. "Ideally I'd love to live in W1," I said, referencing my assigned police district. "But I didn't see anything in the area that allowed pets."

Seth didn't have to worry about Blast impacting his living arrangements. He lived in his grandparents' house in east Fort Worth, along with his grandfather, whom I'd surmised was both an old curmudgeon and had suffered PTSD since the Vietnam War.

Seth backed out of the space and drove to the dog park. Brigit and Blast stood in the back, tails smacking against the backseat with a *whap-whap-whap* as we pulled into a space. Seth and I retrieved our canine partners, led them through the double gates, and unclipped their leashes.

"Hey." I lifted a hand to greet a redheaded woman I knew only as Bruiser's Mom. Bruiser was a small, neutered Boston terrier with big balls, metaphorically speaking. He routinely picked fights with dogs three times his size. Fortunately, none of them took the little pip-squeak seriously.

After giving only a passing glance to Bruiser, Brigit trotted over to say hello to a couple of the other regulars, a poodle-pinscher mix named Delilah and a fluffy-haired chow named Tina, after Tina Turner. The trio wagged their tails, sniffed each other's butts, and chased each other around in circles. Blast, meanwhile, reacquainted himself with a speckled heeler, a black lab mix, and an apricot poodle.

After spending a few minutes in idle chitchat with the

other dog mommies and daddies, Seth and I began to walk around the perimeter of the park.

As we walked, Seth nudged my hip with his. "Valentine's Day is this coming Saturday."

I cut a glance his way and raised a brow in question.

"I thought we could go to Reata," he said.

The Reata restaurant was a famous steakhouse, but it also served an incredible vegetable plate that would satisfy even the most diehard carnivore.

"Sounds great," I replied. "I work that day, but I'm off at five."

"I'll make a late reservation."

We walked back and forth along the park fence a dozen times before our dogs came looking for us, a sign that they'd had their fun, worn themselves out, and were ready to go. After loading them into the car, he leaned in. "You two hungry?"

Woof! Woof-woof!

"I'll take that as a 'yes.'"

We climbed into our seats and Seth drove to a nearby burger place, pulling into the drive-thru lane. He unrolled his window and leaned his head out to call into the speaker. "Two plain double-meat burgers."

A garbled voice came back. "You want fries with that?"

Brigit stuck her head over the seat. *Woof-woof!*

Seth cast a glance at her, chuckled, and leaned out the window a second time. "Sure. Two large fries."

Seth insisted on paying for Brigit's lunch even though the department added an amount to my paychecks to cover the cost of her care. Who was I to argue? The beast ate way more than the stipend would ever cover.

The dogs' lunch taken care of, Seth turned to me. "How's Mexican sound?"

"Muy delicioso."

As Seth aimed his car for Chuy's, a popular Mexican restaurant just west of downtown, I reached into the white food bag, the paper crinkling as I removed the burgers. I tore the burgers into bite-sized pieces and fed them to the dogs. "Wait your turn," I scolded Brigit when she tried to snatch a chunk intended for Blast.

I finished feeding the dogs as Seth pulled into a curbside parking place across the street from Chuy's. Peeking into the burger bag, I groaned and held up my greasy fingers. "They forgot the napkins."

Brigit and Blast seized the opportunity to get one last taste of meat. *Slurp. Slurp-slurp-slurp.* Their tongues might be germy but they were effective.

We left the dogs in the car with the windows cracked and went inside. I made a quick stop at the ladies' room to wash my hands with hot water and soap, then joined Seth at a table near the window where we could keep an eye on the car and make sure Brigit and Blast weren't eating the seats.

We placed our orders and made small talk for a few minutes until the waitress returned with our food. She set our steaming plates down in front of us. "Here you go. Enjoy."

Seth glanced down at the tortilla and turned his plate 180 degrees to face me. "Say hello to Willie Nelson."

I took a look. Sure enough, the brown parts looked like a man with a bushy beard. "I think it's less Willie Nelson and more Karl Marx."

"How do you know what Karl Marx looks like?"

"Randy Dunham," I replied. Randy was the sociopath who'd strapped explosives to my chest. The guy hadn't even bought me dinner first. *Jerk.* "We found a copy of *The Communist Manifesto* in his bedroom when we searched it."

The copy had been worn and dog-eared, several passages highlighted with yellow marker. Because I'd been the one to take Randy down, the higher-ups allowed me to go along with the detectives and crime scene techs when they gathered evidence at his home.

Seth picked up his quesadilla and took a big bite, essentially scalping Willie or Karl with his teeth.

"Pareidolia," I said, with a shrug. "Weird how the brain works, isn't it?"

Seth swallowed, splayed his fingers on either side of his head, and emitted an explosive sound. "Kapow! You just blew my mind."

I read a lot and tended to retain random information, most of it useless. But occasionally some of the information proved helpful.

"Pareidolia is the tendency for people to see faces in inanimate objects."

He nodded and took a sip of his soda. "Is there a word for seeing sexual organs in inanimate objects?"

"Ew." I cringed. "Do we *need* a word for that?"

Seth shrugged this time. "You always hear about people saying something looks like guy junk or girly parts. You know, like butternut squash or tacos."

I shook my head and waved a hand as if to clear the air of this ludicrous conversation. "Moving on topic-wise." I held up the newspaper, which remained folded to the rental section. "I'm going to see three p-places this afternoon. Can you come with me? You might notice things I don't." After all, women tended to focus on things like wallpaper and closet space, while men tended to notice dripping faucets or dry rot. I'd already lived in one hellhole. I didn't want to move into another.

He cocked his head, his gaze heated and intent as he eyed me. "I'll come if you promise me a sleepover."

My eyes flickered to his soft lips, his broad shoulders,

and back again. *Yeah, I can definitely see myself waking up to him.* "Okay. I promise you a sleepover. I just don't promise *when*."

A slow, sexy grin spread across his lips. "I'll take it."

TWO
DOG DAY AFTERNOON

FWPD Sergeant Brigit

The dog days of summer were so called because the star Sirius, also known as the "Dog Star," in the constellation Canis Major, was most visible in the summer months in the Northern Hemisphere. Of course, though Megan knew this, Brigit did not and wouldn't have given a cat's ass about it anyway. All that mattered to Brigit was that she'd been taken for some fun playtime at the dog park, fed a nice lunch, and was now dozing peacefully in the backseat of Seth's Nova, using Blast's butt as a pillow.

If life never got any better than this, she'd still die a happy dog.

THREE
MY TWO DADS

Dub

Sunday afternoon, Dub ran down the basketball court at the YMCA, faking left, then dribbling right. But his moves weren't quick enough. Trent, one of his foster dads, slapped the ball away and took off in the other direction. Dub turned and ran after him.

When Trent reached the basket, he performed a slam dunk followed by a celebration dance involving goofy knee lifts and arm rotations. *Show-off.*

Dub jogged up to the basket. "I didn't think gay dudes were supposed to be good at sports."

"And I didn't think black boys were supposed to suck at them," Trent said, chuckling as he ruffled Dub's dark curly hair.

"I'm only half black."

"Then you should only suck half as much as you do."

Wesley, Dub's other foster dad, finally caught up with them. His face was red and sweaty. He bent over to put his hands on his knees. "You two are going to give me a heart attack."

Trent scoffed. "You're going to give *yourself* a heart attack. I've tried to get you to work out with me and you always say no. You've got no one to blame for your big ass but yourself."

"And Mrs. Butterworth," Dub added.

Wes raised a hand from his knee and pointed a finger at Dub. "You leave her out of this. She's the only woman I'll ever love."

"Her and Aunt Jemima," Trent said. "I caught you having a three-way with them in the kitchen this morning."

Trent and Wes might be a couple, but like all men they gave each other crap. Three months ago, Dub had been released from McFadden Ranch, a halfway house for juveniles. He'd thought going to live with a gay couple would be totally lame. But it turned out to be dope. Trent was an architect who drove a Hummer, worked out every day, and, like Dub, liked to watch sports on TV. Wesley taught biology at Tarrant County Community College. He had more fat than muscles, but he was really smart. He helped Dub with his homework. He didn't even mind when he had to explain things two or three times before Dub got it.

Dub had three burglary convictions and a felony drug offense on his record, and he knew the men had taken a chance taking him in. Both were in their late thirties. With no kids of their own eating up their money, they'd been able to buy some nice things. A house in the historic Fairmount neighborhood. All kinds of exercise equipment, including an adjustable treadmill and a universal gym, which they'd set up in the converted attic. An enormous high-def television and a state-of-the-art stereo, a thief's wet dream. They even had season tickets to Bass Hall and the Dallas Mavericks basketball games, plus matching sapphire-studded cuff links to go with the tuxedos they wore to charity dinners.

The two had once dragged Dub to one of the dinners. Before they'd left, Wes had schooled Dub on manners and the right way to use silverware. *Salad fork on the outside, dessert fork up top.* Wes had learned all of this stuff when he was a kid at something he called cotillion. The only things Dub had learned as a kid were how to pack up and flee in the middle of the night, and to never, ever cry, no matter how bad you wanted to. Oh, yeah. He'd also learned never to talk to cops or lawyers. They only heard what they wanted to hear.

"You stink, kid." Wes wiped sweat from his ruddy face with a white hand towel, then used it to snap Dub's butt. "So do I. Let's hit the showers."

Dub followed them to the men's locker room, bouncing in his brand-new basketball shoes. They'd come with a $130 price tag, by far the most expensive shoes Dub had ever owned. Trent said Dub needed good footwear so he wouldn't end up with blisters or bunions or fallen arches. Dub didn't even know what a bunion was. And Trent hadn't stopped at the shoes. He'd also bought Dub the latest iPhone, a closetful of new clothes, and a laptop computer. He signed them all up for a YMCA membership so Dub would have a place to play basketball, too. What more could a fifteen-year-old boy ask for?

It was the first time in Dub's life that he wanted for nothing.

Well, almost nothing . . .

Wes said he and Trent had been "blessed." Until now, Dub had been nothing but damned. But he was beginning to feel blessed, too.

Despite all the money they'd thrown around, Dub knew Trent and Wes weren't trying to buy him off. They were only trying to make his life easier, help him fit in at Paschal High School and focus on his schoolwork. Not that it was easy to do, especially with girls like Jenna

Seaver around. Dub had been held back once and none of them wanted that to happen again. But flunking sixth grade hadn't been all his fault. *It had been a really bad year . . .*

After showering at the rec center, Dub put on jeans, a blue sweater, and his basketball shoes. He slid his wallet into his back pocket and clipped the attached chain to his front left belt hoop. He probably didn't need to secure his wallet like this. After all, he no longer lived in the ghetto where someone would be looking to jump him or pick his pocket. But, you know, old habits and all that. Besides, he liked the badass look of the chain wallet.

The three of them packed up their gym bags and headed out to Trent's Hummer.

"Can I drive us home?" Dub asked when they reached the car. He gave Trent what he hoped would be a convincing smile. "You'd be the coolest dad ever if you let me drive this."

Wes had signed Dub up for driving school and taken him to get his learner's permit. He'd even taken Dub out for practice sessions every afternoon in his Honda Civic. But the Hummer? That car was Trent's baby. Dub knew his chances of ever getting to drive the Hummer were low. But no harm in asking, right? The worst Trent could do was say no.

To Dub's surprise, Trent turned to Wes. "Whaddya think?"

Wes looked at Dub before turning back to Trent. "He's been doing real well, doesn't go too fast, obeys the rules. If he practiced here in the parking lot first, got a feel for the car, I think he'd be okay."

Dub's heart began to pound in his chest. *Could this really be happening? It is!*

Trent pulled his keys from his pocket and tossed them to Dub. "Don't make me regret this."

"I won't!" Dub said. "I swear."

A minute later, Dub sat behind the wheel of the Hummer. He started the engine and put his foot to the gas.

For the first time in his life, he felt in control.

FOUR
HOUSE HUNTING

Megan

At three o'clock, Seth pulled his car up to a small but cute house on Wabash Avenue in southwest Fort Worth.

I took in the one-story, wood-frame house with bright blue shutters. "Not bad." Though certainly not *quaint*, as it had been described in the ad. *Mental note: quaint = old.*

Seth raised a finger off the steering wheel and pointed down the street. "There's a greenbelt that runs through this neighborhood. You'd have a nice place to walk Brigit."

We climbed out of the car, bringing the dogs with us. Even if she couldn't speak, Brigit should get a say in where we moved, shouldn't she? We met the property manager, a fortyish blond in a plain navy pantsuit, on the steps.

After Seth and I introduced ourselves, she looked from me, to Seth, to the dogs. "Would all of you be living here?"

"Just me." I lifted my end of Brigit's leash. "And my shepherd."

A wary look crossed the woman's face as she gave my

partner a thorough once-over. "She's much bigger than I had expected."

I wasn't sure if the woman was scared of the dog herself or simply of the destruction a huge beast like Brigit could cause, but either way it couldn't hurt to allay her fears. "She's a police K-9," I told her. "We're both officers with Fort Worth PD. She's very well trained."

Trained to sniff out drugs and chase fleeing suspects, that is. When it came to her off-duty time, the dog was a loose cannon, chewing my shoes, knocking over the garbage can and spreading trash all over the place, clawing open the pantry door and helping herself to dog treats. But this woman didn't need to know all of that. I normally believed in honesty, but in this case honesty would only keep me and Brigit from securing a lease. Better to keep my mouth shut.

The woman's lips pursed as she seemed to consider the information. "Well, let's take a tour, shall we?" She pulled a huge key ring from her purse and flipped through the numbered keys until she found the correct one. She slid the key into the dead bolt and turned it, giving it a little jiggle when it fought her. "There we go," she said when the bolt slid home. She pushed the door open and raised a palm, inviting me to lead the way.

I stepped inside and found myself in a small living room with dark wood paneling and mottled brown carpet designed to hide stains. Not exactly the bright, cheery home I would have hoped for, but not too bad, either. Seth, too, glanced around, lifting a shoulder in an *it's okay* gesture when my eyes met his. Brigit and Blast snuffled along the floor, checking things out.

An open doorway to our right led to two small wood-paneled bedrooms and a single bath with a pedestal sink. No room to set out my hot rollers or makeup. Not a deal-breaker, though. I could always add some shelves or a little table.

We continued on into the kitchen. Unlike the dark front room, the kitchen was bright. Outdated, though cheery, yellow tile covered the countertops and backsplash. The cabinets were painted a slightly lighter shade of yellow. Daisy-print wallpaper covered the walls, curling up at the edges and seams. A window over the sink looked out onto a backyard that wasn't large by any stretch of the imagination, but it would at least give Brigit a place to relieve herself and a little room to sniff around and enjoy the outdoors.

While I opened the cabinet doors to assess the shelf space, Seth opened the cabinet and peeked under the sink. "No evidence of a leak."

I stepped to the sliding glass door, unlocked it, and slid the heavy panel open. The concrete patio was cracked and uneven but, again, not a deal-breaker given my limited price range. The shallow yard was enclosed by a four-foot chain-link fence that provided a clear view into the adjoining yards and very little privacy. On the upside, the back of the yard looked out onto a small grassy hill. There was no house behind the rental. One less neighbor to deal with.

The woman, Seth, and Blast stepped outside after us.

While Seth meandered over to check the outside faucet, the woman turned to me, ready to get down to business. "We've had quite a bit of interest in this property," she said, probably lying to get a quick close to this deal and have the rest of the day off. "If you're interested," she continued, attempting to wave us back into the house as a rumbling sound began off to our right, "we should get a credit check started as soon as—"

Clack-clack-CLACK-clack. Clack-clack-CLACK-clack.

The woman's words were cut off by the rhythmic chugging of an oncoming freight train running up the rails that ran at the top of the incline. *Clack-clack-CLACK-clack.*

CLACK-CLACK-CLACK-CLACK! The orange metal of a BNSF engine roared into view, forcing us to cover our ears lest our eardrums burst.

While Blast yelped and darted back into the house, Brigit lowered the front half of her body, raised her head in the air, and began to howl. *Arooooooooooo!*

The outdated kitchen might not be a deal-breaker, but the train tracks were. I couldn't subject the poor dog, with her superior hearing, to this kind of noise on a regular basis. It would be cruel. Besides, I feared a derailment. What if a tank car carrying some type of toxic chemical rolled down the embankment and into my bedroom?

Woooooooo-woo! The engineer laid on the horn. Probably some idiot up ahead who thought he could beat the train by ignoring the warning lights and bells and crossing the tracks. At least I wasn't on duty if the idiot got splattered. I'd been on the force for just over a year, and had somehow been lucky enough so far to avoid a dead body. I'd seen some mangled ones, sure, including a guy with his arm bent the wrong way after a motorcycle– school bus collision—*freaky!*—but I'd yet to see a dead person. Of course I knew my luck would run out at some point, but was it wrong to hope that any dead persons I encountered would be old folks who'd died peacefully in their sleep with a smile on their faces?

"Come on, girl!" I hollered, my words lost in the noise. I tugged on Brigit's leash and we ran back inside, the manager and Seth on our heels. Seth shut the door behind us but the glass only marginally muffled the intense train sounds. The house vibrated like a nightclub playing techno music on a Saturday night. The motion was unnerving.

When the last *clack-clack-CLACK-clack* had clacked, I shook my head. "Thanks for your time," I told the woman. "But I'm going to keep looking."

"It's your decision." Her tone was snitty now. "But

this place will go fast. You better call me right away if you change your mind."

I wouldn't, but no need to irritate her further by saying it.

Seth, the dogs, and I headed back out to his car. We climbed in and he cranked the engine.

Sliding on his aviator-style sunglasses, he cut a glance my way. "Where to now?"

"Crowley."

"That's awfully far, isn't it?"

"We'll see. I can probably get more for my money if I'm willing to sacrifice a little convenience."

Seth drove to the I-20 entrance ramp and took it, heading east until exiting on I-35 south. Thirty minutes later we headed past an elementary school and drove slowly down a suburban street, careful to avoid the abundance of children taking advantage of the unseasonably warm weather to ride their bikes or skateboards. Or perhaps their mothers had forced them out of the house, needing a break. Brigit let out a *woof* and wagged her tail when she spotted a golden retriever lying in a driveway. The dog stood and wagged its tail in return as it watched us drive by.

We pulled up in front of a house made of red brick and ivory siding. An orange and black FOR RENT sign was stuck in the center of the yard. Though bigger than the house on Wabash, this house was nonetheless a relatively modest starter home. The structure appeared to be only about twenty years old and in good shape.

"Not bad," I said.

A middle-aged couple stood in the open garage, waiting. Seth and I climbed out of the car, retrieved the dogs from the backseat, and met the couple in the garage. After we'd introduced ourselves, I again explained that my dog and I would be the only tenants.

The woman bent down and scratched Brigit under the

chin. "Dogs are always welcome. A house isn't a home unless it's got a dog in it." She cupped her hands under Brigit's chin. "Ain't that right, girl?"

Brigit wagged her tail as if in agreement.

"Jack and I lived here when we first married," the woman said as she led us inside. "We outgrew it when we had our second child and moved to a bigger place in Burleson. It's been a great investment property. We've never had any problem finding tenants."

I could see why. Despite being modestly sized for a suburban house, the place was open and clean and bright, with three bedrooms and two bathrooms. The living room had a nice brick fireplace, the backyard a swing set and built-in sandbox, as well as plenty of shade provided by two mature Bradford pear trees.

"What do you think?" the woman asked as we stood on the back porch.

Brigit rolled on her back on the grass. It was clear that my partner liked the place.

"It's very nice," I told the woman. The couple seemed like they'd be easy landlords, too. But I wasn't quite convinced yet. "Mind if I t-take a second look?"

"Be my guest."

Seth and the husband stayed out back talking sports as the wife and I went back inside so I could make a more thorough assessment. The bathrooms had decent counter space and the closets, though not walk-ins, had more than enough room for my limited wardrobe. You don't need much in the way of work clothes when you wear a uniform every day.

Ding-dong.

"Excuse me a moment." The woman stepped away to answer the door.

I puttered in the kitchen, marveling at the cabinet space which, though certainly not excessive, put to shame the miniscule storage at my apartment. As I stood there, a young couple ventured into the house. The wife, who was only a few years older than me, had a gender-indeterminate tow-headed toddler on her hip. The toddler, in turn, had his/her thumb in his/her mouth, and his/her finger up his/her nose. Multitasking.

The young woman's mouth fell open. "Just look at this kitchen!" she called back to her husband. "It's got twice as much counter space as we have now." Her eyes went to the back windows. "There's a swing set out back, too! How great is that!"

The husband stepped to the back window. "There's room for my grill back there. And our picnic table."

Their interest cinched it for me. As nice as the house would be, it was both at the outer end of my geographic range and the upper end of my price range. What's more, given that I was currently single and childless, I'd have little in common with the young families living in the neighborhood. Besides, I could tell this couple loved the place and would fit in here much better than me. I'd let them have it.

"Thanks," I told the older woman, motioning for Seth to bring the dogs back inside when he looked through the window. "But I think this house is better suited for a family like them."

The woman nodded and gave me a smile and a wink. "Someday, hon," she said, casting a knowing glance at Seth.

Sheesh. She was getting way ahead of herself. Heck, Seth and I had only been an official couple for a matter of hours. Still, I knew she meant well so I returned her smile.

Seth and I returned to his car once again, stopping at the elementary school to let the dogs take a quick tinkle at the edge of the playground. We continued on to the last place, which was a duplex in the South Hemphill area.

"This location would be convenient." Seth cut me a smoldering look. "You know, for those sleepovers."

I wagged a finger at him. "Don't push your luck, buddy."

As Seth slowed, my eyes spotted a man standing in the driveway, fooling around on his cell phone. *Ugh.* I recognized the face immediately. *Richard Cuthbert.* A grade-A number-one colossal A-hole if ever there was one. After warning him multiple times about violating the city's water rationing ordinance, he'd threatened to take my badge when I'd issued him a citation for breaking the law. No way would I ever rent a place from this guy.

"K-keep going," I spat.

Seth's brows angled in puzzlement. "Don't even want to take a look?"

"I know the landlord. He's a condescending jerk." Thus, I would not bother to give him the courtesy of a call to let him know I was no longer interested. He could stand in that driveway until Jesus came back for all I cared.

Seth punched the gas and we drove past. I cast one last glare in Cuthbert's direction. *Kiss my butt, jerkwad.*

We returned to my apartment where Seth left me with a contented heart and pair of fully-kissed lips. After he'd gone, I checked my cell phone. Richard Cuthbert had left two voicemails. In the first, which he'd left a mere two minutes after our scheduled appointment, he simply said *I'm waiting. Where are you?* in a short-tempered voice. In the second, which he'd left an hour after the time I'd arranged to meet him, he'd barked, *Don't bother calling me back. It'll be a cold day in hell before I rent to someone who's wasted my time like this!*

Ah, justice.

It's a bitch, no?

FIVE
A HOWLING GOOD TIME

Brigit

Brigit wasn't quite sure why Seth and Megan had driven the dogs all over town today, but she always enjoyed spending time with Blast, whether it was running around with their friends at the dog park or even just riding around in a car. The only thing she hadn't liked was the darn train. The rumble of its wheels and the sound of its horn had been downright deafening. If she'd had opposable thumbs she would've unlocked the gate, run after the damn thing, and sunk her teeth into its caboose.

Brigit hoped she'd get to see more of Blast in the upcoming days. He was a fun and sweet companion. Neutered, so he didn't act like a jackass like some of those male dogs who still had their balls. Really, that Great Dane with the pendulous testicles at the dog park who kept trying to pick fights? What a dumbass.

If Brigit had to guess, she'd say the chances of seeing Blast more often were likely. She'd noticed Megan and Seth putting their mouths together, a sign of affection in both dogs and humans. She'd also smelled the sexual pheromones the two had released when Seth backed Megan against the door. Each of them was hot for the other, that much was aromatically clear.

Now if they could only manage not to screw it up this time . . .

SIX
PANTS ON FIRE

Dub

At six o'clock, Dub rounded up his backpack. He slipped something for protection into the outside pocket. He wasn't sure he'd need it tonight, but a person could never be too careful.

He left his bedroom and went to the den. Trent and Wes were flopped down in their recliners to watch the Bulls/Spurs game on the big-screen television. "I'll be back in a couple of hours. I'm going to see a friend."

Wes raised a hand to stop him. "Hold up a second. What's this friend's name?"

"Mark." The lie slid easily off Dub's tongue. Years of practice had made him an expert. "We're going to study for our history test."

"Mark?" Wes said. "Mark who?"

"Stallworth." His gut clenched with guilt. But no way could he tell them where he was really going tonight.

Trent sat up in his chair. "He live around here?"

Dub hiked a thumb over his shoulder. "Lilac Street." That part was true. Mark Stallworth sat beside him in history class and lived on Lilac. He and Dub rode the same school bus. But *friends?* No.

Wes flopped around like a fish on a dock before managing to get himself out of the chair. "You won't be able to study on an empty stomach." He went to the kitchen, pulled a foil-covered dish from the fridge, and placed it on the granite countertop. "Eat some of this leftover vegetable lasagna before you go."

Trent stepped up behind Wes, made a face, and mouthed the word "sorry." Wes thought he was a gourmet cook. Wes was wrong. The guy must have defective taste buds. Still, Dub appreciated Wes's efforts. Hell, Dub couldn't remember his own mother ever doing more for him than heating a frozen pizza.

Dub yanked open the silverware drawer, grabbed a knife and fork, and cut a square of lasagna from the pan, scooping it onto a plate. He stuck the lasagna in the microwave, punched the buttons to heat it for three minutes—*beep-beep-beep*—and, when it was ready, stood at the counter and wolfed the food down.

Wes handed him a napkin. "Slow down. You'll get a tummy ache."

Dub rolled his eyes. "I'm fifteen, dude. I don't get 'tummy' aches."

"You better not talk back," Trent whispered as he grabbed another beer from the fridge, "or he'll punish you by making you eat more of it."

When Dub finished the lasagna, he washed it down with a glass of tap water, rinsed his plate and glass, and stuck them in the dishwasher. He went to his bathroom and brushed his teeth. After having shared a bathroom with a dozen other boys, the luxury of having his very own bathroom was not lost on him. He slung his backpack over his shoulder once again, and headed to the door a second time.

Wes raised a hand again. "Hang on, Dub. I'll drive you."

Shit. Dub should have seen this coming. "It's only three blocks."

"I know." Wes grabbed his keys from the hook on the wall. "But it's dark outside. I'll worry about you."

That was funny, really. The rest of the neighborhood worried about Dub, too, but in a totally different way. Trent and Wes hadn't told their neighbors about Dub's past. They'd wanted to give him a fresh start. But one of the girls in Dub's math class knew someone who knew someone else who had known Dub at the junior high he'd attended briefly in east Fort Worth before being arrested and shipped off to the Gainesville State School for boys. So, yeah, the secret was out.

Wes grabbed Dub's coat from the hook and held it out. "Put this on."

"I'll be fine. It's ten steps from the door to the car."

Wes jabbed the coat at him. "Put. The coat. On."

Dub offered another eye roll but took the coat and put it on. It was nice to have someone who gave a shit about him. That was a new thing that wasn't yet lost on him, either.

They climbed into Wes's Civic and Wes drove the three blocks south to Lilac. "Which house is it?"

Dub pointed. "That one."

Wes pulled to a stop at the curb.

"Thanks," Dub said as he climbed out.

"Text me when you're ready to come home."

Damn! "Okay."

Dub got out of the car and walked slowly up to the porch, silently willing Wes to drive off. No such luck. Dub was forced to ring the bell. A moment later there was movement behind the frosted glass in the door. A dark-haired woman answered, a leery look on her face as she gave Dub the once-over.

"Hi." Dub's breath made a cloud in the cold air. "Is Mark home?"

The woman didn't invite him in. Instead, she turned and called back over her shoulder. "Mark? There's someone at the door for you."

Mark came down the hall. He was short, skinny, and still waiting for his visit from the puberty fairy. By the looks of him, she'd been out on a long cigarette break.

"Uh . . . hi." Mark's face was confused, like his mother's, and his eyes were wide. Looked like he'd heard about Dub's sketchy past, too.

Mark didn't invite Dub in. Neither did his mother. Poor manners, Wes would say. Dub guessed neither of them had attended cotillion. Behind Dub, Wes still waited at the curb, the engine idling. *Shit.*

"It's cold out here," Dub said. "Could I come in for just a second? I have a quick question about our history homework."

"I guess so."

Mark moved back and Dub stepped inside. Mark closed the door enough to block out the cold outside air, but he didn't push it enough for the latch to click. It was as if he wanted to allow himself a way to escape if Dub suddenly whipped out a weapon. Luckily, it was enough for Wes. Dub heard the Civic's engine rev as it pulled away from the curb.

"Can you remind me what chapter we were supposed to read?" Dub asked.

"Twenty-seven," Mark said.

"Twenty-seven," Dub repeated, buying himself a few seconds of time as he input the information into the notes app on his phone. He looked back up. "Great. Thanks, Mark. That's all I needed to know."

He turned and opened the door. "See you on the bus tomorrow."

As the door swung shut behind him, Dub heard Mark's mother say, "Maybe I should start driving you to school."

Dub stopped on the porch, the heat of rage and shame radiating from his core to the tips of his fingers and toes. It was all he could do not to turn around and put a fist through that frosted glass on the door.

At least he'd soon have a release from the rage.

Two hours later, Dub was back in front of the Stallworths' house. His hand shook so bad as he texted Wes that it took him forever to type just five words. *I'm ready to come home.*

He hadn't meant to do what he'd done. Things had gotten out of control, gone too far.

And he'd been unable to stop himself.

Oh, God! The trouble he'd been in before would be nothing compared to the deep shit he could be in now . . .

SEVEN
NO BOYS ALOUD

Megan

Monday morning I showered, dressed, and ate my standard breakfast of organic oatmeal and fair-trade coffee. Brigit gobbled a bowl of canned beef by-products, probably mostly ears and feet and icky innards, not exactly gourmet fare but she didn't seem to mind.

We stepped out of the apartment to find that yesterday's pleasant weather had moved on, leaving north Texas cold and miserable once again. *Blah.*

Thanks to budget cuts, officers were not allowed to drive their patrol cars home and Brigit and I were forced to make our commute crowded into my metallic blue Smart Car. Thankfully, our drive was a relatively short one. At five till eight, my partner and I rolled into the lot at the W1 station. I lifted a hand to wave to Summer, a bubbly, curly-haired blonde officer who, like me, had joined the force right out of college. She had three years' experience on me, though. She and I had gone out for drinks a time or two after the Fort Worth Police Officers' Association meetings. She responded to my wave by aiming two finger guns at me and pretending to squeeze off a couple of shots. *Bang-bang*.

As my partner and I climbed out of my car, Derek "The Big Dick" Mackey, my former partner, slid down from his black pickup a couple of spots down. Derek wore his flaming red hair in a short buzz cut, and sported a larger than average build. He also had excrement for brains and a personality that stunk just as bad.

He snorted derisively as Brigit and I walked past. "'Mornin', bitches."

As was my morning ritual, I whipped out my baton, extended it with a flick of my wrist—*Snap!*—and gave the rubber testicles hanging from his truck's trailer hitch a solid *whack*.

Derek snorted again, this time with laughter. "I can see that anger management class did you a world of good."

Okay, yes, I'd been forced to take an anger management class after Tasering Derek in the testicles a while back. And, okay, yes, I had an Irish temper, courtesy of my mother, whose maiden name was O'Keefe. But who among us doesn't have some type of flaw? At least I'd decided to put my anger to good use as a cop. Not that I harassed people, mind you. I was more than fair. But when push came to shove and some jackass needed to be brought down to size, I could summon the ire to do it. Anger was like a source of fuel for me.

I reached my specially equipped K-9 cruiser and opened the back door, reaching in to unlock the door to the metal mesh enclosure for Brigit. "In you go, girl. Another day, another dog biscuit."

My partner's tags jingled as she hopped up onto the platform that had been installed where the backseat would be in regular cruisers. She wagged her tail and woofed once, ready to go out on patrol.

My furry partner now situated, I climbed into the front and turned on the car's radio, the laptop mounted to the dash, and the shoulder-mounted radio affixed to my uniform. I cranked the engine and headed out, turning west out of the lot. *Another day, another dollar. Also, another day, another day closer to making detective.*

I'd studied criminal justice and become a cop for a number of reasons. My stutter had rendered me a quiet yet observant child, and I'd realized early on that the world could be a harsh, unfair, and dangerous place. If there was anything I could do to make it less harsh, more just, and safer, I wanted to do it. Around the same time, I'd stumbled upon mystery books in the elementary school library. I'd devoured them like candy, making notes and puzzling out the clues, thrilled when I could solve the mystery before the author's big reveal. I hoped one day to make detective so I could put my investigative skills to work to solve crimes.

I'd previously had the good fortune of working under a couple of FWPD detectives who'd recognized my abilities and dedication and allowed me to be involved in their investigations. I'd helped them take down a bomber and violent pickpocket. But who knew when I'd have the chance to work such a case again? In the meantime, I'd have to bide my time as a street cop, fighting for truth and justice as I racked up the minimum four years of police work required to apply for detective.

A mere twenty minutes into my shift and a dispatcher's voice came over the speaker. "Noise complaint near TCU." She rattled off an address on Shirley Avenue. "Who can respond?"

I was currently cruising down Park Hill, not far from the location. I slid the car's mic out of its holder and pressed the talk button. "Officers Luz and Brigit responding."

I waited on the light, then crossed University, making my way into the older neighborhood that contained a mixture of pretty, restored owner-occupied residences and slightly rundown rentals. As we made our way up Shirley, there was no need for me to check addresses. My window was down and the raunchy rap music blaring from a stone house with a gable over the front door let me know this was the place. The purple and white flag featuring the horned frog mascot further informed me that students lived here.

I climbed out of the cruiser and stepped away from the car, intending to leave Brigit inside, when she emitted a soft whine. Looked like she might need a potty break already. I returned to the cruiser and let her out, giving her the order to stay close to me.

I waited while she crouched in the dry winter grass and relieved herself. When she was done, I headed up the three steps to the porch and pushed the doorbell. The music was so loud neither the *ding* nor the *dong* was audible. I tried again to get the occupants' attention, this time banging on the front door with the outside of my fist. *Bam-bam-bam.*

Still no response from within.

I stepped to one of the front windows and rapped on the glass. *Rap-rap-rap.* "Fort Worth police!" I hollered. "Come to the door!"

Still nothing.

I cupped my hands around my eyes and put my face to the glass. I caught a glimpse of a twentyish guy walking down a hallway in nothing but a pair of tightie whities with a quarter-sized hole in the left butt cheek. "Hey, you!" I yelled. It was of no use.

Both irritated and out of ideas, I stepped back to survey the house. The window on the end was open an inch or two. Young guys didn't tend to be as careful about home security as they should be. Not as concerned about their utility bills, either.

I moved down to the open window and took another

look inside. Judging from the empty pizza boxes littering the floor and the overflowing ashtrays on the coffee table, the tenants had had a party last weekend.

I could not only hear the music now, but I could also hear the guy singing along with it, belting out the four-letter words as if his life depended on it. I removed the screen, leaned it up against the outside wall, and pushed the window open a few more inches.

"Hey!" I yelled again through the open window. "Fort Worth PD! Come out here!"

Nothing but more singing.

I pushed the window all the way up, leaned against the windowsill, and stuck my head inside, scanning the room. Enormous speakers at least four feet tall sat in each corner of the room. The stereo itself sat only a few feet from the window. Maybe I could reach in and unplug it.

Nope.

Try as I might, my fingers could not quite reach the cord. *Dang.* Whipping my baton from my belt once again, I extended it with another *snap!* Amazing how often the metal stick came in handy. Sticking it through the window, it easily reached the cord. One quick upward jerk and the cord came out of the plug. Instant silence.

"What the hell?" came the boy's voice from somewhere down the hall. A moment later he appeared in the doorway and spotted me at the window. "Shit!" he shrieked, his hands instinctively moving to cover his crotch. As if there was anything there I wanted to see. "What are you doing?"

"Putting an end to this cacophony." I placed the end of my baton against the stone wall outside and pushed it closed. I angled my head to indicate the front door. "Come out on the porch. We need to talk."

"Can I put on pants first?"

"Please do." Justice may be blind, but I wasn't.

A moment later, the boy opened the front door, now dressed in a pair of tan shorts so wrinkled they appeared to be made from Shar-Pei skin.

Though I'd been a college kid myself only a couple of years ago, I nonetheless gave him a stern look. Might as well nip this in the bud. I knew how these things went. If I went easy on him, FWPD would be called out here a dozen more times before he'd get the message. "I rang the bell," I told him, "and knocked, and called to you through the window. We received a noise complaint. You can't play your music so loud."

"But it's my getting-ready-for-class music!" he said, as if that excused his behavior. "I need it to get me going."

"Use headphones," I suggested.

As I wrote him up a quick warning, Brigit squeezed past me in the doorway and went as far inside as the leash would allow. She used her snout to push aside a pizza box, found a piece of rock-hard crust, and snatched it up.

The form completed, I ripped it from the pad and held it out to the boy. "You're on the record now. If officers are called out here again, you'll get an expensive citation. Understand?"

"Yes, ma'am," he spat, yanking the warning paper out of my hand.

Ma'am. Nice touch.

Without further adieu, Brigit and I headed back to the cruiser, where she hopped into the back, positioned the pizza crust between her front paws, and began working it.

No sooner had I started the engine and pulled away from the curb than dispatch came over the radio again. "We've got a report of a body found in Forest Park near the zoo. Who can respond?"

A body?

Holy crap!

Every sphincter in my body puckered. I was less than a minute's drive away. But the last thing I wanted to do was take this call. I hesitated, waiting to see if another officer would take it.

Several seconds went by with no response.

The dispatcher tried again. "Who can respond?"

Please. Please, someone, anyone, respond!

No one did.

Instead, the Big Dick's voice came over the radio. "Your last call was right near there, Luz. Ain't you still around?"

I could hear the shit-eating grin in his voice. When we'd been partners, we'd responded to a call involving an assault and robbery at an ATM. One look at the victim's bloody, broken nose and I'd tossed my cookies in the bank's sage bushes. Derek had found my squeamishness nothing short of hilarious.

"C'mon, Luz," he said, when I failed to respond. "Don't be a puss."

Lest I look like said "puss" to my fellow officers, I squeezed my shoulder mic in resignation. "Officers Luz and Brigit responding."

Blurgh.

EIGHT
FAST AND FURIOUS

Brigit

Wheee!

Megan drove fast, the back window down, a rush of cool, crisp air blowing over Brigit. The dog loved the feel of the wind in her fur. She would have loved to stick her head out the window, but the metal mesh enclosure prevented her from doing so. Rather, she stood at the mesh, her snout lifted, scenting the fast-moving breeze.

Her superior olfactory senses detected a number of smells. Some, like car exhaust and Megan's lavender body lotion, held little interest. Others, like bacon and squirrel, caused her mouth to water, easily worth the shrill noise of the siren.

Brigit knew what the speed and siren meant. She and her partner were needed somewhere for something important. And when she and her partner did important work, Megan rewarded her with liver treats, the number of which corresponded with the difficulty of the task.

Liver treats. *Yum.* A drop of drool fell from her chin to the carpeted platform.

Wherever they were going, and whatever they would do, Brigit hoped it would be big.

NINE
TEEN DRAMA

Dub

Monday morning, as Dub performed the balcony scene from *Romeo and Juliet* in his first period theater class, the events of last night seemed as if they'd been acted out by someone else. There were still scratches on his skin, but with any luck they'd heal before anyone noticed. He only hoped that no one would ever find out. Because what happened last night could be as tragic as the ending of this play.

TEN
HARD TO FACE

Megan

Knowing that a body on occasion might not be as dead as it looked, I switched on my lights and siren, zipped up University, and turned right into Forest Park. The crowd of people near the woods flanking the jogging trail made it clear where the body had been found. Taking a deep breath to steel myself, I parked the cruiser and climbed out.

Opening the back door and steel hatch, I motioned for Brigit to hop down. "Come on, girl." I supposed I could have left her in the car, but frankly I wanted her along for moral support. Surprising how much comfort a dog could provide.

As we sprinted up the path, I attempted to mentally prepare myself for what we would find. I forced myself to visualize a body with a bullet in the chest. A body with multiple stab wounds. A body with a bloody scalp from head trauma. I'd seen enough pictures at the police academy and in various files to know what a dead body looked like. Heck, as cadets we'd even taken a trip to the morgue, seen a number of frozen corpses with toe tags identifying them.

As we approached, the crowd erupted in fresh murmurs. A few people stepped back, giving me my first glimpse of the victim, from his chest down to his feet. He wore rumpled blue jeans, scuffed black biker boots, and a fleece-lined denim jacket. From this vantage point, no wounds were visible. What had he died of? A drug overdose? A heart attack? I'd assumed the guy would be a murder victim, but maybe he'd simply died of natural causes, called home by his creator as he took a late-evening stroll at the park. *Could he have been so lucky? Could I be so lucky?*

As I made my way forward, more people stepped aside.

Holy shit.

The photographs and morgue visit did nothing to prepare me for seeing what I saw now.

Oh, God. Oh, God! OhGodOhGodOhGod!

I bent over, hands on my knees, and up came my fairtrade coffee and organic oatmeal.

Bruuup.

As the crowd gasped and groaned, a hot blush rushed to my cheeks. How humiliating. Nothing like a cowardly cop to make the people feel safe and protected, huh?

When Brigit went to sniff my regurgitated breakfast, I pushed her away with my foot. "No!"

Standing up straight, I pulled my citation pad from my pocket, ripped off a page, and used it to wipe my mouth. I looked up to find every eye in the crowd locked on me. *Great.* I clutched Brigit's leash tightly, hoping it would make my shaking hands less obvious. Stepping forward, I took a closer look at the victim, attempting to force myself to think of the situation clinically.

Easier thought than done.

The victim lay ten feet or so into the woods, behind

the trunk of a large tree. He faced away from the trail, as if he were looking into the woods, only the back of his blood-drenched head and blood-soaked shoulders visible from my current angle. *Thank God.* I wasn't ready to see his face yet. I needed to ease myself into this.

His patchy, stringy hair was too soaked with blood to tell what color it might have been before he'd been attacked. He rested on his side, his arms and legs scissored. He appeared to be slightly below average in height and on the thin side, the kind of scrawny person for whom the saying "pick on someone your own size" had been invented.

But who had picked on this man? And why?

Kneeling, I took yet another deep breath and reached out over his shoulder to take hold of his wrist, breaking out in a sweat at the feel of his cold, stiff skin. No pulse. No surprise there. It would have been nothing short of a miracle for someone to have survived after losing so much blood.

I stood and slowly circled around to his front. If there'd been any coffee or oatmeal remaining in me, it would have spewed forth at this point. This guy definitely had not died of natural causes. Not unless having your throat ripped open and your face pulverized beyond recognition counted as natural causes. His face and neck were nothing but shredded flesh covered in a thick ragu of blood.

I'll never eat ziti marinara again.

Wait.

Movement at the man's mouth caught my eye. Was he moving his tongue? Had I somehow missed his pulse?

Two antennae emerged from between the narrow gap in the man's lips, followed by the long, flat brown water bug to which they belonged. *Gah!* My legs turned to wet noodles and I melted to my knees beside Brigit in the moist, leaf-covered dirt.

The dog looked at me with soulful eyes and gave my cheek a soft lick, almost as if she realized how traumatic this scene had been for me and wanted to offer some consolation. But the dog couldn't be that smart, could she?

"What happened to him?" asked a woman in running gear with her red hair pulled up in a ponytail.

I gulped, forcing my throat, which had squeezed itself shut, to open. "I'd only be guessing at this p-point."

Good police work involved gathering evidence, critically assessing the clues, and reaching conclusions based on proof. I wasn't about to engage in idle guesswork here. But between you and me, from the looks of this guy, my money was on werewolves.

Using a tree limb for leverage, I pulled myself to a stand, brushed the dirt and leaf fragments from the knees of my pants, and pushed the button on my shoulder mic. "This is Officer Luz. I need backup at Forest Park, a team from crime scene, and a detective." I also needed another breakfast, given that I'd just lost mine. Mouthwash couldn't hurt, either. Raising my eyes to the crowd, I asked, "Who found him?" My voice sounded as weak and faint as I felt. Some tough cop I was, huh?

A lanky man with wavy black hair and pointed features stepped forward, raising his hand as if he'd been called on in class. He wore running shoes, a lightweight blue windbreaker, and black spandex running pants that hugged and accentuated his naughty bits. *Let's leave that fashion choice to people without external genitalia, shall we?*

"Your name, sir?" I asked, pulling out my notepad.

"Clark Dennison."

I jotted it down on my pad. "When d-did you f-find him?" Here came my stutter in full force. *Great.*

"Just a few minutes ago," he said.

"You were jogging on the trail?"

He nodded.

"And you sp-spotted the b-body from the trail?"

The man looked around as if embarrassed. "Not exactly."

His gaze met mine, imploring me for privacy.

I willed my stutter to screw off and looked at the crowd again. "Anyone with information wait by that tree." I pointed to an oak thirty feet away. "Anyone else p-please move on." They'd only get in the way of the crime scene technicians and detectives.

The crowd dispersed, none of them going to wait by the oak, though several people ignored my instructions to leave and hung out in a group in the parking lot, engaging in speculative chatter.

I turned back to Naughty Bits and arched a brow.

"I came over here to take a leak," he said. "That's when I found the body."

So nature called, then coughed up a dead body. Nature seemed to enjoy toying with us humans today.

"Any idea who he is?"

Dennison shook his head. "None."

"Did you touch him?" I asked. "Move him?"

"Lord, no!" The man shook his head vehemently. "I was too freaked out."

Understandable. "Did you see anyone in the area when you found him?"

He shook his head again. "Only other joggers."

"Anyone running particularly fast?"

"Not that I noticed."

I obtained his contact information and asked him to wait for the detective. "The detective will have more questions for you." Probably better questions, too. I was still having trouble standing upright, let alone performing a proper witness interview.

He pulled his cell phone from its clip on his waistband and phoned his office, explaining that he'd be late coming in today. "I came across a dead person in the park when I was jogging this morning and I need to wait for a detective to come interview me." He paused a moment. "Yep, that's what I said. A dead person." Another pause. "No idea. Looks like his throat was slashed."

Lest he spill a detail the detective would want to keep secret, I motioned for him to zip his lip. He nodded, said "gotta go now," and ended the call.

Sirens wailed and tires screeched as Derek whipped around the corner and into Forest Park. Given that the victim was halfway to heaven or hell by now, there was no need for the hoopla, but far be it from Derek not to make a show of any case he was involved in. The guy was an attention whore.

He stopped his cruiser at the curb, leaving the lights flashing but turning off the siren. He trotted over with a rolled-up ribbon of crime scene tape, took one look at the victim, and chuckled. "Hoo-ee. That is one unlucky son-of-a-bitch."

No puke.

No trembling hands.

No falling to his knees in the dirt.

Derek either had nerves of steel or was a heartless ass. Or maybe he was both. Without another word to me, he tied an end of the yellow plastic tape around a tree and began to mark off a perimeter.

A few minutes later, the crime scene van pulled up, lumbering up over the curb and onto the grass, coming to a stop a few feet outside the taped-off perimeter. Three technicians climbed out, plastic tool kits in their hands. A moment later, an unmarked police car drove into the lot and parked next to my cruiser. Detective Audrey Jackson, a fortyish African-American woman with short, perky braids climbed out. She was dressed in her usual khaki pants and loafers, which she'd paired today with a pink button-down shirt and a FWPD windbreaker.

After donning a pair of blue booties she'd obtained from one of the techs, she walked toward me, raising a hand in greeting. "Good morning, Officer Luz."

Good? Hardly. Nonetheless, I raised a hand in reply.

Circling wide, she watched her step as she came around the front of the victim. "Oh, yeah. He's dead all right."

A choking sound spurted involuntarily from me.

Jackson glanced over at me, her brown eyes soft with concern. "This your first corpse, Officer Luz?"

Despite my attempts to hold them back, tears filled my eyes as I nodded.

"I'd like to say it gets easier," she said, giving me a consoling look before turning back to the victim, "but it doesn't. It can get much worse than this, in fact. And if you remain a cop, it will."

I didn't want to think how much worse it could get, so I refused to let my mind go there.

She pulled out a notepad. "What do you know so far?"

"Not much." I gestured at Clark Dennison, who'd taken a seat on the curb outside the tape to wait. "That's the guy who found the victim. He was jogging and came over here to relieve himself. That's when he spotted the body."

"Did he touch it?"

"He says no."

"Did *you* touch it?"

"Only his wrist to check for a pulse."

Jackson glanced around, her gaze landing on my vomit. "Looks like this guy might have been sick or overdosed before getting his face ripped off. Or maybe whoever did this to him threw up."

I shook my head. "The vomit's mine."

"Ah." Her nose twitched. "I'll let the techs know they don't need to collect it as evidence." She looked my way again. "You're looking awfully green. You're not going to throw up again, are you?"

I shook my head. "My stomach's empty."

"You can go on, if you'd like." She angled her head as if evaluating my condition. "But if you're up to it you're welcome to stick around and listen in. It's not every day we get a homicide investigation."

Thank God. No way could I deal with this type of horrific crime on a regular basis. Still, I knew if I wanted to make detective, I'd have to learn how to handle these types of gruesome situations. "I appreciate the offer, Detective Jackson. I'll stick around."

Detective Jackson had become a mentor to me during the bombing case. She knew I aspired to make detective one day and, despite her hectic schedule, made time to help me out and provide pointers when she could. I appreciated her taking me under her wing.

I followed her over to Clark Dennison.

"Mr. Dennison? I'm Detective Audrey Jackson." She reached out and gave his hand a shake before pulling a notepad, pen, and small digital tape recorder from the pocket of her windbreaker. "Mind if I tape this conversation?"

"Okay with me," Clark replied.

I suspected she was taping the interaction so that she could review it later, see if there were any tidbits that might seem insignificant now but that could provide additional leads later if a suspect could not be identified immediately.

Detective Jackson pushed a button on the device to begin recording. "Interview with Clark Dennison, Monday, February ninth—" she glanced at her wristwatch—"9:13 A.M." She looked up at Mr. Dennison. "Can you tell me how you happened to find the body?"

The man repeated the story he'd told me, that he'd been jogging, felt the urge to urinate, and headed into the woods only to come across the corpse.

"You recognize the deceased?" Jackson asked.

I mentally grimaced. I don't know that anyone would recognize the man now, even the man himself if he were still alive. Kind of hard to identify someone whose face has been pulverized beyond recognition.

"No," Dennison said. "I don't know him."

She asked some of the same questions I had, telling me that, despite my overwhelming sense of panic and nausea, my short interrogation had been on the mark.

"You touch him?" she asked. "Maybe check to see if he was breathing or had a pulse?"

"No," Dennison replied. "It was clear the guy was dead. I mean, he doesn't even have a face anymore and his neck looks like someone took a steak knife to it and tried to saw clean through."

Oh, God.

Never mind that my stomach was empty, it was going to try to purge itself nonetheless. My mouth expelled a loud burping sound, which was only partially stifled by the hand I'd placed over my lips. "Excuse me."

After casting me a pitying look that said she doubted whether I could stomach detective work, Jackson returned her attention to Dennison. "Did you notice anyone leaving the scene?"

"No," Clark said. "All I saw were other joggers and a couple of women pushing kids in strollers."

"Did you hear anything unusual?"

"Like what?"

Jackson shrugged. "Rustling in the woods. Birds cawing as they were scared off. Shouting or footsteps. A car or motorcycle taking off quickly. Anything like that?"

Dennison ran his fingers through his hair and left his hand atop his head, cupping his scalp. "Not that I can recall. Honestly, I was so shocked I'm not sure I would've even noticed anything like that."

Jackson looked Dennison up and down. "You're in good shape. You jog here every day?"

"Most weekdays," the man said. "Weekends I sleep in."

She scanned the vicinity. "Ever notice anything odd when you were here? Someone loitering? People arguing? Anything like that?"

"I've run across some teenagers I suspected were skipping school," he said. "But that's it."

"When was this?"

Dennison looked up in thought. "Week or two ago."

"How many were there?"

"Two boys, one girl."

"What did they look like?"

"One of the boys was black. Average size. Short hair. The other boy was white. Tall. I think he had brown hair but I don't remember for sure. The girl was white, too. Long blond hair. Kind of chunky."

"Did you recognize them?"

"No. I hadn't seen them before and I haven't seen them since."

"What were they wearing?"

Dennison was unsure. "All I can say is they were dressed casual, like kids would dress for school. None of their clothing made a big impression on me."

"Any distinguishing characteristics? Scars? Tattoos? That kind of thing?"

"I didn't get close enough to tell. The two white kids were smoking cigarettes. I remember that."

Detective Jackson reached under her windbreaker to pull a business card from the breast pocket of her pink button-down. "If you think of anything else or see those kids again, give me a call right away."

"I will."

With that, Dennison left.

The detective motioned for me to follow her. "You up for taking a closer look?"

No! "Yes." I took a deep breath to fortify myself and

wrapped Brigit's leash tightly around my hand to keep her from disturbing the crime scene.

Keeping a ten-foot span between herself and the victim, Jackson slowly walked a circle around the body and the tech photographing it. Brigit and I followed along. The detective stopped when she faced the body, bending down to get a straight-on look. When she was done, she looked up at me. "Okay, Padawan. Give me your observations."

Observations. Hmm . . .

I looked around. "I don't see a trail of blood, so it doesn't look like he was just dumped here. He was probably killed here, too."

"Good. What else?"

"The killer used something jagged on his neck. Maybe a serrated knife."

"Not a knife," called the tech, who was crouching next to the body with his camera. He reached out with a hand clad in a blue latex glove and lifted the end of a narrow chain from the wound in the victim's neck. "A chain."

He tugged on the chain, slowly pulling it out from the victim's neck where it was embedded, pieces of bloody flesh sticking to it as it came free. *Ew.*

The chain looked too thick and had loops too big to be a typical necklace, but it was too small for other typical purposes, like towing a car or securing a fence.

Jackson must have had the same thought. "Any idea what kind of chain that is?"

My first thought was that it could be a man's rosary, but it lacked the requisite prayer beads. "Could it be a chain for military dog tags?" Maybe our victim was a veteran.

The tech chimed in now. "No, not dog tags. Those hang from a ball chain. This chain has open loops. Looks to me like something Mr. T would wear. Could be the suspect's a gangbanger."

"We've got plenty of those around here." Jackson gestured to the body. "What about his face? How do you think the killer did that?"

I eyed what remained of the dead man's cheek. It contained four dark bruises spaced at even intervals. The two marks in the center were slightly darker than the outer two. I looked around, noting a few jagged stones and pointy tree limbs on the ground. "Was he hit repeatedly with a rock maybe? Or a stick?"

"Nope. The spacing is too precise. Whoever hit the victim was wearing brass knuckles."

Ouch.

"Look here." Jackson pointed at something small and white lodged in the bark of a tree a few feet away.

I stepped closer. *Oh, my God! It was a tooth!*

The tech pulled a tongue depressor from his tool kit. "This killer was brutal. Take a look at this." He used the wooden stick to lift the dead man's blood-caked upper lip, revealing a set of jagged, broken teeth. "I better collect the fragments." He exchanged the tongue depressor for a pair of oversized tweezers and began to pick small white objects, which I'd originally mistaken for pebbles, from the ground.

Again my stomach attempted to purge itself. I made a mental note to take a Dramamine next time a corpse cropped up on my to-do list.

The second tech joined the first and began to pat down the dead man's pockets. Finding nothing in the pants or outer jacket pockets, he reached inside to check the inside pockets. "No wallet. No ID. Nothing."

Jackson pulled out her cell phone. "I'll call the station. See if we've got any missing person reports that fit his description."

She placed the call, was put on hold for a minute, then said, "Thanks." She put her phone away. "No missing person reports. Not yet, anyway."

Who was this man?
And why did someone kill him?

I felt a tug on the leash in my hand, Brigit trying to pull me over to the body.

"No, girl." She was probably curious, but no way did I want to get any closer. This was just too damn creepy.

Brigit tugged again, refusing to take no for an answer, this time digging her claws into the soft dirt and leaning toward the body.

I nudged her furry butt with my knee. "I said 'no, girl!' "

The techs and Jackson looked our way. An embarrassed flush burned my cheeks. Brigit was making me look like an idiot, like I couldn't control my dog.

Brigit woofed and tugged again. That's when I realized she was trying to tell me something.

I looked from the techs to the detective. "I think she smells something and wants to check it out. Is it okay to let her get closer?"

"Sure," the lead tech said. "Can't hurt anything at this point."

I led Brigit over, letting the leash out a few inches so her head could move freely. She began to snuffle along the body, her nose twitching and wiggling as she sniffed, thankfully starting at the guy's boots. She made her way up his calves, nudged a knee, and thoroughly sniffed his thigh. She sat back then, giving her passive alert.

"She's indicating there's drugs on him," I explained.

The tech frowned. "I already checked his pockets."

Jackson stepped up beside me. "Check inside his pants."

The tech carefully unzipped the man's jeans and pulled them down a few inches, revealing a pair of blue briefs and hairy thighs. Sure enough, a plastic bag containing small white crystals was affixed with medical tape to a shaved spot on the guy's thigh.

"Aha," Jackson said. "Looks like fuzzy-wuzzy discovered a possible motive."

Drugs. Not a surprise, really. Drugs played a huge part in crime. Many of those who committed crimes were high on drugs at the time. Others committed crimes in order to get money to buy drugs.

"Good girl!" I praised my partner, retrieved a liver treat from the stash in my jacket, and held it out to her.

She took the treat from my fingers, wolfed it down, and began to snuffle around in the nearby trees, probably scenting a squirrel or raccoon.

A call came in on my shoulder radio, reporting a disabled vehicle impeding traffic on Rosedale. "I better get back to work."

Jackson lifted her chin in acknowledgment. "I'll let you know what we find out."

As Brigit and I headed back to our cruiser, I found myself wanting to talk to Seth. He'd seen people killed in Afghanistan, seen people die in fires here. Surely he could help me deal with this murder.

What do you know? Maybe I did need him for something, after all.

ELEVEN
HOME, STINK, HOME

Brigit

She'd wanted really bad to roll on that man's dead body. Wasn't that what dead things were for? Rolling on? But given Megan's tight hold on her leash, Brigit knew she'd get in trouble if she tried. She'd had to settle for rolling on a squirrel in the parking lot. The flat, dried-out thing was days old, its odor mostly gone. Not much of a consolation prize, but the dog would take what she could get.

Brigit wasn't quite sure why Megan kept taking her to empty houses, but she liked this one. It smelled great. Like mildew and wood rot. The carpet also bore scents of sweaty feet and spilled milk. The backyard was great, too. Very little grass so she'd have an easy time digging holes if given the chance.

The evening was even better. Seth brought Blast with him to Megan's apartment. While their meal tickets talked on the couch, Brigit and Blast wrangled and wrestled on the carpet. Brigit bested Blast, flipping him over onto his back. She went for his throat. Playfully, of course, mouthing his fur without sinking her teeth into him. From the way he wriggled on his back and begged for more, Brigit suspected he liked it. Megan and Seth ought to give it a try sometime. The two looked like they could use some fun.

TWELVE
FAMILY REUNION

Dub

"Pleeeeeease?" Dub begged. He knew Wes would give in eventually. "Just one burrito. All that basketball made me hungry." Dub had spent the last two hours playing in a drop-in game at the Y while Wes sat in a nearby Starbucks, grading exams. "I'm a growing boy. I need nourishment."

"You can hardly say a fast-food burrito is nourishing," Wes said. "We've got plenty of healthy stuff in the fridge at home. Spinach. Broccoli. Brussels sprouts. Tofu . . ."

The grin on Wes's face told Dub his foster father was only teasing. Sure enough, Wes turned his Civic into the drive-thru lane at Taco Bell.

They waited as a woman with what looked like an entire girls' soccer team in her SUV placed a long and complicated order, turning back to the girls several times to discuss the "hold this's" and "extra that's."

"Girls," Wes said, rolling his eyes.

Dub emitted a grunt of agreement, though actually, their pickiness aside, he thought girls weren't bad at all. Unlike Mark Stallworth, the puberty fairy had visited Dub early, tapping him quite hard with her magical sparkling wand. He'd had facial hair by age twelve and was often mistaken for an adult. The guy who'd come to their door the other day trying to selling them new gutters hadn't asked to see Dub's parents. He'd assumed Dub was the owner of the house.

Their team's order finally done, the woman drove forward and Wes pulled up to the menu board.

A woman's voice came through the speaker. "Welcome to Taco Bell. What can I get you today?"

Holy shit.

That Tennessee twang was unmistakable. What happened Sunday night could land Dub in a world of trouble, and so could the woman whose voice had just come through the speaker.

Wes leaned his head out the window. "One bean burrito," he called.

The woman repeated the order and gave him a total. Wes thanked her and began to pull forward.

"Wait!" Dub cried.

Wes slammed on the brakes. "What is it?"

Dub opened the passenger door. "I'll be right back. I need to go inside and use the bathroom." Dub hopped out the door and slammed it behind him.

He did not want the woman working the drive-thru to see him. He *couldn't* let her see him. If she did, everything he'd worked so hard for would be over.

Yet he wanted to see her.

Needed to.

Dub pulled the white hood of his Tornadoes sweatshirt over his head and walked into the restaurant. He turned left into the dining area rather than right toward the food counter. Keeping his face ducked, he circled around to the drink machine. Taking a deep breath, he dared a look behind the counter.

There she was.

Standing inside the drive-thru window was a small black woman, barely five feet, wearing a colorful Taco Bell uniform. She wore her dark hair in a springy Afro. She'd never been able to afford to have her curls relaxed. Dub was glad about that. She looked cute this way, more real, younger and less processed and pretend.

She turned to talk to one of her coworkers. Her face had no bruises or cuts, no swollen mouth. She still had the thick scar on her upper lip where it had been split open a few years ago, but that had healed as much as it ever would. Her eyes looked clear. She'd put on some weight, too, no longer looking like one of those half-starved refugees on TV.

Thank God.

Relieved, he turned to go. He was nearly to the exit door when her voice came again.

"Wade?" she cried. "Is that you?"

He stopped in his tracks but didn't turn around. Everything in him told him to run. To run as fast as he could out to Wes's car and to never look back. To get away from her and to stay away.

But he couldn't do it. Had never been able to do it.

Slowly, he turned around.

By this time, she'd stepped up to the front counter. He saw tears in her deep brown eyes.

"It is you!" Her smile revealed an incomplete set of teeth. "I knew it!"

She was out the door that led from the food prep area and standing in front of him before he could even take a breath.

And he knew right then it was all over. The basketball

at the Y, the B average in school, the bedroom and bathroom he had all to himself.

He was no longer blessed, but damned.

Damned straight to hell.

And, this time, he could blame no one but himself.

THIRTEEN
HOUSE CALLS

Megan

Thursday morning, the W1 Division captain called the staff in early for a briefing. We officers—uniformed, plainclothes, and detectives alike—crowded into the conference room.

The Big Dick had been lucky enough to snag a chair up front. Summer had been unlucky enough to land the seat next to him. By the time I arrived, it was standing room only. I managed to squeeze myself into a small space between two male officers, a Latino named Hinojosa and a stocky African-American named Spalding, both of whom were veteran cops in their thirties. After offering them a nod in greeting, I turned my attention to the front of the room and Captain Leone, a fortyish guy with spongy dark hair and wiry eyebrows that threatened to reach out and grab you. *Terrifying.* Brigit sat at, and on, my feet, her rigid stance indicating she didn't like being boxed in by the crowd. Couldn't much blame her. With any luck, this briefing would be quick.

The captain stepped up to the podium and scanned the

group, his face blank with a practiced impassivity perfected during years as a homicide detective. If I hoped to make detective someday, I should probably work on my poker face. My emotions tended to be obvious, as evidenced by my gastronomic response to seeing that bludgeoned corpse on Monday.

"Listen up, folks," Leone barked, the crowd immediately quieting in response. "It's been a busy week. We've had reports of two home burglaries, one in Mistletoe Heights, the other in Fairmount. The thieves took the usual. Jewelry. Electronics. Silverware. Both homes were unoccupied at the time. The couple who owns the first house was on a cruise. The second house was owned by a single woman who was away at her cousin's wedding in Sonoma, California. Best we can tell, both burglaries took place in the late afternoon, after school hours but before most people get home from work. Residents of Mistletoe Heights and Fairmount are understandably concerned. Spend a little more time in these neighborhoods, let the people know we're looking out for them. All right?"

Murmurs of assent came from the officers gathered.

"Okay. Item number two, the murder at Forest Park. I'll invite Detective Jackson up here to give y'all an update."

As Detective Jackson stood from her seat and made her way to the front of the room, Captain Leone stepped aside to allow her to take the podium.

Jackson leaned forward, resting her arms on the podium and curling her fingers over the front lip. "A few more details we've found out. Fingerprint analysis positively identified the victim as Brian Keith Samuelson. Samuelson has a conviction for possession of methamphetamines and has long been suspected of doing some occasional dealing in the area. Unfortunately, though we've now identified our victim, we still have no idea who might have killed him. Since we found drugs but no money on Samuelson, we suspect his murder was a drug deal gone bad. The medical examiner put his time of death around eight o'clock Sunday evening."

Eight o'clock Sunday night? That was about the time I'd been kissing Seth good-bye at my apartment. And what a kiss it had been. Soft. Warm. Somehow sweet and sexy at the same time, making my toes curl and my mind visualize white picket fences and vegetable gardens . . .

"We have one potential person of interest," Jackson continued, pulling me from my picket-fenced reverie. "A woman who works at the zoo was walking to the bus stop on University a few minutes after her shift ended at eight. She says a man ran past her down Colonial Parkway headed toward Park Place. He had dark curly hair. He was wearing dark clothing. Average height. She estimated the man to be in his mid-twenties. Given that it was dark outside she didn't get a good look at him, but she believes he's either a dark-skinned Caucasian or a light-skinned African-American, but she said he could be Asian, middle-Eastern, or Latino."

So the only thing we knew for sure was that the guy who ran past her wasn't unusually pale or dark. That didn't narrow it down much. The pinched expression on Jackson's face told me she'd been frustrated by the vague description, too.

She held up a black-and-white drawing penned by a police sketch artist. The drawing showed a young man with lightly shaded skin and short, dark curls.

The Big Dick snorted. "The guy was killed by Bruno Mars?"

"Nah," replied one of the older officers in the middle of the crowd. "That's a mid-eighties Michael Jackson."

Everyone seemed to be chiming in with opinions now, claiming the drawing looked like everyone from Usher to Shemar Moore to a young Barack Obama. Of course my mind went straight to Chris Brown, who had a documented history of violence.

"Enough!" Jackson sliced the air with her hand, cutting off the chatter. "If you interact with anyone fitting this description," she said, "find out where the person was Sunday night. Got it? I'm going out this morning to speak with a couple of men in W1 who have meth convictions on their records." Her eyes met mine through the crowd. "Officer Luz, I'd like you to go with me."

Instinctively I stood up straighter, nodding. *Yay!* Detective Jackson was including me in the case! My first thought was that she'd asked me to accompany her because of my impressive detection skills, but when Brigit shifted on my feet, I realized the detective was probably more interested in my furry K-9 partner. Having a drug-detection dog along on the interrogation could be useful. I was only along for the ride, or, more precisely, because I could give Brigit a ride. I wasn't a cop. I was a chauffeur. *For a dog.*

"Officer Mackey," Jackson said, turning her eyes to the Big Dick, "I want you to escort me. Both of the men we'll be visiting have violent records."

She didn't explain why she'd chosen Derek in particular to serve as her security detail, but she didn't have to. The Big Dick had a reputation for being the bravest cop in W1, maybe the bravest in all of FWPD. Of course there's a fine line between bravery and stupidity, and Derek sometimes crossed it. So far he'd been lucky when he had crossed the line. At any rate, he'd make a good bodyguard for Jackson should things go south during this morning's visits. Part of me felt insulted she didn't think I'd be sufficient backup for her. Another part of me was thankful I only had to worry about keeping myself and Brigit safe.

On hearing the detective announce that I'd be working with the Big Dick this morning, Summer turned around from her seat next to him and offered me a sympathetic expression before forming a gun with her thumb and index finger and pretending to blow her brains out. I nodded in return. Yeah, I'd rather put a bullet in my brain than work with Derek, but I wasn't about to let Detective Jackson down. Looked like my brains would remain intact for the time being.

Jackson stepped aside and Captain Leone returned to the podium. "Stay safe out there. You're dismissed."

While the room emptied, I turned sideways to better shield Brigit from the moving crowd. Didn't want her paws getting stepped on. Once everyone had left the room, only Detective Jackson, the Big Dick, Brigit, and I remained.

Jackson jerked her head toward the door. "Let's go, folks."

Ten minutes later, the four of us pulled up to a house on East Dashwood Street, which lay in the northeastern quadrant of W1 and dead-ended at the railroad tracks that ran just west of and parallel to Interstate 35. An old, boxy sedan sat cockeyed in the front yard. Oxidized chocolate brown paint covered most of the car, though the driver's door, which had been replaced with a door scavenged from a salvage lot, was robin's egg blue. The house, like most others in this area, was around ninety years old. With some TLC and a designer touch, it could make a beautiful home. As is—with its cracked windows, faded white paint, and cushionless couch on the porch—not so much.

Jackson had ridden with Derek in his cruiser. They waited at the edge of the street while I clipped Brigit's leash to her collar and let her out of the back of my car.

Jackson's eyes cut to a trio of black plastic garbage bags sitting on the curb. "Have your dog check the trash."

"Sure." I led Brigit over to the bags and let her give them a thorough sniff. Trash left at the curb was fair game for a warrantless police search. No probable cause needed.

While my partner put her nose to work, Detective Jackson gave me and Derek the rundown.

"This house belongs to Sabina Patterson," she explained, "mother of Darius Patterson. Darius has two drug convictions. The first was for possession of meth. The second was for possession with intent to distribute. He was caught with crystal meth and crack in quantities large enough to indicate he was dealing in the stuff."

Interesting . . .

The detective continued to fill us in on the potential suspect. "Darius has two assault convictions, one for breaking a guy's arm after a dispute at an apartment complex and the other for briefly choking his own cousin with a strand of ribbon snatched off a gift at the family Christmas celebration in 2008."

"Choking, hmm?" I said, thinking back to the ragged neck on the murder victim. "Sounds familiar."

"My thought exactly," Jackson replied. "Luckily for the cousin, their granny intervened and knocked Darius out with a cast-iron skillet." She went on to tell us that, unluckily for Darius, Granny had pulled the frying pan off a hot stove, leaving him not only unconscious, but also with first-degree burns on his forehead.

"Serves 'im right," Derek said.

I was inclined to agree. "Did he get jail time for the assaults?"

Jackson nodded. "Spent four years in the Glossbrenner Unit down in the valley. He was released three months ago."

The question now was whether he was back in the drug game and, if so, whether he was connected to the murder in Forest Park.

Though Brigit had thoroughly sniffed, snuffled, and snorted her way around the garbage bags, she gave no alert. I gave her a nice scratch behind the ears to reward her efforts. "The bags are clear."

"Okay, then," Jackson said. "Let's roll."

We walked up to the porch, which creaked under our collective weight, threatening to give way. Derek positioned himself at an angle, resting his right hand on his belt near his gun. He spread his legs slightly and bent his knees, ready to move fast if needed. Jackson stood next to him, while Brigit and I took up a spot to the rear left.

Jackson rapped firmly on the door. *Rap-rap-rap.*

A moment later, we heard another creak, though this one came from the flooring behind the front door. The door did not open, however.

"I know you're there!" Detective Jackson called. "We heard the floor creak. Open up."

A moment later the door swung in to reveal an unsmiling black woman in a satin head scarf, zippered terrycloth robe, and cheap open-toe house shoes. "What do you want?"

"Good morning, Mrs. Patterson." Detective Jackson handed her a business card. "I'm Audrey Jackson with the Fort Worth PD. I'd like to speak with your son."

Mrs. Patterson gave the card back to the detective. "He's not here."

"Where is he?"

"How should I know?" Mrs. Patterson frowned. "He don't tell me everywhere he's goin'. He's a grown-ass man."

"If he's a grown-ass man," Jackson replied, nonplussed, "why's he still living with his mother?"

Touché.

A door opened down the hallway behind the woman and a man stepped out wearing nothing but a white tank top and a pair of wrinkled XXXL boxers. He certainly was a grown-ass man. His ass had grown to epic proportions. Clearly the guy had not spent his time in prison at the gym or exercising in the yard, sculpting his glutes.

Perhaps he'd chosen to curl up next to the fence with a classic novel, maybe something by Steinbeck or Tolstoy. A copy of *Hustler* was probably more like it, disguised behind an issue of *Golf Week*.

Other than his ass the guy was average sized, his skin the color of coffee with cream. Unlike our suspect, however, Darius had no curls. He wore his hair shorn nearly to the scalp, the burn scar from the frying pan visible on his forehead. Still, the haircut looked fresh. It was possible he'd purposefully had it cut and styled since Sunday.

Darius rubbed his eyes. "Hell, Mama! Who's coming by this earl—" He stopped speaking when he spotted us in the doorway.

Jackson waved him forward. "Come here, Darius. We'd like to talk to you a minute."

"You got a warrant?" Mrs. Patterson asked.

"No," the detective said.

Mrs. Patterson waved her son back. "Then he doesn't have to tell you nothin'."

"That's true," Jackson replied, "but if he doesn't talk to me now, he may find himself talking to me later down at the station."

Mrs. Patterson was not deterred. "He'll take his chances." With that, she slammed the door in our faces.

Jackson pushed past me with a huff. "Well, that was productive."

We climbed back into our cars and drove to the next suspect's place. Owen Haynes lived in a house, too, his being a yellow model with green shutters located on Carlock Street. Though Haynes's home was as old as the one Darius Patterson lived in, it was slightly better maintained. There was no car parked in the drive and the curtains had been pulled tightly shut.

"This is a rental," Jackson explained as we walked to the door. "Haynes's girlfriend leases it."

I wound Brigit's leash tighter around my hand to keep her close. "What's the scoop on Owen?"

"He's racked up convictions for both possession of crystal meth and assaulting the police officers who'd arrested him. Rumor has it he put up a damn good fight. He went after them with a pocketknife. Broke two fingers on one officer and stabbed the other in his upper arm."

Yikes.

Derek's reaction was the polar opposite of mine. He smiled and cracked his knuckles, as if hoping for a brawl. "If he puts up a fight today, he won't know what hit him."

"What does Haynes look like?" I asked. "Anything like the guy in the sketch?"

Jackson pulled out her cell phone, tapped the screen a few times, and held it up to show me the screen. "You tell me."

The photo on the screen depicted a man in his twenties with dark, loose curls surrounding his face. His hair was longer than that on the man shown in the police sketch, but a recent trip to Supercuts could account for the difference. He appeared to be mixed race, with a high percentage of Caucasian relative to African-American. His skin was a *café au lait* tone.

My eyes moved from the screen to the detective. "There's a definite resemblance."

Dare I hope that we'd find Haynes at home bearing scratches or other telltale defensive wounds and put this case to a quick rest? Yeah, I dared. Chalk it up to rookie idealism.

We walked up to the door and assumed the same positions we'd taken earlier at the Pattersons' residence. Jackson knocked on the door. *Knock-knock-knock-knock.* My heart knocked in my chest right along with her.

We stood there a full thirty seconds before Jackson tried again. *Knock-knock-knock.*

Still no answer.

The detective tried one last time. *Knock-knock.* Nothing. "Let's try the neighbors."

The older retired couple who lived in the house on the left had nothing to offer.

"We don't get out much," the woman said. "I can't remember the last time I saw anyone over there."

"Me, neither," her husband added. "It's been awhile."

The detective handed the man her card. "Call me if you see anyone at the house, okay? But it would be best if you don't let them know we've been by. Understand?"

The man dipped his head. "Sure do."

The young, scraggly man who answered the door at the house on the right claimed he hadn't seen anyone at the house recently, either. He scratched at the greasy hair at his temple. "I think Owen may have taken off. For good."

"So you knew him?" Jackson asked.

"Not good or nothin'." The guy's nose twitched. "I mean, I just seen him out working on his car every once in a while. That's all."

Jackson handed him a card, too. "If Owen or his girlfriend show up, I'd appreciate it if you gave me a call ASAP."

"Yeah. Okay."

Despite his assurance, I had my doubts he'd contact the police. He seemed more like the type who would let Haynes know we were on his trail.

We tried a couple of houses across the street, but nobody was home.

"Looks like we struck out," Jackson said, turning to head back to the cars. "You two cruise by here on occasion, give me a call if you see any cars or people."

"Will do," I said.

Derek tugged on the waistband of his pants, jostling his nards, a habitual behavior that disgusted me though it seemed to give him some satisfaction. "Anything you say, Detective."

"How about I give you a ride back to the station?" I suggested to the detective. "Let Mackey and his muscles get back out on the streets."

My compliment was backhanded, meant to manipulate Mackey so he wouldn't fight my proposal to give Jackson a ride back to the office. I wanted to hear more about the burglaries Captain Leone had mentioned at this morning's meeting, and see what I might learn.

Mackey eyed me suspiciously, but Jackson shrugged. "Fine by me. Let's go, Officer Luz."

Mackey continued to watch as the detective, Brigit, and I climbed into my cruiser. I started the engine and pulled into the street.

"So," I said to Jackson, "about those burglaries—"

She let loose a snort. "I should've known you were up to something offering to drive me back to the station."

"I'm eager to learn. That's a good thing."

"You're right," she acquiesced. "It makes you a little annoying at times, though."

I chose to ignore that comment. "Given that the burglaries took place in the late afternoon, the thieves could have been teenagers looking for items they could sell or pawn, maybe to buy drugs."

"Or the thief could be someone who is out of work," Jackson added. "Or someone who is employed but doesn't work a regular weekday shift."

Darn. That could include a lot of people.

I pulled to a stop at an intersection. "The fact that both homeowners were on trips when the burglaries took place seems like it might be an important fact."

Could both houses have been struck by someone who knew the homeowners would be away for prolonged periods of time? Maybe someone from their lawn care or housekeeping services, if they hired such people? I hated to suspect the maids. Cleaning crews were blamed far too often for the theft of items misplaced or wrongfully reported stolen by home or business owners. But sometimes they did, in fact, take advantage of their access in order to pocket things that didn't belong to them. Or perhaps the victims had submitted orders at the post office to have their mail held. Maybe a postal employee was the perpetrator.

As I pulled out from the stop sign, I ran each of these ideas by the detective. "What do y-you think?"

"I think your idle speculation is just that. Idle. I don't have time to run down all those leads."

"I do."

"That's not what you're paid for, Officer Luz. You're paid to patrol the streets."

"I'll make it quick. You know, just ask a few questions and see if anything jumps out at me."

She cut me a look. "You were one of those geeks in school who always did the extra-credit projects, weren't you?"

She'd nailed me. The only extra-credit projects I hadn't done were any that required me to speak in front of the class. My stutter had been too pronounced back then.

She let out a long breath. "I suppose it can't hurt. I'll e-mail you a copy of the files."

"Great!"

After dropping Detective Jackson back at the station, I decided to head down to Berry Street, which marked the southern edge of the W1 division. My partner and I just passed Hemphill when a collision up ahead forced us to slow down. FWPD was already on scene and appeared to have things under control. I lifted my fingers off the steering wheel to wave to Summer, who was directing traffic to detour down Travis Avenue.

I was driving through an intersection a block down

when a flash of red came out of nowhere and passed in front of my car, mere inches between the blur and my bumper. I slammed on my brakes. *Screeech!* What the hell was that?

I switched on my lights and turned left to pursue the offender.

During my stint as a cop I'd pulled over vehicles with four wheels, eighteen-wheeler trucks, and two-wheeled motorcycles. I'd even once pulled over one of those goofy-looking three-wheeled cycles. Seriously, if you need training wheels, maybe you should just drive a regular car. But this was the first time I'd pulled over someone on eight wheels.

The young woman on roller skates zipped ninety-to-nothing down the street. She wore a helmet and pads, but a fat lot of good they'd do her if she kept pulling out in front of moving cars.

I caught up to her, leaving a safe distance between us in case she suddenly fell. She made no move to pull over. Probably she had no idea I was behind her. Skating helmets don't have rearview mirrors, after all.

I grabbed the mic for my public address system and pushed the button. "You on the skates. Pull over to the curb."

The woman glanced behind her, spotted me, and performed a skilled half turn so that she now skated backward while facing my car. She dipped her feet forward to slow herself down and eventually came to a full stop in the street, raising her hands in the air.

I pulled my car over, left the lights on, and climbed out. As I walked toward her, I noticed several things. This woman was in her mid-twenties, like me. She was very tall, five ten or five eleven, I'd guess, and built from solid muscle. The red spandex shirt she wore featured the open-can logo for the Fort Worth Whoop-Ass, the local women's roller derby team. And she was sobbing. Huge tears streamed down her face and her shoulders shook uncontrollably.

I stopped a few feet in front of her. "Are you okay?"

She shook her head, lowered one of her arms to wipe her eyes on her sleeve, and sniffled. "My boyfriend dumped me," she managed between crying fits. "We've been together for two years—" She stopped to gulp back a sob. "And suddenly he says I'm not 'girly' enough for him." She lowered her other arm now, too. "He sure seemed to think I was girly enough last night when he was jackhammering away at my—"

"Okay!" My own hand was up now. Funny how some people don't want to give cops any information and others want to give too much. "I'm sorry about the breakup. But you can't be out here skating around like this, not paying attention to traffic, or you'll get yourself killed."

She bit her quivering lip. "I know. I'm sorry. It's just that I had no idea this was coming and he's moving his stuff out of our place and I couldn't bear to watch."

"What's your name?"

"Francesca Kerrigan. I go by Frankie."

Frankie? Hmm. Maybe her boyfriend had a point about the 'girly' thing. Still, he shouldn't have used her for sex if he planned to dump her the next morning. *Jerk.* I glanced at my watch. "How long have you been out here, Frankie?"

She shrugged. "I don't know. An hour or two?"

"Any chance your boyfriend c-could be done now? I'd be happy to give you a ride home." This woman was in no condition to be out on the streets. I'd feel horrible if I left her out here and she got plowed down by a bus or something.

She nodded and skated toward me. "One of his friends showed up with a truck a couple of hours ago. Between the two of them they're probably done by now."

I opened the passenger door for her and she skated over and climbed into the car, easily filling the seat.

"Wow!" she said. "You work with a dog? How cool is that?"

Sometimes it was really cool. Other times, like when Brigit nearly burst my eardrum barking in the car, not so much.

I circled around to the driver's side and climbed in. I glanced over at her, noticing a few more things up close. She had great cheekbones and her eyes were blue, as were the few jagged pieces of hair sticking out from under her helmet. "Where to?"

She hiked a thumb behind us. I pulled into a driveway and reversed out, turning to go back the way I'd come. In less than a minute we turned onto Travis Avenue and pulled up in front of a bungalow-style home, a type common to South Hemphill Heights and the surrounding neighborhoods, though this one was on the smaller side compared to some of the others. The paint was a subtle mauve with ivory trim, the front door painted a nicely contrasting navy blue. A giant magnolia tree shaded the front yard, making it impossible for grass to grow, but ivy ground cover was doing its best to compensate. A prefab single-car detached garage sat to the right and back of the house, clearly having been added quite some time after the house was originally built. The backyard was enclosed with a six-foot wooden privacy fence. A pickup truck sat at the curb, the bed piled with a sofa, cardboard boxes, a pinball machine, and assorted odds and ends.

"Dammit!" Frankie said. "He's still here."

The front door opened and two large, dark-haired men came out, one on either end of a big-screen TV.

Frankie was out of my cruiser as if she'd been hurled from an ejection seat. "Hey!" she hollered at the men. "You can't take that TV! I paid for half of it!"

"And I paid for the other half," retorted one of the men, who I assumed was the Dumper.

As the two men ignored Frankie and continued toward the truck, I climbed out of the patrol car and raised my palm. "Stop right there. You've admitted that half of that television belongs to Ms. Kerrigan. If you don't return that television to the house I will have to arrest both of you for theft."

"What the fuck?" Dumper spat.

His friend said nothing, though his expression made it clear he was annoyed. He probably had better things to do than get in the middle of a domestic squabble and risk arrest over a TV.

I turned to Frankie. "How much did the set cost?"

"Total? Six hundred dollars. We each paid three."

I returned my focus to Dumper. "You can either pay Ms. Kerrigan three hundred dollars cash right now or you can return the TV to the house."

"That's bullshit!" he hollered.

"That's the law." Or at least I thought it was. When something—a television, a pet, a child—was the subject of debate, law enforcement tended to protect the status quo unless and until one of the parties obtained a court order to the contrary.

"Fine!" He lowered his end of the TV to the ground and his friend did the same. Not exactly what I'd told them to do, but Dumper looked so angry at this point I didn't trust him not to intentionally drop the thing if he carried it back to the house.

Without another word, the two men headed back to the truck.

"Good riddance!" Frankie hollered after them, breaking down in fresh tears. Evidently, big girls *do* cry. A lot.

I patted the gun holstered at my hip. "He's still in range. Want me to shoot him?"

A laugh spurted from her. "Would you? Between the eyes would be good."

"Between the legs would be even better."

The men climbed into the truck, slammed their doors, and drove off. She turned her back, as if it was too hard to watch.

I gestured to the house. "He may be gone, but at least you've got a nice place."

"For now." She used her fingers to brush away her tears. "No way can I afford this place on my own."

"So you'll be looking for a roommate?"

She shrugged. "I guess so."

"Does your lease allow pets?"

She nodded. "I've got a cat."

"Can my partner and I take a look?"

"Sure." She sniffled. "Why not?"

We brought the TV up onto the porch where it would be safe. I rounded up Brigit and the three of us went inside. Rolling through the place on her skates, Frankie took me and Brigit on a quick tour of the house, her fluffy, green-eyed calico cat trotting along behind us.

The living room had lots of windows, hardwood floors, and an empty spot where the sofa had been. Though not large, the kitchen had sufficient cabinet space and an L-shaped counter with a two-seater breakfast bar, as well as a small dining nook. I opened the back door and let Brigit out to explore the yard for a moment or two. When she returned, we continued the tour.

Down a hallway off the living room were two bedrooms and two bathrooms, perfect for a roommate situation. The back bedroom stood empty except for a poster of Kate Upton lying bare-breasted and virtually bare-assed on a sandy beach. The only thing she wore was a tiny, ruffled thong that left nothing to the imagination.

Frankie snatched the poster off the wall, crumpled it

up, and hurled it across the room. "He used to call this room his 'man cave.' Kept all his dirty magazines and porn collection in here."

"Ick. You'll be better off without him."

"You're right. What did that butthead ever do for me?"

I took one last glance around as we made our way back to the front door. Despite its age, the house looked to be in fairly good shape. There was some loose trim here and there and I'd noticed the toilet giving off the telltale sound of a loose seal in the tank, but nothing that couldn't be easily repaired. It had everything I'd been looking for and then some—a fenced yard, off-street parking, convenience. It even had a fireplace.

I stopped on the front porch. "I've been looking for a place with more space and a yard for my dog." Of course I'd been looking for a place I could manage on my own, but going solo didn't seem to be in the cards. "Should we give it a try?"

Frankie gave me a smile and raised her hand for a high five. "Hell, yeah!"

Slap! As my hand met hers, I realized I'd known my new roommate for a grand total of ten minutes. I hadn't asked about her job or run a background check. Moving in here was an incredibly impulsive decision.

But something told me it would prove to be a good one.

FOURTEEN
A YARD OF HER OWN

Brigit

Brigit loved this place!

The front porch was shady and cool, the perfect place from which a dog could keep watch over the neighborhood or lie down for a nap. So much better than their current digs, where she had to stand guard at a narrow window that gave only a partial view of the apartment complex parking lot. Hard to work under those conditions.

The floors were sturdy hardwood in the living room and bedrooms, linoleum in the kitchen and baths. Brigit would have preferred nice, plush carpet to lie on, but she knew Megan would put down a soft rug or bed for her. Besides, her partner let her up on the furniture, so the floors weren't a deal-breaker.

The kitchen contained fading, residual smells of bacon grease and pork chops, making Brigit's mouth water. Too bad her partner was a vegetarian. Still, those soy sausages Megan sometimes made for breakfast weren't half bad. They weren't half good, either. But a dog who'd gone without a meal for several days under the negligent care of a previous owner knew better than to ever turn down food, no matter how it tasted.

When Megan opened the back door for her, it seemed like a portal to heaven. Brigit saw a deep yard with a gnarly live oak and a tall pecan tree that, from the smell, served as home to an extensive squirrel family sure to provide Brigit with hours of entertainment. As soon as Megan unclipped her leash, Brigit had bolted into the space, running around and kicking up her heels, thrilled to have room to roam and romp. The dirt was soft under her feet, perfect for digging and hiding bones in. A *rrrruf!* from next door told her she'd have a friend in the neighborhood, a terrier judging from what she could see through a small gap in the fence boards.

The only downside was that darn cat. The stupid thing had followed them all through the house, had tried on several occasions to get Brigit's attention by swiping at her tail. *Pathetic.* Brigit sensed the poor thing might be lonely. Heck, she'd been there herself, back when she'd lived with her first owner, who rarely gave her attention. While Brigit would have preferred to share her home with another dog, she'd learn to tolerate the feline if she had to.

As Megan led her back to their cruiser, Brigit slowed to sniff the ivy, scenting two rats hiding in the foliage. Had she not been on a leash, she would've eaten one as an hors d'oeuvre, the other for dinner.

Or maybe she would've shared the second one with that cat . . .

FIFTEEN
WRONG NUMBER

Dub

He stared down at the phone number scribbled on the Taco Bell napkin in his hand. He shouldn't dial it. He knew that. Katrina Mayhew was his mother in name only.

But her crappy parenting hadn't been totally her fault, had it? It wasn't her fault she'd gotten addicted to drugs. Some people just couldn't control themselves. She hadn't come from the best family herself and the meth . . . it made her someone else.

Drugs could make a person do horrible things they never intended to do. Dub knew that better than anyone. And the dealers who sold the drugs, who got people addicted, who ruined so many lives? If it were up to Dub, every last one of them would be wiped off the face of the earth.

He picked up the landline phone, willing it to explode in his hand, to stop him from doing what he knew he was going to do.

Okay, so he'd call her. No biggie, right? He would just talk to her for a minute, make sure she was doing all right, catch her up on his life. She'd be proud to know he was making good grades. That he'd played on the basketball team at Gainesville State School—second string and they'd had a losing season, but still. She'd be thrilled to know that, after encouragement from Wes and Trent, he'd auditioned for a role and would be playing Mayor Shinn in *The Music Man* at Paschal High School. It wasn't the lead, but the fact that he'd been chosen at all, that the director had seen something in him, had made him think that maybe change was possible after all. And, of course there was Jenna. She'd seen something good in Dub, too, even if her parents only saw his rap sheet and had forbidden her from dating him.

He'd just call his mother.

Have a quick talk.

And that would be it.

Sure.

Trent and Wes wouldn't find out. There was no record of local calls on a landline phone bill, right?

He began dialing—*8-1-7*—angry to find the phone shaking in his hand. *For shit's sake*, he told himself. *Chill.*

He finished dialing.

He'd nearly hung up when Katrina answered after the fifth ring. Her voice sounded wary, probably because she didn't recognize the number. "Hello?"

"Hi . . . Mom." *God, it shouldn't be so hard to say that word, should it?*

"Wade!" she cried, as if she'd just won a Caribbean cruise on *Wheel of Fortune*. "It's so good to hear from you! I've been hoping you would call!"

He wasn't sure where to start. "It was . . . uh . . . a surprise seeing you the other day."

"It was fate, honey!" she cried. *"Fate."*

Uh-oh. He feared where she might be going with this. *Better take control of the conversation.* "So, uh, I played basketball in Gainesville. And I tried out for a play here. I'm gonna be in *The Music Man*."

"Is that right? That's great, hon. Just great. I've missed you so much!"

"I'm making good grades. "Mostly B's but I've got an A in Hist—"

"You think you could come by? You know, so we can talk in person? I'd love to see you."

Dub hesitated. "I'm not sure that's a good idea."

"What do you mean 'not a good idea'? I'm your mother. Your *mother*, Wade. How can you turn your back on me?"

There it was. The same old guilt trip. "I'm not turning my back—"

"Just come by for a little bit," she said, her voice softer now, sweeter. "Come see where I'm staying. I've got things together now. I just want you to see. That ain't too much to ask, is it?"

There was a long silence during which Dub nearly hung up the phone. But he didn't. *He couldn't.* "*He* isn't there, is he?"

"Oh, hell no! I am done with that sorry son-of-a-bitch."

"You sure?"

She huffed. "Would I lie to you?"

Yes. Yes, you would. Over and over and over again. And I'd be stupid enough to keep believing you . . .

She didn't wait for him to answer. "Come on over. I'll make you dinner. I've got corn dogs in the freezer."

Frozen corn dogs. Dub supposed most teenage boys would be thrilled to eat junk food but, even though Wesley's homemade meals tasted like rubber, they meant something. That Wes *cared*.

"Come on," his mother said. "You'll break my heart if you don't come by." She gave him the address. "You got that, hon?"

Dub felt sick. He put a hand to his eyes. "Yeah. All right. I'll see you soon."

He hung up the phone, rounded up his history book, and slid it into his backpack. Might as well make good use of his time on the bus to get the required reading done. He put on his favorite hoodie, the white one with the black tornado, the Gainesville State School mascot. He didn't dare wear it to school here. Though the name of the reform school appeared only in small print on the top left side, things were bad enough already without him reminding people he had a criminal record. But on the east side of town where his mother lived the sweatshirt could give him some street cred.

Wes was out shopping for groceries, which meant Dub could avoid the usual grilling about where he was going and when he'd be back. Sometimes he wasn't sure his foster fathers totally trusted him. They probably shouldn't. He left a note on the kitchen counter.

Gone to library. I'll be back by dinnertime.
D.

He caught the number 6 bus on 8th Street, switching to an eastbound number 24 on Berry. He'd just finished the chapter in his history book when the bus arrived in the Morningside neighborhood. It pulled to a stop with a *whoosh* of the air brakes.

Dub looked out the window at the rundown apartment complex where his mother lived. The place was made of that god-awful pink brick they used way back. The gray awning over the walkway was torn, a loose corner flapping in the wind. Three young men of various races hung out in the parking lot, sitting on hoods of beater cars, drinking beer. *Damn.* He wished he'd brought something for protection. A piece of pipe. A knife. His brass knuckles.

Dub should get on a westbound bus and head back to Fairmount. That's exactly what he should do. But instead, he found himself jumping up from his seat and hollering "Wait!" as the bus driver began to close the doors.

"Hurry up!" the driver called back to him. "I've got a schedule to keep."

Dub hurried to the front of the bus and climbed down the steps to exit onto the sidewalk. The doors slid closed behind him with a *shwuck*, as if shutting him out of the new life he'd left behind. He slid the back of his hand across his forehead, like he could wipe away the thought. *Stupid.* All he had to do to go back to his new life was get on another bus. Hell, he could probably call Wes to come pick him up. Wes was close to his own mother. He'd understand Dub's need to make sure his mother was safe.

As Dub crossed the street, making his way toward the complex, he noticed the three men stiffen. He knew what that meant. They saw him coming and planned to defend their turf. As much as he wanted to turn and run right now, he knew that was the worst thing he could do. One whiff of weakness and these guys would be on him like white on rice.

As he came near, he mustered his inner tough guy, walking in a loose-limbed swagger, one that said *I ain't scared of you pussies.*

He forced himself to lock eyes with the black man, who seemed to be the leader. Dub knew looking away would be a sign of fear. The man had short hair with a swirl design shaved over each ear and eyes that were dark and dangerous and hard and soulless. The eyes of a man who didn't give a damn about anyone but himself. The eyes of a man who'd make you sorry if you crossed him.

Dub was all too familiar with eyes like that.

One of the others, an Asian guy with a neck tattoo, stepped forward, his eyes narrowed until they were only dark slits in his face. He leaned to the side to take in Dub's backpack, got in Dub's face, and said, "What the hell you doing here, college boy?"

Dub was years away from college, but he wasn't about to let these thugs know how young he really was. For once, he was glad his experiences had aged him, taught him how to take care of himself. And he thanked the puberty fairy for not holding out on him.

"You don't want to fuck with me," Dub said coolly, his eyes locking on the Asian man's now. Wes may have learned how to behave at cotillion, but Dub had learned it on the streets. "I just got out of the joint."

Of course the "joint" had been the state school for juvenile offenders, but these guys didn't need to know that.

The Asian's eyes opened wide now and his brows arched. "Prison? No shit?"

Funny how being incarcerated made people fear him in nice neighborhoods, but got him respect in places like this.

The black guy cocked his head. "What you doin' here?"

"None of your fucking business." No sense telling them he'd come to see his mommy.

The man chuckled, slid off the hood of the Dodge he'd been sitting on, and extended a fisted hand with scabby, skinned knuckles. He'd either been in a fight or worked with machinery. Dub's money was on a fight. If this guy had a decent job, he wouldn't be hanging out in a parking lot like this in the afternoon.

"Welcome, brother," the man said. "I'm Marquise. 'Cause I'm hard and cut—" he lifted his shirt to show off a tight set of abs, "like a diamond."

Dub wondered if Marquise used that lame line on women and whether any of the women were stupid enough to fall for it. He also doubted whether the name was legit. Dub understood guys like this. They might hang together, but sharing personal information? Not gonna happen. Nonetheless, he curled his fingers and bumped fists with the man.

The guy lifted his chin to indicate the Asian. "The nosy one is Long Dong."

The Asian smiled, but it was more evil than friendly. Guys like this didn't make friends. They only hung with people who could provide them with some type of benefit, whether it be sex, drugs, cash, or alibis.

Marquise hiked a thumb toward the Latino. "That's Gato."

Dub knew from his third period Spanish class—in which he'd earned a B+ the last six weeks—that *gato* meant *cat*. He could see why the guy had the name. His moves were sleek and catlike as he slid down the hood of the car and stepped over to give Dub another fist bump.

"WC," Dub said, introducing himself.

"WC?" Marquise asked.

Dub wasn't about to tell him the initials stood for Wade Chandler. His name was none of their business. Besides, they might laugh at the fact that his mother had named him after a character on *Friends*. "WC," Dub repeated. "White Chocolate."

"White Chocolate?" Marquise grinned. "I like that, man."

Dub raised a hand and headed off. "Later."

The men engaged in speculation as he walked away.

"I bet he's going to see Yolanda. Get hisself a little sumthin-sumthin'," said Long Dong.

Dub had no idea who Yolanda was, and he didn't want to find out. The only girl he was interested in was Jenna.

Eyeing the numbers on the apartment doors, Dub spotted 215 and took the stairs up to it. He hesitated again before knocking.

Last chance, dude, he told himself. *Turn around and go back to Trent and Wes's house. What did this woman ever do for you?*

Still, he found himself rapping once on the door. *Rap.* His mother might not have ever done much for him, but that didn't excuse him from doing anything for her. He needed to protect her—not only from Leandro, but from herself.

Dub heard the grating noise of a chain bolt being slid open and the *click* of the dead bolt as it unlocked.

She opened the door only a crack at first, the frown on her face spreading into a wide smile when she spotted Dub on the walkway. "You came!"

He didn't know why she seemed so surprised. He'd told her he would. Then again, a lot of people had made promises to her that they hadn't kept.

"You look good," he told her as she opened the door to let him inside.

"'Cause I'm not using anymore," she said. "Those days are behind me."

Dub had heard those same words before. They'd turned out to be a lie. He could only hope she spoke the truth this time.

She closed the door behind him. "Nice place, huh?"

Nice? Hardly. It was a tiny one-bedroom apartment with stained carpeting and cigarette burns on the kitchen countertop, nothing like the beautiful home Trent and Wes—*and Dub*—lived in. But, compared to some of the other shitholes his mother had rented, this one was a freakin' palace. No sense putting the woman down. She'd do that herself.

"Yeah. Not bad." Dub laid his backpack on the breakfast bar.

"Let me take you on the grand tour." She led him first into the kitchen. He opened the pantry to find only a half loaf of white bread, a jar of store-brand peanut butter, and a bottle of imitation maple syrup. The freezer held only frozen waffles and the corn dogs she'd mentioned earlier, while the fridge contained a quart of milk, a bottle of yellow mustard, and a dozen paper-wrapped Taco Bell burritos. Not a fruit or vegetable in the house, not even a can of peaches. Some things never changed.

But had his mother changed?

She claimed she had, but was it the truth?

She led him from the kitchen into the living room, where a single faux-leather recliner faced a small television sitting atop a plastic bin. No coffee table. No lamp. And no baby grand piano like the one Trent played. He'd even taught Dub a song or two.

Dub stepped to the back of the room and pushed the dusty curtains aside to find a sliding glass door that led to a patio overlooking the apartments' murky pool. He turned back to find his mother looking up at him, her face anxious, like a child seeking a parent's approval. He supposed it made sense. Their roles had been reversed for as long as he could remember.

She led him into the bedroom next. It was a small room, barely wide enough for the full-sized mattress that lay directly on the floor. At least the pink-and-red striped comforter she'd spread over it looked clean. Her Taco Bell uniform hung from a hook on the back of the door. The rest of her clothes were stacked in a plastic bin on the floor of the open closet.

They walked back into the living room. Rather than take the only chair in the room, Dub leaned back against the breakfast bar. "I'm really glad you're doing okay, Mom."

He was happy her life seemed to be going good now. Happy and relieved.

Wondering about the time, he reached for the cell phone he always kept in his jeans pocket. It wasn't there.

Damn.

Had it fallen out of his pocket on the bus? Or had he

been so thrown off balance by his phone conversation with his mother that he'd left it back at Trent and Wes's house?

"What time is it?" he asked.

His mother glanced at the clock on the stove. "Five forty. Why?"

Dub retrieved his backpack from the counter. "I need to get going."

"But you just got here!"

"I know. But it's a long bus ride back home and I've got homework to do."

"No!" Tears brimmed in Katrina's eyes. "Don't leave me, Wade. Please!"

The desperation on her face and in her voice stabbed him in the heart.

"I can't stay," he told her, feeling his resolve begin to break down even as he spoke. "You know that."

Not long before his most recent arrest, which led to him being sent to Gainesville Child Protective Services had, once and for all, deemed Katrina an unfit mother and given up on attempts to reunify the family. She'd been a jobless, homeless drug addict. After being lied to and stolen from time and time again, Katrina's immediate family had cut all ties with her, so Dub had been sent to live with distant relatives in Katrina's hometown of Memphis—relatives who quickly grew tired of the burden and cost of housing and clothing and feeding a young boy. His own relatives had less patience for him and less concern for his welfare than the foster home he'd lived in when he was younger. When they heard Dub's mother had worked things out with Dub's father and now had a roof—*a leaky one*—over her head, they'd put him on a bus back to his mother in Fort Worth.

When Dub had later been arrested, the social worker was enraged to learn the boy had been returned to his mother against court orders. Probably not unusual, though, Dub guessed.

"Give me another chance, Dub!" His mother grabbed his arm, inadvertently digging her nails into his skin. "I'll show you! I'll be a good mother!"

Too late for that. Dub didn't need a mother anymore. He was nearly a man. He could take care of himself. Now it was his mother who needed taking care of.

He felt himself weakening. *She needed him.* And if anyone found out what he'd done last Sunday and wanted to come after him, they wouldn't know to look for him here.

Seeming to sense that Dub was giving in, Katrina wrapped her arms around him in a bear hug, sobbing into his shoulder. "You're all I've got, Dub! Without you I've got nothing!"

He hated to disappoint Trent and Wes, hated to lose all the progress he'd made, but what could he do?

He had to stay. He had to keep his mother safe. Because no matter how Dub's situation turned out, he knew that, at some point, his mother would take up with Andro again. She couldn't help herself.

And this time Andro was liable to kill her.

SIXTEEN
EXTRA CREDIT

Megan

On Saturday morning, in recognition of Valentine's Day, I put a white collar with red hearts on Brigit. Just because the dog was a K-9 officer didn't mean she couldn't look festive, right? Besides, she had a date with Blast tonight. Might as well look like she'd made some effort, even if he wouldn't appreciate it. Her male counterpart would probably prefer she roll in garbage prior to their meet-up.

As I dressed myself, the morning news played on the television, the forecaster mentioning that warm air flowing up from the Gulf of Mexico would create early-spring conditions, but that the Canadians were fighting back by sending a simultaneous cold front down from the north. This international weather war would be fought out over the Southern Plains region which included Arkansas, Oklahoma, and Texas. In other words, we Fort Worth residents should be prepared for the potential of rapidly changing outdoor conditions today. Thus forewarned, I grabbed my rain poncho, my FWPD windbreaker, and my heavier police-issue jacket, preparing myself for any eventuality.

Before heading off to work, I stopped by my apartment manager's office and knocked on the door. Dale Grigsby answered the door, his pimply paunch, as usual, not quite covered by the T-shirt he wore. He held half a cherry Pop-Tart in his hand. The entire other half seemed to be in his mouth. "What?" he said, revealing a mouth full of half-chewed cherry pastry paste.

I handed him an envelope. "I'm giving my notice. I'm moving out at the end of the month."

Frankie had already given me a set of keys for the house on Travis Avenue and I'd paid her prorated rent for the remainder of February. I planned to move my things into the house tomorrow.

Grigsby tossed the envelope onto a table next to the door. "You've got to give thirty days' notice," he said, "You'll owe me for part of March, too. Read your lease."

"So *now* you're a stickler for rules?" I spat. "Need I point out the numerous building code violations you've ignored?"

Grigsby frowned and took another bite of his Pop-Tart.

"Besides," I added, "don't you have a waiting list for this place?"

Few apartments in town offered rent as cheap as Eastside Arms. The low rent was what led me, and every other tenant, to the place. It sure as hell wasn't the ambiance.

Grigsby chewed the bite and swallowed. "All right, all right. You always were a pain in the ass. No skin off my nose if you go."

I blew him a kiss. "I'll miss you, too."

Yeah, right. I'll miss him when hell freezes over.

At 8:00 A.M. the day was already warm. The newscaster on the local NPR affiliate predicted near record-breaking high temperatures by the afternoon. You wouldn't get

any complaints from me. The day before had been cold
and wet and dreary. As short as Texas winters were, I
was already in the mood for spring. With any luck, that
Canadian cold front would stall out over Oklahoma.

Brigit and I picked up our car at the station and headed
out on patrol, our first destination Owen Haynes's house.
The driveway was still empty, the curtains drawn. Detective Jackson had informed me that she'd stopped by the
house twice more during the week, but had no luck.
Looked like Haynes and his girlfriend might have flown
the coop permanently. But whether it was to flee arrest
for Samuelson's murder was unclear. I checked with the
neighbors again, but still nobody claimed to have seen
anyone at the house.

As I waited at the stop sign at Carlock and Hemphill,
an SUV came roaring up the road, nearly running up
on the curb as the driver swerved around a smaller
vehicle.

Not on my watch, buddy.

I switched on my flashing lights and turned right,
going after the SUV. The smaller vehicle pulled over to
let me pass, and I laid on the gas, moving up behind the
still-speeding car. Rather than pull over, the driver put
the pedal to the medal. *Moron.* If he thought his SUV
could outrun my cruiser, he had poop for brains. Still, we
officers had been cautioned against unnecessary high-
speed chases, which posed a risk of injury to innocent by-
standers. The general public had become aware that
officers were less likely than they used to be to engage in
hot pursuit. Looked like this ass was going to put that theory to the test.

I flipped on my siren now. The guy still made no
move to pull over or brake.

I grabbed my mic and pushed the button to activate the
radio. "Backup needed on Hemphill heading north from
Allen. Got a speeder evading arrest."

Probably realizing officers would be waiting for him up ahead, the driver hooked a right turn on Magnolia. Unfortunately for him, he hooked it much too fast, the back end of his vehicle swinging around like a square dancer. Tires squealed as he braked. *Screeeeee!*

Dumbass. Didn't he know to turn into a skid?

His SUV came to a stop in the middle of the road. He glanced around furtively, realizing that, though he'd somehow managed not to hit another car, he was now hopelessly boxed in by traffic.

I pushed the button to activate my patrol car's public address system. "Step out of the car with your hands up."

The man banged his hands on the steering wheel before doing as told. He slid out of his truck, his meaty hands raised to his shoulders.

The guy was Caucasian, with a round body and an equally round, bald head. His lips were full and protruded more than usual. He looked look like a human rubber duck.

"On your knees," I said through the mic, fighting the urge to add *quack-quack*.

He put one hand down to lower himself to the asphalt, then raised it again once he was kneeling.

Brigit stood in her enclosure, breathing down my neck, her tail wagging as I shifted the gear into park. I emerged from my car, standing behind the door until I could extend my baton. *Snap!*

"Any more monkey business," I called to the human duck, "and you will be sorry. Understand?"

His only response was a fat-lipped scowl.

I circled around behind him and pulled out my handcuffs. "Put your hands behind you."

"Godammit!" he spat, though he did as he was told.

Once he was cuffed, I circled back around to his front. "Who do you think you are, driving like that? Jeff Gordon?"

"No!" he snapped. "I think I'm a stupid asshole!"

He'd get no argument from me.

His scowl disappeared, and his big lips began to bounce as he started blubbering. "I must be a stupid asshole if my wife and best friend think they can carry on right under my nose and I wouldn't figure it out."

I groaned. "That's rough. Let me guess. You were on your way to set your friend straight?"

He could only nod now, engaged as he was in an all-out blubber bonanza, big tears rolling down his cheeks.

"I don't blame you for being upset," I said, "but I do blame you for not pulling over. You should always do what a cop tells you."

Another squad car pulled up, Summer at the wheel. When she emerged from the car, she stared at the guy for a moment, a puzzled look on her face. "You look familiar. Have I arrested you before?"

Still blubbering, the man shook his head.

I stepped over to my coworker and whispered, "Rubber duck."

"Ah." She nodded. "That's it."

After explaining the situation to Summer, I let her take over. Because they had no backseat, K-9 cruisers could not be used to transport suspects. It was a nice benefit of being partnered with a dog. Didn't have to listen to the cursing and threats suspects often spewed from the backseat of a patrol car. Less paperwork, too.

As Summer led the man to her cruiser, she called over to me. "We're overdue for drinks."

"I'm moving into a new place tomorrow," I told her. "You'll have to come over and see it. I'll get a bottle of moscato. You can meet my new roommate. She has blue hair."

"Blue hair?" Summer's nose crinkled. "Is she an old lady or a Smurf?"

"Neither. She plays roller derby."

"Ah. That explains it."

While Summer loaded the man into his patrol car, I pulled my cruiser to the curb, then did the same with the man's SUV. I radioed for dispatch to send a tow truck and Brigit and I went, once again, on our merry way.

At ten o'clock, I headed to Mistletoe Heights to meet with the first burglary victims, the married couple who'd been on a cruise when their house had been hit. I left the windows down on the cruiser and admonished Brigit to "be a good girl and wait nicely" while I spoke to the couple on their front porch.

Though the officer who'd responded to the burglary call and completed the report had noted that the two had been on vacation when their house was hit and had listed the items that had been stolen, his report was sorely lacking in details. Truth be told, very few burglaries are ever solved. For one, the people who commit them know to hit quick and get the hell out of Dodge. Even if they're spotted, the person who reports them is advised not to confront them. By the time police arrive the thieves are usually long gone. Secondly, burglaries are a lower priority than drug or violent crimes. Relative to a murder or rape, a stolen laptop seems insignificant. Staff, funds, and time were limited, and the police department simply didn't have the resources to devote to tracking down every burglar. But I saw these break-ins as a challenge, a chance to see if I could put the clues together, figure out who the bad guy or guys were, and bring them to justice. The crimes would give me a chance to practice, to hone my skills so that once I became an official detective three years from now, I'd be the best detective the Fort Worth Police Department had ever seen.

The couple, John Bayer and his wife Elena, were both ginger-haired, both lean and trim, and both dressed in trendy exercise gear.

"I've read over the report," I told them, "but I'm

hoping you can give me more detailed information today. Maybe something that will give me a lead to pursue. Let's start with the trip you were on. Can you tell me more about that?"

Elena nodded, resting her hand on the doorjamb. "When the house was robbed we were on a five-day eastern Caribbean cruise. It left from San Juan, Puerto Rico."

"What cruise line?"

"Carnival. The ship was called the *Valor*."

I jotted down the name of the ship and the dates of travel. "What airline did you take to San Juan?"

"American," Elena said. "We flew out of DFW."

The Dallas/Fort Worth Airport was a hub for American Airlines, with untold numbers of flights departing every day. The airline was also among the area's major employers, and operated both a museum and a training facility/conference center in the area.

"How did you book your travel?" I asked. "By phone? Online? Through a travel agency?" I didn't ask whether they'd booked their flights in person. Nobody did anything in person anymore.

"We weren't sure where we wanted to go on vacation," Elena said, "so we used an agency to help us come up with some options. It's called Go-Go Getaways." She gave me the name of her contact at the agency, as well as the agent's phone number.

"Did you have anyone watching your house while you were gone?"

"Not specifically," she said, "but I did tell both of our adjoining neighbors that we'd be gone for several days. They have our cell numbers for emergencies."

"Do either of these neighbors have teenaged children?"

"No. The ones over here—" she pointed to the house on the right, "have two kids in elementary school. The others—" she gestured left now, "have a grown son in college down in San Antonio."

I explained my theory that, given the late afternoon time frame during which the burglaries were committed, teenagers could be the culprits.

Elena shrugged. "All I know is that our neighbor said the window wasn't broken when she left to take her daughter to soccer practice at three thirty, and that it was broken when she returned at five."

"Are there any teens in the neighborhood that seem suspicious?"

Her husband harrumphed. "Don't *all* teenagers seem suspicious?"

This line of inquiry seemed to be going nowhere. *Moving on.* "Did you have someone watering your plants or picking up your mail while you were on the cruise?"

"No," Elena said. "Since we were going to be gone less than a week I just gave all the plants a thorough watering before we left. We had the post office hold our mail."

I jotted a note on my pad. *Mail hold.*

"Do you have a lawn service?" I asked. "Or a housekeeper?"

"No," she said. "We tend to be do-it-yourself types."

That didn't surprise me. The way they were both jogging in place while we talked told me they were high-energy people.

"Have you had any workers at your house lately? Maybe an appliance repairman or plumber or electrician?"

Both of the Bayers shook their heads.

John followed up with, "I think the last time we had a repairman at our house was last June or July, for the garbage disposal. Remember?"

"How could I forget?" Elena replied before turning back to me. "Something went wrong and the darn thing wouldn't turn off." She put her hands up on either side of her face and wiggled her fingers. "It was so loud you couldn't hear yourself think. I thought my head was going to explode."

I could think of no more questions to ask, so I thanked them for their time and told them I'd let them know if anything panned out.

As I walked back to the cruiser, I wondered. Had anything they told me been useful? Was there some clue in there to cling to? Had the Bayer's home been a random hit? Had the burglar or burglars simply cased houses in the neighborhood, looking for one that appeared to be unoccupied? Or was there some other reason the thief or thieves had chosen their home to rob?

SEVENTEEN
MY KINGDOM FOR OPPOSABLE THUMBS

Brigit

Brigit knew today must be a special day because Megan had exchanged her usual collar for a new one. She had no idea what holiday it might be, but she hoped it was one of the holidays where the humans would eat turkey or ham or barbecue and feed her the scraps. She loved those holidays. Heck, she even liked pumpkin pie. Cranberry sauce, though? The humans could keep that tart and tangy slop to themselves.

The morning had been exciting. They'd engaged in a high-speed chase. Brigit loved to go fast in the car. Of course she liked it better when Megan remembered to put the windows down so she could feel the wind in her fur and bark into the breeze. If only Brigit had opposable thumbs she could take care of such matters herself.

As instructed, Brigit was being a "good girl" and "waiting nicely" in the back of the cruiser while Megan talked to a man and a woman. But she was beginning to get bored. Much longer and she'd have to start barking in protest or see if she could chew her way out of her metal mesh enclosure.

Oh, wait. Here comes Megan now.

EIGHTEEN
HEARTBROKEN

Dub

It was Valentine's Day, and Dub's heart was broken.

Since he'd moved in with his mother, he'd only been able to contact Jenna once. He couldn't risk calling her from his mother's phone and having someone track him down, and he didn't have enough money to buy a prepaid phone. He'd walked all around the neighborhood and finally found a pay phone inside an old laundromat down the street.

He'd tried her cell number first, but it went straight to voicemail. He'd gotten the Seavers' home number from information and tried that next, crossing his fingers that Jenna would answer.

She had.

It hadn't been easy to talk over the *thunk-thunk-thunk* of someone's heavy towels in a nearby dryer, but at least he'd been able to tell her how much he missed her. She'd cried on the phone, which only made him feel worse. He'd hoped they'd be able to sneak away, maybe meet up in a park somewhere, but her parents had grounded her and taken away her cell phone when they found recent selfies of the two of them in her camera roll. Jenna's parents didn't think Dub was good enough for their daughter. They were probably right. Jenna deserved the best, not some juvenile delinquent who'd been caught burglarizing houses and in possession of crystal meth.

And now he was a dropout, too. When he'd left his life in Fairmount behind, he'd had to cut all ties with Trent and Wes and had stopped going to school, where his foster fathers or CPS or the police could have easily found him. He couldn't protect his mother if he were rounded up and taken back to Gainesville or a foster home or a detention facility. He knew that. But it didn't mean he was happy with this decision. Hell, it didn't mean he was happy at all.

He was only doing his duty.

After calling Jenna, he'd placed a quick call to Wes and Trent, dialing their home number rather than calling their cell phones because he didn't really want to talk to them. It would be too hard. He'd left a message on their answering machine that was half lie, half truth.

I liked living with you two. But I think it's best if I go back to my family in Memphis. Thanks for everything, and . . . I'm really, really sorry.

He hoped the message would throw them—and anyone else who might be looking for him—off track. He also wondered how they'd reacted, whether anyone had searched his room. Had they found the brass knuckles he'd hidden? *God, he hoped not.* The things were illegal in Texas. But you could buy anything online. They'd wonder why he had them, whether he'd ever used them . . .

Damn, he was miserable. But just because he was

miserable didn't mean he couldn't make his mother happy. He had twelve dollars in his wallet. Why not go get her a little something to celebrate the day, surprise her when she arrived home from work tonight? Other than the cards he'd made in elementary school, he couldn't remember anyone ever giving her anything for Valentine's Day.

He left the apartment and walked down the street to the grocery store. Weird how warm it was outside. But that was north Texas weather for you. One minute you were freezing your butt off, the next minute you were hotter than hell.

When he reached the store, he looked over the special display of Valentine's gifts at the front.

Flowers.

Bath oils.

Wine.

Nah. He'd stick with candy. His mother looked so much better with some meat on her bones. She could stand to add a little more.

As he looked over the various boxes of candy, he scratched at the tufts of hair on his cheeks and chin. *Dang, it itched.* But he knew the facial hair made him look older, tougher. It would also make it harder for anyone to recognize him if the police or social workers came looking. No sense spending any of his money on a razor or shaving cream.

After thinking things over, he chose the most expensive box of candy he could afford, a $10.99 box of assorted chocolates that came to $11.90 with tax. He took the dime from the cashier and slid it into a charity box with a photo of a sick, bald kid on it. *Maybe he didn't have it so bad, after all.*

As he walked back to the apartment, dark clouds formed in the sky. The wind seemed to be picking up, too, blowing plastic bags and trash and grit around, shaking the trees. Looked like bad weather was on the way.

He tucked the candy heart under his arm and picked up the pace. No sense getting caught in the rain.

NINETEEN
TWIST AND SHOUT

Megan

As the day wore on, the skies began to darken, large clouds forming on the horizon and working their way toward the city. The winds picked up, too, gusting in bursts that had me tightening my grip on the steering wheel and Brigit whimpering in concern as the car shimmied and veered.

"It's okay, girl," I said in my best soothing voice. "It's okay."

Rain began to fall, lightly at first, but quickly gaining momentum until it splattered loudly on the roof and windshield of the cruiser. Even on high speed, the cruiser's wipers couldn't keep up, diminishing visibility of the city around us. It felt as if we were driving through a never-ending car wash.

So much for that Canadian cold front stalling out over Oklahoma. It had hurried on down and was now clashing with the warm air Mexico had sent our way.

On the bright side, few people were out and about in the monsoon conditions. On the not-so-bright side, those who *were* out tended to be people with poor judgment and even worse driving skills. Call after call came in from dispatch regarding motorists who'd slid into each other, off the roads, or down embankments.

I sighed. It was only a matter of time until one of those collision calls would require me to respond.

The female dispatcher's voice came over the radio. "We've got disabled vehicles on Rosedale eastbound at Washington. Who can respond?"

I eyed my partner in the rearview mirror. "You're lucky you're a dog today, you know that?"

Brigit gave me an open-mouthed look and a tail wag that said she felt lucky to be a dog *every* day.

I pushed the button on my mic. "Officer Luz responding."

Carefully, I headed up Henderson to Rosedale, and turned right onto the major thoroughfare. Barely visible through the steady stream of water down my windshield was a dark Mercedes sedan with its emergency lights flashing like red beacons. Sideways in front of it was the red sports car it had hit broadside.

I flipped on my flashing lights and pulled up behind the vehicles. After wriggling into my nylon police-issue poncho, I emerged from the cruiser into a warm, wet hell. By now, the winds had picked up so much that the rain blew sideways across the road. The poncho, which hung only to the middle of my thighs, did nothing to protect the lower two thirds of my legs from being soaked to the bone. Meanwhile, Brigit stood in the cruiser, dry and warm. *Lucky bitch.*

I stopped first at the door of the sedan. The driver, an older lady with layered white hair, rolled her window down a couple of inches. "I don't know what kind of story that little twit might tell you," she snarled through the gap, "but she pulled out right in front of me."

"You two have spoken, then?"

She jerked her head back as if slapped. "Are you crazy? I'm not getting out in this weather."

But *I* had no choice but to get soaked, thanks to these two drivers, sitting in their toasty warm cars. Where was the fairness in that?

I left the grandma behind and scurried to the driver's window of the sports car. The window came down an inch to reveal a woman at the wheel in a long-sleeved pink tee and yoga pants. Her caramel hair cascaded in waves from the crown of her head to her chin, her eye makeup generous yet impeccable, the look combining to make her appear like a human cocker spaniel. Despite her circumstances, her face was serene. She must have been on her way home from class when the accident took place.

She gave me a smile that made me think she was also about to offer a "Namaste." God help her if she did. Given my current mood, which was as sour as I was drenched, I just might beat her to death with my baton.

"What happened here?" I asked.

"I have no idea," the woman said. "The road looked clear and then all of a sudden *bam!* That other car seemed to come out of nowhere."

I went back to my cruiser, retrieved my accident report forms, then trekked back and forth between the two cars with each driver's name and insurance information. This stupid storm had reduced me from tough-as-nails cop to wet-as-a-mermaid secretary.

Fortunately, neither car was damaged bad enough to render it undrivable. The women were on their way, dry as a bone, in minutes. As for me, my pants dripped so much once I was seated again in my cruiser that a puddle formed under my foot pedals. *Blurgh.* Some Valentine's Day this was turning out to be.

Seth was on duty at the fire department, and his day was going as badly as mine. I received a text from him just after noon that said *What part of STAY OFF THE*

ROADS do people not understand? A second text came in a moment later. *Can't wait to see you tonight. Hoping for that sleepover. :)*

I was flattered, my heart pitter-pattering in my chest nearly as loud as the rain on the windshield. I only hoped the weather would let up by tonight. I didn't want anything to spoil our plans to dine at Reata. And after nearly being drowned out in the rain, I was beginning to seriously consider that sleepover. An orgasm might do me some good.

I cruised down Rosedale to Main, went south a couple of miles, then swung by Haynes's place again. Still no signs of life.

Eeert! Eeert!

I nearly came out of my seat when, halfway through Ira Glass's *This American Life* show on NPR, the broadcast was interrupted by the sound of the emergency alert system. The sudden, ear-splitting noise was evidently designed not only to get your attention, but also to cause you to drop a brick in your pants.

A recorded message played. "The National Weather Service has activated the emergency alert system. A severe weather warning has been issued for Tarrant County and the surrounding areas." The message went on to warn of possible flash flooding, hail, rotation in the clouds possibly producing tornadoes, everything short of locusts and frogs. Listeners were advised to take cover in an interior room of their house and to stay tuned for further information. With a final *eeert*, the warning ending.

Knowing the alerts would be repeated ad nauseum, and that my nerves could not take another such jolt, I turned the radio off.

The rain continued to pour down, the white noise accentuated here and there with thunderbolts, the lightning temporarily illuminating the sky and surroundings. I considered heeding the radio's advice and pulling over to wait out the storm, but when Derek passed me in his cruiser going the opposite direction, I figured if the Big Dick was man enough to continue patrolling in this weather then so was I . . . figuratively speaking, of course.

The sky turned an odd gray-green as I reached Berry Street. It was lunchtime now, so I pulled into a Burger King and ordered a plain whopper for my partner, a veggie burger for me. "No mayonnaise, please." *57 calories a tablespoon and 76% fat?* No thanks.

Once we'd received our food, I pulled into a parking spot. I tore Brigit's burger into bite-sized bits, dropped them one by one over the top of her enclosure, and sat back to enjoy my own meal. Not gourmet fare by any means, but I'd get that tonight at Reata.

As we pulled out of the restaurant a few minutes later, the clouds released a barrage of hail the size of dimes. The frozen balls pinged off my hood and roof, too small to do any real damage, but big enough to make a deafening racket. *Ping-ping-ping-ping-ping! Ping-ping! Ping-ping-ping!*

What do you know? Hell had frozen over. Maybe I would miss Dale Grigsby after all.

My eyes scanned the area, looking for something I could pull under until the hail passed. The pharmacy drive-thru at Walgreens was already occupied by a car, as were both lanes at a drive-thru bank. Every covered bay at the gas station was full, too. People in Fort Worth knew to take hail seriously. Twenty years ago, during the annual outdoor Mayfest event, the city had been hit with hail having a diameter of up to ten centimeters. Dozens of people had been injured, and thirteen people died in the storm. In addition to the personal injuries, the property damage was astronomical, the most costly hailstorm up to that point in history. More recently, a nineteen-year-old boy lost his life here when hit in the head with softball-sized hail. *Pleasant thoughts, no?*

The hail grew larger, quarter-sized now. The *pings* became *pangs*. *Pang-pang-pang! Pang-pang-pang-pang-pang! Pang-pang!*

Brigit cowered behind me, whimpering.

"I feel the same way, girl." Mother Nature could be a vicious, scary bitch.

The wind picked up yet again, and the hail grew from quarter-sized to golf ball-sized. The sound of the hail hitting the car was like artillery fire. *Bam-bam-bam-bam-bam-bam! Bam-bam! Bam-bam-bam-bam!*

I was a bit freaked out and figured a prayer couldn't hurt. Given the frozen ice balls raining down, a *Hail Mary* seemed appropriate. "Hail Mary," I began, my voice hardly audible over the sound of the storm. "Full of grace. The Lord is with thee."

The Lord might be with her, but He certainly wasn't with the citizens of Fort Worth at the moment.

"Blessed art thou amongst women . . ."

I passed a liquor store and doughnut shop and turned into the parking lot of a pizza place, pulling under a tree. The leafless limbs offered only a minimum of protection, the hail continuing to bombard my car. My hood was so dimpled now it appeared to suffer a vehicular form of cellulite. Brigit continued to whine, pacing back and forth on her platform as we waited for the storm to pass. It sure seemed to be taking its time.

"I don't know what you're whining about, dog," I said, my tone soft and soothing even if my words were snide. "If this windshield breaks I'll be in big trouble. You'll still have your cage to protect you."

Reeeeeeeeeeeeeee!

My heart sputtered in my chest.

Holy shit.

The tornado sirens had been activated. First a corpse and now a tornado. Could this week get any worse?

I knew a car was the wrong place to be in a storm, but

I couldn't very well take cover in the pizza place. It would be equally dangerous to run through the hail, and I didn't want to risk Brigit being injured. Besides, the poor dog was terrified enough already, pacing back and forth on her platform. Taking her out in this weather, even for a brief moment, would be unwise. Hell, she might panic and try to run away from me. I couldn't take that risk.

Reeeeeeeeeeeeeee!

"It's okay, girl!" I called, my voice sounding as tight and tense as I felt. I turned back to my partner and stuck my fingers through the mesh to stroke her the best I could with my fingertips. "It's okay!"

Like hell it was.

As we sat there, a piece of sheet metal flew by in front of the cruiser, probably the roof to someone's backyard shed. A large plastic garbage can rolled down the middle of the street, bouncing up and over the curb, then being blown back into the street to continue its careening path. The storm drains clogged with globs of hail and the gutters overflowed with rainwater in mere minutes, turning the parking lot into a pond, hailstones floating like miniature icebergs.

And still the hail came down. *Bam-bam-bam!*

And still the tornado sirens wailed. *Reeeeeeeee!*

Another text came through from Seth. *Armageddon?*

Despite my situation, the text brought a chuckle to my lips.

A new sound joined the cacophony now, a *chugga-chugga-chugga-chugga* that sounded like an oncoming freight train. I wasn't far from the tracks, but the sound was louder than I'd expected. Would trains even be running in this weather? Something seemed off.

And then I saw it.

A dark, massive swirl of wind and rain and debris that spanned the entire five-lane span, churning its way up Berry Street as if coming straight for me.

"Oh, God!" I crossed myself, imploring God, Jesus, Mary, and St. Francis of Assisi, the patron saint of animals, to protect me and Brigit. It couldn't hurt to get the entire team on our side.

"Our Father!" I cried, figuring I'd bypass Mary and go straight to the Big Guy this time. The situation seemed to warrant escalation. "Who art in Heaven—"

Clouded by terror, my mind went blank, unable to produce the remaining words to the prayer I'd recited thousands of times during my life, often as penance for one sin or another.

Instinctively, I started the car, my fight or flight reflex telling me to try to outrun the twister. Weather forecasters advise against this, of course, but my mind wasn't exactly functioning at maximum efficiency at the moment. All I felt was a primal compulsion to get the hell out of there.

Mother Nature had other plans for us, however. Before I could drive off, she sent forth a gust of wind shear that rocked my car like thugs in a riot. The car went momentarily airborne before jerking up and flipping over, landing on the driver's side, the left part of my skull impacting the window with a solid *smack*. The glass cracked, weblike fissures reaching to the edges. It was a wonder the hit didn't knock me unconscious. Given what followed, I almost wished it had.

Brigit was beyond panicked now, leaping up and down in her cockeyed cage enclosure, barking up her own storm.

Woof-woof-woof!
Reeeeeeeee!
Chugga-chugga-chugga!

The tornado was on us. With the car on its side, it created a larger plane for the wind. The twirling funnel of air sent the car spinning on the asphalt like a whirligig.

Round and round and round she goes, where she'll stop nobody knows!

My seatbelt kept me glued to my seat, but the centrifugal force threw Brigit against the back of her enclosure and held her there. She was too terrified now to even bark.

Though the spinning motion disoriented me, I had a sense that the car was also moving toward the street.

Oh, God!

What will happen if the car slams into the tree?

The roof will be crushed and Brigit and I will be killed, that's what.

Poor dog. She'd been partnered with an idiot who hadn't had the sense to come in out of the rain. Brigit would suffer for my poor judgment. The guilt of that realization cut me to the core. Her life was in my hands and look what I'd done. Probably put an end to it.

A few seconds later the spinning wound down—*thanks be to God!*—but Mother Nature wasn't done with us yet. She sent another burst of wind shear and sent the cruiser sliding forward in a straight line now, right toward a fire hydrant. I could see it through the now-cracked windshield, a bright red anvil rushing toward my face. At the last second, the car tipped up slightly.

BAM!

The cruiser shook with the impact, causing Brigit to emit a fresh whine. The reinforced bumper knocked the hydrant aside, while momentum carried the cruiser forward a few more feet. Finally, the car came to a rest on the spot where the hydrant had been. The *chugga-chugga* noise became fainter, then ceased completely as the tornado either moved on or dissipated. The *reeeeeeee* of the sirens continued, however, punctuated here and there by a light *ping* of residual hail.

I unbuckled myself and turned in my seat to look at Brigit, who stood on the mesh over the back driver's-side window. Her whining reduced to a whimper.

"We're okay, girl. We're—"

SPLOOSH!

A geyser of water burst from the main where the hydrant had been, sending glass and water rocketing into the cruiser.

HOLY SHIT!

As I choked and sputtered and fought against the roaring tidal wave, the car began to fill with water.

OH!

MY!

GOD!

I had to do something or Brigit and I would drown in here! Maybe *I* deserved to die for my actions, but *she* didn't.

Pinching my nose to prevent the gush of water from rushing up my nostrils, I used the force to my advantage, allowing it to push me to a stand. One of my feet was hooked inside the steering wheel for leverage, the other braced against the passenger door. Reaching up, I grabbed the hand strap mounted above the window and threw my torso against the passenger seat in an attempt to rock the car. As the water rose to my shins, then knees, I repeated the action over and over, again and again, until the car began to shift. With one final hurl of my body, the car fell back to earth, righting itself, the water flowing in another *swoosh* to the floorboards.

I was out the door in an instant, Brigit's leash in my hand. I opened the back door and unfastened her enclosure, giving her the order to stay. Probably not necessary given the way she was cowering on her platform, drenched and shaking like a paint mixing machine.

I reached in and clipped the leash to her collar lest she change her mind and attempt to bolt. "I'm so sorry, girl. It's okay now. We're all right. We're okay. We're all right."

I repeated the words like a mantra—*we're all right, we're okay*—stroking my hand down her back until both she and I calmed. Finally, I ventured a look around me.

The rain and hail had let up, though the hydrant geyser continued to spew ten feet into the air next to the cruiser. The sky grew lighter, the clouds beginning to thin. The tornado siren stopped its wail, replaced by an eerie quiet.

As my eyes moved up to the sky my mouth fell open. "I'll be damned."

Off in the distance, over the downtown skyline, arced not one, but two, vivid rainbows, almost as if Mother Nature were issuing a colorful apology to the city of Fort Worth.

TWENTY
WHAT THE HAIL?

Brigit

Holy dog biscuits! What just happened?

All Brigit knew was that things had been too loud and too shaky and too wet and too scary. She'd even peed on her platform. Not that anyone would be able to tell. The water that had gushed up through the window while the car had been turned on its side washed the evidence away.

After clipping the leash onto Brigit's collar, Megan coaxed the dog to the open door of her enclosure, lifting her up to carry her over some broken glass on the asphalt. After Megan put her down, Brigit gave herself a good shake, ridding herself of some of the water that had doused her. She nuzzled the pocket where Megan kept her liver treats. If ever she'd earned one, it was today.

Megan pulled out three liver treats and fed them to Brigit, telling her she'd been a "good girl." If Brigit could communicate verbally with Megan, she'd tell her partner that Megan had most definitely *not* been a good girl. Megan had ignored all of Brigit's warning whines and whimpers, continuing on their patrol despite the threatening weather. *Dumbass.*

Brigit's sharp eyes scanned their surroundings. The world around them looked nothing like the world she was used to. This world lacked its usual order. This world was messy and haphazard and chaotic. She was reminded of the time her original owner had taken her with him to a makeshift barrio just this side of the Mexican border. He'd visited with a prostitute while Brigit played with the woman's bug-eyed Chihuahua. Her owner brought some souvenir crabs back with him, necessitating a trip to the county medical clinic. Sure, he'd treat his pubic lice, but Brigit's irritating flea infestation? Forget it. She'd scratched herself nearly bald in places and the dipshit didn't give a damn.

The annoying and constant high-pitched warning siren had stopped, replaced now by multiple sirens on numerous emergency vehicles responding to calls nearby. Brigit could hear screams and cries coming from houses in the neighborhood behind the damaged businesses across the street. She knew the sounds meant people were either hurt or scared or both. She also knew the sounds meant she and Megan would be very busy for the rest of their workday.

TWENTY-ONE
CRIMES OF OPPORTUNITY

Dub

Sometimes opportunity knocks. Sometimes it knocks things down.

Once the storm passed and he crawled out of the closet where he'd taken shelter, Dub's first thought was to try to call his mother at work, to see if she was all right. Her apartment had no landline, though. He no longer had a cell phone, either. He'd wanted to get a new cell. Hell, he'd wanted to get a second pair of underwear. But his mother had no cash until payday on Monday. All she had was a bus pass and a fridge full of burritos. Dub used to love the things, but after eating them three meals a day since he'd arrived, he'd be happy if he never saw another burrito again in his life.

His mother's apartment complex had been spared the brunt of the storm and suffered no damage other than some trash being tossed about, but the sirens in the distance told Dub that the area just to their west had been hit hard. The electricity was out, so there was no point in trying the television for reports.

He slid into his Gainesville State Tornadoes hoodie. Seemed right, what with today's weather. Besides, he had nothing else to wear other than the T-shirt he'd had on under it when he'd first come here, and that one was dripping dry in the bathroom. His mother didn't even have enough change to wash a load of laundry, so he'd had to rinse the shirt out in the sink.

He opened the door and went down the steps, through the open walkway, and into the parking lot. Marquise, Long Dong, and Gato were back on their cars, sitting on the hoods like the storm had never happened.

Dub had never liked taking what wasn't his, but he'd done what he'd had to do to survive. Begged neighbors for food when his mother was too high on meth to feed him. Stolen shoes off a porch so he wouldn't have to go barefoot. Pocketed a tip left for the waiter as he made his way out of a café after going inside to use the restaurant's bathroom. That time they'd run out of soap and he needed the money to buy a bar.

But a storm like this? It could be a godsend of sorts. Looting was stealing. Dub knew that. But insurance would cover any losses, wouldn't it? He didn't want to commit yet another crime, but what choice did he have? Morals and ethics were for those who could afford them. Someday, when he got on his feet and had a real job, he'd find a way to repay what he'd taken, to make his wrongs right.

But there were some wrongs that could never be righted.

Dub lifted his chin at the three men. "Hey."

"'Sup?" asked Marquise, his arms crossed over his chest.

"Sounds like the storm caused some trouble," Dub said. "Could make it easy to find some loot."

Marquise stood and slapped him on the shoulder. "Good thinking, WC." He turned to the others and waved them down from the cars. "Let's roll."

Ten minutes later, they were cruising down Berry Street in Gato's silver Sentra. Not exactly a tough gangsta car, but it was the least likely to fall apart on the drive.

The condition of the buildings got worse as they made their way west.

"Ho-o-ly shit," Marquise said. "Looks like a tornado went right through here."

Roofs had been ripped off houses and businesses, leaving only wood framing and pink foam insulation. Trees and fences and signs were down, electric wires, too, some sparking on the wet ground like fireworks. All kinds of stuff was scattered along the streets, sidewalks, and parking lots, everything from overturned shopping carts to children's toys to mailboxes. There was even one of those outdoor Redbox machines resting at an angle against a smashed car.

When a downed sign from a doughnut shop blocked the road and they could drive no farther, Gato pulled down a side street and parked at the curb. The four climbed out, slamming their doors shut behind them.

They picked their way down the street, checking things out, keeping an eye out for anything that might be useful to them or that could be resold for cash.

"Check that out." Dub pointed to a building a half block ahead. It was a liquor store missing half its roof, its front windows shattered, the burglar bars on one span of glass twisted out of place. The store was dark inside and looked abandoned.

Led by Dub, the young men headed to the store. As they peeked through the opening where the front window had once been, a fiftyish black man came through a swinging door at the back.

When the man saw Dub and the others in the window, his eyes went wide and he raised his hands in the air. "I don't want no trouble!"

"Neither do we!" Dub called back. No sense letting the guy get a close look at them. Better to move on and find a store that was unoccupied.

But the others had a different plan.

Dub heard a metallic rattle and click, and turned to find Marquise, Long Dong, and Gato with guns in their hands, the barrels pointed at the man. *Damn.* This was *not* what he'd had in mind.

"Take whatever you want!" the man cried. "I won't stop you! Just please don't hurt me! I've got a wife and kids!"

Shit. Things had already gone further than Dub had intended. With guns involved, the cops would take this crime more seriously. The last thing he needed right now was the police on his tail. If they started snooping around, asking questions, things could get bad for him. *Very* bad.

"Hold on." Dub pointed at a security camera mounted over the register. "If we go in there we'll be caught on tape."

"No we won't," Marquise said. "The camera don't work when the electricity is out."

Dub wasn't so sure. Thieves were known to cut off power to security systems. The thing might have a battery backup. But every time they showed security videos on the news the pictures were pixilated and blurry. If he put up his hood, the camera wouldn't be able to get a good shot of him, right?

He pulled his hood up and over his head, tugging on the edges until it shaded his face like he were some type of Grim Reaper.

"Be careful not to leave fingerprints," he told the others. "Any one of us leaves a print, we'll all go down."

Gato pulled the sleeve of his sweatshirt down to cover his fingers, then grabbed the burglar bars with his covered hand and swung under them like a Latino chimpanzee.

Marquise was next, followed by Long Dong. Dub was the last to squeeze through. He was careful not to touch the bars with his hands.

The store carried a row of household items at the front. Dub looked over the merchandise until he found what he was looking for. Latex gloves. He grabbed four packages.

"Yo," he called to the others. "Here. Take the bag with you when we go." He tossed them each a package of gloves. He tore his package open, removed the gloves, and shoved the empty package into his pocket. Sliding his hands into the bright orange gloves, he was ready now.

A life-sized cardboard cutout of a blonde in a red bikini lay cockeyed across a display of canned beer. "Check out these tits!" Gato grabbed the cutout with his gloved hands. He turned it to face the others, then groped and humped the cardboard woman from behind. "Oh, baby! Is it good for you, too?"

Long Dong snickered. "You suck at this!" he cried in a fake woman's voice, pretending to be the blonde. "I want the Asian guy!"

Holding the cardboard woman in front of him, Gato charged at Long Dong.

Long Dong sliced the air with a bladed hand. "Hi-yah!" When his hand met the woman's neck, the cardboard bent and her head folded over backward.

Gato grabbed her head, ripped it off, and tossed the headless body aside. "I never liked her anyway. Too bitchy."

Marquise headed to the front checkout counter. "The cash register is mine!"

Dub watched as Marquise jabbed buttons on the machine but couldn't get it open.

Marquise slammed a fist down on the register but it remained closed. "What's the code?" he yelled, waving his gun at the clerk.

"Two-two-seven!" the man cried. "Then hit the *Enter* key."

Marquise punched the keys and the cash drawer dinged open. "Now we're talking." He grabbed a plastic bag from under the counter and shoved handfuls of money into it.

Long Dong and Gato went to the back storeroom and returned with cardboard boxes. They grabbed bottles of liquor from the shelves and packed them into the boxes.

Dub wasn't interested in alcohol. He walked up to the customer side of the counter and held out a hand to Marquise. "Give me a bag, man."

Marquise yanked another bag from under the counter and tossed it to Dub. Dub pulled packages of beef jerky and nuts and sunflower seeds from the metal hooks at the display by the register and dropped them into the bag.

Once he'd taken all of the jerky and nuts, Dub looked around, trying to figure out what to take next, how to make the most of the situation. Should he grab cigarettes? He could probably resell them at the apartment complex or at the bus stops.

As he tried to decide what to take next, he looked over at the bag in Marquise's hand. Didn't look like the dude had gotten much cash from the register. Not many people used cash these days. *Ha.* Dub felt better knowing Marquise wasn't getting rich here today. It wasn't fair the guy had called dibs on the cash. But guys like Marquise didn't give a crap about fairness.

The register was empty now, and Marquise headed to the back room, probably to get a box.

"Hey, man," Dub said. "Bring me a box, too."

"Get your own damn box!" Marquise barked over his shoulder.

Asshole. Dub hurried to the stockroom, grabbed a box with a Smirnoff Vodka label, and went to the cigarette display behind the checkout counter. He'd planned to grab cartons of cigarettes from the shelves, but his eyes landed on something that could be way more valuable.

Scratch-off lottery tickets.

Ha! Marquise hadn't thought to take the tickets. *Dumbass.* But would he try to take them from Dub? Dub didn't trust the guy.

Dub grabbed the rolls of lottery tickets, yanking the entire spool from the display, starting with the $10.00 10X Mega Money tickets and working his way down to the $1 Tic Tac Toads. He'd just removed the final roll when Marquise emerged from the end of an aisle, his open-topped box tinkling as the glass bottles inside rattled against each other.

Marquise cut a look at Dub. "Don't touch the Kools or Marlboros. Those are mine."

Dub grabbed several boxes of Camels and lay them longways in the box to hide the lottery tickets.

Marquise stepped up next to him and looked down into Dub's box. "Shit, man. I meant to say the Camels are mine, too."

He grabbed a box of cigarettes out of Dub's cardboard box. Before he could take another Dub pulled the box away. "Get your fucking hand out of my box."

Marquise laughed. "A'ight, man. Relax."

When each of them had filled their box, they headed to the front door.

Marquise took one last look at the store clerk and held up his gun. "You never saw us. Got that? Don't make me have to come back here and set you straight."

The man nodded like a bobblehead doll. "Whatever you say."

Marquise shoved the barrel of his gun into the front of his jeans, picked up his box, and climbed back out the broken window. Long Dong went after him, then Gato, then Dub.

Gato stopped suddenly on the sidewalk and Dub

bumped into his back. He noticed Marquise and Long Dong were standing still, too. Dub stepped to the side to figure out why none of them were moving.

Oh shiiit.

Twenty feet away stood a soaking wet female police officer with a German shepherd on a leash. The cop raised her hand. "Hold it right there."

TWENTY-TWO
LOOT-N-SHOOT

Megan

I'd spent the last half hour dripping and shivering, partly from nerves, partly from the cooler air that had now settled over the city. My soaking shoes emitted a wet *skwunch* with each step as I gingerly picked my way around the area, calling into the wreckage, trying to figure out whether there were any survivors who needed immediate help. With my cruiser out of commission and the roads fully blocked with debris, I couldn't do much other than radio reports into dispatch to help them determine where to direct the emergency crews.

Brigit trotted along beside me, stopping occasionally to shake moisture from her fur. She sniffed at the rubble, probably hoping to find food scraps or an errant squirrel who'd been caught up in the storm.

The windows at the pizza place had all shattered and the dining room furniture had been scattered by the storm, chairs and tables positioned haphazardly about the space, some still standing on their legs, others lying on their sides. Luckily, the five customers who'd been eating lunch and the seven employees who'd been on duty had all taken cover in the freezer. They'd emerged slightly frostbitten but without a scratch on them. I'd advised them their best course of action would be to wait for the city's street crews to clear the roadways before trying to leave, but that if they wanted to attempt to walk home they should be extra careful given the wreckage strewn about.

The doughnut shop had fared much worse, its entire roof missing and two of the walls caved in. Bricks mixed with squashed éclairs and rain-soaked napkins lay in a messy pile. Brigit had helped herself to a squashed, rain-soaked bear claw as I'd called into the rubble—*"Is anyone in there? Hello? Anybody?"*—but heard no response. According to the hours posted in the part of the front window that was still intact, the place was open only from 6 to 10 A.M. each day. With any luck, nobody had been in the place when it came down.

My next stop had been the Bag-N-Bottle, where I discovered a surprisingly integrated street gang exiting the space after having looted the store.

I raised a palm. "Hold it right there."

The four men who'd just emerged from the Bag-N-Bottle stopped in their tracks and stared at me. All carried cardboard boxes, all appeared to be in their twenties, and all wore orange latex gloves, blue jeans, and hooded sweatshirts, like some type of hip-hop cleaning crew. *DJ Tidy and the Kleen Machine.*

Their attire was where their similarities stopped, however. The first who'd come out was a well-muscled African-American, with hard, soulless eyes, the color of which matched his dark-roast skin. The next was a skinny Asian with a neck tattoo and a flinty glare. The third was a lanky Latino with a somewhat pointy, lightly bearded chin that gave him a feline appearance. He was far more predatory panther than happy housecat, though, his gaze powerful and penetrating and pissed as hell.

The last one was a little harder to pinpoint, race-wise. His hair was dark and curly, like a Labradoodle's, with a cowlick on the left. His skin was the color of cappuccino, approximately two shades darker than my own latte color. His face bore approximately three days' worth of dark stubble. He resembled a scruffy version of the singer Prince. If I had to guess, I'd say that, like me, he was of mixed race. He wore a white hoodie with a black cartoon tornado on the front. Fitting, I supposed. A few inches of chain hung down from under his hoodie. Looked like he carried one of those chain wallets popular with bikers.

Something about this last guy seemed familiar. Had I crossed paths with him before? Maybe pulled him over for speeding or running a red light? Who knew? Certainly not me. Not at the moment, anyway. My thoughts were as scattered as the debris around me. But the fact that he'd taken pains to wear gloves told me he his prints could be on file with law enforcement. Then again, maybe he was just a smart cookie who knew better than to leave any evidence behind, record or not.

My first instinct was to tell the four to put the boxes down and their hands up, but then I realized that as long as they were holding on to their boxes none of them would be able to pull a weapon on me, should they have one. My mind attempted to access my police training, to remember how to handle a situation like this, but my mind was still rattled. The last half hour of my life had been terrifying and traumatic and, honestly, the only thing I wanted to do right now was curl up in a nice, warm bed and cry. It took everything in me not to fall to pieces in front of these thugs.

Should I order them to stay still, then frisk each of them? Frankly, getting closer to the group didn't seem wise. One of them might attack me while I was searching another.

Should I have them spread out? Divide and conquer? That could work, though I couldn't have them spread too far apart or I wouldn't be able to watch them all at once. For the first time since I'd been partnered with Brigit, I found myself wishing I had a human partner to consult with.

"You." I pointed to the one in the tornado hoodie. "Take two steps to your right."

He exhaled a long, frustrated breath, but did as I told him.

"You on the other end," I said, pointing to the Asian, "take two steps to your left."

He, too, did as he was told, though he cast a glance at the large black guy before doing so, as if seeking permission or forgiveness.

"You," I pointed to the cat man now, "take a big step forward."

After several seconds' hesitation he took a step toward me, but calling it a big step would have been an exaggeration.

My eyes met those of their leader now. I'd seen eyes more full of hate, eyes more full of rage. But what I hadn't seen before were eyes so cold and uncaring. This guy didn't give a shit about anything, maybe not even himself. And people who didn't care about anything could do some very vile things.

His upper lip quirked in a sneer. "If you think I'm gonna play your game of *Mother May I?* you are sorely mistaken, sister."

Before I could realize what was happening, he set his box on the ground, pulled off his right glove, and whipped out a handgun from under his sweatshirt. He aimed the gun at my face.

Holy.

Shit.

I had to fight to keep from wetting myself. Not that these hoodlums would have noticed, what with me being soaked to the skin. My hand shook as I pushed the button on my shoulder-mounted radio. "Backup needed at the Bag-N-Bottle on Berry Street. Armed robbery in progress."

The dispatcher's voice came back a few seconds later, her response loud enough for the men to hear. "Access to the area is still limited. It may be awhile."

The sneering man laughed full out now.

I'm in trouble here.

BIG trouble.

My Kevlar vest would protect my chest, but my head was totally exposed, and Brigit had no protection at all. I probably should have pulled my gun from my holster then, but as I'd mentioned, my brain was still swirling like the twister that had just passed through. Instead, my hand reflexively went for my weapon of choice. My baton. I yanked it from my belt and extended it with a flick of my wrist. *Snap!*

The man with the gun laughed again and shook his head. "What's your plan, chickee chickee? Gonna hit my bullet away with your stick?" He made a swinging motion with his left hand, mimicking a batter taking a swing at a baseball.

"Maybe I am." *Yeah, right.*

Okay, so I'd just made a fool of myself. Time for some redemption.

I bent down and used my left hand to unclip the leash from Brigit's collar, but gave her the order to stay by my side for now. Realizing things were heating up, she quivered next to me, ready for action. I transferred my baton to my left hand and pulled my gun from my holster, pointing it back at the guy. Well, I *sort of* pointed it at him. I was shaking so hard I couldn't keep my aim straight. *Damn!*

"Let me help you out." The bastard chuckled, performing a sort of shimmy dance now as he leaned left, then right, then left again, following the quivering of my gun.

The guy's teasing brought back memories of the kids in school, making fun of my *st-st-stutter*. My body temperature rocketed as my fear turned to anger. Given my wet uniform and hot skin, it wouldn't have surprised me to see steam coming off my uniform.

"Set your gun on the ground," I demanded through gritted teeth, "or I'll sic my d-dog on you."

The black guy didn't move, continuing to sneer and raising a brow in challenge.

The Asian guy slid his box on top of a newspaper machine that was chained to the front wall of the store. His hands now free, he, too, removed his gloves and pulled out a gun, also aiming it at my head.

Okay. Back to fear now.

My head felt fuzzy and my throat constricted, closing off my air supply. I swallowed hard, attempting to force my throat open before I passed out from lack of oxygen.

The Latino guy plunked his box onto the asphalt at his feet, the bottles inside giving off loud tinkles as they rattled against each other. Like the others before him, he took off his gloves, dropped them into his box, and pulled a gun from his waistband, though he aimed his weapon at Brigit. "Move on, bitch, or I'll shoot your dog."

"No!" My stomach clenched into a hard little ball. The woman in me told me to step in front of Brigit and protect her. The cop in me acknowledged that doing so would go against our training. Although she was a dog, Brigit was also a fellow officer and, as such, was expected to do her job, to accept the risks that came with it, and to not impede her coworkers.

In my peripheral vision, I saw Brigit look up at me, probably wondering why I'd cried out. She was lucky she didn't understand the gravity of the situation. These guys could shoot us dead and very likely get away with it. There were no witnesses out here on the street and no security cameras in sight.

"Nobody's shooting the dog." The one in the tornado hoodie put his box down and stepped forward, blocking the Latino's bead on Brigit. He turned back to address the other men. "Ain't nobody shooting nobody here. This lady cop can't fire on any of us or the others will take her out, and none of us is stupid enough to fire on her over liquor and cigarettes."

The guy seemed confident, but I wasn't so sure. The other three did, in fact, look stupid enough to sacrifice their lives for a few bottles of hooch and some cartons of cigarettes.

"You're the brains of this operation, huh?" I said.

Turning back to me and my partner, Tornado Hoodie cut me a grin. He reached down into a plastic bag that sat among the cigarettes in his box. He removed a wrapped piece of beef jerky and ripped off the wrapper, having a little trouble with his dexterity given the gloves he wore. He tossed the trash aside. Littering, a citable offense. But not one I planned to do anything about. Especially since this guy seemed to be the voice of reason among the group.

"Here, girl!" he called to Brigit, holding up the jerky. "Come get a treat."

Brigit lifted her nose, scented the meat on the air, and stepped forward, seeming to forget all of her training.

"Brigit!" I hollered, issuing her the order to return to my side.

Over her shoulder she tossed me a look that said *Quit*

being so bossy. But fortunately she obeyed and stepped back in place.

The young man crouched down to dog level. "You're a pretty girl," he murmured in a high, soothing voice, as he ripped the jerky slice into quarters. "A pretty, pretty girl."

Next to me, Brigit wagged her tail, responding unashamedly to his flattery. *Furry, four-footed twit.*

One by one, he tossed the bite-sized pieces of dried meat to Brigit, and she snatched each of them out of the air. *Schomp. Schomp. Schomp. Schomp.*

A sad look flickered over the young man's face as Brigit finished the last of the jerky. Unlike his cohorts, who all had hard, mean eyes, this man had eyes that seemed troubled and disillusioned, but not yet completely hopeless. His skin and his actions illustrated a critical point I'd learned early on in my police career. Few things were entirely black or white.

"When I was little," he said wistfully to Brigit, "I had a dog like you. Her name was Velvet."

As if sensing his sorrow and trying to cheer him up, Brigit bent down on her front legs and offered a playful growl and a bark. *Rrrrowl-arf!*

The man laughed, retrieved his box, and stood. With a final, oddly polite nod to me, he turned to the rest of the gang. "Let's roll."

Ordering them to come back or stop would be futile, so I didn't bother. There was nothing I could do but watch the four men walk away with their spoils and snap a picture of their departure with my cell phone. I felt stupid and useless and utterly powerless.

And I didn't like it one bit.

The looters on their way, I stepped to the window, careful not to touch the metal burglar bars and disturb any prints that might be on them. I hadn't heard any gunshots, but the gang might have pistol-whipped customers or the store staff, maybe tied them up inside.

My reflection gazed back at me from the broken glass. "Yikes." I looked like a crazy person. My makeup was smeared all over my face, my hair half in and half out of its bun, sticking out in odd, droopy loops all over my head. But my appearance was the least of my worries right now.

I attached the leash to Brigit's collar, tied her to a pipe out front where she'd be less likely to get hurt, and squeezed through the bars and shattered glass. "Hello? Fort Worth Police! Anybody in here?"

"Just me!" came a male voice.

A moment later, an older black man stepped into view at the end of the shelves.

"Are you okay?" I asked. "Any injuries?"

"I'm fine." He cast a look out the window as he made his way over to me. "The storm scared the bejeezus out of me but that was it."

"Were you the only one on duty?" It seemed odd there would be only one person running the store on a Saturday when business was likely to be brisk. And, with today being Valentine's Day, shoppers could be expected to stop by for a bottle of wine or champagne to celebrate.

"There were two others," he said, "but when we heard on the radio that the storm was picking up I let them go home. I stayed behind to empty the register and lock up, but that twister was on the ground before I could finish."

"You own the store?"

"Sure do."

"May I have your name?"

"Roland Wilson."

"Are you aware that you had looters, Mr. Wilson?" I asked. "I caught four young men sneaking out this window with cardboard boxes full of liquor and cigarettes."

Wilson shrugged. "I was hiding in the back. I didn't see anyone."

I gestured to the security camera mounted in the corner over the register. "The camera would've picked them up. Let's take a look."

"No point," he replied. "The camera's electric. No electricity, no footage."

I made my way over behind the counter to take a look at the camera.

Wilson followed me over, pointing up at it. "See? It's not running. The green indicator light is off."

Damn. Odd that the man seemed relieved by that fact. *Hmm . . .*

I eyed him closely. "The looters threatened you, didn't they?"

He shrugged, but the flash of alarm in his eyes told me his nonchalance was as phony as the breasts on the headless, bikini-clad cardboard woman lying on the floor near the beer display. "Look, lady. How I run my store is my business, okay?"

"And fighting crime is *my* business," I retorted. Realizing I'd sounded harsh, I raised a conciliatory hand. "Look, I saw the guys, talked to them. If they get busted, it's on me, not you. They'll know that."

He seemed to think things over for a moment, but offered only a shrug again.

"All right, then." He wasn't the first reluctant witness I'd come across, and he wouldn't be the last. I removed a stack of soggy business cards from the breast pocket of my uniform, peeled one off the top, and handed it to him. "If you decide you want to talk or file a report, call me. Okay?"

I eased myself back out the window and untied Brigit from the pipe.

Woof!

A bark from behind caught my attention and Brigit's as well. We turned to see two men and one woman from the Fire Department picking their way up the street with a team of dogs. One of the dogs was a shepherd, like Brigit, though noticeably smaller than my hundred-pound partner. The second dog was a black lab. The third was a golden retriever. All of the humans wore hard hats and fluorescent yellow suits. The animals wore fluorescent yellow vests with printing identifying them as trained search-and-rescue dogs.

Although these people weren't armed, the presence of other authorities brought me some comfort. At least Brigit and I weren't alone anymore. I headed toward them, taking a look back to make sure the gang was still leaving the area. No sense letting these first responders walk into a dangerous situation . . . or a situation that was any more dangerous than it already was given the downed electric wires, shifting wreckage, and broken tree limbs teetering in trees. Fortunately, the looters had already disappeared from sight.

I held up a splayed hand in greeting. "Hi, there! I'm Officer Megan Luz." I lifted Brigit's leash, glad to see my shaking had subsided a bit. "Sergeant Brigit, my p-partner. Can we help in any way?"

As Brigit and the other dogs gave each other a friendly sniff-over, the female member of the team handed me a spare walkie-talkie. "If you could work ahead of us, tell us if you hear survivors in the wreckage, that would be great."

I informed them that everyone in the pizza place and liquor store were okay, and that the doughnut shop appeared empty. "There's one man in the Bag-N-Bottle, but he's not hurt."

"Good." She raised a hand and pointed down the road. "Try the gas station next. But don't take any chances. You don't have a hard hat and these buildings can be unstable."

I nodded in acknowledgment and issued a warning in return. "I've run across some armed looters. They seem to have left the area, but they could return or there could be others. Keep an eye out."

"Thanks," she said. "We will."

Brigit and I weaved our way around broken tree branches, an overturned ice machine, and a twisted, pink girl's bicycle to the gas station. By the time we reached the structure, a woman was stepping out of the doorway, the man next to her holding a bloody roll of paper towels to his bleeding forehead. They were followed by three other men, two of them in shirts bearing the gas station's logo.

"Is he the only one injured?" I asked.

The woman nodded. "He was hit by flying debris. The gash is pretty deep."

"Sit down here." I took the man's arm and helped him to the curb. "I'll get you an EMT as soon as possible."

I radioed dispatch with details.

A news van with a satellite dish on top pulled up on a side street. Trish LeGrande, a bossy, bosomy reporter with butterscotch hair stepped down from the passenger seat. She was dressed in her trademark pink, today's outfit consisting of pink rubber rain boots, a pink vinyl raincoat, and a ruffled pink umbrella.

I heaved a sigh. Trish and I had crossed paths before, and our interactions had never been good for me.

Her cameraman climbed out of the sliding side door with his equipment, lifting it to his shoulder. He said something to Trish and pointed my way.

She raised a waving hand in the air and scurried my way. "Can we get a statement, Officer . . . ?"

"Luz," I huffed. The woman had spoken to me after the bombing at the mall last fall and the purse snatchings at the rodeo mere days ago, but she didn't seem to remember me at all. *Twit.* "I don't have time for an interview. I need to help search for survivors and secure the area."

"Can I at least get a quick intro with the dog?"

Knowing the woman was speaking about her, Brigit wagged her tail.

"Make it quick. And then move back. Emergency crews will need to get into the area."

Trish stepped into place on the other side of Brigit and signaled her cameraman to start rolling. "Trish Le-Grande reporting from Berry Street in Fort Worth where it's been raining cats and dogs." She bent down, flashed a coy smile at the camera, and ruffled Brigit's fur before standing and stepping away. "As you can see, folks, this area was hit hard by a tornado only minutes ago. Though the official word is not yet in, sources at the National Weather Service have told us that this tornado was likely an EF5."

While Trish continued her report, I slunk quickly and quietly away. As I moved on to the bank next door, my eyes spotted Derek weaving his way up Berry, driving up over the curb and on sidewalks when necessary to avoid debris. When he could come no farther, he parked and climbed out, making long, quick strides toward me. "Your backup's here."

The saying *better late than never* did not apply in this case.

When he reached me he glanced around. "Where's the robbery suspect?"

"Off with his three friends spending their take."

"There were four of them?"

"Yes," I spat, "and they pulled guns on me."

Derek actually had the nerve to laugh at that. If he knew how close I was to beating him over the head with my baton, he might've held it in.

"So, what?" he said, raising his palms. "You just let them walk away?"

"What part of 'four armed gang members' did you not understand?"

"Don't get your panties in a wad." He looked me up and down, taking in my wet uniform and my messy hair. His lip quirked in an expression that was half disgust, half amusement. "What the hell happened to you?"

Before I could answer, his eyes moved to my cruiser in the parking lot of the pizza place down the street. The entire driver's side was dented and scraped, the still-flashing light bar cracked and askew, the driver's window gone.

His lips went slack, but his brows rose. "Jesus Christ, Luz! What did you do to your cruiser?"

"I didn't *do* anything," I spat. "In case you didn't notice, a tornado went through here."

Derek pulled out his cell phone, activated the camera, and ran a finger across the screen to zoom in on my cruiser. *Click.*

"What are you doing?" I asked.

He didn't respond, but instead sent a quick text then pulled up a name on his contacts list and placed a call. "Check your texts, Chief," he said into his phone. "I sent you a photo. You'll never believe what Luz did to her patrol car."

Jackass.

TWENTY-THREE
SEARCH-AND-SNIFF

Brigit

She'd been terrified by the storm and the sudden, unexpected fountain spouting up through the overturned cruiser's window, but just as quickly as the supercell moved on, things began to look up. The man who'd shared the beef jerky with Brigit sure was nice, and he had an entire bag full of the meat. The dog hoped she and Megan would see him again. And then she got to meet three new dogs. How fun was that?

Like Brigit, these search-and-rescue dogs were trained to perform important tasks. No pampered house pets here. Nope, these were smart dogs, serious dogs, dogs that sniffed around for injured people, scenting for blood. They also knew to listen carefully for calls for help that might be coming from inside piles of rubble.

Once again, canine skills filled in where human capabilities fell short.

What would people do without dogs?

Brigit could sense that Megan had become tense ever since that other officer had arrived. Brigit knew the guy was a jackass. He had a barking laugh and spoke in staccato bursts. Brigit might not always treat Megan with respect, yet, as members of the same pack, they had a right to push each other's buttons on occasion. But when someone outside the pack pulled a fast one on a member, Brigit wasn't about to let it go unchecked.

The jackass issued a derisive snort and spoke into his phone. The dog decided to take advantage not only of his distraction but also his wide-legged stance. She sneaked up to him and, with all the force she could muster, rammed the top of her hard skull into his soft, squishy scrotum.

With a retching sound, he buckled to his knees, one hand instinctively going to his groin, the other still clutching his phone. "Goddamn dog!" he gasped between labored breaths.

When the man reached out a hand to grab her, Brigit scurried back to Megan's side. As expected, her partner surreptitiously slipped her a liver treat.

You don't mess with these bitches.

TWENTY-FOUR
CASHING IN

Dub

The second Gato's Sentra came to a stop in the apartment complex parking lot, Dub was out the door. No sense giving Marquise the chance to take more of the merchandise that Dub had snatched.

"Later." Dub walked away as fast as he dared. If he went any faster, they might realize he had something special hidden in his box.

He slid his mother's spare key into her apartment door, unlocked it, and stepped into the empty, lonely space. When he'd come home to Wes and Trent's house in the afternoons after school, Wes would always meet Dub at the door, ask about his day, offer him a snack or drink, and make sure he did his homework. Since Dub had been here, the only thing his mother had asked was whether he had any cash on him. When he said he had none, she'd suggested he might be able to earn a few bucks raking leaves at houses in the neighborhood—bucks they could spend on a set of bedroom furniture for her. Never mind that Dub didn't even have a mattress and had been sleeping in the recliner. His back was so sore he felt like an old man.

He set the box on the kitchen floor, removed the cartons of cigarettes, and stacked them on the countertop. Then he took the lottery tickets to the bathroom, locked the door just in case his mother got home from work early, and sat down on the closed toilet seat to go to work on the scratch-offs.

Most people used a coin to scratch off the shiny silver surface but, at the moment, Dub literally did not have a penny to his name. Instead, he used his key to Trent and Wes's house. He figured it might bring him more luck than the key to his mother's crappy apartment, which so far had only opened the door to regret. But maybe these tickets could change that.

The more expensive tickets probably gave higher payouts, so Dub started with those. He scratched and scratched and scratched, holding the cards over the plastic bag so the residue wouldn't end up on the floor. *Scritch-scritch-scritch-scritch-scritch.* An hour later, he had a bag full of losing tickets and scratch-off shavings.

But he also had a handful of winning tickets worth $865.00.

Wow. The tickets represented more money than he had ever had in his life. They also represented freedom. Nobody knew he had these tickets, and nobody could tell him what to do with the money. The cash would be his to do with as he pleased.

Dub gathered up the tickets and trash and returned to the kitchen. He glanced at the clock on the stove. Two thirty. He'd better cash these tickets before his mother got home and before the store owner could report them stolen and have them voided.

Dub tucked the winning tickets into the ankle of his high-top basketball shoes, grabbed his keys, and went back out the door. Rather than risk running into Marquise,

Gato, or Long Dong in the parking lot, he stuck close to the wall so he could exit through the back way by the laundry room. Luck was with him. He saw none of the guys. They were probably in their apartments drinking and smoking their take.

The neighborhood around the complex was still without electricity, but Dub could see lights on in a strip center a half mile down the road. He jogged to the shopping center. *Good.* The end space was taken up by a convenience store with a lottery decal on its front window.

Dub ducked around the back of the building and pulled out $150 worth of cards. The clerk might become suspicious if Dub tried to cash all the winning cards at once. Better to cash them at several different places.

He removed his hoodie and turned it inside out so the Gainesville State School tornado logo wouldn't be visible. He'd been stupid to wear the identifiable clothing on the looting spree. Of course, having no other clothing, he'd had no choice. With the cop standing twenty feet away, she probably hadn't been able to read the words printed on the sweatshirt. Even if she had been able to read them and the police figured out he'd been one of the looters, how would they find him? Nobody had any idea where he'd gone after running away from Trent and Wes's place and, if the police decided to contact his mother for information, they'd have a hard time finding her. The apartment and phone service were in Dub's aunt's name. After defaulting on rent and payday loans and bouncing a dozen checks, his mother's credit was shot. She'd used her sister's name and Social Security number to apply for the lease. And even if the police traced his mother to Taco Bell, he doubted his mother had used her real address on her job application. Like Dub, she trusted no one. If the police confronted her at work, she'd lie and say she hadn't seen Dub since he'd been arrested way back.

Yeah, Dub and his mother were virtually untraceable.

Still, he knew that somehow, some way, his father could find them.

Would find them.

It was only a matter of time . . .

Forcing the thought from his mind, he stepped up to the checkout stand and laid the tickets on the counter. The guy behind the counter looked from Dub to the tickets then back to Dub. "Got lucky, did ya?"

"Yeah. Very lucky."

The clerk ran the tickets through the machine to verify them. Once he'd made sure they were all legit, he opened the register and counted out the cash.

"One-twenty, one-forty, one-hundred-and-fifty," he counted as he slapped the last bills onto the counter.

"Thanks." Dub scooped up the cash and tucked it into his wallet, the chain that attached it to his pants jingling with the movement.

He left the convenience store and continued down the road, cashing in several more tickets at a car wash, a few more at a large grocery, and the rest at a couple of gas stations.

The $865 in his wallet, he turned to head back to the apartment. He'd walked quite a ways by then, probably two miles or more, and it would get dark soon. He'd noticed a bus go by a few minutes earlier, so it looked like mass transit was running again, at least in this neighborhood. He was headed to the nearest westbound bus stop when he saw it.

An old van sat in the fenced lot of a car repair shop. Its black paint was scratched and scuffed in places, but the words painted on the side in bright yellow were intact. PLUMBING PROBLEMS? CALL (817) 555-CLOG. Next to the words was a smiling cartoon man wielding a toilet plunger.

Dub stepped over to the fence to take a closer look. The van had four bald tires, a single dented hubcap, and a cockeyed front bumper. Expired registration and inspection stickers, too. But it also had the words $400 OBO written on the windshield in white shoe polish.

One of the doors to the three-bay auto repair shop stood half open, a light on inside. Dub let himself in the unlocked gate and walked to the open doorway, ducking to look inside. "Hey!" he called to a man in coveralls working under the hood of a white car. "This van out here. Does it run?"

The man looked over at Dub and stood. He pulled a greasy rag from his pocket and wiped his hands on it. "Yeah. It runs. You interested?"

"Maybe," came out of Dub's mouth, though his mind screamed *Hell, yeah!* If he bought the van, he could use some of his remaining cash to buy lawn care tools and a ladder. Then he could make money raking leaves and trimming bushes and cleaning out gutters. Once the grass began to grow again in spring, he could buy a mower and cut lawns.

It was a short-term plan. He knew it. But his life had never been stable enough to think beyond the immediate future. Or at least it hadn't been until he'd been placed with Trent and Wes.

But his mother needed him. And she was the only family he had left. He couldn't turn his back on her. Besides, she seemed to have pulled herself together now.

Maybe there was hope for her. For him. For the two of them to be a real family.

The man walked over, ducked under the door, and pulled a set of keys from his pocket. "Want to take it for a test drive?"

"Yeah."

Dub didn't have a driver's license, but he'd practiced enough to know how to operate a car. Luckily, the man didn't ask to see his license. Looking older than he really was had worked in his favor.

The man handed him the keys, slid open a wide panel in the fence, and walked around to the passenger side. Dub climbed into the driver's seat. The van sat much higher than Wes's Civic, but was similar to Trent's Hummer. He should be able to manage it.

Dub stuck the key in the ignition and turned it. The engine hesitated a moment, came to life for a brief second, then sputtered out.

"Pump the gas pedal a couple of times," the mechanic said.

Dub did as the man had told him to and this time the engine roared to life.

The man pointed down the road. "Drive out onto the street and hook a left."

Dub slid the gear into drive and pushed lightly on the gas pedal, not sure how much pressure to give it. The van lurched.

The mechanic huffed. "You gotta release the parking brake."

"Oh. Right." Dub looked around but saw no hand brake.

The mechanic pointed to a lever under the left side of the dash. "There. Give it a pull."

Dub pulled back on the handle and noticed the parking brake light go out on the dash. He drove slowly forward, stopping at the edge of the drive, and waited for cross traffic to pass before pulling onto the road.

The engine sounded louder than it should and the van trembled like it was having a seizure, but it made it down the road and around the block without stalling. It even had a quarter tank of gas left in it.

Dub pulled back into the lot of the repair shop, barely missing the fence support.

"Watch it!" the mechanic cried.

"Sorry," Dub said. "I'm not used to driving something this big." He pulled to a stop and turned off the engine. "How about three-fifty for the van?"

"The price is four hundred," the mechanic said.

"Four hundred *or best offer*," Dub said, pointing to the OBO written on the windshield. If anyone had offered the seller four hundred the van would have been gone already, right? And OBO meant there was room to haggle. Dub might only be fifteen years old, but he'd seen enough movies to know how these things were supposed to go.

The mechanic frowned. "I put nearly three hundred dollars in parts in the engine. Plus, there's my time to think about."

"Three-seventy-five then," Dub said.

"Nope," the mechanic replied. "Four hundred or nothing."

Dub felt his face go hot with anger. Again, he felt cheated and powerless. *He wasn't going to put up with this shit.*

"I'm walking." Leaving the key in the ignition, he opened the driver's door and climbed out. He thought the mechanic would change his mind, say something. But the man said nothing.

Dub slammed the door behind him and walked to the gate. He looked back to see the man slipping back under the half-closed bay door.

Dammit!

Frustrated and humiliated, Dub turned and stomped back to the door. He bent over to holler under it. "Three ninety-nine!" *Asshole.*

The mechanic chuckled and waved him in. "Close enough."

Dub ducked and went inside, where he counted out the money from his wallet. Dub gave the cash to the man and the man handed him two sets of keys for the van.

Dub started to go when the man stopped him. "Hold on, there. You're forgetting your title."

The man retrieved a small rectangular certificate from a metal filing cabinet and handed it over. Dub looked down at the paper. It had the word SALVAGE printed on it. He wasn't exactly sure what that meant, but for three hundred and ninety-nine dollars he didn't much care.

Dub folded the title in half and tucked it into his back pocket. "Do me a solid and put a new inspection sticker on it."

"That wasn't part of the deal."

"Don't be a dick."

The man chuckled again. "All right." He walked over to a drawer, pulled out a current inspection sticker, and handed it to Dub. "You're on your own for the registration."

TWENTY-FIVE
LENDING A HAND

Megan

My cell phone buzzed with an incoming text from Seth. *Working overtime. Rain check for tomorrow?*

So much for our romantic Valentine's dinner plans. *Damn tornado.*

I responded *sure* and sighed. I supposed I shouldn't be surprised about the rain check. It was all hands on deck after the devastation the storm had caused. In fact, Derek had informed me that all day-shift FWPD officers had been ordered to stay out on patrol until further notice. Still, after the run-in at the liquor store, I'd love the comfort of Seth's strong, safe arms around me. I hadn't even had a chance yet to tell him what had happened.

I motioned to one of the K-9 teams working a pile of cinder blocks, mortar, and glass that, only an hour ago, had been a nail salon. "There're search-and-rescue teams in the area. They've asked me to head west and see if I can hear anyone in the rubble."

As usual, Derek seized control of the situation. As weary as I felt, I didn't mind, for once.

"I'll work the north side of the street," he said, gesturing to our right. "You take the south side."

We retrieved our bullhorns from our cruisers and made our way around the vicinity, calling into demolished buildings and running our gaze over the wreckage, looking for any signs of a buried body, a possible survivor. I hoped that if I did spot a body part it would still be attached to a body. I wasn't sure I could handle finding a severed limb.

Though the debris had yet to be removed and emergency vehicles could not get into the immediate area, multiple teams of EMTs with portable gurneys swarmed about, some of them carrying injured down the street to ambulances waiting at the edge of the debris field, others running with their equipment to help dig survivors from under collapsed walls and roofs. The constant wail of distant sirens and the flashing lights in the distance made the area feel like some type of warped carnival midway.

I stopped in front of a dry cleaner that was missing the top half of its four brick walls. The only things still standing were half a sign that read VER & SON, the countertop in the customer service area, and a huge pressing machine. Garments in clear bags had been tossed around like items at Neiman Marcus Last Call, the protective plastic covering torn. So much for *dry clean only.*

Though it would be a miracle if anyone who'd been in the store had survived, I pushed the button on my bullhorn. "Fort Worth PD. Anybody in the cleaners?" *Or in what remained of the cleaners?*

I cupped a hand around my ear and listened, feeling like Horton trying to hear a Who.

Nothing.

Just in case there was a Who in Whoville who had not yet spoken up, I tried a second time. "Anyone in there?"

When I cupped my hand around my ear this time, I heard a faint sound, a female voice calling "Here!", the word carried on a cry.

"I hear you!" I hollered into my bullhorn, the result-
ing sound so loud it caused me to cringe even though I'd
caused it. "Call out again!"

Another faint, "Here! I'm here!" came from behind the
countertop.

I grabbed the walkie-talkie from my pocket and
pushed the button to activate the mic. "I've got a survivor
at the dry cleaners."

One of the male search-and-rescue team members responded. "What's the closest cross street?"

I looked over to where the street sign should be but it
was gone, evidently torn away by the winds. I pulled out
my cell phone. Thank goodness mobile service was still
operative. After checking my current location on the
GPS app, I relayed the information to the team.

"On my way."

I looked around for something to tie Brigit to, but
none of the structures looked stable. I ended up tying the
end of her leash to the door handle of an upside-down
Mercedes in the parking lot. "Stay here, girl."

Brigit's eyes shined bright with anxiety but she
obeyed, sitting down on her haunches with only a small
whine in protest. I gave her a quick kiss on the snout. As
scary as today had been, it would've been worse if she
hadn't been with me.

My partner now situated, I began making my way
through and over the rubble to the counter, talking the
entire way, partly to reassure the person buried under the
wreckage, partly to make sure I wasn't stepping on someone else buried under the debris. "Here I come!" I called.
"Almost to you!"

Scuttling and crawling over shifting debris wasn't
easy. Bricks slid and smashed my fingers twice, and a
piece of drywall I'd mistaken for concrete gave way
under my foot, jamming my ankle against an unforgiving

strip of metal roof flashing. It felt as if I were in some type
of carnival fun house—minus the fun.

When my eyes spotted one of the rescue teams heading our way, I raised my arms and waved them. "Over
here!"

The man rushed over to the edge of the debris field,
unclipped the leash from the collar of his golden retriever, and issued an order. The dog scurried onto the
pile, quickly sniffing and snuffling his way past me, having a much easier time balancing on the shifting debris
with his four legs than I'd had on my two. He stopped
behind the counter, his nose shoved into the rubble, his
back end sticking up in the air. A second later he raised
his head, looked back to his partner, and barked. *Ruff!
Ruff-ruff-ruff!* His tail wagged vigorously. To humans,
search-and-rescue work was a matter of life and death. To
the dog, his work was playtime, an elaborate game of
hide-and-seek. Still, despite the differences in approach,
human/canine partners made amazingly effective teams.

The man, whose embroidered name badge read J. REED,
ordered his dog to continue his search for other survivors
while he joined me in trying to get to the buried woman.
Reed had an easier time than I'd had, having been trained
for this type of work and also being equipped with knee
pads, shin guards, heavy gloves, and other protective
gear.

He began to pull bricks off the pile and stack them on
the counter. "Careful," he advised. "The last thing we
want to do is make things worse."

One wrong move and the stack of debris could tumble
down like a house of cards or blocks in a game of Jenga,
but with devastating consequences.

After three minutes of careful digging, Reed pulled
away a section of uprooted floor tile to reveal a tiny white
woman cowering against the back of the counter. Her

gray hair was matted with blood, her face crisscrossed with deep scratches, her pink sweater soggy and stained.

"Thank God!" she cried. She reached up to grab me, nearly pulling me into the hole with her.

Reed and I helped her to her feet, and she looked around in horror. "Where's my son?" she said, softly at first, her words escalating to a shriek as the enormity of the damage sunk in. "Where's my son? Where's my son!?!"

The retriever had moved twenty feet back, indicating he'd found another person. But whether that person was still alive was unknown. The area where the dog stood contained an even deeper, denser pile of remains, including heavy machinery that had been tossed and toppled like children's toys.

Reed helped the woman to the top of the counter. "Stay here until we complete our search."

He radioed for paramedics to come tend to the woman.

As we turned to head to the back of the space, his eyes met mine. From the expression therein, it was clear he thought the chances of anyone surviving in the wreckage would be nothing short of a miracle.

It took us a full five minutes to reach the dog, another ten to figure out how to unearth the buried person with the risk of dropping machinery on him. Two large washing machines were counterbalanced at odd angles on top of the ruins. One wrong move and we could cause an avalanche that might not only crush the man trapped below but us as well.

Minutes later, when we finally uncovered a leg, Reed called into the rubble. "Search-and-rescue here. How you doing in there?"

There was no response. The man was either dead or unconscious. I prayed for the latter.

"Is he okay?" cried the woman from where she now knelt on the countertop, trying to get a better look. "Is he okay?"

As much as I wanted to give the woman good news, I had to tell her the truth. "We don't know yet!" I called.

We continued to pull debris away from the man, keeping one eye on the machines towering over us. *Creeeaaak.*

Uh-oh. One of the machines had begun to shift.

"Get back!" cried Reed, scurrying to his left. "It's gonna fall!"

I scurried in the opposite direction.

The machine wobbled atop the pile for a moment, letting out another *creak*, before toppling over backward and sliding away from us. While the machine had exposed the man buried below, it had also removed the main means of support for the other washer, which had started to inch its way down a slope of debris.

The rescue worker reached down and wrapped his hands around the prone man's left ankle. "Grab a leg and pull!"

I reached down, wrapped my hands around the man's right ankle, and yanked with all my might. We managed to pull him toward us and out of the way a mere instant before the washing machine slammed down into the space with a resounding *BANG!* A second later and the man would've been crushed to death.

Back on the countertop, the woman put her hands to her mouth and screamed.

"We got him out!" I called to her, hoping my words didn't give her false hope. We'd gotten the man out of the rubble, but whether he was alive was yet to be determined.

The man looked to be in his late forties or early fifties, with salt-and-pepper hair and a few lines beginning to form around his closed eyes. The rest of his face was slack, as if he were taking a restful nap. I only hoped it wouldn't be a permanent nap. A large, oozing gash on his left temple indicated he'd suffered major head trauma.

Reed put two fingers to the man's neck and exhaled a

quick, sharp breath. "We've got a pulse. It's weak, but it's there."

I looked over at the woman. "He's still alive!"

"Thank God!" she cried, putting her left hand on her heart and raising the other to the sky. "Thank God!"

A paramedic team ran up with a stretcher. While the three of them finagled the man's limp body onto the device, I picked my way back to the woman, helped her down from the counter, and gave her a shoulder to lean on as she limped her way through the rubble to join her son in the ambulance.

Brigit and I worked the rest of the day and late into the evening before being relieved from duty. During that time, I helped to pull three more seriously injured people from structures in the area. EMTs had set up a makeshift morgue in the bank building, one of the few structures that had suffered only minor, cosmetic damage. Several times I spotted teams going by, the limp forms on their stretchers covered with sheets. I nearly lost it when a woman's hand flopped out from under the sheet, the sparkly diamond ring and festive pink nail polish at odds with the dark situation.

Captain Leone stopped by in person just before nine, giving me a once-over. "You look exhausted," he told me. "We've got officers en route to relieve you. Go on home."

He'd get no argument from me. My muscles were so sore and tired they quivered. I was no use to anyone in this condition.

Brigit and I rode back to the station with Derek. I didn't bother to thank him for the ride. It was his job to help out a fellow officer, after all. Besides, he'd complained the entire time that my furry partner and I were making his patrol car smell of "wet bitch."

I loaded Brigit into my Smart Car and drove back to my apartment. I'd never been so happy to get out of my uniform and into a warm shower. Afterward, I took a brush to Brigit, running it over her fur until her hair was tamed.

I set the brush aside and cupped her face in my hands. "That looter was right. You are a pretty girl."

She gave me a sloppy kiss, then trotted across the kitchen to munch on her kibble. *Crunch-crunch-crunch.*

I, on the other hand, had no appetite. I did what I'd been longing to do all day. Curled up on the futon and cried.

TWENTY-SIX
PARTNER PITY

Brigit

Her partner lay on the couch, curled up in a fetal positon, bawling and shaking. Tired as Brigit was, she knew she had to try to cheer Megan up. Heck, she could use some cheering up herself.

She abandoned her overdue dinner of dry kibble and walked over to the couch. Ignoring Megan's cries of protest, Brigit cleaned the tears from her partner's face with her warm, wet tongue. *Shlup-shlup-shlup.*

Eventually, Megan unfurled, stretching her legs out on the sofa and patting the space in front of her, inviting Brigit to lie down with her. Brigit hopped up and flopped down, turning her back to Megan so her partner could scratch her chest while they cuddled and comforted each other.

Megan dug her fingers into the fur just below Brigit's neck and gave the dog a nice scratch.

Ahhh. That's the ticket.

TWENTY-SEVEN
BLOWING SMOKES

Dub

Dub parked the van in the back lot of the apartment complex. He didn't want to tell his mother about the van. At least not yet. She'd wonder how he'd gotten the money to pay for it and then she'd want to know whether he had any money left over. Dub didn't mind helping her out. But he wanted it to be on his terms. Besides, if he gave her any cash, he was afraid what she might buy . . .

He walked fast up to the apartment. It was nearly five o'clock now, and his mother would be home in half an hour.

Inside, he slid the second set of car keys into his backpack and looked around the apartment for places to hide his remaining $466. The toilet tank was too obvious. Same went for his mother's mattress. He thought about taping it under one of the kitchen drawers, but with his mom's history of delinquent rent payments he didn't want to risk them being evicted and someone else ending up with his cash.

Where should he hide it?

He realized then that the safest place to stash the cash was in the van itself. He rushed back out of the apartment, down the stairs, and was almost past the laundry room when Marquise stepped out of the doorway and blocked his way.

Shit.

Marquise's upper lip quirked. "Where you going in such a hurry, WC?"

None of your fuckin' business. "Where d'you think?" Dub snapped, bumping shoulders with Marquise as he pushed past him. "To see a girl."

"Ah." Marquise laughed. "Gonna get you some, huh?"

"You know it."

Dub continued on into the parking lot, looking back to see if Marquise was still watching him. Luckily, the guy was no longer in sight.

Dub climbed into the van. Though the vehicle might be a safer place to hide the cash than the apartment, Dub knew thieves sometimes broke into cars looking for electronics or drugs, especially in neighborhoods like this one. Dub also knew the glove compartment would be the first place someone would look if the van were broken into. He needed a better hiding spot.

He looked around. There were no floor mats to hide the cash under, and the back of the van had only straight metal walls. Spots of clear, dried glue told him there had once been carpet in the back of the van, but it was gone now. As he leaned back to check out the cargo bay, he noticed the vinyl backing on the passenger seat had separated at the seam, leaving a gap just wide enough to shove the money through if he folded it into a wad. He pulled the cash from his wallet, folded it in two, and shoved it into the seatback.

Good.

He turned back to the door and almost screamed

when Marquise, Long Dong, and Gato stood at the driver's door, staring in at him.

Had they seen him hide the cash?

Would they take it from him?

Before he could decide what to do or say, Marquise yanked the door open. "What's this, WC? You been holdin' out on us?"

"Yeah, man," Gato said. "You got yourself some wheels and didn't tell us?"

So they'd seen the van but not the cash. *Good.*

"Just got it." Dub slid down from the driver's seat and pushed down on the manual door lock. "Traded my twelve cartons of Camels for it." He was blowing smoke, but he didn't want these guys to know about the lottery tickets. He knew how these relationships worked. As the newest member of their gang, it wouldn't take much for the other three to turn on him.

"You move fast," Marquise said, watching Dub closely. "No grass growin' under your feet."

"You got that right." He closed the door behind him. "I'm going to use this van to start a lawn business."

Long Dong scowled and waved a hand. "A business? Shit, man. You should be having a party in there!"

TWENTY-EIGHT
THE SUN WILL COME OUT TOMORROW

Megan

Sunday dawned warm and bright, not a cloud in the sky, almost as if Mother Nature were mocking us. *Scared ya, didn't I?*

After a late breakfast I had no real appetite for, I checked my work e-mail and the news reports for updates. Seven people were confirmed dead, three more were still missing, and over a hundred had been injured. Weather experts verified the tornado as an EF5, the strongest possible category of tornado. The only saving grace was that the twister, though strong, had been narrow and stayed on the ground only a short time, giving the city a quick bitch slap before vaporizing.

My emotions were all over the place. When someone was hurt in a violent crime, it was easy to assign blame. But a natural disaster was an entirely different story. Who was at fault here? God? Satan? Corporate polluters whose emissions caused climate change? All of us who drove cars that decimated the ozone layer, leading to more frequent and extreme weather conditions? And, while catching a criminal and bringing him to justice could provide some closure, where was the closure here? When would this tragedy be "over?" When the last victims had been either buried in a cemetery or released from the hospital? When the grief of those who'd lost loved ones became manageable, if ever it would?

Blurgh.

Though I could certainly use a spiritual fix this morning, I'd slept too late to make it to Mass with my family. Maybe I could hit the Wednesday evening service this week.

The only thing lifting my spirits after yesterday's tragic events was the fact that I'd be leaving this crappy apartment behind by the end of the day. Even mean Mother Nature couldn't put a damper on that.

I dressed in a pair of yoga pants and a long-sleeved tee—moving attire—and began to pack up my apartment, glad to have the distraction. Given that I wore uniforms to work, had a limited off-duty wardrobe, and virtually no remaining shoes thanks to Brigit's chewing habit, it didn't take me long to pack my clothes. My coffeepot, toaster, and blender went into a large box with my small collection of plates, pots, pans, and utensils. The few items from the bathroom fit in a recyclable shopping bag.

My books were another story. I had an entire bookcase full of them. Rather than pack them in a large box, which would quickly become too heavy to lift, I stacked them in a series of smaller boxes and, when I ran out of those, slid the remaining few into a rolling suitcase.

A knock sounded at my door a few minutes before one o'clock. Brigit normally announced a visitor's presence long before they reached our door, but today she'd been sound asleep on the futon, snoring even. She was as drained by yesterday's events as I was.

Seth and Blast stood on the walkway. Seth looked as

tired and defeated as I felt. Being a first responder wasn't easy, physically or emotionally.

His green eyes met mine, clouding with concern as he seemed to assess my mental state. I must have looked even worse than I'd realized, because Seth immediately stepped forward and gathered me into his arms. I'd thought I'd cried every tear I had by then, but it turned out a few more had been hiding in reserve. I wet Seth's shoulder with them as he stroked my hair and held me. Neither of us said anything. But, really, what was there to say? Words couldn't change anything that had happened. But Seth's strong, comforting arms could make me feel safe and secure, give me some hope.

When my reserve ran dry, I gently pushed him back and wiped my eyes on my sleeve. Time to focus on the task at hand. Moving. "Thanks for getting the truck."

Seth had rented a small Budget truck this morning and driven it to my place.

"No problem," he replied, following me into my apartment. After he and Blast gave Brigit their standard greetings—a head pat from Seth and a butt sniff from Blast—Seth gestured to the futon. "Let's start with the big pieces."

We waved the dogs off the couch. While our canine partners wrestled and wrangled noisily on the floor, Seth and I folded the oversized cushion in half and performed our own wrangling, carrying the cushion out the door, down the stairs, and to the truck, laying it on top of a clean tarp Seth had spread across the floor.

At the back of the truck sat a huge rectangular gift more than three feet long and nearly as tall and wide. It was covered in red Valentine's wrap covered with cartoon cupids, as was another flat box wrapped in the same paper. I had a Valentine's gift for Seth, too, though mine was small enough to fit into my purse.

Seth caught me eyeing the gifts. "Not yet," he said with a coy smile. "Not until we've got you moved into your new place."

I stuck my tongue out at him. "Party pooper."

My current next-door neighbor, Rhino, was sitting on the wicker loveseat I'd bought secondhand several months ago and placed by the pool. He put down the guitar he'd been noodling around on and stepped to the chain-link fence that surrounded the pool. Rhino, so named because he wore his hair glued to a point over his forehead, had played in a seemingly endless list of alternative rock bands with such illustrious names as Crotch Rot and Toe Jam. Though his late-night practice sessions often impaired my sleep, he was otherwise a decent guy.

He draped his forearms over the fence. "You moving out?"

"Yeah," I told him. "I found a roommate with a house. Brigit needs a yard."

"Sweet!" he called. "I mean, not sweet that you're moving but sweet that your apartment will be up for rent. Our drummer's been looking for some new digs. If he moved into your place we could carpool to gigs." He stepped out of the gate. "Y'all need some help?"

"We'd appreciate it," I said. "Thanks, Rhino."

He followed us up the stairs to my apartment. While he and Seth each took an end of the futon frame and finagled it out the door, I folded the legs on the cheap card table that served as my dinette set and collapsed the chair that went with it. I returned to the truck with these light-weight items and slid them into a space behind the futon.

Seth and Rhino brought the bookcase down next, while I carried the big box of kitchen utensils. After a couple more trips to load the boxes of clothing and books, the last thing I brought down were my most-prized possessions, my twirling batons and fire batons. I'd recently performed with my fire batons at the stock show and rodeo, earning loud applause and even a few catcalls from the audience.

I ordered Rhino a pizza as a show of my gratitude and, while Seth kept the dogs entertained outside, vacuumed the dog fur off the carpet and performed a quick cleaning of the apartment. It was a tiny place, so it didn't take long.

Once the vacuum and cleaning supplies were stashed in the moving truck, I went to Grigsby's apartment to return my keys.

He answered the door with a television remote in his hand. "You clean the place?" he asked without preamble.

"Yes," I said. "You can go check if you want."

I knew he wouldn't. The guy was as lazy as they come.

He waved a dismissive hand, which he then held out to me. "Keys?"

I dropped my apartment and mailbox keys into his hand. "Did you lease my apartment yet? Rhino has a friend who's looking for a place."

"I thought I had it rented," Grigsby said, "but the guy's deposit check bounced." He leaned out the door and hollered across the lot to Rhino, who'd settled back on the wicker love seat and resumed his noodling. "Rhino! Come on over here!"

I left the two of them to their negotiations, rounded up Brigit, and put her in my Smart Car while Seth loaded Blast into the cab of the truck.

As I pulled out of the lot, I took one last look back at Eastside Arms, expecting a tug at my heart, a brief sense of melancholy. Nope. Couldn't muster up any feelings for the place other than a big sense of relief that I wouldn't be living there anymore.

C'est la vie.

Seth followed me in the truck to the rental house. We had to detour a few blocks out of the way to avoid the crews still working on Berry Street and the surrounding areas. Unlike yesterday, many of those working today were civilians. Tree trimming services. Contractors boarding up broken windows. Plumbers capping off leaking pipes. Store owners trying to salvage what they could from the remains of their shops. Insurance adjustors assessing damage.

I turned into the driveway of the house while Seth pulled the truck to the curb. Brigit and I climbed out of the car and met Seth and Blast in the front yard, which bore a scattering of broken tree limbs, leaves, and trash, evidence of yesterday's storm. The magnolia tree was missing several branches and the mailbox stood crooked now, but fortunately, the house itself was intact.

Seth's gaze traveled from the sidewalk, then across the front of the house. "Nice-looking place."

The front door opened, and Frankie stood there, still wearing flannel pajamas even though it was the afternoon. Her short blue hair, which had mostly been covered by her helmet when I'd met her, stuck up all over the place, looking as if she'd styled it with a cheese grater. Her eyes were still pink and puffy, which meant she'd shed a few more tears over her ex, but at least she was able to smile today. Her cat stuck his head between her calves and mewed.

"Welcome, roomie!" she said.

I introduced her to Seth and Blast.

Frankie picked up her cat and bounced her gently in her arms. "This little girl is Zoe."

Introductions complete, Frankie and I took Seth on a quick tour of the place.

When we'd shown him around, Frankie said, "I'll throw on some clothes and help y'all get the stuff out of the truck."

"That'd be great. Thanks."

We let Blast and Brigit out into the backyard to play

while we worked. We started with the futon, which we placed in the empty spot where Frankie's ex's sofa had been before he'd left with it. I'd slept on the thing at my old place, but it was time to move up to a real bed. Especially for that sleepover I'd promised Seth.

It took Zoe less than five minutes to claim the futon as her own, and us humans only half an hour to unload my meager possessions. When we finished, I glanced around my new bedroom. The only furniture in the room was the card table and bookcase, unless you counted the plastic crates I kept my lingerie and socks in. I needed not only a bed, but also a dresser and a night table.

"Mind if we do some furniture shopping while we've got the truck?" I asked Seth.

"I'm all yours today," he said, sliding me a sexy glance. "Do with me what you will."

I slid him a sexy glance right back. "That's an open-ended offer." One of these days—*soon*—I was going to take him up on it.

On our way out, I poked my head into the kitchen to let Frankie know we were leaving for a bit. "Need anything while I'm out?"

"Nah," she said. "I work nights stocking groceries at Kroger so it's easy for me to pick things up after my shift."

Good to know.

Seth and I loaded the dogs into the rental truck and set out for the nearest mattress store. Minutes later, Seth and the salesman were loading a plastic-wrapped queen-sized mattress and box spring into the rental truck, along with a metal frame and a padded headboard that would be great for sitting up to read in bed.

Next, I directed Seth to the home of Honeysuckle Sewell, an older woman who lived in an ancient wood-frame house on the east side of town and ran a perpetual yard sale on her front lawn. When one of the Tunabomber's explosives had detonated at the country club last fall,

Honeysuckle had lost her left eye and three fingers on her left hand. She hadn't let the injuries slow her down, though. She was back in business and as busy as ever. More so, really. After the local paper ran an interview with her, people in Fort Worth had begun taking their gently used but no longer needed furniture to Honeysuckle to sell.

Dressed in her usual denim overalls and red Keds sneakers, Honeysuckle was discussing a framed oil painting with a woman as we pulled up. The painting featured an orange-and-white horned steer standing among bluebonnets, standard art fare in Texas. Honeysuckle's left eye socket was covered with a white patch, but her right eye performed double duty. She spotted my familiar face in the truck's window and gave me a smile and a wave. I sent a smile and wave back her way.

Seth and I leashed the dogs and climbed out of the truck to check out today's selection of furnishings. With the yard still soft and moist from yesterday's storm, Honeysuckle had her wares set out on tarps today. I found a tall maple dresser that looked promising, though the drawers seemed to stick when I tried to open them.

"Darn," I said. I liked the look of this one but I didn't want to wrestle the thing for a clean pair of undies every day.

Seth lifted a shoulder. "It just needs a little sandpaper and wax."

"You know how to fix things like this?"

"Sure," he said, sliding me another sexy smile. "I'm good with my hands."

Honeysuckle glanced our way and I pointed at the dresser, then myself, letting her know I'd called dibs on the piece. She nodded in acknowledgment before leading the woman to another painting, this one of a black-and-white striped lighthouse surrounded by seagulls in flight.

Seth and I walked farther into the yard and came upon

a couple of bedside tables. Neither matched the wood on the dresser, but that was okay with me. At this point in my life, price and function were more important than style. "I think I like the white one with the oval top best."

Finished bargaining with her other shopper, Honeysuckle traded the lighthouse painting for some bills, slid the cash into a fanny pack at her waist, and moseyed over. "How are you, Officer Megan?"

"Doing good," I told her. I gestured to Seth. "This is Seth."

She held out a hand to Seth, the eye patch raising along with her brow.

"I'm Megan's boyfriend," he clarified.

Boyfriend. Yeah, I still wasn't used to the sound of that. I mean, it's not like I'd never dated, but I hadn't been in a serious relationship since I'd finished college and started work at the police department over a year ago. Besides, given my unstable relationship with Seth, it felt a little strange to finally put a label on it. But maybe I was overthinking things. Every couple had their ups and downs, right?

Honeysuckle shook Seth's hand. "Nice to meet you."

I glanced around, noting none of the pieces showed signs of hail or water damage. "What did you do with all of this stuff yesterday when the storm hit?"

The woman gestured to the house next door. "My neighbor was kind enough to move it all into the back of his carport for me. I covered it up with plastic and crossed my fingers."

I was glad she hadn't lost her inventory. She relied on the income from her secondhand sales to supplement her social security.

"I'd like this night table in addition to the dresser," I told her. "I just moved into a house so I need some new things."

"Congratulations on the new place," she said. "Any

chance you need end tables? I just got in a nice pair. Lamps, too, if you're interested."

While I'd made do with next to nothing in my tiny studio apartment, there was no sense in doing without at my new place. There was plenty of space in the living room for a couple of end tables and a lamp. A lamp would come in handy in the bedroom, too. "Show me what you've got."

By the time I'd finished shopping, I was down two hundred bucks and up a dresser, a night table, two end tables, two lamps, and a full-length mirror on a stand. Honeysuckle even threw in a slightly wobbly park bench for free.

"Thanks!" I called after we'd loaded the last of it into the truck.

"Keep in touch!" the old lady called, giving me a final wave before stepping over to attend to a young mother with a baby on her hip who was checking out the children's toys.

We arrived at my new residence and returned the dogs to the backyard while we unloaded my new possessions. Frankie was gone. She'd left me a note in the kitchen letting me know she'd gone to roller derby practice and wouldn't be back until late.

When Seth and I finished putting the new furniture pieces into place, I gazed around. The house was beginning to look like a home. All I needed now was new bedding. For tonight, though, I'd tough it out with the blankets I'd used on my futon.

After I spread them on the bed, Zoe trotted in and hopped up onto the blankets, flopping onto her side and rolling back and forth. Seth flopped down next to the cat, rolled onto his back, and cocked a brow, reaching out a hand to me. "Come here."

"If you think I'm going to jump right into bed with you, you're sorely mistaken."

"Aw, come on. It's the least you could do after I helped you move your stuff. Hell, all Rhino did was carry a few things out to your truck and you bought him a pizza."

"You want a pizza?"

He shook his head, climbed off the bed, and wrapped his arms around my waist. "I'd never be satisfied with pizza."

He put his soft, warm lips to mine and I nearly melted in his arms. Would things work out between us? I wasn't sure. I only knew that, either way, I was willing to find out.

It was well after seven by then and neither of us was much in the mood to get dressed up and go out for dinner. Instead, we picked up Italian takeout and a bottle of red wine and brought it back to the house, eating it at Frankie's pine dinette set in the kitchen, a vanilla votive in the middle to provide romantic ambiance.

While Zoe lay on the floor, swatting at the dogs' tails, Brigit and Blast ignored her and sat next to the table, staring hopefully up at me and Seth, licking their lips, clearly hoping for a scrap or two.

"Go away," I told Brigit. "It's bad manners to beg."

Of course she wasn't the only one to blame for her bad manners. I used the dog as a garbage disposal so it was no surprise she'd taken to hanging around while I ate to see what might be tossed her way.

Brigit's eyes followed my hand as I tore a bite from my garlic bread and carried it to my mouth. She smacked her lips and pawed at my leg.

"Oh, all right. I give in." I ripped off a chunk of bread for her and another for Blast. Some disciplinarian I was, huh?

After we finished our meal, Seth retrieved the wrapped boxes from the truck and the two of us took seats on the couch to exchange our overdue Valentine's gifts. He picked up the flat box and handed it to me. "This one's for you."

I tore off the wrap. "A hammock! What a great idea."

The hammock was made of bright, colorful rope and big enough to accommodate two people. Seth had done it again, found me a perfect gift. Once the weather warmed up, the hammock would be a wonderful place to lie and read in my new backyard. The hammock could also provide some romantic cuddling opportunities . . .

"I love it, Seth." I put a hand on his cheek and a kiss on his lips. "Thanks."

He cocked his head to indicate the larger box. "That one's for Brigit. From Blast."

"Is he as good a shopper as you?"

"You tell me."

I called Brigit over to the enormous box and ordered her to "shake" so she'd raise her paw. Once she'd lifted it, I used her claws to tear open the wrap, then pulled the rest off myself. Inside was a bright red Snoopy-style wooden doghouse, complete with her name in black letters over the arched doorway.

"Did you build this?" I asked.

Seth nodded. "Found plans online. But Blast helped. See?"

He pointed to several strands of Blast's fur that had stuck in the paint. *Some help.* That was like when Brigit helped me with laundry by dragging all of my dirty socks out of the basket.

Brigit sniffed the doghouse, circling the outside completely before stepping inside. She turned around and stuck her head out the door, issuing a happy *woof* as her wagging tail slapped the interior walls. *Slap-slap-slap.*

"She loves it!" I gave Seth a smile. "Thanks so much."

Blast trotted over to the door and licked at Brigit's mouth. Puppy love.

"I'll carry it out back," Seth said. "We can find a spot to hang the hammock, too."

"But first," I said reaching into my purse and retrieving the small box, "you have to open your gift."

Seth took it from me and pulled off the wrap. Inside was a waterproof swimmer's training watch that would count and time laps.

"This is great." Seth slid the watch onto his wrist. "'Course now I'll have to up my game, improve my times." He cut me a smile that said he appreciated the challenge, then gave me a soft kiss in gratitude.

I flipped on the back porch light and carried the hammock through the dusk while Seth finagled the doghouse out the back door. After trying the doghouse in several places—on the patio, against the back wall of the house, next to the house by the gate—we collectively decided that placing the doghouse catty-cornered in the back of the yard was the best option. The corner would be shady once the leaves grew back on the trees, and it gave Brigit a vantage point over the entire yard, which would better allow her to perform squirrel patrol.

Locating the hammock was easier given our more limited options. There were only two trees in the yard, the pecan and the oak, so of course the hammock had to be strung between them. The only question was which limbs looked the sturdiest.

After it was hung, Seth made a broad sweep of his arm. "Your seat, milady."

Turning sideways next to it, I flopped back into the woven cocoon, wriggling until I was lying longways. A moment later, Seth joined me.

I snuggled up next to him, enjoying the feeling of warmth, comfort, and connection. If this moment never ended it would be okay with me.

We lay there quietly for several minutes, staring up at the stars, before the dogs decided to join us on the hammock.

Fwump.

Brigit was on us in one leap that knocked the air out of our lungs and sent the hammock swinging out of control. She flopped on top of me, her legs splayed as she tried to balance herself against the motion. I supposed I could have been annoyed with her for interrupting my romantic interlude with Seth, but frankly I was surprised she'd given us as long as she had before pushing her way into our space.

Once she settled down, Seth invited Blast onto the hammock, and the two dogs lay butt-to-butt between us humans, who now lay on our sides, facing each other.

I ran a hand down Brigit's back and told Seth what happened at the Bag-N-Bottle yesterday.

His eyes went wide and he pushed himself up on one elbow. "They pulled guns on you?"

"Three of them did," I said. "They might have shot me and Brigit, too, if not for the fourth one stepping in."

I left out the part where my hand shook so violently the men had laughed at me. It was too embarrassing. I was supposed to be the leader of a tough K-9 team, not a fraidy cat.

"Any idea who they were?" Seth asked. "Or where to find them?"

"Not yet," I said, "but I plan to look into it."

Those four might have bested me at the Bag-N-Bottle, but they hadn't seen the last of Officers Megan Luz and Sergeant Brigit yet. I'd do everything in my power to track them down and bring them to justice. Looting was one thing, but threatening Brigit's life and mine was another thing entirely. Of course the only clue I had to go on at the moment was the tornado hoodie.

I gave Blast a scratch at his favorite spot at the base of his tail. "One of them wore a white hoodie with a black tornado on it. It seemed to be a logo of sorts, or maybe a picture of a team mascot."

"The mascot for Ball High down in Galveston is the

Golden Tornadoes," Seth said. "Our swim team com-
peted against them back when I was a freshman. And
Iowa State's mascot is a cyclone."

I mentally filed away the information. It could prove
useful later. Or not. It was often hard to tell which clue
would be the one to catch a culprit.

The night had begun to grow chilly, and both Seth and
I had to work the next day, so we called it a night. We
ended our postponed Valentine's celebration with a prolonged kiss at the door. If the organ pumping blood in my
chest had been a candy conversation heart, it would
have read I'M ALL YOURS, SETH.

Cupid might have been late this year but, boy, had he
delivered.

TWENTY-NINE
MY FURRY VALENTINE

Brigit

What a great day!

Megan had shared her people kibble, and Seth and Blast had brought Brigit a nice house that she could chill in out in the yard. And, speaking of yards, Brigit finally had one of her own to run around and dig in! Yippee!

Megan hadn't even noticed the sizable hole Brigit and Blast had started digging along the side of the house. Brigit realized Megan might be miffed about the digging, but yesterday's rain had left the dirt soft and supple, making for easy work. Heck, it would be a crime not to take advantage of such perfect digging conditions. Besides, Megan had her own annoying people habits. She wore too many floral scents, bathed too often, and ate too much fruit that Brigit had no interest in sharing. It was only fair that Megan tolerate some of Brigit's bad habits in return, right?

THIRTY
DOCTOR JEKYLL AND MISS HYDE

Dub

After another bean burrito for lunch on Sunday—*God, he was sick of those things!*—Dub lay down on the stained carpet to watch football, leaving the recliner for his mother. She sat, but didn't relax, her foot jiggling nervously.

"You know I'm glad to have you back home, honey," she said. "But I don't make much money. It's gonna be hard for me to have another mouth to feed. Think maybe you could catch a bus and go over into Fairmount or one of those nice areas around the university and see if anyone needs some help with sumthin'? Bet you could make a buck or two to chip in around here."

For the millionth time since agreeing to stay, Dub doubted—no, *regretted*—his decision to move in with his mother. Just days ago she'd begged him to stay, but now she was treating him like a burden. For God's sake, he was only fifteen. He shouldn't be having to worry about putting food on the table or clothes on his back. That was *her* responsibility. It wasn't that he minded working.

Hell, he'd been doing it as long as he could remember. It's just that he'd like the chance to be a kid. Besides, the lottery winnings would hold him over for a little while. Of course she didn't know about that money.

He stood. "I'll see what I can scrounge up."

He went out to the van, climbed in, and drove to the nearest Walmart store. Carefully, he pulled the wad of cash from the back of the passenger seat.

Inside the store, he headed straight to the electronics department. He bought two prepaid cell phones, the cheapest ones that had Internet access. He paid for a month of unlimited service in advance for both phones.

No ID required. No credit check.

He went to the garden section next. The spring yard tools were already on display. He put a rake, a set of pruners, and a pair of hedge clippers into his cart. He also grabbed a pair of heavy-duty work gloves and a roll of masking tape from the home improvement department. In the men's clothing section he snagged a package of underwear, a package of socks, a pair of basketball shorts, and a couple of printed T-shirts. A Dallas Mavericks jacket, too. It wasn't much, but at least he'd have something to wear other than the jeans, T-shirt, and hoodie he'd had on when he'd first come to his mother's apartment.

In the health and beauty department, he bought a combination bottle of shampoo/conditioner/body wash, a four-pack of razors, shaving cream, toothpaste, and a toothbrush. He'd been using his finger since he'd moved back in with his mother. It would be nice to actually have a real toothbrush again. He snatched a small box of laundry detergent as he passed the cleaning aisle, too.

In the grocery section, he stocked up on food, most of it stuff that wouldn't go bad right away. Cereal bars. Peanut butter. A loaf of whole wheat bread, the kind that Wes had made him eat. Funny, he'd pushed back before, but now, well, the bread seemed to give him hope, like he was staying healthy for the future. Stupid, huh? He wasn't even sure he had a future anymore. He also got a box of spaghetti, a jar of marinara sauce, and some canned vegetables.

He passed the sporting goods department on his way to the checkout. A display of basketballs caught his eye. He grabbed one and dropped it into his cart. He picked up a sporty duffel bag, too. It wasn't as nice as the one Trent had bought him, but it would do.

When Dub emerged from the store, he was down three hundred dollars, but he still had a little over a hundred fifty, enough to last him another week or so if he was careful.

Using the car charger, he plugged his new phone into the cigarette lighter in the van and searched the Internet. He found a print shop not far away that was open on Sundays. He drove to the shop and used a computer in their foyer to draft a quick flyer.

YARD CARE AND HAULING.
NO JOB TOO SMALL.
QUICK SERVICE AND CHEAP RATES.

He added a clip art cartoon of a man with a hoe, and listed his new phone number repeatedly on tear-off tabs down the right side.

Returning to his van, he headed west and posted the flyers on the poles of streetlights in the University Place, Mistletoe Heights, Berkeley Place, South Hemphill Heights, and surrounding neighborhoods, skipping the Fairmount area. No sense risking Trent and Wes stumbling upon him trimming bushes. He wasn't sure what would happen if they did. Would he be returned to juvie and sent back to Gainesville State School? Placed in a high-security group home? He had no idea what they did with runaways. But he didn't want to find out. He didn't want his life to be someone else's decision.

He dialed Jenna's home number from his cell phone. With him living at his mother's place across town and Jenna grounded at home without a cell phone and forbidden from seeing him, he hadn't even been able to wish her a happy Valentine's Day yesterday.

The phone rang three times before a man answered. Jenna's dad. *Damn!* Dub knew that if he hung up it would only make Jenna's parents suspicious.

"Hello, Mr. Seaver," Dub said, talking in a voice that wasn't his. "I'd like to tell you about a great deal I can offer you on—"

Click.

Yeah. Nobody wanted to talk to telemarketers. It had been a smart trick.

Dub knew he couldn't go back to his mother's apartment right away or she'd be suspicious. He decided to give it a few hours. When he returned, he'd tell her that he'd made a hundred bucks helping a couple load furniture into a moving truck. He'd got the idea when he'd passed a Budget rental truck on Travis Avenue. A blond guy, a woman with long black hair, and another woman with blue hair had been carrying furniture from the truck into a house. He'd still keep the van a secret. If his mother saw it, she'd know he'd been holding out on her.

To kill time, he drove to the YMCA. He passed through the parking lot to make sure Trent's and Wes's cars weren't there. They hadn't had a membership before they'd taken Dub in, so it was unlikely they'd be at the Y now. But better safe than sorry.

He pulled through a spot, making sure he could drive straight out and make a quick getaway if he had to. He shoved one of the T-shirts and his basketball shorts into his duffel bag and went inside, flashing his card at the attendant at the front desk before going to the men's dressing room.

He yanked the price tags off his new clothes and put them on, stuffing his jeans and tornado hoodie into the sports bag, and stuffing the sports bag into a locker. Dressed now, he went to the basketball court, hoping to get in on a pickup game.

No such luck.

The courts were quiet. He supposed it was because Sunday was a family day for most people. They'd go to church, eat a late lunch, maybe play a board game or watch a movie together or shoot hoops in the driveway. He could see the image in his mind. A smiling mother serving fresh-baked cookies. A father with a receding hairline and fat gut cracking corny jokes. Two kids who groaned at their father's jokes and thought he was a total embarrassment, but who loved him anyway.

The thought left him feeling cheated and empty and sad.

No.

He forced the picture from his head and the feelings from his heart. No sense getting all worked up about the stupid image in his mind. Not every family was as happy as the ones in minivan commercials. He'd survived all this time without a family, and he'd continue to survive. He wasn't some soft loser who needed to be babied. Dub could take care of himself.

Always had.

Always would.

With no one to play with, Dub settled for shooting hoops by himself. He practiced his layups, his slam dunks, his free throws. He even tried some shots from the three-point range. He sank half of them. He hadn't been nearly this good when he played for the Tornadoes. Dub knew the coach had given him a spot on the team not because he had skill or talent, but because he loved the game, showed up for practice on time, and because the coach thought it might build Dub's self-esteem. Somehow it had, even though Dub's performance on the court was nothing to brag about. But for the first time in his life, he'd felt like he was part of something bigger than himself, like he belonged, like he was wanted, like he had a part to play even if that role was a minor one as benchwarmer.

Two white boys strolled in, both dressed in athletic pants and blue and yellow tees printed with the logo for the Arlington Heights High School Yellow Jackets basketball team. Their eyes moved over Dub, sizing him up. He must have looked much fiercer than he felt, because they challenged him to a game of two-on-one.

He bounced the ball hard against the court. *Thunk.* "Prepare to meet your doom."

But no doom was to be met.

When they easily ran away with the ball, one of them switched to Dub's side. "Where's that doom you promised?"

Dub lifted a shoulder. "I just don't want to embarrass you crackers."

"Yeah," said the other, chuckling. "Right."

They went on to play a game of Horse, trouncing Dub once again. But why shouldn't they? They probably had personal coaches and every weekend free to practice. They probably hadn't been forced to roam the streets looking for odd jobs, to buy their own toothbrushes and underwear. He wanted to hate these boys for everything they had, for everything they were, for everything they would be. But how could he? He'd trade places with them if he could. They were just lucky to have been born into a good situation. They weren't at fault for that. No, Dub knew who was to blame for his current situation.

One man.

The man who had ruined Dub's life, his mother's, too.

Though the man had laid low lately, Dub knew he wasn't done fucking things up for him and his mother. That man wouldn't stop until he was put away for life . . . *or dead.*

Dub could kill him himself.

He knew he could.

One of the boys glanced up at the clock on the wall. "Gotta go. My mom will kill me if I'm late for dinner."

Dub chuckled at the irony and raised a hand. "See ya."

After shooting hoops on his own for a while, Dub went to the locker room, changed back into his jeans and Tornadoes hoodie, and drove back to the apartment complex. He worked on his story on the way, hoping his mom would buy it. *The people I helped had a lot of furniture. Heavy stuff. One of those big china cabinets and an entertainment center that took up an entire wall. I used the money to get groceries for us.*

He pulled the van into the parking lot of the apartment complex and there was his mother, sitting on the curb outside, smoking a cigarette. Probably one of the Camels he'd stolen from the liquor store. She tilted her head as she saw him drive in.

Shit. So much for keeping the van a secret.

He pulled into a spot nearby. No need to hide the van around back anymore.

As he climbed out, his mother gestured at the van with her cigarette. Ashes fell to the asphalt at her feet. "What's this?"

He closed the door behind him and shoved the keys deep into his pocket. "I got some new wheels."

"How'd you—" She stopped herself, closed her eyes, and shook her head. "Never mind. I don't want to know how you got the van."

She assumed he'd stolen it. His first reaction was to be angry she'd think so low of him, but how could he be mad? He'd paid for the van with cash from stolen lottery tickets. Not much better than stealing the van, if at all.

She reached a hand up to her face and scratched at her cheek.

Oh, no. No, NO, NO!

"Mom?" He stepped closer.

Sure enough, her eyes were glassy. Fury and frustration and fear shot through him, so hot and intense it was a wonder he didn't burst into flames on the spot. He wanted to grab her and shake her, shake some sense into her, shake her until she disintegrated in his hands and was no more.

"You're using again!" he hollered. "Aren't you?"

He wasn't sure why he even bothered to ask. He already knew the answer. His mother could live without furniture or food. She could live without a husband. She could even live without her only child. But she couldn't live without crystal meth. Not for long anyway.

She didn't answer.

"Did you see him?" Dub demanded. "Did you?"

His mother scratched her cheek again and looked past him. "What I do and who I see are none of your business."

None of his business? How the hell could she say that? Her drug use had been his business since the day he'd been born. How many times had he been up all night, left alone in whatever shithole they'd been living in at the time, waiting in the dark for his mother to come home? How many times had he gone hungry because she'd spent the last of their money on a hit? How many times had child protective services taken him away because she was an uncaring, unfit mother who allowed herself and her son to be brutalized? How many times had he heard her lame excuses and apologies?

But maybe the real question was, how many times would he put himself through this?

He was done.

The money he had left wasn't enough to get his own apartment, but as soon as he had enough cash to get his own place he was out of here.

And he would never look back.

THIRTY-ONE
LOOK-ALIKES

Megan

Early Monday morning, Frankie and I chatted at the dinette table and shared a toasted bagel. I'd swiped my half with a fruit spread, while she'd topped hers with a quarter inch of cream cheese. While the bagel was breakfast for me, given that Frankie had just come off a night shift I supposed hers counted as dinner.

I licked a bit of strawberry goo off my thumb. "What's it like to work in a store late at night?"

"Quiet, mostly," she said, taking a sip of her orange juice. "But sometimes on the weekends we'll get a bunch of rowdy college students coming in to buy beer. I was stocking toilet paper once and when I went to round up the empty boxes I found a guy asleep in one of them, drunk off his ass."

I'd worked many a night shift myself. The wee hours seemed to bring out all sorts of oddballs.

"How long have you worked there?" I asked.

"Six years," she said. "I started as a sacker back in high school. I moved to the floor after I graduated. It pays better and you don't have to deal with so many grumpy customers."

"What's your plan?" I asked. "Are you hoping to m-move up into management?"

She shrugged. "I don't know. I guess I'm still trying to figure out what I want to be when I grow up."

Her situation wasn't unusual. Lots of people didn't find their calling until later in life. I supposed I was lucky to have discovered mine early on.

"What about you?" She took another sip of her juice. "What made you want to be a cop?"

"Being mercilessly t-teased and helpless to do anything about it." I'd already seen her at her worst, bawling over a man who'd dumped her. No harm in opening myself up a little, too, right?

She obviously hadn't expected me to bare myself like that. Her mouth went slack, her lips parting slightly to reveal a bit of half-chewed bagel. She finished chewing. "The stutter?"

"Yeah."

"That sucks." She huffed. "Sounds about as fun as being five-eleven and a 38D as a high-school freshman. At least I didn't get teased to my face, though. No one had the guts to do that. But I knew what the other kids were calling me behind my back. *She-Hulk.*"

"Jerks."

She shrugged again. "I suppose it wasn't all bad. I channeled my anger into the derby. Youngest player on the team and MVP three years in a row."

"That's the way you do it." I raised my hand and we exchanged a congenial high five.

When we were done eating, Frankie helped me tie Brigit's cage to the top of my Smart Car. My specially equipped K-9 cruiser had been towed off for repairs, but Brigit and I could make do with a regular cruiser so long as I had her kennel to keep her restrained and safe. We garnered a few odd looks and a couple of smiles as we drove to work, but that was pretty typical for us.

Leading Brigit on her leash, I walked into the W1 station to speak to the receptionist/office manager/administrative assistant/queen-of-the-police-universe about my cruiser situation.

"Hi, Melinda," I said as I stepped up to the counter.

Melinda was a fluffy-haired blue-eyed bleached blonde in her early forties with a smart mind and, on occasion, a just-as-smart mouth. Not a bad thing, really. Working the front counter in a police station required her to deal with some rather unsavory types on occasion, and she had to be able to hold her own.

"Mornin', Megan. What can I do you for?"

"My patrol car suffered some water damage on Saturday." That was putting it lightly, huh? "They towed it to the shop."

"Yeaaah." She gave me a knowing look over the top of her computer monitor. "I heard about that."

"Let me guess. Derek told you?"

"Of course. That guy's worse than the women at my hair salon. I'm tempted to buy him a stylist's chair and one of those old-fashioned hair dryers so he can sit under it and blah-blah-blah all day."

I didn't consider Derek so much a gossip as a tattletale and an ass-kisser. One false move on my part and he went running to the chief to discredit me and score brownie points. "Can you get me a replacement car?"

"Honey, I can do anything." She turned to her computer, hit a few keys, and consulted the screen. "Three-oh-one is available."

"Is that the Barf-mobile?"

"Mm-hm."

Car 301 had worn shock absorbers and suffered a perpetual alignment problem, meaning it swayed and bounced and shimmied like those dance teams on *America's Got*

Talent. More than one criminal prone to car sickness had filled the back floorboards with the contents of his stomach. One had even tossed up a latex balloon filled with cocaine.

"There's nothing else?"

"Not unless you want to go on bike patrol. I can get you a nice Schwinn with a banana seat, a flowered basket, and a shiny bell." She made flicking motions with her thumb. "Ching-ching."

Damn.

I let out a long breath. "Guess I'll take the Barfmobile."

She unlocked a cabinet behind her, exposing a pegboard with rows of hooks and keys, and retrieved the set for car 301, holding them out to me. "Here you go."

"Thanks."

She cocked her head. "I'm assuming you'll need a new laptop, too?"

I nodded and she slid a clipboard onto the counter with a property damage form attached. I snatched a pen from the cup on the counter, completed the form, and returned the clipboard to her.

Melinda stood and went to another locked cabinet, where she pulled out a brand-new black laptop and padded computer bag. *Cool.* New equipment. Looked like getting your ass kicked by a twister had some advantages.

She handed the laptop and bag to me. "You know the drill. Don't download any new programs to it. Don't use it for personal purposes. Don't upload photos of yourself naked to the hard drive."

"Got it."

As I took the laptop from her, my eyes spotted the police sketch of the possible murder suspect tacked to the bulletin board behind her.

Holy guacamole.

Now I knew why the guy at the liquor store seemed

familiar. He looked just like the guy in the sketch. Well, except for the cowlick. But a detail like that would be easy for an eyewitness to miss, especially when she only saw the potential suspect in motion and caught just a quick glimpse.

As I stood there, mouth gaping, the door to Captain Leone's office opened behind Melinda. Chief Garelik stepped out, along with Detective Jackson.

"We need some movement on the murder case," Garelik barked at Leone and Jackson. "Soon. The damn media's breathing down my neck demanding to know why we haven't been able to identify a suspect yet. They're playing things up like we've got some kind of drug war going on in Fort Worth."

Detective Jackson's lips pursed. "We're doing our best, sir."

Chief Garelik turned his charm on me now. "Officer Luz. Good God a'mighty! Next time a tornado's bearing down on you have the sense to pull into a safe place. Those cruisers don't come cheap and we've got enough idiots out on the street without our own officers adding to it."

He didn't wait for me to reply, instead pushing past me to head out the door.

Jackson's eyes met mine. "Always nice to start the workweek with an ass-chewing, isn't it?"

I offered her an empathetic chin lift. "Can I talk to you a minute?"

"Is it important? I'm swamped."

"It's important."

"All right, then." She waved me to follow her down the hall to her digs. The chief might not trust my judgment, but it was flattering to know Detective Jackson did.

She slid into her rolling chair behind her desk, while I closed the door and took a seat in one of her wing chairs. "When I was patrolling on foot after the tornado Saturday,

I ran into a gang looting the Bag-N-Bottle liquor store on Berry Street."

"You're not the only one," she said. "We had gangs hit a Radio Shack and a jewelry store, too. To be expected. Criminals see an opportunity, they're going to take it."

Her tone was short, telling me to get to the point.

"One of the men who l-looted the store looked like the police sketch of the man who'd been seen in Forest Park."

She leaned forward now, putting her hands on her desk. "This is getting interesting now."

"Here's the thing," I said. "The guy was the only one who didn't p-pull a gun on me. In fact, he defused the situation. He didn't give off a violent vibe."

She raised a shoulder. "Just because someone doesn't draw on a cop doesn't mean he wouldn't willingly kill a civilian, especially if he had a good reason to."

"True." Still, the guy had shared beef jerky with Brigit. Even if the snack was stolen, it was still a sweet gesture, wasn't it? "I noticed the guy had one of those wallets with the chain that attaches to his pants. Do you think the chain that was used in Samuelson's attack in Forest Park could have been that type of chain?"

She cocked her head. "I think it's a distinct possibility." She picked up her phone receiver. "Is the guy still in lockup or has he been released already?"

"He was never arrested."

"Why not?"

"Because they weren't cooperating and backup wasn't able to get there in time to help me. I couldn't take in four men by myself. I had no choice but to let them walk off."

She dropped her phone back into the cradle. *Clunk*.

I pulled out my cell phone. "I got a photograph of them, though." I pulled up the picture and showed it to her. The man in question was the shortest of the bunch. He walked to their left and slightly apart from the others.

She heaved a sigh. "All it shows are the backs of their heads."

An angry flush warmed my cheeks. "Well, I couldn't very well take a picture when they were facing me. For one, I had my gun in my hands. And for two, they might have shot me."

She raised a conciliatory palm. "I didn't mean to rub you the wrong way, Officer Luz. I realize you did the best you could under the circumstances. All I'm saying is that the photo doesn't help much."

I took a breath to calm myself and sat back in my chair.

"Any idea who the guy might be?" the detective asked. "Or any of the men with him?"

"The guy who looks like the murder suspect wore a white hoodie with a black tornado on it." I went on to tell her that I'd spent an hour on the Internet last night, trying to track down the logo or mascot on the hoodie. "There's a brand of vacuum named after the tornado, as well as a protein shake. The tornado is a mascot for a number of high schools and colleges from as far south as Key Largo, Florida, to Anoka, Minnesota, and even way out in Washington State."

Her lips pursed again. "So what you're saying is that the hoodie, and our suspect, could be from anywhere."

My ire began to rise again but I tamped it down. The detective was only stating facts. No need to get my knickers in a twist.

"Wouldn't the odds be greater that he'd be from somewhere close?" I suggested. "Texline High School has a tornado for a mascot." The small town was located in the panhandle, just south of the Oklahoma line on the Texas-New Mexico border. "So does Texas State Technical College." The college had numerous campuses throughout the state. "Ball High in Galveston also has a tornado for a mascot."

"The Golden Tors," Jackson said, nodding. "I drove past the school once on summer vacation. I remember thinking a hurricane would've made more sense than a tornado."

Galveston Island had suffered a massive hurricane in 1900 that killed over 6,000 people, making it the deadliest natural disaster in U.S. history. Beyond tragic. The seawall was put into place thereafter, to protect the island from future storm surges. More recently, Hurricane Ike, which struck Galveston in September of 2008, claimed over three dozen lives. Okay, maybe I could see why the high school wouldn't want to have a hurricane as a mascot. Maybe it would have been better to avoid storm references all together—call themselves the Sharks or maybe something more original like the Jellyfish or the Sunburns.

Jackson pulled a pen and legal pad from her desk drawer to take notes. "What else can you tell me about these looters?"

"One was Asian with a spiky neck tattoo. Another was a black guy with lots of muscles and one of those swirly designs cut into his hair." I circled a finger over my ear to indicate the location of the design. "The last guy looked to be Latino. He had pointed features and a thin mustache and beard."

Jackson tapped the point of her pen on the pad. "So we've got a guy of apparent mixed race, a black guy, an Asian, and a Latino. Sounds like the kind of diverse group they'd feature in a brochure for military recruitment. The only thing missing is the white boy." She jotted down a few notes before looking up at me again. "You file an incident report?"

"I filed one online Saturday night." After spending a half hour curled up on my couch, crying. "But I didn't put it together until just now that the guy in the hoodie resembled the man in the sketch."

"We need to get crime scene techs over to the Bag-N-Bottle ASAP."

"It's unlikely they'll find any fingerprints for the murder suspect," I said. "He was wearing gloves. The others were, too."

Her brows rose. "That so? Maybe he's already got a record and doesn't want to get caught. And even if they wore gloves, it's still possible he or one of his cohorts left a print before they put them on. If we can find one of them, maybe he'll lead us to the guy we're after."

She picked up her phone again and punched a button, relaying the information to someone in forensics and requesting they send a team to the Bag-N-Bottle immediately. When she hung up, she hit some keys on her computer keyboard, pulling up my report. She read through it and cut her eyes my way. "*'The fourth suspect exuded an aura of despair and melancholy that seemed to run as deep as his soul?'* What the hell kind of report is that?"

I shrugged. "I'd just faced down death. I was feeling poetic."

She exhaled a long breath and waved for me to come around to her side of the desk. "Bring your chair and laptop with you. This may take a while."

I dragged the wing chair and my computer around her desk. Brigit followed me, flopping down at our feet to take a nap.

Jackson gave Brigit a scratch behind the ears. "Hey, puppy."

Brigit responded with a *swish-swish* of her tail.

The detective maneuvered her computer mouse and addressed me while gazing at her screen. "You familiar with Gangnet?"

"A little." I knew Gangnet was a database maintained by the Tarrant County District Attorney's Gang Prosecution Unit to share information on gang activity in the state, but I'd never had reason to access it before. I told the detective as much.

"Well, you'll learn it now," she said. "I want you to help me look through the database and see if you spot any of the men from the Bag-N-Bottle. Of course the fact that the group was interracial is unusual and may make it harder to track them down."

She went on to tell me that most gangs tended to form within a single race. Latinos made up Tango Blast, the state's fastest-growing gang, as well as the Texas Syndicate, the Texas Mexican Mafia, the Latin Kings, and Barrio Azteca, a particularly dangerous gang with ties to drug cartels. The Aryan Brotherhood operated in the state, along with a support group who called themselves the Solid Wood Soldiers. Needless to say, whites made up these gangs. Whites also made up the majority of the membership in the Hells Angels and, despite the Spanish name, the Bandidos. The biker gangs often coordinated charity events to gain favor with the public and put a fresh patina on their tarnished images. Asian gangs included the Asian Boys and Asian Pride. The black gangs were more creative with their names. Hoova Crips. Bustin Heads Daily. Untamed Gorillaz. Playas Afta Cash. There was even a gang called the Fuck You Clique.

How charming.

Still, while gangs tended to separate along racial lines and used to engage in often violent rivalries, they'd recently learned they could sometimes profit by working together. Members of the Aryan Brotherhood had even set aside their racism—temporarily—to engage in crimes with members of other racial groups.

"We've seen more of these gangs teaming up," Jackson said. "It's possible the four men you saw are members of different gangs and joined up solely to do some looting."

During the police academy, the instructors had informed us that gangs were such a problem in the big cities of Texas that the state had formed the Texas Anti-Gang (TAG) Tactical Operations Center in Houston. The team included representatives from the DEA, Homeland Security, the Texas Department of Public Safety, the ATF, Houston city police, the Harris County Sheriff's Department, U.S. Marshals, and the Harris County DA's office.

Gangs were ranked by the Department of Public Safety under a three-tiered "Threat Index" that took into consideration eleven factors including, among other things, the gang's links to drug cartels, the type and frequency of crimes committed by the gang's members, the level of violence, the prevalence of the gang throughout the state, whether juveniles were involved, the gang's organizational effectiveness, the extent to which the gang was involved in human trafficking, and the threat posed to law enforcement. Gangs who posed a threat to law enforcement only if fleeing apprehension were considered a lower threat than those gangs who intentionally targeted members of law enforcement.

Jackson showed me how to log in to the Gangnet database. "Run a search to see if you can find any gang members who attended any of those Texas schools you mentioned that have a tornado mascot."

It was a long shot, but it was the best shot we had.

I moved my cursor to the search box and typed in *Texline High School*. There were no matches. I typed *Ball High School* next. One entry popped up, a listing for an African-American guy who'd graduated from Ball High in 2003. He'd gone on to an illustrious career moving marijuana in the nearby city of Houston. Though the man depicted in the mug shot was too old to be the person at the Bag-N-Bottle, it was possible the two might know each other, right? After all, they were potentially from the same hometown.

I continued to read down his bio until I reached the

field depicting his *Last Known Address*. Rather than a
street name and number, the field contained the words
Deceased 03/24/15. He'd been only thirty years old when
he'd died. *Sheesh*. The report noted that he'd been shot in
the back of the head and left in the brush next to a high-
way outside of Houston. His killer or killers had yet to be
found.

So much for that potential lead.

Next, while Brigit snored and twitched at my feet,
dreaming her doggie dreams, I searched for gang members who'd attended Texas State Technical College. There
was only one, also an African-American, a young man of
twenty who'd dropped out of the TSTC Welding Tech-
nology program in Waco and been sucked into gang
activity up the road in Dallas. He'd been caught last year
with four pounds of heroin, a sizable stash. Per the report, he was currently serving time in the Telford Unit in
New Boston, which sat three hours to the northeast of
Fort Worth.

I looked over his picture.

Darn. Not my guy, either.

I mentioned him to Detective Jackson. "Think there's
any point in trying to contact him at the jail?" I asked.
"See if maybe he knew the looter at TSTC?"

She mulled it over a moment. "Not yet," she said. "It
takes forever to get an inmate on the phone. We'd have to
jump through a bunch of hoops. Besides, we don't even
know for certain that the tornado you saw on the sweatshirt was the TSTC mascot. There are several TSTC campuses and multiple programs. The chances of that man on
your screen knowing the looter are probably equal to the
chances of winning the lottery."

True again. *But somebody wins the lottery, right?*

I spent another two hours looking through the Gangnet files, trying a variety of searches that might unearth
any of the four men. I searched by location, approximate

age, and physical characteristics. The more photographs I looked at, though, the more muddled my memory seemed to become. Did the Asian guy have a shaved head, or was his hair spiky like his tattoo? Did the Latino have a silver cap on his front tooth or not? Did the black guy have pierced ears?

Hell if I could remember.

Although I found some gang members in the Fort Worth area who could possibly have been the men I'd encountered, I wasn't sure about any of them. The only thing I was sure of at the moment was that, no matter what it took, somehow, someway I'd track these men down.

THIRTY-TWO
DOGGIE DREAMS

Brigit

Zzzzzzzz . . .

THIRTY-THREE
SICK DAY

Dub

He woke with a start, surprised to find the apartment so light. He'd been unable to sleep and had stayed up late watching television and reading through his history book. He'd have the entire thing finished soon, for all the good it would do him.

He rolled out of the recliner, walked to the kitchen, and glanced at the clock on the stove. 9:00 A.M. *Uh-oh.* His mother's shift had started at eight.

He stepped to her bedroom door. "Mom? It's past nine. You're late for work."

She didn't answer.

He tried again, knocking this time. *RAP-RAP-RAP.* "Mom? You up?"

Still no answer.

He tried the knob. The door was locked. *Dammit.* He couldn't even get in the bathroom to take a piss. "Mom! Open the door!"

Still nothing.

He knocked full out now. *Bam-bam-bam!* "Mom!" He put his ear to the door.

He heard no rustling.

No snoring.

No breathing.

No signs of life whatsoever.

Gulping back the thick lump that had formed in his throat, he ran to the kitchen, found a paper clip in the junk drawer, and pulled it straight as he rushed back to the bedroom door. He jammed the end of the metal strip into the hole on the doorknob, poking and poking and poking until he heard the *click* of the lock releasing. Tossing the clip aside, he threw the door open and ran to his mother, falling to his knees next to her mattress.

Her face lay slack, her mouth hanging open just enough to allow a small puddle of drool to collect on the pillow beneath her head.

His ears roaring in panic, Dub put a hand to her shoulder and shook her. "Mom? Mom, are you okay?"

Guilt slammed him when he realized he would be nearly as relieved to find she had passed away as he would to find her alive. At least then he would no longer be sucked into this recurring nightmare. It would be over once and for all.

Her right eye fluttered, then opened to a slit. "Why you carryin' on like this?" she mumbled. "Someone dead?"

He choked back a sob. "I thought you were."

Her eye slid shut again.

He stood and kicked the side of her mattress. "Get up! You have to go to work."

"I'm not going," she said. "I'm sick."

"You're not sick!" He gave her mattress another kick. "You're wasted."

She was using again. She'd lose this job, just like she'd lost so many others before. She'd lose the apartment, just like she'd lost so many before. She'd lose herself again, too.

Same song, same verse.

And he was sick of it.

Trying to get her out of bed in this condition would do no good. He stood and gave her mattress a final kick. *Sorry excuse for a mother.*

After using the bathroom, he found the phone number for the Taco Bell on the Internet and called the manager. "I'm calling for Katrina Mayhew. My mother won't be able to come into work today," he said. "Sorry, but she's not feeling well."

"I didn't realize Katrina had a son."

"That's all right," Dub said softly. "She doesn't seem to realize it, either."

"Excuse me?"

He didn't explain. He just said, "Have a nice day" and hung up the phone.

He ran a hand through his hair. Why was his mother like this? Why wasn't she like those other mothers, who actually enjoyed caring for their children, who cooked and cleaned, who licked their fingers and styled their children's hair with their saliva? He'd seen mothers do that. Lots of times.

Okay, maybe the whole spit-style thing was gross, but he couldn't remember his mother even once trying to fight his crazy cowlick with a brush or comb. And now she was missing work and would probably lose her job. It would be one thing if she were on her own, but she'd convinced Dub to stay with her. How could she not care at all?

Screw it.

Someone needed to go to work and earn a few bucks, and it clearly wasn't going to be his mother. Not in the condition she was in.

He grabbed his cell phone, hoping that maybe someone had left a message for him, wanting to hire him for an odd job. No such luck.

He took a quick shower, dressed, and brushed his teeth. *Bam!* Dub slammed the door of the apartment as he headed out. His mother probably hadn't even heard it, but it made him feel better anyway.

He walked out to his van, trying to figure out what to do to earn some money. The only thing he could think to do was to go to the day labor site and see if someone might hire him.

On his way, he made a quick stop at Paschal High, parking in a visitor's spot and waiting until he heard the bell ring. *Bzzzzzzzt.* He hopped out of his van and hurried into the building, keeping his head down in case any of his teachers happened to be in the halls. The last thing he needed was one of them asking why he hadn't been to class and calling the police.

He turned down a noisy, crowded hallway and stopped.

There she was. At her locker.

Jenna Seaver, with her pretty reddish hair and her baby blue eyes and her way of making him feel like he was more than his rap sheet, that he was someone who mattered, that, no matter what anyone else thought or said, she knew the real him and that he was special and wonderful and good.

She could've been with another boy, one with better grades, better looks, less baggage. But she'd chosen him, seen something in him that he'd only caught glimpses of himself.

He was crazy for her.

His heart twisted. Probably the best thing he could for her was to turn back around and walk out of her life forever. What did he have to offer a girl like her? He'd only bring her down.

But he couldn't leave her.

Not yet, anyway.

Especially when she turned and saw him and her eyes got all bright and her mouth got all smiley and she squealed.

She rushed toward him. "Dub! Oh, my God!" She dropped her books at their feet and grabbed him in a hug so tight he couldn't move his arms. The hug even hurt a little, but in a good way.

When she stepped back, there were tears in her eyes. "I've missed you so much."

His throat seemed to shrink and his voice squeaked. "I've missed you, too." *Oh, hell, he wasn't going to start crying here in the hall, was he?* "Here." He handed her the prepaid phone he'd bought for her. "Be sure to keep the ringer turned off and hide it from your parents. I put my new number in the contacts for you."

She looked down at the phone, then back up at him. They stared at each other for a few seconds. Dub had so much more he wanted to say to her. She looked like she had things she wanted to say, too.

But not here, not now.

He coughed to clear his throat. "I gotta get out of here before the tardy bell rings."

"Okay." A tear running down her cheek, she stood on her tiptoes to give him a kiss. "I love you, Dub," she whispered.

He didn't say anything back. He couldn't. But he nodded and she smiled again because she knew what it meant. She *got* him. *God, that felt good.*

He left the school and drove to the industrial area where the day laborers gathered each morning. Most of the men were Latino and spoke limited English. When he pulled up in his van, a group of them hurried over, thinking he had come looking for helpers.

"Sorry," he told them. "I'm looking for work, too."

He parked his van and climbed out, standing at the edge of the group.

Several contractors came by, looking for workers with experience in roofing, framing, masonry, and drywall. Dub had never done any of those things. Unfortunately, nobody was looking for a fifteen-year-old dumbass who was qualified to do nothing.

He began to step up to the trucks as they stopped. "Do you need somebody to clean?" he asked. "I can pick up nails and sweep or whatever."

Nobody took him up on his offer. Eventually, it was down to just Dub and an ancient man with a stooped back and a single tooth.

A man in a pickup pulled up, a roll of carpeting sticking out the back of the bed. He looked over at Dub. "Either one of you know how to lay carpet?"

The old man nodded and stepped over to climb into the truck. They drove off, leaving Dub standing in their dust.

Alone.

THIRTY-FOUR
POST THIS

Megan

Tuesday morning, I climbed back into the cruiser and drove to the second burglary victim's house in Fairmount.

Unlike the Bayers, this victim, Tessa Gilpin, was single. Her wood and stone home had to be worth at least two hundred grand. Tessa must do pretty well for herself. Curious, I consulted her file. The record noted that Tessa was an engineer with Bell Helicopter. *Impressive.*

Tessa had arranged to go into work late this morning so that we could meet first. I led Brigit up to the front door and rang the bell. Tessa answered a moment later. She was dressed in black pants and a red turtleneck, her sleek blond hair pulled back in a barrette. She held a docile dachshund in her arms. He, in turn, was dressed in a blue sweater with little hot dogs all over it.

When the woman noticed Brigit, she emitted a cry of delight and exclaimed, "A K-9! Cool!" She bent down and introduced her dog to Brigit. "Hello, Officer," she said in an animated voice as if speaking for her dog. "I'm Oscar. Would you like to come in and play with me?"

I wasn't sure what the protocol was here. Was I supposed to respond on Brigit's behalf in a simulated dog voice? And, who, exactly, would Brigit sound like if she could talk? Angelina Jolie? Charlize Theron? Queen Latifah? *Hmm.* Maybe Whoopi Goldberg.

Realizing I'd wasted too much thought on the ridiculous topic already, I decided to skip the dog-speak and simply stepped into Tessa's house. The place was beautiful, with lots of windows, impeccable paint, and tasteful contemporary furnishings. Far more finished and classy than my eclectically furnished rental, though I was perfectly happy with my new place. I'd never been the Martha Stewart/HGTV type.

At least a dozen dog toys lay haphazardly around the room, most on the shiny wood floors, others lying on the couch and coffee table. Oscar was definitely one spoiled dog. Brigit nuzzled a stuffed raccoon toy on the floor and looked up at me as if to say *How come you never bought me one of these? Cheapskate.*

"Please," Tessa said, holding out a hand in invitation. "Sit wherever you like."

I took a seat on a boxy gray chair and pulled out my notepad. Tessa sat on the couch, positioning Oscar on her lap now.

I twirled my pen in my fingers. "I realize you were questioned already," I told her, "but I'm hoping this follow-up will provide some new leads."

"Me, too," she said. "I haven't felt safe here since. I had a security system installed as you can see." She gestured to motion sensors mounted on the ceiling in each corner of the room. "It cost a small fortune."

"Smart decision," I told her. "Security systems can be a good deterrent." They could also be a pain in the ass. Fort Worth PD received dozens of false alarm calls each day, mostly people who'd accidentally set off their own alarms or whose motion sensor systems had been triggered by a pet or a floating helium balloon left over from a birthday party.

I launched into my questions and listened carefully to her responses. As Tessa had stated previously and repeated now, her house had been robbed when she'd flown to California to attend her cousin's wedding in the wine country. A meter reader had come into her yard the afternoon she left, noticed the broken window, and phoned police when his knocks on the front door went unanswered. Tessa had left her house around one thirty and the meter reader had found the broken window approximately three hours later. The burglary had obviously taken place in the interim.

"Who arranged your travel?" I asked.

"I did it myself," she said, ruffling Oscar's ears. "The bride and groom had reserved a room block for guests at a specific hotel. I made my reservation online. Same with my plane ticket and rental car. I did everything on the Internet."

"What airline did you take?"

"American," she said. "I flew into San Francisco and drove to Sonoma from there."

Though they'd made their reservations via different means, both the Bayers and Tessa had taken the same airline. Did that mean anything? Maybe. Maybe not.

"Was someone watching your house for you? Maybe babysitting Oscar?"

"No," Tessa said. "I was only going to be gone for the weekend. I didn't think it was necessary to have someone watch the house." She lifted her dog up an inch or two. "This little boy went to stay at the kennel."

"Which kennel?"

"Paw Dee Da Pet Resort."

I jotted down the name of the kennel.

"What about your mail?" I asked. "Did you have the post office hold it?"

"No," she said. "It was only going to be two or three days' worth. Most of my mail is junk anyway. Sale ads and coupons, that kind of thing. I do all my bill paying on-line so I wasn't worried about anyone stealing my mail and getting a credit card number off a statement or anything like that."

When she'd answered all my questions, she walked me and Brigit to the door. I told her the same thing I'd told the Bayers. "We'll let you know if we find anything out."

"Thanks." She looked down at her dog. "Wave good-bye, Oscar." She grasped her dog's paw between her fingers like a puppy puppeteer and made him wave good-bye.

Poor dog. The sweater had been goofy enough, but he looked humiliated by this little command performance. Maybe it was time for him to put his itsy-bitsy, teeny-tiny foot down.

My mind whirled in thought as I walked to the car. I pondered where to go from here as I opened the back door for Brigit.

Should I go speak to someone at the airline? No, that would be taking things too far. The airport and the air-line headquarters sat miles away, outside my jurisdiction. I couldn't justify leaving W1 during a scheduled work-day, especially for such a weak tip. However, I could call the airline from my phone without having to leave my district.

I slid into my seat and retrieved my cell phone. I placed a call to the airline's legal department and ex-plained the situation, hoping my inquiry didn't sound ac-cusatory. "The only commonality between the cases is that both of the victims had taken flights on American."

The attorney was polite, but it was clear he not only thought I was barking up the wrong tree, but that, even if an employee of the airline had accessed the bookings, it would be impossible to identify who that person had been. "We have approximately 60,000 employees," he said, "thousands of those here in the Dallas–Fort Worth area. Around eight hundred flights a day take off from DFW."

In other words, *needle/haystack/can we end this call now so I get back to more important things?*

"Well . . . thanks for your t-time."

I ended the call and decided, what the heck. Why not stop at the post office? Maybe the carrier who handled Tessa's route had noticed her mail stacking up in her box and realized she was gone. Maybe that same carrier delivered to the Bayers' house and knew they'd put a hold on their mail while they'd gone on vacation. Of course this could be another dead end, but the radio was relatively quiet this morning. It wasn't like I'd be neglecting my duties by making a quick stop at the post office.

I drove to the post office on 8th Avenue, parked at the end of the lot, and went to let Brigit out of the back. When I opened the mesh door to her enclosure, I found her mouthing the stuffed raccoon that belonged to Oscar.

"Brigit!" I wagged a finger in her face. "You should be ashamed of yourself!"

First Tessa had been robbed, and now her dog had, too. Brigit had committed this misdemeanor act of thievery right under my nose. Some detective I was. I couldn't see clues when they were right in front of my face. Then again, Brigit was more at knee level.

Despite my admonishment, Brigit continued to mouth the raccoon, which she held between her paws. She looked up at me, not with shame, but with a look of indignation, as if she had every right to be chewing on the stolen toy. She even gave me her signature up-down *screw-you* tail wag.

I clipped her leash onto her collar and led her into the post office. She proudly carried the raccoon with her. I cut her a disapproving look. "I hope you know we are taking that back to Oscar when we're done here."

We went inside, where a line of people a dozen deep waited for service. *Yeah, I'm not waiting in that line.* Pulling rank, I lifted a palm to the next available clerk and stepped forward to speak with her. "I need to talk with the manager of this branch, please."

The woman looked down at Brigit, her eyes narrowed, her lips set in a firm line. Not a dog person, apparently. I supposed few postal employees were. Too many nips in the ass. "Let me get him for you."

She left her spot at the counter and disappeared through an open doorway that led to the back rooms. A minute later, she returned, a man in a navy blue sweater-vest tagging along with her. He had salt-and-pepper hair, as well as a thick mustache that curved down on either side of his mouth. If he were a dog, he'd be a schnauzer.

He, too, sent Brigit a death glare. I'd heard of racism and sexism, but what was it called when people were prejudiced toward dogs? Dogism? Caninism?

Having sent his hate beams at Brigit, the man turned his attention to me. "Is this a private police matter?"

"Yes, it is."

He gestured to his right. "Meet me at the door."

I stepped out of the customer service area and back into the main lobby. The man's face appeared in a small glass panel in a metal door on the wall. There was a *clunk* as he released the bolt. "Come on back."

He led me to his office, which was a small, window-less space. A dreary place to work, but the perfect place to hunker down in a tornado. Maybe I should reconsider my public service, resign from the police force, and take a job with the post office. It would probably be much safer than being out on the streets. And I could always buy a pair of chaps to protect myself from the ass nips.

The office was stuffy, with poor air circulation. The décor consisted of framed pictures of stamps issued through the ages and a metal desk with so many scrapes and scratches it looked like it had been in place since the branch opened decades ago.

I took a seat on a hard plastic chair. Brigit flopped down at my feet, perfectly content to chew on her contraband while I took care of business.

I pulled my notepad from my pocket and flipped through it until I found what I was looking for. "Can you tell me the names of the carriers who deliver mail to these addresses?" I held out my pad so the manager could see the streets and house numbers written there.

He logged onto his computer, and input the Bayers' address. "Their carrier is Stefan Nicolescu." He input Tessa Gilpin's address next, hit enter, and consulted the screen for the results. "Same carrier. Stefan Nicolescu."

Coincidence? Or not? I turned my notepad back my way and jotted down his name, asking the man to spell it for me to make sure I got it right. "Any chance he's here now?"

"Depends on whether he's finished loading his truck. I can check." The manager picked up his phone, punched a series of three numbers, and put the receiver to his ear. "Has Stefan headed out yet?" He paused a moment. "All right. Thanks." He returned the receiver to the cradle and addressed me again. "He's already out on his route. I can give you his cell number if you want to try to catch him out on the road."

"I'd appreciate that."

The manager grabbed a green certified mail card off a stack on his desk and jotted the number down on it. He held the card out to me. "Here you go."

"Thanks."

Brigit and I returned to the cruiser, where I promptly dialed Stefan's number. The man who answered sounded like the count from Sesame Street. A Romanian, I surmised, given the name and accent. Maybe I could put clues together, after all. When I told the man who I was and that I had some questions for him, he agreed to meet me.

"Ten minutes," he said. "At the corner of Edwin and Jerome Streets in Mistletoe Heights."

Ten minutes later, I pulled my cruiser to a stop behind the postal delivery truck. I left Brigit in the car and walked up the left side of the truck. When I reached the window, I realized my blunder. Postal trucks were equipped with the driver's seat on the right side of the vehicle rather than the left, allowing carriers to stick mail into boxes without having to exit the truck. I wondered if it was difficult to get used to sitting on the other side to drive.

I circled around the front of the vehicle to the other side.

An odd-looking man looked down at me. He had a Jay Leno chin and the large, bulbous eyes of an iguana. His hair was thick and coarse and wavy and in need of a trim. His skin was the rich tone common to Eastern Europeans.

I gave him a friendly nod. "I appreciate your meeting me here."

"You are a police officer," he said. "Did I have a choice?"

Hmm. Why the defensive tone?

Assuming his question was rhetorical, I didn't bother to answer. Instead, I showed him the two addresses. "These homes belong to John and Elena Bayer and Tessa Gilpin."

"I know," he said.

"You do?"

His iguana eyes circled in their sockets. "I have had this route for seven years. I can tell you the names of everyone who has lived here for any length of time." He pointed down the street in front of him. "Starting on the left are the Roberts, the Jeffers, and Justine Blevins. She is recently divorced."

"How do you know that?"

"Her husband's mail is being forwarded to an apartment and she has received correspondence from attorneys. Also she joined a wine-of-the week club."

Heck. This guy was better at putting clues together than I was.

He resumed his virtual trip down the street. "Then we have the Yousefs, Terrence—"

"Okay. You have a good memory. I get it. That's a great skill to have." I cocked my head, eyeing him closely. "The Bayers and Miss Gilpin were both robbed recently. Do you know anything about that? Did you maybe see anything odd in their neighborhoods?"

"I knew someone broke into Tessa Gilpin's house," he said. "Her street is one of the last on my route. The policemen were there when I drove up. Their car was blocking the mailbox. I had to get out of my truck to place her mail in her box."

He seemed none too happy about the inconvenience, either.

"Were you aware that the Bayers and Miss Gilpin were on vacation?" I asked.

"I seem to recall that the Bayers asked for their mail to be held." He narrowed his bulging eyes. "Why are you asking me such questions?"

"Because you're familiar with the neighborhoods and might have noticed something that looked out of place." *And because you could be the burglar.*

He stared at me for several seconds. "Well?"

"Well, what?"

"Are we done here? I have mail to deliver."

I took a step back and swung my arm to indicate he could proceed. "Enjoy the rest of your day, Mr. Nicolescu."

THIRTY-FIVE
WHAT A WEENIE

Brigit

Brigit had watched as the woman forced the dachshund to wave his paw.

Ridiculous.

She thanked her lucky stars she hadn't been born a wiener dog. They were the laughingstocks of the canine world, what with their disproportionately long ears and stretched-out bodies and too-short legs. They looked as if they'd been assembled with spare parts.

Yes, shepherds were a far superior breed. Stealthier, too. That's how Brigit had gotten away with that poor little schmuck's raccoon toy.

It was the law of the canine world.

Alphas rule.

Megan didn't seem to understand that rule, however. After taking Brigit to the place where everyone hated dogs and meeting with the mailman at the truck, she drove back to the house where Brigit had snatched the raccoon toy, forcefully taken the toy from Brigit, and left it on the porch.

Brigit had been plotting revenge until Megan stopped at a pet supply store, took Brigit inside, and found her a suitable substitute—a stuffed mallard duck.

Yeah. Brigit had Megan wrapped around her paw.

Sucker.

THIRTY-SIX
SLAVE LABOR

Dub

After a peanut butter sandwich for breakfast, Dub brushed his teeth and got dressed. His phone rang as he was tying his basketball shoes. An older couple who lived only a few blocks from the tornado's path needed someone to clean up the broken tree limbs in their yard and replace a few fence boards that had blown away.

"Attic needs a little cleaning out, too," the old man said. "Shouldn't take you more than an hour or so. We'd be willing to pay you twenty dollars."

Twenty dollars wouldn't get him far, but at least the work would get him out of the apartment for a while.

As he walked out to his van, he came across Long Dong and Gato putting bottles of liquor into the trunk of Gato's Sentra.

Long Dong waved Dub over. "We're going to the high school later to see if we can sell some of this shit. Grab your cigarettes and come with us."

"Thanks, man," Dub said. "But I got some things I gotta do today."

"Like what?" Gato asked.

Like it's none of your damn business, Dub thought. But he said, "Got a girl to go see." *If only.* He didn't want these jerks to try to horn in on his odd job business.

Gato cocked his head and narrowed his eyes. "You'll be missin' out. Sellin' this stuff to those kids will be like shooting fish in a tank."

"Where's Marquise?" Dub asked. If this was such a great opportunity, why wasn't their leader involved?

"He's already unloaded his take," Long Dong said. "He's got some friend who works at a restaurant. Bought all his liquor and cigarettes."

Looked like Marquise had cut the others out of the deal. Dub didn't point that out, though. It could come back to bite him in the ass. So could giving Gato and Long Dong the brush-off. Guys like this, you were either with them or you were against them. "I'll try to meet up with you if I can," Dub said. "What time you going over there?"

"When school lets out at three," Gato said. "We'll be in the lot."

"Okay," Dub said. "But if I don't get by there today, count me in next time?"

Gato cut him a sharp look. "We'll see."

You people be crazy, Dub thought. *An hour's work, my ass.*

The attic was packed with box after box of kids' toys, old clothing, and kitchen stuff. Their stepladder shook each time he carried a load down. He wouldn't be surprised if the thing folded up under him. The couple watched him closely, like they thought he might pocket some of their precious possessions. What the hell would he want with a dozen sets of animal-shaped salt and pepper shakers?

It took him two and a half hours to empty the attic, and another fifteen minutes to sweep it out to the old lady's satisfaction. The fence—*whoa*—that was a whole 'nother story. It was no wonder the dang thing blew over. Most of the boards were so weathered they'd split, and the support posts were rotted around the bottom. He drove to the closest Home Depot and spent sixty dollars of his own money on fence boards and nails. The old man wouldn't give him cash up front. He probably thought Dub would take the cash and never come back. Hell, if anyone was getting robbed here it was Dub.

He returned with the boards and gave the receipt to the old man, who hung over him in the backyard while he worked.

"Make sure that nail's straight," the man said. "Get that board flush up against the one next to it."

When Dub finally left five hours later with the twenty-dollar profit, he felt cheated again. He'd made only four bucks an hour, far less than minimum wage.

Why did life keep kicking him in the balls?

THIRTY-SEVEN
SHOOTERS AND CHASERS

Megan

After speaking with Stefan Nicolescu, I'd driven to a nearby church, pulled into the lot, and ran a background check on the guy. He had no prior convictions, no arrests, not even a fine for an overdue library book.

Hmm.

Nicolescu might have a clean record, but he definitely seemed like an odd duck. Being the sucker that I am, I'd then stopped by a pet supply store and bought Brigit a stuffed duck. A run-of-the-mill mallard, nothing odd about this one. I didn't normally shop while on duty, but since Brigit was my partner and, thus, an official cop, I figured tending to her needs counted as legitimate police work. I'd also driven back to Tessa Gilpin's house and tossed the soggy raccoon onto her porch. Restitution.

Later Tuesday afternoon, as I cruised by Owen Haynes's place for the bazillionth time, dispatch came over the radio.

"We've got a report of thugs selling liquor in the

parking lot at Trimble Tech High School. Who can respond?"

My "Officer Luz and Brigit responding" crossed Derek's response on the airwaves. "Officer Mackey on the way."

Not one to back down, I put the pedal to the metal and hightailed it over to the school. The tree-shaped pine-scented air freshener I'd picked up at the gas station swung to the side as I careened around the corner that led to the school.

It was easy to tell where the illegal pop-up sale was taking place. A dozen kids were gathered around a silver Nissan Sentra at the back of the parking lot. Fortunately, they were too distracted by the promise of liquor to pay attention to the cop heading their way.

I turned on my flashing lights as I drove across the half-empty lot. My eyes spotted the Big Dick coming in from the other side. He, too, turned on his lights. Both of us drove as fast as we dared through the lot, nearly colliding as we pulled our cars to a V behind the crowd.

I grabbed the mic for my public address system just as Derek grabbed his. Our orders came out like this.

Me: "Don't—"

Derek: "Stop—"

Me: "—move—"

Derek: "—right there!"

Me: "—or else!"

Ignoring our garbled demands, most of the teenagers who'd been lined up scattered like fire ants from a mound that had been poked with a stick, disappearing among the remaining cars in the lot or running off down side streets. As they scattered, they revealed two men facing the open trunk, their backs to me.

As I leaped from the Barfmobile, the two men turned around and my eyes met those of the men selling the booze. *Holy Mary, it's the Latino and the Asian from the Bag-N-Bottle.*

"Put your hands in the air!" I pointed at them with my left hand while using my right to yank my baton from my belt. I flicked my wrist and extended the stick with a *snap!*

The men looked from me to Derek, lifting their hands, but only as high as their chests.

The Big Dick stepped up on my right. "Put your hands in the air!"

I slid a glare to Derek. "I already said that."

"They clearly didn't listen to you."

True. *Dammit.*

"These guys drew on me Saturday," I told my former partner. "They might be armed."

Derek raised his chin in acknowledgment and pulled his gun from his belt. "I said to put your hands in the air! Don't make me tell you twice."

"Technically," I told Derek, "you already have told them twice."

"Shut up, Luz," he muttered.

When the men still failed to raise their hands, Derek stormed toward them. The Latino took off running in one direction, the Asian in the other. Derek dashed after the Asian. That left the Latino for me.

I let Brigit out of the cruiser and gave her the command to stay close by my side. With so many inexperienced teenaged drivers in the vicinity, I wasn't about to send her down the street alone. We set off after the guy, the two of us chasing him down the road, past a row of medical offices, and into a neighborhood. The guy was fast and nimble, darting around parked cars, garbage cans, and small children. When a school bus pulled through an intersection, the big yellow roadblock gave him an advantage. By the time my partner and I could circle around the behemoth, the guy had disappeared.

"Shit!"

A little girl who'd climbed out of the school bus gave me a stern look. "You're not s'pposed to say that word."

Sheesh. "Cut me some slack, kid," I said as I glanced around, trying to figure out where my quarry had gone. "I'm t-trying to make the world a safer place for you."

Derek pulled up in his cruiser, the Asian man secured in the back. The suspect's nose was bloody, his forehead scraped raw. Looked like he'd taken a nice skid across the asphalt.

A snide grin spread Derek's lips when he saw me empty-handed. "Mackey one," he said, "Luz zero."

Jackass.

"It's not over yet." I gave Brigit the order to follow the scent. She put her nose to the ground and began to sniff her way forward, with me following on her furry heels.

Derek trailed us in his cruiser, acting like the ass he was the entire time. "Come on, bitch!" he called. "Let's see what you've got! Let's see what your dog can do, too!"

When he barked with laughter, I turned to him. "You want me to tase you again?"

He narrowed his eyes. "You wouldn't dare."

He was right, of course. The last time I'd lost my temper and used it on Derek the Chief had nearly canned me. One more wrong step on my part and I'd be out of a job, my dreams of becoming a top-notch detective down the toilet.

I returned my attention to my dog. She sniffed and snuffled her way up to a six-foot privacy fence that enclosed the backyard of a house that sat on a corner lot. Standing on her hind legs, she leaned up against the fence and sniffed along the top. She sat down, letting me know the guy had gone over the fence.

I stepped closer and peeked between the fence boards.

I saw nothing in the backyard other than a rusty metal garden shed. *Could the man be inside?*

I turned back to Derek. "Go see if anyone's home who can let us into the backyard."

He scowled, but did as I asked, parking his car at the curb as he went around to the front of the house. A minute later he came back around the corner. "Nobody's home."

We checked the gate, but it had a solid padlock on it. Looked like there was only one way to get past this fence—by going *over* it.

Realizing Brigit wouldn't be able to jump the tall fence on her own, I bent over to form a human vault and issued her the order to scale the fence. With her love for the chase, she was more than happy to oblige.

The hundred-pound dog took a running leap toward me and bounced off my back, sailing gracefully over the top of the fence while I fell to my hands and knees on the sidewalk. *Oomph!*

My partner sniffed her way up to the shed and began to bark wildly at the door, her tail whipping back and forth in excitement.

"He's in there," I told Derek. "Now the score is even."

"Not yet it's not." He grabbed the top of the fence and pulled himself up in an instant, swinging his legs over and dropping to the lawn on the other side.

Oh, hell no.

I darted back a few feet and took a running leap at the fence, my feet scrabbling against it as I pulled myself up and over, ignoring the rough wood digging into my palms.

The two of us ran for the shed, reaching it simultaneously. "We know you're in there!" I yelled. "Come out now or I'll send my dog in after you!"

I really didn't want to send Brigit in. This guy was the one who'd threatened to shoot my partner the other day.

If he hurt her, God help him. I'd beat the guy with my baton until he was nothing but a fleshy mess on the lawn.

There was no response from within the shed.

"Get your ass out here!" Derek ordered. "Or I'll send my dog in there, too!"

"What the hell are you talking about?" I whispered. "You don't have a dog."

Derek cut me a snarky smile and squatted, his hands on his knees. "Bow-wow!" he barked, the sound deep and scary and surprisingly doglike. "Bow-wow-wow!"

A small voice came from within the shed. "All right! I give up! Call off your dogs!"

"Down, boy," I said to Derek.

He chuckled and stepped aside. "Come out with your hands in the air."

I called Brigit back to my side and we backed a few feet away. I pulled out my gun and held it at the ready just in case the guy tried to pull a fast one. When the metal door slid open and he stepped out, I issued the order for Brigit to take him down. For one, she deserved to have the fun of bringing this guy down after tracking him here. And, for two, she could get to the guy faster than either Derek or I could.

Brigit ran around behind the man and jumped onto his back like she was playing a rough game of leapfrog. The man careened forward and fell to the ground, his chest hitting the dirt with a *fwump*.

I stepped over, put a foot on the man's rump, and cut Derek a snarky smile of my own. "This one belongs to the bitches."

THIRTY-EIGHT
ALL JERK, NO JERKY

Brigit

Brigit was surprised to hear Derek barking. Of course, if translated, his attempts to speak the canine language would translate roughly as "I'm a human idiot who should be neutered so that I cannot reproduce." Dogs could understand around 165 human words, but humans? They could never seem to pick up dog language. *Poor, dumb creatures.*

After Brigit had taken down the man who'd been hiding in the shed, Megan held up her palm and Brigit tapped it with her paw, giving her partner a high five as she'd been trained to do. She didn't much see the point in the exercise, but she could tell it was a celebration of sorts and she didn't want to deny her partner her bragging rights, even if Brigit had done the bulk of the work here.

While Megan cuffed the man Brigit had taken down, the dog sniffed him up and down. She recognized his scent. He was one of the men who she and her partner had encountered on Saturday at the store. Unlike his friend, who'd given Brigit a nice treat of dried meat, this man had

no jerky in his pockets. Well, then. Brigit had no use for
him.

She trotted along behind Megan as her partner led the
man to the cruiser and shoved him into the back. Megan
led Brigit around to the other side then, and directed her
to climb back into the car and into her cage. Brigit did as
she was told, though she didn't like the cage. It was much
smaller than the enclosure in their special K-9 cruiser
and less comfortable. She also had a harder time seeing
outside the car.

"Good girl!" Megan said, dropping liver treats
through the bars of the cage. "Good Brigit!"

Brigit snatched up the treats and gobbled them down.
One, two, three, four, five. Interesting. Five treats meant
the man she'd taken down was a big haul, someone important.

She glanced over at the man. *Hmm.* He didn't look like
much to her. But, whatever. It was Megan's call.

THIRTY-NINE
SPITTING IMAGE

Dub

It was four o'clock by the time Dub returned to the apartment. He wondered whether his mother would be up by now or whether she'd still be sleeping off her meth high.

He slid the key into the lock. As always, he had to jiggle it to get the door open. As he stepped inside, an arm grabbed him and pulled him down into a headlock. His heart hammered in his chest. A face appeared next to his, a face he found so ugly but that was so much like his own, all the way down to the cowlick.

Spitting image, people said.

Appropriate, Dub thought. *After all, spit is disgusting.*

A loud, obnoxious laugh filled his ears. "Hey, there, sonny boy! Daddy's home!"

Daddy. What a fucking joke. Leandro had never been a father to him. His name didn't appear on Dub's birth certificate in the space designated for *Father.* That part had been left blank. Hell, Dub didn't even known Andro's last name. The man had never played ball with Dub, or read him a story, or taught him how to ride a bike, all those things normal fathers did with their sons. He'd never paid to put a roof over Dub's head, or food in his mouth, or shoes on his feet. Hell, he'd heard Andro threaten his mother with a beating if she filed for child support and forced him to take a paternity test.

Paternity test or not, there was no doubt Andro was Dub's father. From the tips of their toes—with the curled-under pinkie— to the tops of their dark, curly heads, the two were as alike as any father and son could be. But their similarities were only skin deep. Andro was a total sleaze, a scumbag, a waste of carbon and oxygen and nitrogen and calcium and all the other elements that make up a human being. Dub had learned all about that in science class.

Leandro was Portuguese-American, the second generation to be born on American soil. His ancestry gave him olive skin and dark hair. His drug use gave him an unpredictable, often explosive temper. This afternoon, he appeared to be in one of his rare good moods.

"Can you believe it?" Andro let Dub out of the headlock. "I ran into your mother Friday night. What are the odds of that?"

Pretty good, Dub thought, *given that she'd probably gone looking for Andro at those skanky, piss-scented pool halls where he liked to hang out.*

Dub took a look at the man who'd fathered him. His black boots were scuffed. His jeans were faded and worn through in places. His striped cotton shirt hung wrinkled and unbuttoned over a dingy white undershirt. Andro wasn't tall, but at five feet seven he was still two inches taller than Dub. Dub guessed the man outweighed him by a good forty pounds, too. Not that Andro was overweight. He was in good shape. Some might even call him ripped. Looked like he'd been working out.

Dub wanted to kill the man.

Right then, right there.
But he knew he couldn't take him.

Dub felt hot tears in his eyes. Rather than be called a *pussy* or a *homo* or a *candy ass* or whatever insult his father would throw at him, he went to the fridge, pulled it open, and stared into it until he could blink the tears away. He grabbed a burrito and hurled it into the microwave, jabbing the buttons to set the oven to cook for ninety seconds. *God, he'd love to jab his finger right through his father's eye.*

"That's my boy!" Andro laughed again, came over, and grabbed Dub by the back of the neck in a hold that felt like a death grip. "Always hungry!"

Andro got that right. Dub had been hungry. He'd *gone* hungry. A lot. But there'd been nothing funny about it.

Andro walked out of the kitchen, grabbed Dub's mother, and pulled her into the recliner with him. She giggled like a girl. Sure, she was laughing now. But it was only a matter of time before those laughs would turn to cries of terror and pain.

The recurring nightmare.
How the hell could she forget?

When the microwave beeped, Dub removed the burrito and ate it standing at the kitchen counter, having to swallow hard to force it down past the tightness in his throat. It burned his tongue but he hardly noticed.

"Where you been all day, boy?" Andro called from the chair, where he sat with an arm around Dub's mother, the two of them cuddling like longtime sweethearts.

Where I've been is none of your fucking business, Dub thought.

"He's got himself some work," his mother answered for him, her burden suddenly a source of pride. "He does odd jobs. You know, raking leaves and yard work and whatnot. He even got himself a van!"

"A van?" Andro's head snapped back in Dub's direction. "I gotta see this."

Shit.

Andro unwrapped his arm from around Dub's mother, got up from the chair, and came to the kitchen. "What are you waiting for, son? Show your dad your new wheels!"

A minute later, they stood before the old van.

"Suh-weet!" Andro ran a hand over the side and kicked one of the bald tires. "This will hold way more stuff than my car. I'll get my tools. You and I have a house to hit."

Andro always kept a toolbox in the trunk of whatever piece-of-shit car he was driving at the moment. Today, the piece of shit was a blue 1998 Subaru Impreza with an aftermarket spoiler welded on the back. After retrieving his red metal toolbox, he held out a hand. "Give me your keys."

"I'll drive," Dub said. After all, the van belonged to him.

"Like hell you will." Andro stepped up to Dub, got right in his face, so close Dub could smell the tuna fish sandwich he'd had for lunch. "Give me the goddam keys or I will rip that tongue right out of your mouth."

So Dub gave him the goddam keys. Climbed into the passenger seat as he was ordered, too, even though he'd rather be anywhere than there, in that van, with Andro.

Andro stuck the keys in the ignition, started the van, and pulled what looked like a paper luggage tag from his pocket. He took a look at the address printed on it before tossing it onto the dashboard.

As Andro drove across town, Dub plotted ways he could kill Andro and never be caught. Too bad he didn't have his brass knuckles. A couple of fists to the face and he could knock out every one of Andro's teeth. Maybe Dub could put rat poison in Andro's liquor, tie some cinder blocks to his arms and legs and dump his body in the Trinity River. Or he could take a screwdriver out of the toolbox and jam it through Andro's ear, shoving it straight into his brain. Or he could grab the steering wheel right now and turn the van into the path of the oncoming dump truck.

Tempting . . .

"After all these years," Andro said, pulling the van to a stop at a red light. "We're back in business."

"Business?" Dub snapped from the passenger seat. "Since when does robbing houses count as a business?"

The hand came out and smacked Dub upside the head. "Don't get smart with me, boy."

Smart? Andro wouldn't know smart if it bit him on the ass.

Andro looked over at Dub. "You haven't asked me what I've been up to since the last time we seen each other."

'Cause I don't give a shit.

Despite the lack of interest Dub had shown, Andro continued to speak. "I've been busy."

Busy getting drunk and high on meth and womanizing, no doubt. Dub looked out the side window. *Maybe I can find an anvil somewhere, drop it off a building, and crush him to death.* He turned to Andro. "Do you know where they sell anvils?"

Andro scowled and ignored Dub's question. "I got me a job at the airport. Handling baggage."

That explained his father's new muscles. Moving fifty-pound suitcases around the Dallas/Fort Worth Airport all day would be a workout. It was also a better job than the ones he'd had before, which had mostly involved delivering some type of food. Pizza. Chinese. Sub sandwiches. He'd worked all over the city. Dub remembered his father saying he knew the streets of Fort Worth better than any bus or taxi driver.

"I'm in a union now," Andro added. "Got a card and everything. Nobody can't hardly fire me, even if I screw around."

Dub had to fight to keep from rolling his eyes.

"Look at me when I'm talking to you, boy."

Uh-oh. Andro's voice had taken on that familiar, unforgettable edge. Dub glanced in Andro's direction, hoping it would be enough for the bastard. He hated that, at fifteen, he still feared his father, still let the asshole tell him what to do, boss him around. But he knew what his father was capable of. Until Dub was sure he could best him, he'd be an idiot to take on Andro.

Andro pulled forward when the light turned green. "I've saved up nearly two grand. I'm thinking about taking me a vacation to Hawaii."

With any luck, Andro would get drunk and fall into a live volcano.

"Maybe I'll take your mother with me."

"She could use a vacation."

Dub only said it because he knew it would never happen. Andro would never be so generous. Hell, Dub couldn't remember a single time when Andro had taken his mother out for dinner or even to a movie. The only thing Andro ever did was bring his mother meth, and he only did that because she'd give him sex in return. Dub had figured that out years ago.

Andro consulted the GPS app on his phone, slowed down, and took a right turn onto 8th Avenue. "You remember the drill?"

How could he forget? From the time he'd been old enough to climb through a window his father had been forcing him to go along when he burglarized houses. Dub had hated every minute of it. Going into houses where photographs of smiling families hung on the walls, knowing they wouldn't be smiling when they came home and found their televisions, game consoles, laptops, and jewelry missing. Funny, he'd never envied them for their valuables. But he'd felt a painful squeeze in his heart when he saw the children's handprints in hardened clay sitting on bookshelves, bronzed baby booties on the mantle, perfect attendance awards and third-place field day ribbons proudly hanging on the refrigerator.

Andro turned onto Elizabeth Boulevard, driving past the tall columns at the entrance to the Ryan Place neighborhood. The area included several streets of nice, older homes with perfect yards.

The man's lip curled back in a smile that looked more like a snarl. He patted the dash. "This van will make us look legit. Anybody sees us, they'll just think we're at the house doing plumbing work."

Dub would love to do some plumbing work. He'd love to shove a pipe down Andro's throat until the man choked to death.

Andro took another right onto Willing Avenue, driving slowly past the house he'd picked out, his head tilting first one way, then the other as he cased the place. "They've got one of them fancy doors with the glass in it. That'll be a cinch."

A cinch for Andro. He wasn't the one who'd have to reach through jagged glass to release the deadbolt.

Andro gestured at the house. "These folks flew out to Paris, France. Ooh la la, eh?"

He must have obtained their address from the tag on their luggage. Probably he looked for tags with addresses in central Fort Worth. Andro had never liked to go out of his way for anything, even to commit his crimes.

Lazy ass.

"Don't see nobody around. Looks like we're good to go." Andro backed into the driveway, pulling up so close to the garage door he nearly hit it. "Get out and do your thing, boy."

Dub slid his hands into the work gloves he'd purchased, grabbed the toolbox, and climbed down from the van. It took everything in him not to take off running. But where would he go? Who would help him?

He had nowhere to go.

No one to turn to.

And if he ran his father would catch him and beat the shit out of him.

Dub stepped up to the front porch and rang the bell. Better to make sure the people who lived there hadn't hired a house sitter to keep an eye on things while they were gone. The last thing he wanted was for someone to stumble upon him and Andro robbing the place. Dub would run, but Andro . . . Well, Dub didn't want to find out what he might do.

Dub rang the bell a second time and, when nobody answered, used the hammer to smash the etched glass. He paused for a moment to see if an alarm would sound. None did. He reached through the opening, his new Mavs jacket snagging on the pointed shards. "Dammit!"

He felt around with his gloved hand until his fingers found the lock. He turned until it clicked, then opened the door. Stepping back to the driveway, he motioned to Andro that the house was open.

Andro hopped out of the van, leaving the keys in the ignition. "You go open the garage door and the back of the van. I'll start looking around."

As Dub went inside, he spotted an orange long-haired cat spying on him from behind a potted plant. "Hello, kitty." He squatted down and held out a hand, but the cat skittered off down the hallway and ran into one of the bedrooms.

Dub found a door at the back of the kitchen that led to the garage. He stepped inside and pushed the button to raise the door. It slid up with a noisy rattle.

Ten minutes later, Andro and Dub had filled the van's bay with a big-screen TV, an Xbox, two dozen video

games, a laptop computer, a jewelry box, two mountain
bikes, and an electric guitar and amp. Andro had even
grabbed the family's Keurig coffeemaker and their box
of coffee pods from the kitchen counter. They carried
everything through the garage to load it into the van's
cargo bay.

"Well, well, well," Andro said. "Would you look at
that?"

Dub followed Andro's gaze. At the back of the garage
sat a tall black cabinet with a built-in lock. *Uh-oh.* Dub
had seen the damage his father could cause with his fists
alone. He didn't even want to imagine what his father
could do if he had a gun.

Andro put a hand on Dub's back and shoved him
toward the cabinet, following after him. "Looks like
these folks enjoy their Seventh Amendment rights."

"The right to a jury trial in civil cases where the
amount in controversy exceeds twenty dollars?" Dub
said.

"No, dumbass." Out came Andro's hand again, smacking Dub upside the back of his head. "The right to bear
guns."

Andro was the dumbass. The right to bear arms was
the Second Amendment, not the Seventh. Dub had studied the Constitution in American History. Earned an A
minus on the test, too. But no sense getting a concussion
over it.

"If we take these guns," Dub said, "the cops will come
looking for them. They don't care much about most burglaries but they're going to pay extra attention if guns are
taken."

Andro mixed it up this time, backhanding Dub across
the cheek. "Did I ask you what you thought?"

Of course he hadn't. Andro didn't give a rat's ass
what Dub thought about anything. And there was no use
arguing about it.

"It'll be easier to carry longways." Andro put both of his hands behind the top of the cabinet and pulled it toward himself, moving out of the way as it toppled forward. It fell to the floor, barely missing Dub's toes.

Dub grabbed one end of the cabinet while Andro picked up the other. The thing was heavy as hell, probably a hundred and fifty pounds or more, more than Dub himself weighed. Andro had no problem carrying his end, but Dub struggled, feeling a pull in his groin. He hoped he wouldn't get a hernia. He wouldn't be able to go anywhere for treatment. Luckily, they got the cabinet into the back of the van before Dub's guts split open.

Andro climbed into the driver's seat. "Close the garage door," he said. "If the neighbors see it open they'll get suspicious."

Dub walked back into the garage and hit the button to lower the door, walking back through the house to exit. As he stepped out the front door, he heard police sirens in the distance. His heart ramped up to warp speed when he realized the sound was growing louder.

The cops were on their way.

Shit!

Dub ran toward the van. But Andro must have heard the sirens, too. He punched the gas, and with a shrill *screeee* left both tire marks and his son behind in the driveway.

FORTY
TWO DOWN, TWO TO GO

Megan

Derek and I took the men we'd caught to the station for booking. According to the driver's licenses in their wallets, the Asian man was Lahn Duong and the Latino was Gustavo Gallegos.

Detective Jackson interviewed them one at a time, allowing me to be present. I sat next to her, twirling my baton in my hand, an exercise that both calmed me and allowed me to burn off excess energy. *Swish-swish-swish.* Brigit lay on her back at our feet, paws up, clearly seeking a tummy rub. I used the toe of my left shoe to ease my right shoe off, and ran my foot up and down her belly.

Jackson separated the men, speaking with Gallegos first. "Officer Luz says she saw you at the Bag-N-Bottle Saturday after the storm. You pulled a gun on her."

"I don't know nothing about that." Across the table, Gallegos lifted his shoulders. "Wasn't me."

Jackson rolled her eyes. "You were selling liquor at the high school. The very liquor you looted from the Bag-N-Bottle."

At least we assumed it was the same liquor. Neither of us knew for sure. Since the liquor store used a scanner, there were no identifiable price tags on the bottles. I supposed the only way to prove for certain that the liquor had come from the Bag-N-Bottle would be to check the glass for fingerprints and see if any of the prints matched the store staff who'd stocked the shelves.

"We found two guns in your car. Officer Luz said they looked just like the guns you pulled on her Saturday."

They did. They were shiny and scary and had a hole at the end that bullets could come out of. Other than that, I actually had no idea whether they were the same guns. But police officers weren't required to be entirely truthful with suspects. Though the law did not allow us to fabricate evidence for court, we could create all the stories we wanted when interrogating a suspect, to see if it would lead a suspect to spill the beans.

"We've got video footage from the store," the detective said. "Shows you and your buddies packing up liquor and cigarettes, hitting the cash register."

Again, it was a lie. Jackson had informed me privately while the men were being booked that, per information relayed by the crime scene techs, the security camera at the store had been disabled when the storm knocked out electricity to the area.

A smirk crossed Gallegos's face, almost as if he knew Jackson's statement about the camera was untrue. "You got video? Show me. Bring me some popcorn to eat while I watch it. I like mine with butter."

Jackson didn't hesitate or bat an eye. "We'll have to wait on the video just a bit. It's being logged into evidence and has to be downloaded to the server."

Wow. I hoped someday I could be as good as her at keeping a poker face while lying my butt off.

Jackson needled Gallegos some more, but he wasn't biting. She called an officer to take him to the holding cell, and had Lahn Duong brought in. Once Duong was seated at the table, she gave him a smile and shook her head. "With friends like Gustavo Gallegos, who needs enemies? That boy sang like a canary."

"Oh, yeah?" Duong said, looking nonplussed. "What did he tell you?"

"That you and two of your buddies looted a liquor store on Berry Street last Saturday, pulled guns on Officer Luz here." She gestured in my direction.

His already hard eyes hardened even more, giving off a flinty glint. "Not buying it."

I supposed I shouldn't have been surprised. This guy didn't seem to *buy* anything. He stole things instead.

Jackson angled her head, her expression calm and matter-of-fact. "Doesn't matter to me whether you buy it or not. We caught you with the contraband from the liquor store and Officer Luz can make a positive ID. Plus we've got you for selling alcohol to minors and bringing alcohol onto a public school campus. Any one of those charges alone is enough to send you down the road for a bit. But if you give us the names of the two others were who were with you on Saturday, we might decide to go easy on you."

"Can't say." Duong raised his shackled hands, palms up, in a feigned gesture of innocence. "Wasn't there. Got no clue what you're even talking about."

Jackson tapped her pen on the legal pad in front of her. "Where do you claim you were on Saturday afternoon, then?"

He performed a lewd pelvic thrust in his seat. "Boning my woman. Call her. She'll back me up. And while you're at it, ask her about my performance. She'll tell you I'm the best she's ever had."

"That's saying a lot," I snapped, "because she's got, what, a few hundred men to compare you to?"

It was a snarky comment and probably a rude thing to

say about a woman I'd never met. I should've kept my mouth shut. But I was beyond tired of this man's BS. I was sorely tempted to swing my baton at his head, see how he liked someone lording a weapon over him, threatening his life. After all, he'd done it to me and turnabout is fair play, right?

The door to the interrogation room opened and Melinda poked her head in. "Got some news."

"Good news or bad news?" Jackson asked.

"Good for you, bad for him," Melinda said. "A deputy pulled Owen Haynes over just south of Hillsboro for a traffic violation and found a meth pipe in his car. When they saw he had a record and was wanted for questioning, they hauled him in."

Jackson glanced at the wall clock—5:12—before returning her focus to Melinda. "Arrange a time tomorrow morning for me to go down there and interview him." The detective turned to me. "You want to come with me?"

Heck, yeah! "Sure."

"I want to go, too," Duong said. "We can hit the outlets after, get some new shoes or a purse."

Smartass.

"Shut your piehole." Jackson turned back to Melinda. "Tell them Officer Luz and Sergeant Brigit will be along, too."

"Will do," Melinda said. "Also, we've got officers en route to another burglary. This house was in the Ryan Place neighborhood."

"Same M.O.?" Jackson asked. "Homeowners on vacation?"

"Supposed to be," Melinda said. "Their flight was delayed a few hours. While they were waiting at the airport they got a call from a neighbor asking if there was supposed to be a plumber at their house. The neighbor told them a van was in their driveway and the garage door was open."

Jackson exhaled a long sigh and turned to me. "I'll have to head out there. So much for getting home in time for dinner. You're welcome to come along if you'd like."

Technically, my shift had ended twelve minutes ago. But I wasn't about to miss the opportunity for some on-the-job training in detective work, even if it would be unpaid. "Count me in."

Jackson hiked a thumb at Gallegos. "Get one of the officers to do something with him."

"Okey-doke," Melinda said.

I slid my shoe back on, shook Brigit awake, and followed Detective Jackson to the door.

We arrived at the house to find the perimeter of the yard marked off with yellow crime scene tape. A woman in her late thirties stood on the front porch, her face contorted with anxiety, a nervous hand clutching her hair as she spoke with Officer Hinojosa and a crime scene tech. A dark-haired man who was likely her husband stood in the open garage, speaking with another tech.

Lest Brigit steal another dog toy, I left her in the cruiser with the windows cracked a few inches. Jackson and I stepped up to the waist-high tape. While I ducked to go under it, Jackson used her hand to push the tape down a few inches and stepped over it. Again, different approaches to the same problem.

As we walked over to the woman, Detective Jackson called out to the man in the garage, "Are you the home-owner, sir?"

He looked our way. "Yes. I am."

She waved him over. "Officer Luz and I would like to speak with you and your wife."

He excused himself and came over to the porch, taking a spot next to his wife, putting a reassuring hand on her lower back.

Jackson pulled a small notepad out of her breast pocket and so did I, the diligent Padawan.

She clicked her pen to write. "State and spell your names for me, please."

"I'm Neil Harrington," the man said, following his words with the spelling.

"Nancy Harrington," the woman said.

The detective and I jotted their names on our pads.

Jackson continued her questions. "I've been told you were at the airport when you got a call from a neighbor telling you someone was at your house?"

"That's right," Nancy said. "We were supposed to be on our way to Paris right now."

"Which airline were you taking?" Jackson asked.

"American," Nancy replied.

Jackson and I exchanged glances. Both of the other victims had taken flights on American, too.

"Did you use a travel agent to arrange your trip?"

"No," Nancy said. "I'm a flight attendant for the airline. People who work in the industry tend to travel a lot so I just asked for tips from my coworkers."

"Any chance one of those coworkers might have tipped off the burglars that you wouldn't be home today?" Jackson asked. "Maybe even unintentionally?"

"I don't see how," she said. "We didn't even know when we'd be traveling until two days ago. Neil wasn't sure when he'd be able to get time off from work but one of his projects was canceled. Our employee flight benefits require us to fly standby. No one could have been sure that Neil and I would be able to get on a flight today."

Hmm.

The detective's head swiveled as she eyed the surrounding houses. "Which neighbor called you?"

"Mrs. Fancher." Nancy pointed across the street at a

gray-haired woman who was watching the activities from the bay window on the front left of her house.

Jackson raised a hand in greeting at the woman and motioned for her to come over. The woman came outside and walked over. We met her at the perimeter tape. She was dressed in a casual, elastic-waist sage green pantsuit with a coordinated scarf. Easy wear but stylish.

Jackson asked the woman to state and also spell her name.

"Helga Fancher," she said, spelling it out. "F-A-N-C-H-E-R."

"Got it," Jackson said. "Can you tell me what you saw over here today?"

"Certainly," Mrs. Fancher replied. "I was watering the houseplants I keep on a stand near my front windows when I noticed a van in the Harringtons' driveway. It surprised me because I knew the Harringtons were out of town. They'd asked me to bring in their mail."

That answered the question as to whether the Harringtons had put a hold on their mail. They hadn't. Either this burglary was unrelated to the others or the post office was a false lead.

"What did the van look like?"

"It was black," Fancher said, "and it looked old. It was dinged up and the paint wasn't very shiny. My eyes aren't good enough for me to see the license plate, but I could read what it said on the side. I wrote it down."

She pulled a slip of paper from her pocket and handed it to the detective, who held it out so that I could read it, too. Written on the slip was: *Plumbing problems? Call (817) 555-CLOG.*

"Okay if we keep this?" Jackson asked.

"Of course," Mrs. Fancher replied. "There was a picture on the side of the van, too. A smiling man holding a toilet plunger."

As the woman spoke, Jackson eyed me, formed a phone with her thumb and index finger and held it to her ear, the gesture indicating she wanted me to call the number.

I whipped out my cell, dialed the number, and stepped aside.

A woman answered on the second ring. "Hello?"

"Is this the plumbing service?" I asked.

"No." Her voice was irritated. "This isn't their number anymore. Hasn't been for years."

When I explained who I was and why I'd called, her tone became more congenial. "Sorry," she said. "I don't know anything other than that we've had this number for seven years. We used to get calls for the plumber constantly, but it's slowed down some over time. I guess he went out of business."

I thanked her and, when Jackson lifted her brows in question, informed the detective that the phone number was a dead end.

"Rats." She frowned and turned her attention back to Mrs. Fancher.

As we learned, when Mrs. Fancher had spotted the van in the driveway, she'd phoned Nancy Harrington on her cell. The Harringtons' flight had been delayed while mechanics took care of a maintenance issue, so their plane hadn't taken off yet. After speaking with Mrs. Fancher, Nancy had phoned the police. The Harringtons put their travel plans on hold and returned home to find their house ransacked.

Jackson's head bobbed as she jotted some notes. She looked back up at Mrs. Fancher. "Did you get a look at the people who were over here?"

"I tried," she cringed with apparent guilt, "but I was afraid to come outside."

Jackson raised a palm. "You did exactly what you

should have done, ma'am. Burglars can sometimes be violent if they realize someone has seen them. They don't like to leave witnesses."

Mrs. Fancher nodded, looking somewhat appeased. "Best I could tell there were only two of them. I saw a man with dark hair get into the driver's seat. I suppose it's possible there were others who'd climbed in the back, but I didn't see anyone else."

"So the second man climbed into the passenger seat?"

"No," Mrs. Fancher said. "By that time you could hear the police sirens and the driver sped away. He left the other guy standing in the driveway. The man stood there a few seconds, then took off running down the street."

"Any guess as to the age of the men?"

"Maybe in their twenties? I don't know for sure."

"What about their physical characteristics? You mentioned the dark hair. How big were they?"

"Neither one was very tall," she said. "The driver looked heavier, more muscular. The other one looked thinner. The driver wore jeans and a dark shirt. The one who got left behind was wearing jeans, a blue jacket, and work gloves."

When the detective finished with Mrs. Fancher, she thanked her and told her she could go back home.

As the woman left, Nancy Harrington whispered, "I'd always considered Mrs. Fancher to be a little nosy, but I've got to say I'm glad to have her around now."

"Yep," Jackson said. "A nosy neighbor can be a good thing."

The conversation turned from the burglars to the items they'd taken.

"My electric guitar and amp," Neil said. "And my laptop. Our TV."

"My jewelry box," Nancy added.

"My Xbox," Neil said.

"Our mountain bikes." Nancy turned her head to look into the garage, where the bikes presumably had been stored. "Oh, my gosh! The gun cabinet is gone!"

FORTY-ONE
NO FUR, NO FUN

Brigit

While her partner and the detective spoke with the man and woman, Brigit subtly snuffled around their yard and sniffed their shoes and pant legs. While she could tell a couple of dogs had relieved themselves on this couple's mailbox recently, she could tell this man and woman had no dog of their own. The pieces of stray fur on their pants and the unmistakable scent of feline told her they were slaves to a cat.

Poor schmucks.

Brigit sniffed along, pulling her leash fully taut as she scented the driveway. *What is that smell? Could it be? Yes!*

Her tail swung side to side in happy surprise. The boy who'd fed her the jerky had been here in the driveway not long ago. She could tell he had no dried meat on him today but, still, she was sorry she'd missed him. He'd seemed very nice and she sensed that he could benefit from a dog's unconditional love.

Disappointed and bored now, she flopped down in the grass and heaved a long, doggie sigh.

FORTY-TWO
LEFT BEHIND

Dub

Unbelievable.

His father forces him to burglarize a house, then leaves him behind to be arrested. *Asshole.*

If that wasn't bad enough, Andro now had Dub's cash and his van. Dub couldn't report the van stolen because someone had obviously seen it at the house and would connect him with the crime. Besides, he couldn't prove he owned the van. The title was still in the van's glove compartment. Hell, he didn't even have a driver's license and was only fifteen. Could he even legally own a vehicle?

So, once again, his father got away with his crimes and Dub was left holding the bag. With any luck, the police would catch his father fleeing in the van and arrest him. He deserved to be caught, to spend some time in prison, to pay for his crimes. So far, the only one who'd paid for Andro's crimes were Dub and his mother.

Dub still had his bus pass in his wallet. At least he wouldn't have to walk all the way back home.

FORTY-THREE
THE MURDER CASE TANKS

Megan

Wednesday morning, Brigit and I met Detective Jackson at the W1 station at 8:00. Rather than fill the detective's unmarked car with Brigit's fur, she suggested we take my cruiser.

I believed she deserved due warning. "I'm driving the Barf-mobile."

"Thanks for the heads-up. The shaking I can handle, but that smell?" She grimaced and pulled a small jar of VapoRub from her desk drawer, scooping up a smidge with her index finger and spreading it over her upper lip. "Works like a charm, especially when you're faced with a decomposed corpse."

Yuck. "Thanks for the tip."

She held the jar out to me and I snagged a swipe. The stuff would not only mask a scent and clear your nostrils, but with all the oil it contained it was probably a great wrinkle fighter, too.

We piled into the car and shook and shimmied and bounced our way down I-35 to the Hill County jail in

Hillsboro. A stocky female sheriff's deputy checked us in and led us down the hall to an interrogation room. Haynes was already seated inside. Next to him sat a young white male attorney who looked to be fresh out of law school. He wore a suit a size too big and a few years out of date. A public defender, no doubt. They performed an important service, but weren't exactly paid the big bucks to do it. He'd probably borrowed the suit from a friend.

Jackson and I introduced ourselves and shook hands with the attorney, who'd stood from the table. Haynes refused to stand, merely glaring at us from under thick, dark brows. His curls were much shorter today than they had been in the photograph Detective Jackson had shown me on her phone days ago. With the shorter hair, he looked very much like the person of interest depicted in the police sketch. He also resembled the guy from the Bag-N-Bottle who'd fed jerky to Brigit. But while the guy who'd looted the liquor store had sad eyes, Haynes's eyes glowed with evil, as if the fires of hell burned within him.

After we took seats, the attorney said, "I hope you two—" he cast a glance at Brigit, "—or *three*—haven't wasted your time coming down here. I've advised my client not to say anything."

Detective Jackson raised a shoulder. "That is his right. But if he doesn't give us a good alibi we might soon be charging him with murder."

The attorney's eyes went wide. "I thought you were coming down here to discuss a drug offense."

"I suppose it's a drug offense, in a way," Jackson replied. "The man who was killed was a known dealer of methamphetamine."

Her eyes locked on Haynes, probably to get a reading on his response. I turned my eyes his way, too.

"His name was Brian Keith Samuelson," she told Haynes. "You know him?"

"I'd like to speak privately—" the attorney began, but his words were interrupted by Haynes saying, "Never heard of him."

There'd been no flicker of alarm in Haynes's eyes when Samuelson's name was mentioned, no noticeable change in posture or respiration. Either the guy was an emotionless sociopath or he truly didn't know Samuelson. Of course I supposed both things could be true, too.

"He was killed in Fort Worth on Sunday, February eighth. Someone repeatedly slammed his face into a tree."

The detective didn't mention the broken chain embedded in his neck or the telltale marks on his face caused by brass knuckles. Those were facts the department had decided to keep in reserve.

"Sunday, February eighth?" Haynes repeated. A slow, sick smile spread across his face. "Oh, hell yeah, I got a good alibi." He expelled a nasty chuckle and leaned forward across the table. "I was on a double date with Beyoncé and Rihanna."

Another dumbass being a smartass. Forget siccing Brigit on him, I was tempted to bite this guy myself.

Detective Jackson, on the other hand, kept her cool. "I'm having a little trouble believing your story, Mr. Haynes. You want to tell me what you were really doing?"

He sat back in his chair. "I was in the city jail down in Austin."

His attorney cocked his head. "You sure about that, Owen?"

"Of course I'm sure!" Haynes spat. "Whose side are you on?"

"Yours, Owen," the attorney said resignedly. "Yours."

"Anyways," Haynes continued, returning his attention to the detective and me. "I went down there to visit my cousin. Him and me went to a bar on South Congress, and when we came out two punk-ass guys started some shit. The cops took us in, too, even though we weren't the ones who started it. I thought people in Austin were supposed to be cool but they're just as big o' pricks as they got anywhere."

"What time were you picked up?" I asked. If it wasn't until late in the evening, it would still be possible he'd committed the murder and then made the three-hour drive down to Austin.

His evil eyes looked up in thought. "Around five o'clock."

Jackson and I exchanged glances. Assuming what Haynes was telling us was true, we could rule him out as a suspect.

The detective stood. "I'm going to verify this information."

Haynes sneered at her. "Knock yourself out."

I stood, also, and gave a low whistle to rouse Brigit. Jackson and I exchanged a final handshake with Haynes's attorney, bade good-bye to the deputy manning the front desk, and returned to the Barf-mobile.

"What now?" I asked once we were seated inside.

"We follow up on Gallegos and Duong. Their curly-haired buddy may or may not be our killer, but I'd at least like to snag their black friend. Anyone who's pulled a gun on a cop needs to be reckoned with."

While I drove back to Fort Worth, Jackson phoned the Austin Police Department from her cell phone and verified that Haynes had, in fact, spent Sunday night in jail for assault. When the detective completed her conversation with Austin PD, she called Melinda from her cell to obtain home addresses for Gallegos and Duong. The detective activated the speaker feature so her hands would be free to jot down the addresses.

Melinda's voice came across the line. "Looks like they live in the same apartment complex. They've got the same street address but different unit numbers."

Jackson wrote down their addresses, thanked Melinda, and thumbed a button on her phone to end the call. "They live in West Morningside."

The neighborhood began just north of Berry Street and continued eastward for several blocks, in close proximity to the Bag-N-Bottle.

Forty-five minutes later, I turned into the apartment complex. The place was constructed of a salmon-hued brick that had been popular decades ago. The gray awnings were faded and frayed. Oil spots and potholes dotted the parking lot.

"Bring your laptop with you," Jackson advised. "We may need it."

We checked in with the on-site manager, a haggard woman in her fifties with monotone jet black hair and deep facial lines that told of numerous summers spent basking in the Texas sun. *Let's Make a Deal* played on the small television set sitting on top of a modern black lacquer credenza that didn't match her classic oak desk.

She gestured for us to take a seat.

Detective Jackson explained that we'd arrested Gallegos and Duong. "We're looking for two other young men who might live here. A black man with a swirl pattern cut into his hair and another who may be mixed race."

"I can go over the current list of tenants with you," she said. "Would that help?"

Jackson nodded. "Sure would."

"We've got sixty-three units," the woman said as she turned to her computer. "Most of them are occupied now. Just a couple of vacancies."

For the next fifteen minutes, the woman went methodically down the list, giving us the names and birth dates of all male tenants. Several of them sounded like possible matches, but when I pulled their driver's license pictures up on my computer, it was clear that none were either of the men I'd seen at the Bag-N-Bottle on Valentine's Day.

Jackson harrumphed. "What can you tell us about Gustavo Gallegos and Lahn Duong?"

The woman pulled up their records on her screen. "Gustavo Gallegos has lived here since last June. Duong moved in last November. Their names are the only ones on their leases. Of course that doesn't mean someone else might not be shacking up with 'em."

"Is there anyone here they're friendly with?" the detective asked. "Male or female?"

"Wish I could help you," the woman said, "but with the way people come and go around here I don't bother to pay much attention. I do my job, show apartments, and post eviction notices, and in between I just collect rent and do the bookkeeping. I don't socialize with the folks here. The management company I'm employed with offered me a discounted apartment at the complex, but who wants to live where they work? My own place is a couple of miles up the road."

Jackson nodded. "Understood. You don't mind if we ask around, do you?"

The woman made a broad sweep with her hand, indicating the buildings outside the window. "Be my guest."

We stood and went first to Duong's apartment, then to the one belonging to Gallegos. There was no answer at either place, though Brigit performed a voluntary snuffle around the bottom and sides of each of their doors. I wondered if she recognized their scents from the Bag-N-Bottle. I wished I could ask her whether she smelled the other two men in the vicinity. Too bad the dog couldn't tell me.

We tried the doors on either side of their apartments, too. While neither of Duong's adjoining neighbors was home, we had better luck at Gallegos's place. A young woman with a chubby baby on her hip came to the door.

She glanced around the courtyard as if to make sure none of the other residents could spy her talking to the police. Couldn't much blame her. Talking to law enforcement wasn't considered the neighborly thing to do in places like this.

"The curly-haired guy doesn't ring a bell," she said, "but I've seen the black guy you're talking about. He's totally ripped. I don't think he lives here, though. I think maybe he's just friends with some of the guys here."

We thanked her for her time and returned to the stinky cruiser.

"All right, aspiring detective," Jackson said to me. "If this were your case, what would you do now?"

"Does that mean you're out of ideas?"

She chuckled. "You're a smart cookie. And speaking of cookies, I'm hungry. Let's get some lunch."

We stopped at a sub shop, went inside, and ordered sandwiches. I chose a healthy veggie sandwich for myself. For Brigit, I ordered one with a variety of meats. "No veggies, no condiments."

After obtaining our food, we carried our trays to a booth in the corner. Brigit hopped up on the seat next to me. I unwrapped the paper from her sandwich and tore the enormous sub into bite-sized pieces that I placed on the tray. Knowing she'd try to eat the wrapper, too, I wadded it up and set it on the table to my other side.

As I dug into my sandwich, I mulled things over. "Let's pay a visit to Roland Wilson," I suggested. "Might as well let him know we've arrested two of the m-men who looted his store."

Jackson swallowed her bite and raised her cup of diet soda in acknowledgment. "Sounds like a plan."

When we'd finished our lunch, we drove to the Bag-N-Bottle. Plywood boards covered the windows and a wide swatch of clear plastic now served as the roof.

While the detective and my partner waited in the cruiser, I went to the door and tried it. Locked. Cupping my hands around my face, I peered inside. No signs of life.

"Nobody's here," I called back to the detective.

As I settled back into the patrol car, Jackson pulled up Wilson's home address on the laptop. "He lives just a little southwest of here."

She navigated the way, and we arrived at his home ten minutes later.

Wilson answered the door in a blue bathrobe, white socks, and a pair of corduroy slippers. An attractive woman also dressed in a robe stepped up behind him. The slightly embarrassed looks on their faces told me that our visit might have interrupted the two engaging in a little afternoon delight.

Since I'd been the one to interact with Wilson previously, I introduced Detective Jackson. Wilson, in turn, introduced the woman behind him as his wife.

"We arrested two of the men who looted your store," I told him. "The Asian and the Latino. We caught them selling the liquor at a high school yesterday afternoon."

Wilson's wife put a hand to her chest and said, "Oh, my." She seemed more concerned about the arrests than relieved. As for the man himself, he merely shook his head.

"I was hoping maybe you'd changed your mind about things," I said. "Your testimony would go a long way in putting these guys behind bars where they belong."

Wilson frowned. "I told you I didn't see them."

"I'd like to believe you, Mr. Wilson. But I don't."

"You've got some nerve," he said. "Coming to my home, calling me a liar."

He began to shut the door but I put out a hand to keep him from closing it.

"We think one of the group could have been involved

in an unrelated murder." I removed my hand. "If people like you don't speak up, guys like them will keep getting away with their crimes, hurting other people."

"Not my problem," Wilson said. "I'm going to take my insurance check and call it a day. I should've sold that place and retired years ago."

With that he shoved the door closed.

Seth texted me that afternoon. *Watch Mavs game at Ojos Locos tonight?*

I sent a quick reply. *Perfect. I could use a margarita. Who we playing?*

The Thunder.

Huh. That was ironic.

Seth swung by my place at 6:30 to pick me up.

"Want to come with us?" I asked Frankie. "There's liable to be quite a few available guys."

She sighed from where she sat, Indian-style, on the futon, still wearing her pajamas since she slept during the day. "I'm still at the all-men-suck phase. I'm not quite ready to get back out there yet."

"When you are," I told her, "just say the word." It was the least I could do for her. After all, she'd taken a chance on me, too, letting me move into her place without knowing much about me.

"Yeah," Seth added. "I could bring along one of my buddies from the firehouse."

Frankie's face brightened. "Got one that's over six feet?"

"Sure."

"Give me another week or two," she said. "My pity party should be over by then."

We left Blast and Brigit at the house with Frankie and Zoe and a couple of chew treats apiece. As we left, I admonished my fluffy partner to "be good" and gave her a kiss on the snout. She replied with a swirling tail wag that told me she'd consider being good, but wasn't going to make any firm promises.

As we headed to the sports bar in Seth's Nova, I caught him up on the burglary, looting, and murder cases. "All of the leads have petered out. I'm feeling frustrated."

He slid a sly smile my way. "I can relieve that frustration for you."

I slid him a sly smile right back. "I just might take you up on that."

"We could do it in the hammock," he suggested. "That would be daring and dangerous. I know how you like a challenge."

Normally, I did enjoy a challenging task. There was little reward in work that could be accomplished easily and quickly, and I enjoyed putting my intellect to work, analyzing clues, assessing evidence. But I feared that if the murder case wasn't solved soon, we'd end up with another body on our hands. Anyone violent enough to punch someone's face with brass knuckles, smash their face repeatedly against a tree, and attempt to saw their head off with a chain could be capable of anything.

The waiter took our order and, a few minutes later, plunked a frozen margarita in front of me, a draft beer in front of Seth, and a platter of nachos between us. We'd made only a small dent in the pile when it was time for tip-off.

While I was only a fair-weather sports fan, tonight's game against the Thunder was exactly the mindless entertainment I needed to give my brain a break. Plus, it felt nice to be with Seth, to see him getting a chance to relax. Like my job, his work with the fire department could be both physically and emotionally demanding. He deserved some downtime, too.

Two margaritas and approximately two thousand calories later, we'd polished off the nachos, as well as a basket of fried pickles and jalapeños and a couple of churros for dessert. I hadn't just fallen off the health food wagon, I'd dived off it headfirst.

The Mavericks had trounced the Thunder, making the crowd happy and the night lively. Seth draped an arm around my shoulders as we walked back to his car. When I stepped up to the passenger door, expecting him to open it for me, he instead backed me up against the side of the car.

"Hey!"

His soft, warm mouth was on my neck. "Hey, yourself," he mumbled into my flesh, stepping closer to press himself gently against me.

Maybe it was the margaritas, maybe it was the stress of work, or maybe it was because fooling around can be a lot of fun, but I found myself tilting my head back to allow Seth better access to the sweet spots on my neck and shoulders. He inched closer, the pressure of his body no longer gentle but insistent and thrilling. When I arched my back he emitted a moan and sunk his teeth into my skin. The feeling was so hot it wouldn't have surprised me to see actual fire shooting down the side of his car along with the painted flames.

He moved his mouth to mine, his kiss the perfect blend of sweetness and seduction. When we came up for air, I turned my attention to his neck now. After all, turnabout is fair play. I trailed a line of kisses down under his chin, his five o'clock shadow rasping lightly on my lips, and stopped to suck gently at his Adam's apple.

He offered a husky chuckle. "Remind me to take you out for margaritas more often."

A car passing by let loose a loud *honk* followed by wolf whistles from the inhabitants.

I raised my head and put a hand on Seth's chest to force him back. "It's getting late and I have to w-work tomorrow."

He groaned. "But things were just getting good!"

I gave him a chaste peck. "Patience is a virtue, Seth."

"And blue balls is a recognized medical condition."

"No man ever died from it."

He groaned again. "Are you sure?"

FORTY-FOUR
A NIGHT IN

Brigit

Blast and Brigit had begun their evening together lying on the futon and chewing their respective treats. Brigit made short work of her first treat and, when Blast wasn't looking, stole his remaining snack. He sniffed around for it a few minutes later, but put up no fight when he realized Brigit had taken it.

Ah, beta males. Gotta love 'em.

When Frankie had gotten up to get ready for work, she'd turned the television to *Animal Planet*. The sounds coming from the television included birdcalls, a lion's roar, and the *chimp-chimp-chimp* of a group of chimpanzees. Much more interesting than the usual *blah-blah-blah* of the news shows or the dings and bells and buzzers of the nerdy game shows that Megan liked to watch. *Jeopardy! Wheel of Fortune. Who Wants to Be a Millionaire?* Brigit didn't give a cat's ass about being a millionaire. All she needed was a soft bed to sleep on, decent food, and a yard to dig in, though she did admit that having another dog around could be fun. Too bad Blast couldn't stay here all the time.

Oh, well. At least Brigit had Zoe, who, despite being a cat, had begun to grow on her. She also had her stuffed mallard, which Megan had taken to calling Duckie. Duckie was no Blast, but he gave Brigit something to do while they were out on patrol.

Speaking of Duckie, where was he?

Brigit got up and went in search of her stuffed pal. *Aha.* There he was, on the floor in the kitchen next to her food bowl where she'd dropped him earlier. *Come on, Duckie. You're missing all the fun!*

FORTY-FIVE
HOME IS WHERE THE HURT IS

Dub

It was Friday evening, and Dub hadn't seen Long Dong, Gato, or Marquise in several days. Maybe the cold weather was keeping them inside. Or maybe they'd been busy selling off their liquor inventory. Dub really didn't care. If he never saw those guys again it would be fine with him.

Dub also hadn't seen his father since they'd robbed the house earlier in the week. Dub had felt furious when his father had taken off in his van, and his fury had only festered, like an untreated infection. Dub knew what that was like. He'd had strep throat for days once, every swallow feeling like broken glass, before his mother finally took him to a clinic for antibiotics.

Earlier in the week, a woman had seen Dub's flyer, called, and offered to pay him fifty dollars to move some things to a storage unit for her. He'd had to turn her down. She drove a car too small to fit some of the furniture items and, without his van, he had no way to haul them. That bastard Andro had taken so many things from Dub, and now he'd taken away his ability to earn a living, too.

Andro would never take anything from him again.

When Dub had told his mother what went down, she'd made excuses for Andro's behavior, as usual. *He panicked*, she said. *Nobody thinks straight when they're in a panic. Or maybe he was trying to draw the cops away in the van so Dub could escape on foot.*

What a load of shit.

Dub's mother had given him a twenty-dollar bill and sent him to the grocery store to pick up a few things. Toilet paper. Soap. Soda. Frozen dinners. A loaf of white bread and a package of processed cheese slices. He could hardly believe it, but he missed the times he'd shop with Wes, who'd take forever looking over the apples and lettuce and tomatoes and bananas, checking them for signs of worms or bruising.

The cashier finished ringing up the items and turned to Dub. "That'll be twenty-one forty-three."

He was short. *Damn.*

He ran his eyes over the bags, trying to figure out what they needed the least. "Take the soda off."

The woman offered him a look of both pity and judgment before removing the bottle of soda from the bag, punching a button on the register, and scanning the bar code again. *Bloop.* She eyed the register for the revised total. "That brings it down to nineteen eighty-two."

He handed her the twenty-dollar bill and took the eighteen cents change in return.

He grabbed the plastic grocery bags and walked back to the apartment. The night was dark. There was no moon and a nearly frozen drizzle was falling. Good thing he had his tornado hoodie to keep him warm.

He walked around the corner that led to the apartment building and came to an instant stop.

His van sat at the back of the lot, its motor giving off

small *tinks* as it cooled. There was a new dent on the back left fender. Andro must have backed into something. He'd also taped silver duct tape over the plumbing logo. Like that wasn't obvious and couldn't easily be pulled off. Paint would have been better. *Idiot.* With Andro's DNA, it was a wonder Dub had done as well as he had in school.

Dub felt fresh anger well up in him, but then he remembered the spare set of van keys in his front pocket. He let loose a laugh. Andro might have taken the van from Dub, but Dub was going to take it right back. That would teach Andro. His days of fucking up Dub's life were over.

Dub set the bags on the ground, pulled out the keys, and opened the van. The smell of alcohol greeted him. Sure enough, a half-empty bottle of whiskey lay under the driver's seat.

Dub wriggled the bottle out from under the seat, carried it to the garbage Dumpster, and hurled it in. He smiled at the sound of the glass breaking and the liquid running down the side of the metal bin. Returning to the van, he tossed the grocery bags inside and climbed in after them. He glanced into the back of the van. The rake, pruners, and hedge clippers were gone. Andro had probably thrown them out somewhere. *Dammit!* He could've used them as weapons against Andro.

He reached behind the passenger seat and stuck his hand through the seam.

Please be there. Please be there!

Aha! The remaining cash from the lottery tickets was still hidden inside the seatback. It wasn't much, but it was something.

He turned back to the front of the van. It took him seven tries to get the van started and it gave off a burning smell, but the engine finally caught. Dub would have loved to drive off and never come back. But he couldn't leave his mother alone in the apartment with Andro, especially

when he knew Andro had been drinking. So Dub drove
the van a few blocks over and parked it down a dark side
street. With the streetlight broken, Andro would have a
hell of a time finding the van here.

God, it felt good to give the bastard a little payback.

Dub grabbed the grocery sacks and jogged back to the
apartment, his jeans and hoodie soaked with cold drizzle. He shifted the bags to his left hand as he stuck the
apartment key in the door lock. As he jiggled the key,
he heard Andro's voice from inside.

"Don't you talk back to me, bitch!" The words were
followed by a *slap* and a *bam*.

Dub dropped the groceries on the walkway and used
both hands to get the door open. He ran inside to find his
mother cowering on the recliner, her arms held up to
block her face. Her eyes were glassy from meth and fear.
Blood oozed from both her nose and her bottom lip.
Andro stood over her, his face red with rage, his fist
cocked for another blow. At least he wasn't wearing his
brass knuckles.

"Stop it!" Dub launched himself at Andro. A sick
thrill surged through him when he felt Andro go down
beneath him. *He'd kill him. He would. He'd beat him
until his head cracked open and his brains spilled out on
the floor. And it would be too good for the man.*

Andro looked up at Dub, his eyes bloodshot and
shocked. He hadn't thought Dub had it in him to put up a
fight. He'd been wrong. His days of pushing Dub around
were over.

The element of surprise gave Dub an advantage. He
wailed on Andro, beating him with his fists, each punch
a small victory. "Don't you ever touch my mother
again!"

Andro turned under him, trying to cover his head.
God, it felt good to see his father scared for a change.

As Andro squirmed, his work ID card fell out of his

back pocket. For the first time, Dub learned his father's last name. *Silva.*

Dub's mother jumped up from the recliner. "Stop! Stop it!"

She grabbed Dub by the shoulders. She wasn't strong enough to pull Dub off Andro, but she threw Dub off balance. Taking the opening, Andro shoved Dub's shoulders. Dub and his mother fell back to the carpet. Andro put a hand on the recliner and pulled himself to his feet.

He looked down at Dub with eyes so full of rage Dub was sure he'd lived his last day. "Boy, I'm going to make you sorry you ever touched me." Hauling his foot back, he kicked Dub in the stomach with his steel-toed boot.

Dub felt as if he'd been gored by a bull. He bent in half, turned onto his side, and rocked back and forth.

"You gonna cry, boy? Huh? You gonna cry?" His father grabbed at him and yanked the damp hoodie off Dub, taking away what little protection the fabric provided. His father pulled his foot back again. This time he aimed for Dub's head.

Woo-woo-woo! Before Andro could kick him again, police sirens sounded through the open front door. The sound seemed to be the soundtrack of Dub's life lately.

Andro put his foot down and pointed down at Dub. "This isn't over." He ran out the door with Dub's hoodie in his hand, his footsteps *thud-thud-thudding* down the stairs.

Tires screeched in the parking lot as the police arrived. Dub was in no shape to run, but he couldn't risk being caught in the apartment and returned to juvenile detention. He wouldn't be able to protect his mother if he were returned to the lockup.

He crawled to the sliding door that led out to the balcony. "I'll be . . . out here," he told his mother, barely able to get the words out. "Close the curtains."

Arms over his bruised belly, Dub hunkered down in a dark, cold corner of the balcony. Through the glass, he heard a male officer holler, "Fort Worth police! Everyone on your knees!"

Dub's mother was the only one left in the apartment, but the police had no way of knowing that.

"It's just me!" he heard his mom cry. "I'm the only one here."

"Check the bedroom," the cop said, speaking to his partner over the sound of Katrina sobbing.

A moment later another male voice replied, "All clear."

"How bad are you hurt?" the first officer asked. "Do you need an ambulance?"

"No," Dub's mother said. "I'll be okay."

"Are you sure?"

Dub heard no response, but he guessed she must have nodded because the officer didn't ask again.

When the cop spoke again, his voice was softer. "Who did this to you, ma'am?"

She didn't answer. She just continued to sob.

The cop tried again. "I know you're upset, ma'am. You have every right to be. But we need to know who did this to you."

Leandro Silva, Dub willed his mother to say. *LEAN-DRO SILVA! Say it! Say his name!*

Her sobbing slowed, and Dub heard her sniffle.

"Please, ma'am," the cop persisted. "We can't help you if you won't tell us who hurt you."

When she finally spoke, her voice was so soft Dub could hardly hear it. "It was my . . ."

What did she plan to say? She couldn't refer to Andro as her husband. He'd refused to marry her. Did she consider him her boyfriend?

His mother paused for a long moment before completing her sentence. "My son. It was my son. He's hiding on the balcony."

Splash!

Dub was over the railing and in the pool in an instant, instinct telling him to flee. Utterly confused and totally terrified, he hardly noticed the near-freezing temperature of the water. He swam to the side, climbed out, and took off running as fast as he could. He was a block away when he realized his wet clothing was leaving a trail that would lead the cops right to him. He hopped over a curb and ran into a yard, hoping the water drops would be harder to see in the dead leaves and grass.

After what seemed like years, he reached the van. He struggled to pull the keys from his pocket. The wetness had sealed the fabric shut and made it hard for him to get his fingers into the pocket. Finally, he got the keys free. With shaking arms, he pulled himself into the van. He tried the engine three times. Each time it died. *Come on, come on, COME ON!* On the fourth try, the engine roared. Dub put his foot to the gas and took off.

Four miles later, when he was sure the police weren't on his tail, his mind calmed enough for him to think.

How? How could his mother have betrayed him like this?

And why?

Dub had done his best to be a good son, to take care of his mother, to be a help instead of a burden. Yet she'd thrown Dub under the bus for Leandro Silva, the man who'd gotten her hooked on meth, the man who'd knocked her up then knocked her down, the man who refused to support her or the child he'd fathered.

Dub had never felt so alone and so helpless in all his life.

And—*God!*—he'd never felt so cold either.

The heater in the van was cranked full blast but the air coming from the vents was barely warm. Dub spotted the Walmart ahead and turned in, pulling his stash of cash from the seat. He went inside and headed straight to the men's department. Though it was warmer inside the store, his damp clothes kept the heat from getting to him. His entire body was shaking as he grabbed a pair of fleece sweats and a sweatshirt, along with more underwear and socks. He rang up his purchases at the self-checkout line and all but ran to the men's room, where he changed out of his wet jeans and tee and into the sweats.

He'd forgotten all about his cell phone until it slid out of the pocket of his pants and onto the floor. He picked it up, jabbed a button, and looked at the screen. It was still working. *Thank God*.

His basketball shoes were soaked. He held them under the electric hand dryer for a full fifteen minutes. The warm air helped to dry his shoes and warm him up, too.

With his wet clothes in the plastic bags now, he went back into the store. His shoes were noisy, *skluck-sklucking* as he walked. The hand dryer hadn't been able to get all of the water out of the padding. He yanked a shopping cart from the line of nested carts and *sklucked* his way to the shoe department, where he picked out an inexpensive pair of sneakers. In the sporting goods department, he looked over the sleeping bags. He found a shiny black nylon one that was rated for outdoor temps as low as twenty degrees. He'd forego a pillow. He could make do without one. He needed his meager cash to last as long as possible.

In the home improvement department, he grabbed a can of black spray paint, another in a glittery silver shade, and a package of lettering stencils. He also picked up a bottle of cleaner guaranteed to remove even the most stubborn sticky substances, including tape residue.

In the health and beauty section, he grabbed the cheapest toothbrush and toothpaste the store offered. He could go without deodorant and shaving cream and shampoo for a while, but he'd feel nasty if he couldn't at least brush his teeth.

He rolled through the grocery department next, filling his cart once again with a jar of peanut butter, wheat bread, bananas, cereal bars, and a can of alphabet soup with a pull-top lid. He also picked up a box of assorted plastic eating utensils, a roll of paper towels, and a jug of drinking water.

This time through, he used a regular checkout.

The cashier was a girl of about eighteen. She was cute and flirty as she rang up his purchases. "Going camping? You forgot the marshmallows."

Her happy smile was almost more than he could take. He forced a smile back at her when all he really wanted to do was break down and cry.

He left, down $119. He had only $31 to his name now, but at least he had warm bedding and enough food to last him for a few days.

He opened the back doors of his van, put his bags inside, and climbed in after them. The parking space was near the edge of the lot, away from the lights. Dub supposed it was as good a place as any to stay for the night. The store was open twenty-four hours. It was probably safer here than on the streets, and less likely the police would stumble upon him.

He removed his shoes, put on a dry pair of socks, and spread his sleeping bag in the cargo bay. Then he zipped himself into the bag and wondered what the hell he was going to do.

FORTY-SIX
OUTDATED

Megan

Lucky me.

It was my weekend to work the night shift. I always had a hard time adjusting to the change in schedule. I'd managed to force myself to take a nap Friday afternoon by downing a dose of the ZzzQuil Frankie offered me, but, despite the nap, I'd still had trouble staying awake all night, especially with the heater running in the cruiser and the hypnotic sound of the wipers swishing back and forth as they wiped away the drizzle. Today, napping had been a little easier, tired as I was from the previous night's shift. But spending a Saturday night cruising the streets of Fort Worth was hardly my idea of the perfect weekend, especially when the Big Dick was also working the night shift.

Brigit didn't seem much bothered by the late-night schedule. No wonder. She slept through most of the shift, curled up on her platform in the back, Duckie lying next to her. It didn't make much difference to the dog whether she was on our bed at home or in the back of the patrol car. In fact, the white noise and vibrations of the patrol car seemed to lull her to sleep, as if she were a human baby.

On the bright side, Brigit and I had our K-9 cruiser back, the Barf-mobile returned to the fleet. And, while it was just as cold as it had been the night before, at least the drizzle had stopped.

Several times on Friday night I'd driven through the parking lot at the apartments where Gallegos and Duong lived, looking for the as yet unidentified muscly black guy and/or the curly-haired young man who'd been with the others at the looting. I'd had no luck. Here I was again tonight, cruising the lot. Still no luck. Nobody was crazy enough to be out in this cold.

The dispatcher came over the radio. "We've got a report of gunshots in Park Hill." She rattled off an address on Winton Terrace West. "Who can respond?"

Before I could get to my mic, Mackey's voice came over the line. "Officer Mackey responding."

It was no surprise he'd jumped on the call. Mackey thrived on risk, volunteering for the most dangerous calls, always trying to prove how macho and manly he could be. Of course chances were good that the reported noise wasn't actually gunfire. More often than not, such reports turned out to be fireworks or merely a car back-firing. I'd once taken a call regarding an alleged machine gun and found only a ten-year-old practicing a tap dance routine in a garage. I'd suggested she close the door next time so as not to alarm the neighbors.

A few minutes later, as I was heading south on Henderson, a northbound SUV passed me, its headlights off despite the late hour. I hooked a U-turn and trailed after him as he merged onto Interstate 30. I followed the car for three miles with my lights and siren on. The driver drove at a speed of only twenty miles an hour, probably thinking he was being very careful. In reality, a car moving at such a sluggish rate on a freeway could be dangerous, too. Other drivers wouldn't expect someone to be going so slow and could easily crash into him before they realized how slowly he was going. Hence, the posted minimum speeds.

Finally, the guy seemed to notice me behind him, his brake lights illuminating. He pulled his SUV over as he went under an overpass, the right side of his car scraping against the concrete wall as he rolled to a stop.

I turned off my siren and spoke to the man on my public address system. "Turn your car off."

There was a *craaaaagh* sound as the car's engine protested the man's attempt to start the already running motor.

I sighed and spoke through my mic again. "Turn the key *toward* you."

He had better luck this time.

I requested backup from dispatch, knowing this guy would be going to jail. The only question now was whether he'd be one of those goofy drunks or a belligerent one.

I checked my side mirror for oncoming traffic before getting out of the cruiser. When the road was clear, I stepped out and walked up to the car.

A thirtyish man looked out at me from the driver's seat, his expression dopey, his movements slow. "Why'd you pull me over?" he asked through the glass.

"It would be easier to have this conversation," I rapped a knuckle on the closed window, "if you rolled this down."

With unintentionally exaggerated movements, he raised his index finger, placed it on the control, and pushed the button. The window slid down.

"Why'd you . . ." He trailed off, as if he'd lost his train of thought for a moment, but then he found it again. "Why'd you pull me over?"

"I'll give you three guesses." Hey, if I had to work the

crappy night shift, I might as well have some fun at it, right?

His brows lifted. "If I guess right do I get to make a wish?"

Goofy it is.

"I'm a cop, not a genie. Where are you headed?"

"Home." He circled his arms in an outdated dance move. "I've been at a par-tay!"

This guy was much too old to talk like a frat boy. "Must've been some '*par-tay*'."

"You know it!"

"I need to see your driver's license and registration, please."

He reached behind him, nearly giving himself an atomic wedgie before managing to get his fingers around his wallet and pulling it out of his pocket. He held the entire thing out to me.

"I only want to see your license."

"Oh. Okay." He opened his wallet and began to thumb through it. "Hey, here's a picture of my girlfriend." He held up a photo of a busty brown-haired woman wearing approximately two inches of clothing and ten pounds of makeup. He ran his eyes over my face and down my chest. "She's prettier than you." He made a pinching motion with his index finger and thumb. "But only by a little bit. 'bout this much."

"Gee," I said. "Thanks." The woman might be prettier than me, but if she was dating this idiot she was certainly not smarter.

He pulled a condom from his wallet next. "This is in case I . . . in case I meet a girl and get lucky."

"I thought you had a girlfriend."

He waved a floppy hand. "Only sometimes." The condom slipped out of his hand and fell to the floorboard. He bent down to pick it up and banged his head on the steering wheel. "Ow!"

"Leave the condom on the floor," I ordered. I wanted this guy's hands where I could see them. For all I knew, he could have a gun under his seat.

"Okay, okay!" he cried. "No need to . . . no need to yell. Jeez, you sound just like . . . just like my mother."

"Do I now?"

"She was a great mom," he said. "She used to . . . used to cut the crusts off my sandwiches."

"When she wasn't yelling, you mean."

"Right."

He continued to riffle through his wallet, pulled out a white plastic card, and held it out to me. "Here you go."

I took a look. "That's your health insurance card. See?" I pointed. "It says 'Blue Cross Blue Shield' right there."

"Oh." He looked down at the card. "Yeah. I had a kidney stone once, you know. Hurt like a motherfu—."

"Wonderful." I made a circular motion with my hand, signaling him to speed things up here. "Your license?"

After showing me his library card, his Visa credit card, and his business card—MARTINDALE'S MOLD REMEDIATION—he finally managed to find his license. I took it from him and motioned to his glove box. "I need to see your registration, too."

He opened his glove box and pulled out his owner's manual, an ice scraper, and a tire gauge before finding his registration. He held it out the window as my backup pulled to a stop in front of his vehicle. "Here ya' go. Hey, did I ever . . . ever get my three wishes?"

"If your wish was for Officer Hinojosa to haul you off to the drunk tank, it's about to come true."

"Jail?" The man scowled. "But I only had one drink!"

"It must've been a big one."

He used both hands to measure now. "It was yay big. 'Course my girlfriend kept refilling it."

Hinojosa stepped up. My eye roll told him all he

needed to know. He pulled out a penlight and shined it in the man's eyes. Sure enough, his pupils reacted slowly.

My coworker opened the man's door. "Step on out here, sir."

The man attempted to slide out, only to find himself held back by his seatbelt. He unclipped it and emerged, wobbling on his feet.

Hinojosa snorted and gave the man a *can-you-really-be-this-stupid?* look. "I'll take it from here, Luz."

"Thanks."

While Hinojosa led the drunk to his cruiser and took him off to jail, I waited for the tow truck. Once the SUV was on its way to impound, I returned to my car and glanced back at Brigit. Her head was still down but her eyes were open now. "You're lucky you don't have to try to reason with these idiots."

She merely took Duckie in her mouth, rolled over, and went back to sleep. Obviously she was already aware how lucky she was.

The Big Dick was back on the radio a moment later. "I need backup and an ambulance for two gunshot victims."

Whoa.

Looked like the reported gunfire wasn't firecrackers or a tap dancer after all. Probably it was a robbery, or maybe an attempted murder-suicide that had somehow been botched. Whatever it was, it wouldn't involve me. By the time I'd grabbed my mic to respond, two other officers had already indicated they were on their way to the scene. Any more would just get in the way and leave the rest of W1 without coverage. Saying a quick and silent prayer for any innocent victims, I returned my mic to its holder and set back out on patrol.

The next few hours were typical. I issued two speeding tickets and one warning for a broken taillight. Took a report at a twenty-four-hour eatery involving a dine and dash. Pulled a busted mattress out of the intersection of

Main and Rosedale. *For goodness' sake. Tie these things down, people!*

After three o'clock, when most of the bars had shut down and the patrons had made their way home, I cruised through several of the apartment complexes near TCU to keep an eye on the after-party action. Couldn't hurt to let the college kids know the police were around to either keep them in line or provide assistance, depending on the circumstances.

As I was about to pull out of a complex, my eyes spotted a black van parked in the visitors' area. Although the inspection sticker was current, the registration was out of date. I pulled up in front of the van, turned on my flashing lights, and stepped out of the cruiser to take a look, taking my flashlight with me.

I turned the flashlight on and ran it over the side of the van. A local phone number and the words ODD JOBS, YARD WORK, & HAULING—CHEAP RATES were spelled out on the side in silver lettering, along with a phone number. Stepping up to the passenger window, I shined my flashlight into the van. The beam picked up a jar of peanut butter, a half loaf of wheat bread, and something shiny, black, and rumpled spread on the floor. Looked like a garbage bag.

Returning to my cruiser, I retrieved my roll of orange warning stickers. Brigit was standing on her platform now, her tail whipping side to side in excitement. There were a number of trees and bushes around the place. She probably smelled a squirrel out here, or maybe a possum taking a late-night stroll.

Woof! Woof-woof!

"Quiet, girl!" At this late hour, she better shut up or someone would be calling the police on *us*.

I peeled off one of the stickers, used a fine point black marker to fill in the date, and slapped it on the windshield of the van. *Smack.*

Brigit was still standing when I returned to the cruiser again. There was little traffic at the complex this time of night, only an occasional resident pulling in, so it seemed safe to let her out of the car without leashing her. She probably needed to pee.

I opened the back door and let her out of her enclosure. With a jingle of her tags, she hopped down to the pavement and trotted over to the van. Her tail continued to wag as she sniffed around the side doors and circled around to the back. She barked again—*woof-woof!*—as if ordering the doors to magically open.

"That's it!" I hissed, swinging a pointed finger. "Back in the car!"

Only half obeying, she trotted back to the car, but took a detour into the bushes first for a quick tinkle.

"Loudmouth," I muttered.

She gave me a look that was the canine version of *So? Sue me*.

When my shift was finally over at 8 A.M., I returned my cruiser to the lot at the W1 station and loaded Brigit into my Smart Car. As I slid into my seat, Seth texted me. *Swimming at the Y. Meet me for breakfast?*

I texted him back. *Keep swimming. I'll meet you there.*

More exercise would be good for Seth. My plan to meet him at the YMCA had nothing at all to do with the fact that Seth had incredible shoulders, a nice chest, and tight abs, and that meeting him at the pool would give me a chance to ogle them.

Okay, even I didn't believe myself on that one.

But after a long night of dealing with drunks and diner dashes and disabled vehicles, didn't a girl deserve to ogle a little?

FORTY-SEVEN
GOOD BOY!

Brigit

Her partner could really be stupid sometimes. Didn't Megan realize the boy with the beef jerky was inside the van? Well, he didn't have beef jerky anymore, but he did have peanut butter. She could smell it. That stuff was almost as good as meat. It stuck to the roof of her mouth, but she didn't mind.

If Megan wasn't going to let her visit with the boy, Brigit supposed she might as well go back to sleep. These night patrols were sooooo dull. She spun around three times and flopped to the floor of her enclosure. Resting her head on Duckie, she exhaled a long, bored breath and closed her eyes.

FORTY-EIGHT
BLOODY SUNDAY

Dub

Dub woke Sunday morning feeling stiff and sore. The sleeping bag was thick, but the metal floor of the van had been hard underneath it. He felt like he'd slept on a rock.

At least he was still free. A security guard employed by Walmart had apparently noticed Dub's van had been in the lot all night on Friday. When Dub went inside the store Saturday morning to use the bathroom, the guard stopped Dub and told him that overnight parking was not allowed. Dub had been forced to find another place to park on Saturday night. He'd chosen an apartment complex near the TCU campus. He figured college kids would be less likely to report the van.

He'd nearly panicked last night. He'd woken to police lights flashing outside the van. He'd pulled the sleeping bag over his head and laid as still as possible. A cop had shined a flashlight in the window and slapped a violation sticker on his windshield. He'd heard a dog bark and sniff around the doors, and a female voice ordering the dog back into the car. Thank goodness the cop hadn't noticed him inside the van and he hadn't been arrested.

He couldn't be sure whether the officer and the dog had been the same ones he'd run into at the Bag-N-Bottle, but chances were good. There were way more male cops than female cops, and probably not many K-9 teams. But if he were going to be caught and taken into custody, he'd rather it be by those two than some dickwad who'd rough Dub up first.

Dub found his keys, climbed into the driver's seat, and drove to a gas station to use the restroom and brush his teeth. When he finished, he splashed some warm water on his face and scratched at his scruffy beard. He wished he could afford to shave. The damn thing was itchy and made him look like a terrorist. Sometimes he wished the puberty fairy hadn't been quite so generous with the facial hair and had instead made him a few inches taller.

The clerk frowned at Dub as he walked to the exit. "Next time you come in to use the bathroom," the man said, "buy something."

Ignoring the clerk, Dub returned to his van. As he pulled away from the curb, he caught a whiff of himself. *Phew.* He could really use a shower.

Remembering his membership card, Dub drove to the YMCA. He parked his van in a spot next to an old blue Nova with orange flames painted down the side. He flashed his card to the attendant at the counter and headed to the men's locker room. He had no soap, no shampoo, and no towel, but figured he could make do with a handful of the liquid soap from the sink dispenser and a dozen or so paper hand towels.

After the cold, uncomfortable night in the van, the hot shower felt beyond good. He washed his hair and body with the hand soap, and just stood under the spray for a good twenty minutes. What else did he have to do? When he was done, he had no choice but to put his sweats back on, despite the stench. At some point he'd find a Laundromat and wash his clothes. For now, his funds were too tight to splurge on detergent.

He exited the locker room into the indoor pool area and stopped still. *Holy crap!* That female cop and her shepherd were standing by the pool, talking to a blond man who was in the water, his arms hooked over the edge.

Dub ducked his head and hurried by, keeping one eye on the cop, hoping she wouldn't see him. The dog turned, sniffed the air, and wagged her tail. She looked at Dub and let out a loud *Arf!* that echoed in the enclosed space.

The officer looked down at her dog and wagged her finger. "Brigit, hush!"

Yes, dog! he thought. *Please be quiet!*

Once he was in the hallway, Dub jogged as fast as he dared to the exit and ran to his van. He pulled out of the parking lot and lurched down the street, one eye on his rearview mirror.

Good. Nobody was on his tail. It looked like the cop hadn't spotted him.

FORTY-NINE
A BANG-UP JOB

Megan

Seth and I were halfway through our pancakes, Blast and Brigit halfway through their bacon and sausage, when my cell phone rang. The readout indicated it was Detective Jackson calling.

I tapped the screen to accept the call. "Good morning, Detective Jackson."

"You hear about the shooting in Park Place last night?"

"I did," I told her. "I worked the night shift. I was tied up with a DUI while it was going on."

"Turns out the victims came home late and surprised a burglar."

Tragic, of course, though unfortunately not unusual. "Did they get a good look at him?"

"The husband is unconscious," she said, "but the wife gave a detailed description. Get this. She said the shooter was a young man with light-brown skin, dark curly hair, and a white hoodie with a tornado printed on the front."

My looter and the possible murder suspect.

Whoa.

Brigit took advantage of the fact that I was temporarily discombobulated to snatch a hunk of pancake from my plate. *Bad dog.* I pushed the plate over in front of her, basically rewarding her naughty behavior, but she'd left several hairs stuck in the syrup. I wasn't above picking a dog hair or two out of a plate of spaghetti and pretending it didn't happen, but I drew the line at fishing fur from sticky syrup.

"I'm heading over to the hospital," the detective continued. "I need to ask the wife some questions while things are still fresh. Want to come with me?"

"Of course."

She gave me the room number and hung up.

"I have to go," I told Seth. "It looks like the curly-haired looter was involved in a shooting last night."

"I thought you said he was the only one who didn't pull a gun on you? That he seemed nonviolent?"

I raised my palms and shook my head. "Maybe I was wrong."

Seth stood and gave me a quick peck on the cheek. "Let me know what happens."

"I will. Can you take Brigit home for me?" Surely the doctors would frown on me taking an animal into the intensive care unit, and if I left her in my car she might eat the floor mats.

"Be happy to," Seth said.

I finagled my house key off my chain. "You can leave it under the mat when you go."

Twenty minutes later, Detective Jackson and I met in the lobby of the hospital. We checked in with the nurse on duty in intensive care.

"There's been no change," she said, "but the good news is he's still hanging on."

Hanging on with the help of life support. Despite the beeps from the heart monitor that indicated he was still alive, Mr. Prentiss looked deathly pale and lifeless in his bed.

Jackson and I continued to the room where Mrs. Prentiss had been taken. Now that her bullet had been removed and she was in recovery, her condition had been upgraded from critical to serious.

The woman lay in her bed staring straight ahead as if dazed. Her eyes were pink and puffy, her fox-red hair mussed, her makeup streaked with tears. An IV bag at the head of her bed dripped what I assumed was a low dose of morphine into her veins, enough to ease the pain of her wound but not so much as to render her unconscious.

Jackson rapped on the door frame. "Mrs. Prentiss? May we come in and speak with you?"

The woman turned her head our way and, noting my uniform, motioned for us to come in. We pulled a couple of chairs up next to the bed and took a seat. The detective pulled out her digital recorder as well as her notepad. She turned the recorder on and positioned it on the rolling, adjustable table situated over the bed.

Her preparations done, Jackson put a compassionate hand on the patient's arm. "I am so sorry about all you're going through, Mrs. Prentiss." When the woman nodded and said a soft "Thanks," the detective removed her hand and picked up her ballpoint pen. "I've been told that you got a look at the shooter. Did he look familiar at all?"

"No," Mrs. Prentiss said. "I don't think I've ever seen him before."

"Can you describe him for me?"

Mrs. Prentiss spoke slowly, her voice warbling with emotion. "He was a little shorter than average," she said. "Curly black hair. Olive skin."

"Olive?" the detective repeated. "Any guess as to his race or ethnicity?"

"It's hard to say," the woman said. "He looked sort of like Johnny Depp except for the hair."

Jackson and I exchanged glances. I'd told her about Stefan Nicolescu, the odd mailman who seemed to know so much. Maybe *too* much. Nicolescu had Johnny Depp's coloring, sure, but with his buggy eyes and Jay Leno chin, he looked more like a caricature of Johnny Depp or a reflection of the actor in a funhouse mirror.

Jackson jotted the Depp reference on her notepad. "Could he have been eastern European?"

"I really don't know." Tears welled up in the woman's eyes when she noticed the frustration on the detective's face and mine. "I'm trying. I really am."

The detective gave her arm another reassuring pat. "We know you're doing your best, Mrs. Prentiss."

The woman closed her eyes for a moment as if trying to blink back the tears. When she opened them again, the detective continued her questions.

"What was his build? Thin? Heavy? Average?"

"It was hard to tell for sure since he was wearing a bulky sweatshirt," she said, "but he had the sleeves pushed up and his forearms looked pretty muscular."

Hmm. I hadn't seen the looter's arms, of course, and his upper body had likewise been obscured by the hoodie, but the looter's legs had definitely been thin.

Jackson pulled up a photo of Stefan Nicolescu on her phone. Given that he was wearing his post office uniform, the picture appeared to be a photo taken for a work ID. Obviously, the detective had taken my concerns seriously and followed up on the man. She showed the picture to Mrs. Prentiss. "Is this the guy?"

Mrs. Prentiss looked at the phone and shook her head. "No. I hate to say this, but if I had seen the man who shot us under different circumstances I would say he was attractive."

A violent criminal with good looks. It just didn't seem right. Still, everything that this woman was telling me pointed to the looter. He'd been scruffy, sure, but still what most women would consider handsome.

"What about this man?" Jackson pulled out a folded copy of the black-and-white sketch of the murder suspect, opened it up, and showed it to Mrs. Prentiss.

The woman nodded, fresh tears in her eyes. "That's a very good likeness. Who is he?"

"That's the problem," the detective said. "We don't know. But maybe you can tell us something that will help us narrow it down."

She continued with her usual line of questions. Who knew that Mr. and Mrs. Prentiss were going to be out Saturday evening? Had they had any work done at their house lately, any repairmen in their home? Did they employ someone to take care of their lawn or clean their house? Had she seen anyone unusual in the neighborhood recently? Did she notice any cars parked near her house when they pulled up? Maybe a truck or van?

The responses gave us little to go on. They'd had no work done at their house in recent weeks. While they had a professional lawn care service, they'd put services on hold for the winter and none of the workers had been to their house since late October, when the grass went dormant. They hired a housekeeper, but she had been with them for years with no problems. Mrs. Prentiss hadn't noticed anyone unusual in the area. There might have been a vehicle of some sort parked across the street and down a ways, but since it sat past their house they hadn't paid it much attention. She didn't think it had been a black van though.

"A van might have stuck with me," she said. "That would be unusual for our neighborhood at that time of night."

Jackson turned to me. "Anything you'd like to ask, Officer Luz?"

Giving the late-night timing, this burglary seemed different from the others that had taken place in W1 recently. Were they unrelated? Or could there be a link? The burglars in the other cases hadn't hurt the homeowners but, of course, the homeowners had all been away on trips during the robberies. There was no telling what could have happened had the residents surprised the burglars like Mr. and Mrs. Prentiss had. And, while Mrs. Prentiss seemed to believe the shooter was the only person involved, there had been at least two men involved in the Harrington robbery.

I sat forward in my chair. "Are you certain the man who shot you and your husband was alone?"

"I didn't hear anyone else in the house," she said, "and he didn't call out to anyone or anything like that."

"Any chance you'd had a trip planned that you canceled for some reason?"

"No. Why?"

"There have been some other burglaries in the area. In those cases, the victims were all out of town when their houses were broken into."

When we'd obtained all of the information we could from Mrs. Prentiss, we stood to go. Jackson wished the woman and her husband a speedy and thorough recovery and I nodded in agreement.

I followed Jackson out the door, turning in the hallway to look back one last time at the fragile woman in the bed. *I'll find the man who hurt you,* I silently promised. *Don't you worry.*

I might not have all the clues I needed yet, but I did have one critical thing.

Dogged determination.

FIFTY
HAVING A BLAST WITH BLAST

Brigit

Blast's partner drove Brigit home from breakfast, making a stop by a home improvement store on the way. When they returned to the house, she thought Seth would merely drop her off and leave. She was thrilled when he and Blast stuck around. Zoe wasn't bad company but, in the end, Zoe was still a cat. She'd rather sharpen her claws on the furniture than chew on toys or shoes. *Boring*. She pooped in a box inside the house. *Uncivilized*. And she threw hissy fits when Brigit tried to share her tuna. *Stingy*.

While Seth puttered around the house, Brigit and Blast frisked about in the cool air outside. They chased each other around. Wrestled. Sniffed for squirrels. And when they tired of those things, they put their paws to the ground and began to dig.

FIFTY-ONE
SUFFER THE CHILDREN

Dub

Rather than waste gas driving aimlessly around town, Dub drove to a strip center and parked. He sat there for a few minutes, staring blindly at the window of the closed hair salon. He had no schedule. No plan. He'd love to see Jenna, but she was still grounded. The best they could do was send texts and pics to each other.

His ringtone sounded and he scrambled to find his phone among the bags in his car. "Hello?"

A male voice came over the line. "You the guy who does the hauling?"

"That's me."

"I got a broken refrigerator. Can you take care of that?"

"I'll do it for thirty dollars."

"I'll give you fifteen."

Dammit, didn't this guy know Dub needed to eat? To wash his smelly clothes? "Twenty."

"Fifteen." The man didn't wait to see if Dub would agree, he just went on to give an address.

Dub drove to the address the man had given him. Together, they loaded the fridge into the back of Dub's van. The wide appliance barely fit, taking up the entire space. When it was loaded, the man gave him a ten, four singles, and a handful of change.

Dub returned to the driver's seat, counted the change, and realized the man had shorted him a nickel. *Ugh.* He accessed the Internet on his phone to see where he could dispose of the refrigerator. Looked like he could dump the fridge for free at any of the three city sanitation stations. But he'd have to wait until tomorrow. None of the stations was open on Sunday.

After being stuck in the van all night and most of the morning, Dub wanted to stretch his legs, get a change of scenery. But without money to spend, his options were limited. He couldn't hang at a restaurant or go to a movie. So he decided to do what teenagers all over America did when they were broke and bored. Hang at the mall.

He drove to the Shoppes at Chisholm Trail and parked his van outside Macy's. He held the door open for a mother and daughter to go inside, then followed them into the store. Passing the clothes he couldn't afford and the cosmetics he didn't need, he headed out of Macy's and down the mall walkway to the home theater store. Maybe they'd be playing a movie on one of the big screens.

He reached the store and, sure enough, one of Matt Damon's Jason Bourne movies was playing on a fifty-five-inch ultra-HD unit. *Score.*

A man in khaki pants and an argyle sweater sat in an oversized chair in front of the screen. He looked like he'd just come from church. Dub took a seat on a recliner-rocker next to him.

The man glanced over at Dub. "Your wife off spending your hard-earned money, too?"

Dub forced a chuckle. "Yeah."

The two watched the movie for several minutes.

Although the salesmen seemed to have no problem with the man in the argyle sweater, Dub noticed that they all seemed to be eyeing him. He knew he looked bad. He'd slept in the sweats so they were wrinkled, and the beard probably made him look homeless—which he supposed he actually was at the moment. Still, what did they think he was going to do, tuck a big-screen television into his pocket and walk out with it?

A commercial came on, a confusing one for some type of feminine product. The man turned to Dub and struck up a conversation.

"You hear about that shooting? What a shame, eh?"

The radio in Dub's van didn't work, and he hadn't seen a newspaper or watched TV in a couple of days now. "There was a shooting?"

"Yup. A couple came home to their house and caught a burglar red-handed inside. The robber shot the man in the chest and the woman in the back. They're in the hospital. Last I heard they were both in critical condition."

Dub's stomach twisted. "Where did this happen?"

Dub knew that Andro stuck to the neighborhoods he was most familiar with to the south of I-30 and west of I-35. Mistletoe Heights. Fairmount. Ryan Place. Park Hill.

"It was over by Forest Park," the man said. "In one of those nice older homes behind the zoo."

Park Hill.

"Did they catch the guy?" *Please say "yes." Please say "yes!"*

"No," the man said. "He got away before the police could get there."

The feminine hygiene commercial was over now, replaced by a Cialis commercial, something the man seemed more comfortable with. As he turned his attention back to the big-screen TV, Dub pulled out his phone and accessed the Internet, searching for information about the shooting. He found a short news report issued only three hours before. The information said the police initially responded to a report of gunshots in the area and had noticed a broken window on the side of the house. They found the man and woman inside on the floor. The woman had lost a lot of blood, but was conscious enough to give the police a description of the shooter.

A young man with light brown skin and curly dark hair, wearing a white hooded sweatshirt with a tornado depicted on the front.

Holy shit.

Andro had really gone and done it now.

FIFTY-TWO
IDENTITY CRISIS

Megan

When I arrived home from interviewing Michelle Prentiss at the hospital, I found Seth at my house. He surprised me by sanding and waxing the dresser drawers, fixing the annoying toilet that wouldn't stop running, and affixing the loose trim more firmly to the wall.

"Wow!" I gave him a warm kiss as a thank you. "I didn't realize you were so handy."

"I can fix just about anything," he said. "My grandfather was a tank mechanic in Vietnam. A Mister Fixit type. He taught me everything he knows."

An unsolicited tidbit of personal information from Seth. Would wonders never cease? I took the revelation to be a sign that, despite his attachment issues, he was beginning to trust me, to open up. I rewarded him with another warm kiss, hoping the gesture would imprint on his subconscious. *The more you tell me about yourself, the sooner you'll get that sleepover.*

When I opened the back door to check on Brigit, I found her rear end sticking up out of the yard. The front two-thirds of her had disappeared inside a freshly dug hole. Evidently the dog was looking for a shortcut to China.

"Brigit! Bad girl!" I marched over to the hole. The thing was so deep I half expected a hand to pop up through it with a to-go box of vegetable lo mein and a pair of chopsticks.

Seth stepped up beside me. "Oops. I guess I should've kept a better eye on the dogs."

"It's not your fault," I told him. "She knows better than this."

She also knew I was a softy who was all bark and no bite. She looked up at me with an insolent grin and did her rebellious up-down *screw-you* tail wag.

Brat.

After another warm kiss, Seth packed up his things and left so I could get some sleep. I brought Brigit inside. I didn't want her digging a hole so deep she couldn't get out while I napped.

Of course sleep didn't come easy. My mind kept alternating between visions of Mr. Prentiss on life support, his wife in her bed, and the young man in the tornado hoodie. Despite all the facts pointing at the looter as being the burglar and shooter—his history of theft, the physical description, the unusual clothing—my mind kept telling me that we didn't have the full story. The guy might very well have saved both my life and Brigit's at the Bag-N-Bottle. Would he then go on to senselessly shoot two people in their own home?

Maybe he would. Maybe I was being suckered in. Maybe he had simply known that criminals who killed cops were very often given the death penalty, especially here in Texas.

It was driving me crazy that we hadn't yet been able to identify him. Who was he? With any luck, we'd soon find out. Jackson had told me they'd informed the media about the tornado hoodie and asked them to instruct viewers to call the police department with any leads.

The guy might be able to hide from the police. But it was doubtful he could hide from the entire city of Fort Worth.

Monday morning, as I left the house, I passed Frankie on her way in.

"You look tense," she said. "What's up?"

Between our odd work schedules and her derby bouts, my roommate and I hadn't been able to exchange two words lately.

I caught her up to date on the investigation.

"I heard about that shooting." She grimaced. "So heartless."

Heartless was definitely one word for it. *Frustrating* was another. I wanted the person who'd done this apprehended and put away. *Now.*

"Don't worry." She formed a loose fist with her hand and gave my shoulder a playful jab. "You'll get 'em."

"I hope you're right."

At work, I led Brigit into the W1 station to get an update on the Prentiss case before I went out on patrol. Melinda had stepped away from her desk, so I headed straight for Detective Jackson's office. She glanced up as I stopped in her doorway.

"Any word on Mr. and Mrs. Prentiss?" I asked.

"No change," she said with a frown. "No calls, either. I'd hoped someone would have seen the news reports yesterday and phoned in with a tip."

"Damn."

"Soon as I hear anything," she said, "I'll be in touch."

"Thanks."

I turned to head out to my cruiser, Brigit at my heels. As I came up the hall, two white men stepped up to the reception desk. One was tall and slender, the other short and pudgy. Both were dressed in business casual attire. The shorter man held a tablet covered in a striped sleeve.

Melinda appeared, a stack of papers in her hand, and dropped into her desk chair, sliding the documents into her inbox. "How can I help you gentlemen?"

Brigit and I were almost out the door when I heard one of them say, "We're here about the robbery in Park Hill. We think we might know the person who did it."

I did a prompt about-face, inadvertently yanking Brigit back with me. She gave me an irritated, confused look but followed me back into the building.

While Melinda contacted the detective on the intercom, I introduced myself to the men. "I've been assisting in the investigation."

The taller man introduced himself to me as Trent, the shorter one as Wesley. When Melinda gave me the word, I led them back to Detective Jackson's office.

The detective was standing behind her desk when we arrived, though she stepped around it to shake hands with the men and exchange introductions. She gestured to her two wing chairs. "Have a seat, please."

The two men sat down, their expressions anxious and reluctant, their posture rigid. With no other chairs in the room, I settled for leaning back against Jackson's credenza. Brigit sat at my feet.

Jackson readied her pen and notepad. "The receptionist told me you might know who the man was who burglarized the Prentiss home?"

"Yes," said Wesley, exchanging a glance with Trent. "Only he's not a man. He's a boy."

"Our foster son," Trent said, a moment later clarifying with, "Our *former* foster son, I guess you'd say. He ran away from our house in Fairmount about two weeks ago. He left a message on our answering machine saying he was going back to be with family in Memphis. We reported the situation to the social worker at Child Protective Services."

"What makes you think it was him?" the detective asked.

Wesley unzipped the tablet sleeve, removed the device, and pulled up a photo. "This."

He held up the screen. Pictured were the two men before us. Between them was the young man I'd seen at the Bag-N-Bottle. Though his face was clean shaven in the photograph, there was no mistaking his thin physique, his telltale cowlick, and the white hoodie depicting a twirling tornado. I felt both vindicated and sick at the same time.

Jackson glanced up at me. I nodded, letting her know the photo was the man—*or boy*—I'd seen.

The detective asked Wes to e-mail the photograph to her. "I'll take this to the victims, see if they can make a positive ID."

"What's his name?" I asked.

"Wade Chandler Mayhew," Wes said. "He's fifteen, but he can pass for much older if he skips a shave. He's got quite a bit of facial hair for a boy his age."

Trent spoke now. "He got the hoodie when he played basketball for Gainesville State School."

Though I'd dealt with only a few juveniles during my tenure as a cop, I knew the state school in Gainesville served boys with felony records. "Why did he spend time in Gainesville?"

"Burglaries and drug possession," Trent said.

"What kind of drugs?"

"Meth," Trent said. "But as far as we could tell he had no involvement with drugs while he lived with us."

Jackson cut a glance my way. How many times had we heard parents adamantly defend their children's innocence when their kids were clearly guilty of one thing or another? Too many. Teenagers could be chameleons, being one person at home and another person entirely elsewhere.

"Any violent crimes?" I asked.

"No," Wes said. "We wouldn't have agreed to take him in if he'd had a violent record. He never seemed to get out of control, either. I mean, he had the normal teenage angst, but he was surprisingly well adjusted given his history." He went on to tell us that the boy, whom they called *Dub*, had been released from a halfway house a few months prior, then come to live with the two of them. "We really don't understand what happened. He seemed happy at our place. He was thriving, doing well in school, had a sweet girlfriend. He'd even landed a role in an upcoming theater performance. He was really proud about that and excited."

"Could he have gotten back into drugs?" I asked.

"I guess anything is possible," Wes said, "but I don't see how. We kept pretty close tabs on him and I searched his room regularly. He didn't know about that, of course. Or at least I assume he didn't. But he never exhibited any of the usual symptoms. He wasn't unusually moody or tired or glassy-eyed or anything like that. And he seemed very motivated."

The detective chimed in again. "Did you ever hear back from CPS?"

Wes nodded. "We've checked in with them several times. The social worker called all of Dub's extended family back in Memphis. None of them have heard from him. They said that his mother had a falling-out with them years ago and the family is estranged."

"So the assumption is the Memphis story was a fabrication," Jackson said, "a cover-up."

"It looks that way," Trent said, "but we don't know for what."

The detective leaned back in her chair, her expression

thoughtful. "You can't identify an incident that might have upset him? Triggered something in him?"

"No," the two men said in unison.

I cocked my head, thinking. "Is it possible something happened at school? Something you didn't know about?"

"I suppose it's possible," Wes said, "but we tried to create an open and nonjudgmental environment for him. We encouraged him to be honest with us, just as we were with him."

Trent reached into his pocket and pulled out a cell phone and charger. "This was Dub's phone. It shows his call history. I don't know if that will be helpful or not. We tried all of the numbers in his contacts after he left, hoping we might find him at a friend's house but we didn't have any luck."

Wes, who'd been gnawing his lip, spoke up again now. "There's something else, too." He and Trent exchanged another glance. "A few nights before he ran away, I dropped him off at another boy's house, a kid named Mark Stallworth who rode the same bus and lives a couple of blocks over. Dub said they were going to study for their history test together. After Dub disappeared, I went by to speak with Mark. He said Dub came inside that night, but only long enough to ask him what chapters they were supposed to read for homework. When I picked Dub up later that night, he was waiting out in front of Mark's house, not inside. He seemed nervous, but when I asked him about it he said he was only worried about the upcoming test."

The detective and I exchanged another glance.

"What night was that?" she asked.

"Sunday, February eighth."

The night Samuelson had been beaten to death in Forest Park, which lay only a mile or two to the west of Fairmount, within easy walking distance.

The detective asked them if they had any other information to share, but they said they'd told us all they knew. The detective stood and we all exchanged handshakes again.

"Thanks, gentlemen," Jackson said, walking them to her door. "If we find Wade we'll let you know."

Once the men had gone, Jackson called Melinda on the intercom. "I need a juvenile record ASAP. The name is Wade Chandler Mayhew. M-A-Y-H-E-W." She turned to me. "While Melinda's rounding up the records, let's you and me go see Michelle Prentiss."

She grabbed her blazer from the back of her chair and the two of us headed out, Brigit trotting along with us.

At the hospital, I left Brigit in the cruiser with Duckie, knowing our visit would be short.

As expected, Michelle Prentiss identified the boy as the person who'd assaulted her husband. "He looks younger in the photo," she said, "but I suppose everyone looks older with a gun in their hand. That's the hoodie, though, for sure. And he's even got the cowlick."

While I was glad that we had a firm suspect now, part of me still felt like something was off. Then again, maybe I just didn't want to think a fifteen-year-old was capable of this kind of violence.

As we returned to the car, Jackson received a text from Melinda, informing her that she'd sent Dub's juvenile and CPS records to Jackson via e-mail. Jackson forwarded a copy to me.

We sat in the car for nearly an hour, reading through the records and taking notes. My heart squirmed in my chest and it was all I could do not to cry.

The kid never stood a chance.

Wade's mother, Katrina, was an on-again, off-again meth-head. Wade had first been removed from his mother's care due to neglect at the tender age of three, but was returned to her at age five after she completed a rehab program and passed a series of blood tests. This process was repeated again a couple of years later.

Wade was treated for physical injuries including a black eye and belt marks on his buttocks at age nine. Katrina claimed the injuries had been caused by an unknown intruder, but the social worker doubted her story. Who whips a kid they don't know? Wade lived with a foster family for a year before being returned to his mother again.

At age twelve, Wade was taken into custody when he bought a packet of meth at a house that was under surveillance. Wade said his mother's boyfriend had given him the money and told him what to do. He also identified the boyfriend as a man named Andro. Katrina claimed she had no boyfriend and that her son was lying to implicate her and protect himself. More drugs were found at the residence. Katrina was convicted of possession and served two months in jail. The family dog, a pit bull mix named Velvet, had been taken to animal control. After a short stint at a juvenile facility, Wade was sent to live with Katrina's relatives in Memphis, but was returned to his mother without the knowledge or consent of Child Protective Services.

At age thirteen, he was taken into custody after burglarizing a neighbor's home. Again, he claimed that he'd acted only on the orders of a man named Andro whom he now identified as his suspected biological father. He didn't know Andro's last name. Again Katrina claimed that her son was lying to protect himself and that no such person as "Andro" existed. When questioned about the identity of Wade's father, she claimed she was uncertain, that he was the result of a single night of indiscretion with a stranger she'd met at a bar. She explained the bruises and lacerations on her son's body as the result of street fights.

At age fourteen, Wade was arrested again in connection with two burglaries. His story was the same. He'd been knocked about and forced to commit the crimes by his alleged father. Again his mother said there was no father in the picture. It was at that time that Wade was placed at the state school in Gainesville. He'd spent a year at the school, another six months at the McFadden Ranch halfway house, and three months with Trent and Wes before disappearing.

"What do you think?" I asked the detective when we'd finished reading the reports. "You think Andro is real and that he's back? That he and Wade might have worked together on the burglaries?" The Harringtons' neighbor had mentioned seeing at least two men at their house.

"I think it's a distinct possibility," Jackson said, "and I think we need to pay a visit to Katrina Mayhew."

I looked up Katrina's driver's license record, and we drove to the address listed. The place was a four-plex, with two units in front and two in back. We went to Unit C. A pink cardboard heart that said BE MINE hung on the door, having yet to be taken down after the Valentine's holiday. We rang the bell and knocked repeatedly, but got no answer.

Eventually, a person in the unit next door poked his head out the door. "You looking for Emily?"

"No," Jackson said. "We're looking for Katrina Mayhew."

The man's nose quirked in disgust and he stepped outside now. "Katrina was evicted from that unit a year ago."

"Any idea where she lives now?" I asked.

"None," he said. "Frankly, I was glad to see her go. I'd had enough of her and her scuzzy boyfriend."

"Boyfriend?" the detective said. "You remember his name?"

The man looked up in thought. "Andrew, I think. Or Andy. He was a total ass, pardon my French."

I fought the urge to tell him that the word "ass" was not French, but English. Then again, I supposed if it were English, it should be "arse."

"How was he an ass?" Jackson asked.

"He'd get angry and call her all kinds of names. Whore. Bitch. Slut. I think he might've beat her, too. She always seemed to have bruises on her face or arms when he was around."

"Can we get the name of your landlord?" the detective asked.

"Sure."

While we waited on his porch, the man went into his unit, returning a moment later with a name and phone number written on a napkin.

"Thanks," Jackson said, taking the napkin from him.

We returned to the cruiser, where Jackson promptly placed a call to the landlord. "No forwarding address?" she said, cutting a glance my way. "All right. Thanks." She ended the call. "The landlord has no idea where Katrina went after she was evicted."

Damn.

I logged on to my laptop and tried to find a current address for Katrina Mayhew. There was no motor vehicle registration in her name, no voter's registration, either. No account in her name with any city utility. She didn't even seem to have a Facebook page. I wondered what she would have listed as her "status." *High on meth? Beaten? It's horrifying?*

"Try the arrest records," Jackson suggested. "Maybe she got busted again recently."

I ran the search. "Nothing. Should I try the police reports?"

"Couldn't hurt."

Bingo. A report popped up, a recent one dated Friday

night. "We got something. Officers Mackey and Spalding responded to a domestic violence call at the same apartment complex where Gallegos and Duong live." That explained how Dub had met his fellow looters. "The report says Katrina claimed her son had beaten her. He'd been hiding on the balcony but jumped into the pool and ran off. The officers couldn't locate him."

Jackson harrumphed. "What kind of kid beats his own mother?"

One who'd seen his father do the same thing, maybe. Still, given Katrina Mayhew's history of questionable reports, I wasn't yet convinced that her story was true.

We drove to the apartment complex and parked. I let Brigit out of her enclosure to stretch her legs and tinkle. When she'd relieved herself, the three of us made our way up the stairs to the apartment.

"You think there's any chance he could be here now?" I asked.

"I think we'd be smart to be prepared for anything," the detective said.

Jackson went to put her finger on the doorbell, apparently noticed what I did—that there was no button, only an empty hole with an exposed wire—and opted to knock instead. While we waited with our hands hovering near our holsters, Brigit sniffed around the door, her tail whipping side to side in excitement. If she thought she'd get another beef jerky treat, she was sadly mistaken.

It took three rounds of knocking to finally bring Katrina Mayhew to the door. She wore a pair of grungy pajamas and one pink sock. Her lip bore a thick scab where it had split and was healing over. A similar-sized scar next to it told me the punch that had landed last Friday had not been the first.

The woman looked totally strung out, gaunt with dull eyes. When she spoke, the condition of her teeth pegged her as a methamphetamine user. The chemicals in the drug

were particularly hard on tooth enamel, and users were
prone to grinding, as well.

"Why are you here?" she asked us.

"We'd like to speak to you about your son Wade,"
Jackson said. "May we come inside?"

"I suppose so." Katrina backed away from the door to
let us in.

The place had too few furniture pieces to feel homey
and smelled of dirty dishes left too long in the sink. Flies
darted about in the kitchen, feasting on the remains of a
half-eaten burrito left sitting on the counter. Brigit pulled
her leash out as far as it would go and sniffed around on
the carpet and walls, her tail continuing to wag. *Sniff-
sniff, sniff-sniff.*

Jackson got right to the point. "Your son is a suspect
in a burglary and shooting that took place Saturday
night in Park Hill. You know anything about that?"

Katrina's dull eyes flared in alarm. "Was anyone
killed?"

"Too soon to tell," Jackson said. "We've got a victim
clinging to life in the hospital, another in serious condition."

Katrina's posture slumped and she put a hand to her
forehead. "That's not good."

Jackson cast me a look that said *no shit, lady.* She returned her focus to Katrina. "Have you seen your son
since the incident Friday night?"

Katrina shook her head. "No."

"How about your boyfriend Andro?" I asked.

Katrina's eyes flared again. "I . . . I don't . . . I don't
have a boyfriend."

"Who's Andro?" I'm nothing if not persistent, huh?
"And where is he now?"

She hesitated just a moment too long. "I have no idea
who you are talking about."

"Sure you do," I said. "He's the one who gave you that fat lip."

Jackson tossed me a cautionary look, but didn't stop me.

Katrina shook her head. "My son did this."

Again, I had trouble visualizing the young man who'd been so kind to Brigit beating someone. And, like the social worker, I surmised his mother might not be the most truthful person on the planet.

"Andro is your son's father." I didn't ask her this time. I told her. "We know that."

"I'm not talking to you anymore," she said, stepping back to the door. "I don't know anything and . . . and I'm through talking to you. I'd like you to leave."

Jackson raised her palms. "Whatever you say, ma'am."

As we walked out the door, I looked Katrina in the eye. A big part of me felt sorry for the woman, another part of me wanted to throttle her myself.

What kind of woman puts a man before her own child?

I simply couldn't fathom such a thing.

FIFTY-THREE
WHERE'S THE BEEF?

Brigit

Brigit's nose told her that the boy from the liquor store, the one who'd shared his beef jerky with her, had been in this apartment. His scent was fading, though. She wondered if he were back in the van she'd smelled him in, or whether he was back at the YMCA.

She also smelled an old burrito. She spied it up on the counter, being eaten by flies. Why should mere insects be permitted to eat something that size? She strained at her leash but Megan wouldn't budge.

Although her nose detected a faint remnant of methamphetamine, this scent, too, had faded, the drug no longer on site. No point in giving an alert.

A few minutes later, they left the apartment. Brigit put her nose to the air as they stepped out the door. She could sense a change in the weather coming. It was already cold, but it would get much, much colder soon. Wet again, too.

She forgot all about the weather when, on the way back to the cruiser, she heard Megan say one of her favorite words. *Lunch.*

FIFTY-FOUR
OUT OF LUCK

Dub

Dub had spent another night in his van. Last night he'd parked in the industrial area near the day labor site, hoping his van would look more at home there. He was still stuck with the damn fridge. He'd thought about dropping it in an empty lot or down an alley so that he could have more space in the back of the van, but he was afraid someone would spot him and report him for illegal dumping. The last thing he needed right now was to attract attention.

To make matters worse, Jenna wasn't responding to his texts or calls. Had her parents found her secret phone? Or had Jenna decided he wasn't worth the trouble and moved on? He couldn't blame her if she had.

He'd thought about leaving town, but he had only an eighth of a tank of gas left. The way this old van sucked down gas he'd only get as far as Dallas before running out. And he couldn't afford to put more gas in it. The small amount of money he had left would be needed for food. He'd already gone through half of the cereal bars, all of the bananas, and most of the peanut butter and bread. Today for lunch he'd eat the alphabet soup, just as soon as he could heat the stuff up with the van's cigarette lighter. It was taking forever. The dang thing only stayed hot for fifteen seconds at a time. Still, he kept trying, pushing the lighter back into the socket to heat, stirring the soup, then holding the lighter back under the can when it popped out, glowing orange.

Funny, after enjoying his freedom while living with Trent and Wes, he hadn't wanted to go back to the state school. But here he was, a prisoner in this van. He couldn't show his face for fear of being hauled to jail for shooting that couple in their home.

It was freezing in the van and getting worse by the minute. As much as he would've loved a hot meal, he gave up on trying to heat the soup and decided to go ahead and eat it cold. When he looked down into the can he wasn't sure whether to laugh or cry. Floating in the orange broth at the top of the can were the letters F U.

"Story of my life," he muttered to himself.

He shoved his plastic spoon into the soup and stirred it up.

FIFTY-FIVE
SNEAKY

Megan

It was straight up noon by the time the detective, Brigit, and I left Katrina's apartment. As the weatherman had forecasted, the day was growing colder rather than warmer. Freezing temperatures were expected tonight, along with precipitation—probably mere snow flurries but they couldn't rule out the possibility of an ice storm. Brigit and I could stay home, curl up in front of the fireplace with a good book, or maybe build a snowman.

We returned to the same sandwich shop we'd eaten at the last time we'd been out to the complex. As we ate, I scrolled through the list of contacts in Dub's cell phone. There were only a handful. Cell numbers for both Trent and Wes, along with work numbers. A number identified as "Home" that, when I tried it, turned out to be Wes and Trent's landline. The only other contacts listed were for a Zach, a Fitzsimmons, and a Jenna, all of whom were presumably the friends Wes and Trent had contacted, looking for Dub.

"Think we should try these numbers?" I asked the

detective. "I mean, I know Trent and Wes said they spoke with everyone on Dub's contacts list, but people might give the police more information. Plus, I see that Wade made a call to Jenna on Sunday the eighth in the early afternoon. That could mean something."

"It's definitely worth a try," Jackson said. "One of them may have heard from Wade since they spoke with Trent and Wes."

Because the kids in Wade's contacts list would be in school until later in the afternoon, we returned to the police station to attend to other aspects of the case.

Jackson contacted the crime scene techs to see what evidence they'd found at the scene, frowning as she listened on the phone. "Not a single print? Well, I guess that was to be expected. Mrs. Prentiss said the guy was wearing latex gloves."

We also placed a call to Gainesville State School and spoke with Dub's basketball coach.

"He was a good kid," the man said. "Always showed up for practice on time, never complained about all the running I had them do. We had a few altercations among the players, but Dub wasn't involved in any of them. He was friendly, well liked. I can't imagine him shooting anyone. 'Course I've been surprised before. Never say never, right?"

The staff at the McFadden Ranch halfway house were just as complimentary. "Dub always made his bed without being asked," the male counselor noted. "He pitched in around the place. He wasn't afraid of hard work. Had good study habits. I really thought he'd be one of those who'd make it out. Looks like I was wrong."

Or was he?

I chewed on the end of my pen. "Where do runaways go in Fort Worth?" I asked Detective Jackson.

She shrugged. "There's not really one primary place I can think of. Some of them end up in the parks or under the overpasses with the other homeless folks. Others, well . . . you know."

I was glad she didn't fill in her sentence. *I did know.* And it was too hard to think about.

When it was a half hour past the time high school let out, the detective phoned Zack, activating the speaker button so I could join in the conversation. After we identified ourselves, Jackson asked the boy if he'd heard from Dub.

"Not since the day before he took off," Zach said. "We used to hang together at lunch. But he hasn't texted or called or sent me a message on Facebook or IM'd or anything."

"All right," Jackson said. "Let us know if you do hear from him, okay?" She gave him both her number and mine.

We repeated the same basic conversation with Patrick Fitzsimmons. He hadn't heard from Dub via any of the myriad means of communication since Dub had run off.

Jenna was a different story.

While the contact number for *Jenna Cell* went straight to voicemail, we got an answer at the number identified as *Jenna Home.*

Her voice was tentative and wary. "Is he in trouble?"

"Unfortunately, yes," the detective said. "How about we come over to your house and talk to you about it?"

"Can you come now?" Jenna asked. "Before my mother gets home? She went to run some errands but she'll be home in an hour."

Jackson looked at me and raised a brow. "We're on our way."

We scurried to the cruiser, loaded Brigit in her bay, and took off for Jenna's house. She lived at Berkeley Place, about a half mile from Lilac Street, where Dub had lived with Trent and Wes. She was watching from an upstairs window of the traditional brick and wood home as we pulled up. By the time we'd exited the cruiser and made our way to the front porch, she'd opened the front door.

I gave the girl a once-over as we stepped into the foyer. She was a petite thing, maybe five feet one inch tall, and probably weighed less than my furry partner. Her copper-colored hair hung in a straight sheet down to her teeny-tiny boob buds. Like me, she had a scattering of freckles on her face. Her blue eyes were bright with worry.

"Is Dub in trouble for running away and missing school?" she asked. "Will he be sent back to juvie if he's found?"

"Wade Mayhew has far bigger things to worry about than missing a few days of school," the detective said. "He's been implicated in a burglary and shooting."

"What?" Jenna shrieked. "That can't be true!"

"You ever see him wear a white hoodie with a tornado on it?" Jackson asked.

Jenna swallowed, looking as if she knew exactly the garment Jackson had referenced but as if she wasn't sure whether she should admit it.

The detective didn't wait for an answer that probably wasn't coming anyway. "The young man who shot the couple was wearing it."

Jenna shook her head. "No, no, no! Dub's not like that! I mean, he's had it really hard and all, but he only did those things before because if he didn't his father would beat him."

"He told you about that?" I asked.

The girl nodded. "We were close."

"Were you dating?" I asked.

She nodded again.

Jackson eyed the girl closely. "We also think your Dub might have killed a man in Forest Park on the evening of Sunday, February eighth."

Jenna's face contorted and her eyes went wide. She shook her head. "No. He couldn't have!"

Jackson tilted her head. "And how do you know that?"

"Because he was *here* that night," Jenna said, tears spilling down her cheeks. "In my room. My mother told me I couldn't see him anymore once she found out he'd been in juvie and the state school and all that. She wouldn't believe me that he's a good guy."

Jackson's brow furrowed. "If you weren't allowed to see him, how could he be here at your house?"

"My parents were gone," she said. "When they came home early, he snuck out my window."

I motioned for her to follow me outside onto the lawn. I looked up at the house. "Which window is yours?"

"It's around the side."

The wind had picked up and bit into us as we stepped across the yard.

After rounding the corner of the house, Jenna pointed up to a second-story window directly above the outdoor A/C unit. Jackson and I looked up at the window. The screen was a little bent on one side, as if it had been pulled off and replaced. Scuff marks were apparent on the wood siding, too, as if someone had scrabbled on the wall with their feet, seeking purchase. I almost felt sorry for the children I didn't have yet. With a mother like me who noticed clues like this, they wouldn't be able to get away with anything.

Jackson turned back to Jenna. "You're sure it was the eighth? A hundred percent sure?"

"Positive," she said. "Since my parents wouldn't let me see Dub, he and I had to sneak around and plan in advance. I knew my parents were going to a political fundraiser dinner that night at the Worthington Hotel. The invitation had been on our fridge for weeks."

I pulled up the Internet on my phone and verified that

there had, indeed, been a political fundraising event at the Worthington on the eighth. It was doubtful now that Dub had been Samuelson's killer. But if not him, then who? And even if he hadn't killed Samuelson, that didn't mean he wasn't the one who'd shot Mr. and Mrs. Prentiss.

We thanked the girl for having the courage to talk with us.

"If you find Dub," she said, her lip quivering with emotion, "tell him I miss him. And tell him that . . . that everything is okay now."

Uh-oh.

"Jenna," I said, "did you and Dub—"

Before I could even finish she looked down but nodded.

"But you're not—"

She shook her head. "I thought I might be pregnant but I found out this morning that I'm not."

"You didn't use protection?" If kids were going to do something stupid, they should at least be smart about it.

"Dub had a condom, but . . ." She teared up again, hunched her shoulders, and shook her head.

In other words, their raging teenage hormones had gotten the best of them. But I couldn't fault them too much. It took quite a bit of restraint for me to resist Seth's advances.

Jenna opened her mouth as if to say something, then closed it again.

"Jenna," I asked. "Are you in contact with Dub?"

"I was," she admitted. "My mother took away my cell phone and laptop, but then Dub came to the school a few days ago and brought me one of those prepaid phones."

Hmm. Even though Dub had run away from home, he hadn't run out on Jenna. That showed character, didn't it? He seemed to have real feelings for the girl. Dub had never had anyone to hold on to. Or maybe I was giving him too much credit. Maybe Jenna was nothing more than a booty call. I supposed I couldn't really be sure.

"Can you show us the phone?" I asked.

"My parents found it last night and took that away, too."

"What's the number for Dub's phone?" I asked.

"I don't know. He'd already put his number in the contacts list when he gave me the phone. I didn't think to memorize it."

"Do you know where he bought the phones?" If so, we could try to track down his number and trace his phone.

She shook her head.

"Do you know where your parents put the phone they took from you?" If we could get her number, we could contact the provider and find out who'd called her phone.

"Yes," she said. "My dad stomped on it and then threw it in the trash in the kitchen."

"Can you get it for us, please?"

She left the door open, returning shortly with a handful of phone bits. The tiny SIM card was shattered. It would be impossible to get any information from it.

"Should've known," the detective said, sighing. Though it was likely hopeless, she held out a plastic evidence bag and Jenna dropped the pieces inside.

"If you hear from Dub," I told Jenna as we turned to go, "try to find out where he is and let us know, okay? If he's innocent, we can help him."

And if he wasn't, we could take one more killer off the streets.

FIFTY-SIX
IDITAROD

Brigit

It was snowing!

While dogs didn't like water much in its liquid form, turn it into frozen flakes and they're all over it. While Zoe the cat watched from the kitchen window, Brigit ran back and forth all evening in the yard, leaving paw prints in the snow. She'd even rolled around on her back and made a dog angel.

Seth had brought Blast over, too, and while the dogs frolicked, their meal tickets built a snow dog. Frankie helped them. It was only the size of a Chihuahua, but that was the best they could do given the limited supply of the white stuff.

When the humans finally forced the dogs to come inside, Frankie set off for work. The others curled up in front of the fireplace, where three logs were burning. The dogs lay side by side on the rug Megan had bought to cover the wood floor. Zoe slinked up and joined them, taking a preferred spot closer to the fire. *Cats. So arrogant.* The humans snuggled on the couch with mugs of hot chocolate laced with something that smelled like peppermint and made Megan giggle a lot. Brigit was glad to hear her partner giggle. It had been a while.

FIFTY-SEVEN
ICE, ICE BABY

Dub

Dub wore three pairs of socks and had even put his jeans and T-shirt on under his sweats. They reeked of mildew, but what choice did he have? Still he shivered uncontrollably. He tried the key in the ignition again, even though he knew it was a waste of time. Either the van had an engine problem or the battery had frozen. Either way, he couldn't get the motor started to run the heater.

His bones ached from the cold and he could barely feel his fingers and toes. His skin was turning blue. All he had to do was shave his head, learn how to play drums, and he could join the Blue Man Group. No face paint needed.

He grabbed his last remaining pair of clean underwear and slid them over his head, wearing them like a hat. He slid socks over his hands like mittens and hunkered down in his sleeping bag, curling up in a ball on top of the fridge in the cargo bay.

The world was too quiet. It was weird, and kind of scary, too. The roads were too slick to drive on, so there was no traffic noise from Interstate 30. There was only the sound of the sleet accumulating on the van and Dub's jagged breathing, which left puffs of steam hovering inside the van.

"Fuck, it's cold!"

He slid farther down in the sleeping bag, pulling the end closed over his head. He might suffocate, but that would probably be better than freezing to death. He felt a strong urge to cry, but he was afraid the tears would freeze on his cheeks and give him frostbite.

His breathing slowed, and slowed, and slowed some more, until finally the world turned black.

Dub woke early the next morning to an eerie gray glow. He peeked out of the sleeping bag to see the windows of the van covered in a sheet of ice so thick he couldn't see through it. With the iced-over windows and the fridge taking up so much space in the van, he felt claustrophobic.

He checked his phone. Still nothing from Jenna. He sent her another quick text. *Miss you. Are you okay?*

He stared at the phone for a full minute, but no reply came.

He slid out of the sleeping bag and crawled to the driver's seat. He reached over, pulled up the manual lock, and turned the handle to open the door.

It didn't budge.

He pushed on the door. Still nothing.

He rocked back and forth in the seat. Maybe the motion would make the ice fall off the van.

Nope.

Nothing.

This time when he tried to open the door, he put his whole body into it, slamming his shoulder against the door. It was useless. The entire van was coated in a thick sheet of ice.

Dub was trapped inside his own little snow globe of horror.

He threw his head back and laughed. "Fuck *me*!"

He was trapped in ice, but his drinking water supply had dwindled to nothing. It was just as well. He needed the jug for other purposes now.

When he was done, he slid back into his sleeping bag. He thought about things as he lay there. About his mother and her sick, warped relationship with Andro. About Jenna, and how much he cared about her. He hoped she wasn't feeling ashamed about what they'd done, and he prayed she wasn't pregnant. He wondered why she hadn't texted him back. He wanted to see her, but how could he let Jenna see what he'd become? She'd *believed* in him. How could he tell her that he was homeless? That he was broke? That he'd looted a store? He had told her about the burglaries his father had made him go on, the drug buys, but the liquor store? That was all on Dub.

He lay there for an hour or so, sometimes sleeping, sometimes daydreaming of Jenna, his room back at Wes and Trent's place, a fire to warm his toes, when he began to hear cracking and dripping sounds.

The world behind the ice had become brighter.

North Texas was thawing out.

Thank God.

As he stared through the ice, watching it melt, watching the world get lighter and lighter, he made an important decision. He was going to turn himself in. What's the worst they could do to him? He was still a juvenile. They couldn't keep him in jail past the time he turned eighteen, right? Even if they could, prison couldn't be any worse than living like this.

Maybe he could somehow prove that he hadn't been the one to shoot those people in Park Hill. He would tell the police about how Andro had taken his hoodie from him the night before, how Dub had been sleeping in his van the night of the shootings, about hearing the police dog sniffing around the doors. He still had the orange sticker the cop had put on his windshield. The date was written on it in black ink. That was evidence, right?

Relief flooded through him. He feared what might happen, but at least now he had a plan. He slid the orange sticker into his wallet, rolled up his sleeping bag, and waited for the ice to release him.

It was midmorning by the time the ice had thawed enough for Dub to force the door open on the van. He climbed out, taking his sleeping bag with him, and walked to the nearest bus station. He planned to turn himself in, but first he had to go to his mother's place and tell her a final good-bye. She couldn't be a part of Dub's life anymore.

Dub had to do this. He needed . . . what did they call it? Oh, yeah. *Closure*.

Dub didn't worry about running into Andro at the apartment. He knew the drill. Any time Andro smacked Dub's mother around, he'd disappear for a few weeks, give Katrina time to get over the physical pain and some of the emotional pain. The emotional pain never fully went away. But with time it dulled enough that she was willing to set it aside, especially if Andro showed up with meth.

The bus arrived and Dub climbed on, raising his face to the warm air blowing from the heater. He sat down, putting the sleeping bag in the empty seat next to him.

Two transfers and an hour later, he walked up to the door of his mother's apartment, stuck his key in the lock, and jiggled it until the lock released. *Click*.

He pushed the door open. "Mom? You home?"

"She's here," hissed Andro as he pulled Dub down into a headlock again. *"And so am I."*

FIFTY-EIGHT
SLIPPERY SLOPES

Megan

The streets had iced over last night, but as Texas weather was wont to do, it changed drastically this morning. The sun rose warm and bright, putting a quick end to the ice in the places it touched. The shady areas took longer, but between the sunshine and the sand trucks that were out and about, most of the major roads were safely passable. *Good.* I wasn't in the mood to be dealing with traffic accidents.

I found myself wondering where Wade had spent last night. Had he found an open church to hole up in? A homeless shelter? A twenty-four-hour diner? I also found myself wondering where the facts ended and the fiction began with Wade Chandler Mayhew. Was he a violent juvenile delinquent as his record and the evidence seemed to reflect and as his mother portrayed him? Or had her false testimony led to her son receiving harsher sentences than he deserved?

I could only hope that someday the boy would be

found and the facts would be ferreted out. Call me an idealist, but I still hoped for truth and justice.

Brigit and I set out on patrol. As we cruised through the neighborhoods, we spotted the slushy remnants of yesterday evening's snowmen. Scarves and carrot noses and charcoal eyes lay in yards, the snowmen they once graced having committed snowicide. *You're not alone, Frosty.*

My first call of the day involved a frozen pipe that had burst in a shopping center parking lot, creating a potential traffic hazard. I put out a semicircle of orange cones and directed cars around the area until a city works crew came and took over.

My second call involved documenting property damage on a corner lot in the Colonial Country Club neighborhood. Someone had lost control of their car when driving last night and taken out a brick mailbox and a decorative fountain, leaving muddy tire ruts in the yard. The culprit failed to own up to his or her blunder, however, leaving the homeowner furious and facing a bill of a couple of thousand dollars to replace the damaged property. I took down notes for the report I'd complete later.

I was starting to ponder lunch options when dispatch came on the radio, asking for an officer to respond to a call in the neighborhood just north of R. L. Paschal High School. A 9-1-1 call had come in, but the caller had hung up immediately after the dispatcher answered.

I grabbed my mic. "Officer Luz and Brigit responding."

The call could have been a false alarm. Some people had the 9-1-1 emergency number programmed on speed dial and inadvertently hit the number on occasion. Other times, people thought they were having an emergency, but the situation resolved itself before their call was answered. I remember hearing of such a call last Easter, when a father had challenged his sons to see who could

stuff the most marshmallow Peeps in their mouth. The
father won with thirteen, but found himself suddenly
unable to breathe with a baker's dozen of fluffy yellow
chicks lodged in his trachea. He managed to upchuck the
chicks before the dispatcher got to the call.

Of course there was always the possibility that today's
call had been purposely ended, such as in cases of domestic violence where the perpetrator might wrestle a phone
from his victim's hands.

At any rate, any time someone called 9-1-1 and hung
up, the operator attempted to contact the caller. In this
case, when the operator returned the call, there was no
answer.

I pulled my cruiser to a stop in front of the house and
took a look. The house was a single-story white brick
model with cheery, bright red shutters and a wooden
rocking chair on the porch. A line of red-berried holly
bushes flanked the front of the house. A large oak tree sat
in the front yard, its gnarled roots reaching out from its
base for a few feet before disappearing into the earth.

Nothing immediately looked amiss. Though the front
curtains were all pulled closed, that wasn't necessarily
unusual, especially given the frigid temperatures of last
night. Why leave the windows uncovered and let all that
cold in?

My eyes made a quick survey of the surrounding
area. There wasn't much to see. Nobody was out and
about at this time of day in winter. They were either at
work or huddled inside watching soap operas. A sand-
colored Suburban sat across the street a few houses
down. On this side of the street, the only vehicle in sight
was a blue Subaru Impreza parked near the corner.

I climbed out of the patrol car and let Brigit out of her
enclosure in the back, wrapping her leash several times
around my hand to keep her close. The two of us walked
up the winding brick pathway to the door. Brigit had her

head raised, her nose twitching as it scented the air. Whatever she smelled excited her to no end. She launched into a prancing dance, her front legs coming off the ground like a saloon girl performing, her tail wagging so hard it whipped against the back of my legs.

Something had my partner agitated. But what?

Gasp! My heart ping-ponged in my chest when a squirrel darted out from the bushes a few feet away. He ran up the oak tree and squatted on a branch, swishing his bushy tail in indignation as he chastised me and my partner with a call of *chik-chik-chik-chik-chik!* Heck, I was tempted to *chik-chik-chik* him right back. The damn rodent had scared the snot out of me.

As Brigit and I drew closer to the front door, my eyes spotted a small, hand-lettered sign in the front window that spelled out MEEMAW'S DAY CARE in primary colors.

Kids. Hmm.

Maybe one of them had been playing with the telephone and accidentally called 9-1-1. Or maybe one of the kids had gotten his tongue stuck to a frozen barbecue grill in the backyard. Or maybe Meemaw had suffered a coronary. Or maybe I should stop speculating and go to the front door and find out, huh?

Determined to do just that, I took a few steps forward before being yanked to a stop by my partner. Brigit had stopped in her tracks, her ears pricked. Her head made jerky movements to the left and right as she processed whatever auditory data I, as a mere *Homo sapiens*, could not detect. The only thing my ears detected was the *drip-drip-drip* of the icicles melting at the edge of the roof.

Brigit set off to the left, leaning with the effort, pulling hard on the leash. Okay, I knew I was supposed to be the pack leader and take charge, but the truth of the matter was that my gut had begun to churn with a very bad feeling. I'd also learned to trust my partner's instincts, as different as they might be from mine.

Brigit led me around the side of the house. Melting icicles dripped onto my face, head, and shoulders as we sneaked around. Brigit stopped walking and rose to stand on her hind legs at a window.

Wait. I could hear something now. Was it a child crying?

I stepped closer to take a look. Through a small gap in the curtains, I saw three young children huddled in the center of a bed. All of them appeared terribly frightened, one sucking his thumb with tears rolling down his face, the other two bawling outright. The door to the bedroom was closed.

I supposed it was possible that these three children were in time-out, having done some minor act of mischief that had gotten on Meemaw's last nerve. But something didn't feel right about this.

Brigit dropped down from the window and yanked me once again, pulling me along the side of the house to the back. We circled around and she led me to a back door with a square window in the upper half. The curtains on this window were lace, giving me a mottled view into the house.

Holy shit.

Was I seeing double?

FIFTY-NINE
A BAD SMELL

Brigit

Brigit didn't like the scents her nose picked up at this house. The place reeked of human fear pheromones, an olfactory cacophony of them coming from the crying children, an older woman, and the boy who'd fed her the beef jerky.

Her nose detected the presence of another man, too. She recognized his odor. She'd picked it up at the apartment Megan and Detective Luz had taken her to the other day, the one where the lady lived, the one that the beef jerky boy had once lived in, too.

This man smelled of sweat and booze and meth. The meth smell was especially strong. In fact, he probably had some on him right now. She sniffed again at the door. Yep, definitely meth.

She plunked her hindquarters down on the back patio and issued her passive alert.

SIXTY
ARM WRESTLE

Dub

His left eye throbbed. It was swollen almost shut. He couldn't see much out of it, and what he could see was blurry. With that solid hit Andro had delivered with his brass knuckles, Dub wondered if he'd ever see straight again. But no sense thinking too much about it. Dub had a feeling he wasn't going to be alive much longer anyway. He'd seen Andro on violent highs before, but today Andro had reached a new level.

Before Andro had dragged him along on this home invasion, he'd slammed Dub's head so hard against the wall in the apartment it had left a hole in the Sheetrock. Dub's mom had begged Andro to stop, but that only made Andro madder. He'd backhanded her across the face and she'd fallen, hitting hit her head on the breakfast bar with a sickening *crack*. Her lifeless body was the last thing Dub saw before his father dragged him from the apartment and out to his car.

Andro had held a gun on him the entire way here. Dub had considered jumping from the moving car, but his father had told him he'd shoot him if he tried to get away. Dub didn't doubt it. Knowing Andro, he'd not only shoot Dub but run his body over with the car, too.

Dub also stayed with Andro because he feared what Andro was going to do. He knew his father had shot that couple in their home. He was afraid his father was going to hurt someone else now. Dub had to do whatever he could to prevent that from happening.

That's how he'd ended up here, in this woman's home, with Andro.

Andro had dragged Dub up to the house and waved a hand at a sign in the front window. MEEMAW'S DAY CARE. "See that? These old bitches always got lots of nice stuff."

Andro had been wrong. This woman didn't have much at all. Her furniture was old and her clothes looked like the kind you'd buy at a discount store. And if she was rich she wouldn't be babysitting children at her house for money. Andro was a dumbass.

The children had been terrified when Andro, posing as a utility worker, had forced his way into the house. At least Dub had been able to convince Andro to let him put the kids in a bedroom where they'd be safer and wouldn't witness whatever brutality Andro planned for the old lady. Of course Andro didn't give a shit about the kids' safety, but Dub had convinced him they'd get in the way.

Dub had grabbed a phone in the bedroom and dialed 9-1-1, but had to drop the receiver back in place when Andro stepped to the door and told him to hurry his ass up.

Dub hated this feeling of helplessness, of not knowing what to do. If he fought his father, Andro would shoot him and Dub wouldn't be able to protect anyone. But if he didn't fight his father, what might Andro do? It was so much—*too much*—to deal with.

Andro stepped in front of the woman, who had pulled herself back in the corner of her couch as if trying to disappear into it. "Where's your silver?"

On the television to their left, the noon news was on, that bimbo reporter with the big boobs looking out at them from the screen, talking about last night's ice storm. Dressed in a pink winter coat with fluffy pink trim, she stood next to a snowwoman built to look like her, with two double-D-sized snowballs on its chest. Like the reporter, the snowwoman wore a pink knit cap and a pink scarf.

Out here in the real world, Meemaw looked up at Andro, her eyes blinking fast like she couldn't believe what she was seeing. "I don't have any silver!" she cried. "We've never had any!"

"You're lying to me!" Andro raised his right hand, which held the gun. "I know it. Now tell me where your silver is or I'll put a bullet in your head and find it myself!"

Dub couldn't take this anymore. He'd probably die here today, bleed out on this woman's rug, but he couldn't just stand here and do nothing. He'd seen Andro beat his mother too many times. Even if it meant losing his own life, he wasn't about to watch Andro beat this innocent woman.

"No!" Dub rushed Andro from the side, grabbed his father's arm with both hands, and forced it upward.

Bang! The gun fired a hole in the ceiling. White dust and drywall dropped to the rug.

The woman shrieked as Dub and his father fell to the floor, fighting for the gun. Andro gave Dub an elbow to the jaw, the hit so hard he'd probably never eat solid foods again.

The woman stood frozen by her couch, her hands over her face like she was trying to catch the scream coming out of her mouth.

"Go!" Dub yelled at her. "Get help!"

She ran out of the room.

Andro and Dub rolled across the floor. Dub gained an advantage when he slammed Andro up against the entertainment center. *Bam!* DVDs fell from the shelves. *The Wiggles. Shrek. How to Train Your Dragon.* Dub had liked that one.

Andro grabbed Dub by the shoulders and rolled him over onto his back. He swung his knee into Dub's gut so hard it knocked the wind out of him and made him retch. Before Dub could recover, Andro raised the gun over his head and brought it down on Dub's temple. Dub's head exploded in pain. His brain wobbled inside his head. *Shit!* The vision through his right eye was blurry now, too. *How could he fight a man he could barely see?*

When his eye cleared, he saw Andro standing over him. Andro smiled a sick, evil smile and aimed his gun at Dub's face. Dub turned his head toward the frozen snow boobs on the television. If he were going to die, he would not give his father the satisfaction of seeing the fear on his face.

Jingle-jingle.

Dub saw a flash of black and tan in his peripheral vision.

Bang!

Arf!

A woman's voice cried, "No!"

Holy shit! Had Andro just shot a dog?

SIXTY-ONE
GO, DOG! GO!

Megan

The *bang* reverberated through the house as I rushed forward. The man had fired the gun again.

My mind whirled in panic.

Was Brigit hit?

PLEASE, GOD, NO!

The dog had been faster than me, of course. The instant I'd kicked in the back door she'd been off and running, rushing past the old woman who was heading toward us. By the time I'd made it through the kitchen and into the living room, Brigit had tackled the man I presumed to be Andro to the floor. There was no blood on her fur. *Thank God!*

The man wriggled and writhed under her, his gun still clutched in his hand.

Not for long.

I whipped my baton from my belt and flicked my wrist to extend it. *Snap!* With an air-splitting *swish*, I brought the baton down on the man's forearm. *Whap!*

"Drop the gun!" I yelled.

He didn't drop it.

Whap! Whap!

I felt the man's arm fracture under my stick, but still he didn't let go. People on drugs seemed almost immune to pain. This guy had likely premedicated with crystal meth.

I supposed I could have shot the guy now and been totally justified. But I'd seen him terrorize the woman on the couch, seen the boy I now knew as Wade Mayhew try to stop him. A quick and easy death would be too good for this asshole.

I stomped and kicked at his hand now, my steel-toed loafers effectively prying his fingers from the gun. When the gun was free, I kicked the gun itself, sending it sailing across the wood floor out of his reach.

Other than a bullet, the only way to disable someone like him was with pepper spray. I yanked the canister from my belt, ordered Brigit off the man, and hollered, "Everyone back!"

The woman, who'd been watching from the doorway, scrambled back into the kitchen. Dub could only manage to get to his hands and knees. He crawled toward the kitchen, too. "Here, doggie!" he called to Brigit, his voice weak and raspy. "Here, doggie!"

She looked up at me for direction. I motioned for her to go with him.

Averting my face, I held my breath, closed my eyes tight, and pushed the button.

Pshhhhh.

The cries that came from the man at my feet gave me no small amount of pleasure. Why not give him a double dose?

Pshhhhh.

"Aaaaaaaah!" he wailed, the knocking sounds telling me he was writhing blindly on the floor.

As my *coup de grâce*, I treated him to a final spray in

the tune of shave-and-a-haircut-two-bits. *Pshhh psh-psh psh-pshhh, pshhh pshhh.*

With my eyes still closed, I yanked my handcuffs from my belt, waved a hand in front of my face to clear the air, and opened my eyes. Enough of the spray lingered in the air to burn my eyes, but I continued to hold my breath and was at least able to get the guy's hands cuffed before backing away, gasping for air. He continued to squirm and roll back and forth on the ground. When he did, his wallet slid out of his back pocket, two inches of broken rolo chain dangling from it.

Aha! Samuelson murder case. Exhibit A.

Eyes watering, I stepped to the kitchen doorway, pulled my gun from my belt now, and kept it aimed at Andro. It was doubtful he could cause any more trouble now that he'd been cuffed and sprayed, but better safe than sorry.

Terrified wails came from the bedroom down the hall. *Poor kids.* They had no idea what was going on out here. That was probably a good thing, though.

"Can I go check on the children?" asked the woman, whom I knew only as Meemaw.

"Sure." After the woman left, I glanced down at Dub, who lay curled up on his side on the linoleum, hugging himself as if he knew nobody else would and crying silently as he stared off into space.

I knelt down next to him and put a hand on his shoulder, unsure what to say. Fortunately, Brigit knew exactly what to say to the boy, and she spoke with her tongue.

SIXTY-TWO
HIGH-SODIUM DIET

Brigit

Slup-slup-slup-slup.

Brigit did her best to lick away all of the boy's salty tears, but they seemed to keep coming and coming and coming, as if he'd saved up a lifetime's worth of them.

Slup-slup-slup-slup.

The boy reached up and wrapped his arms around her neck. No sense making it hard on the kid. She flopped down next to him and continued her ministrations. *Slup-slup-slup.* Too bad tears didn't come in multiple flavors, like chicken and turkey and beef. *Slup-slup.*

Megan reached out to the boy, putting a hand on his hair and smoothing the cowlick Brigit had premoistened with her saliva. For some reason, the gesture made the boy cry even harder.

Brigit continued to tend to the boy until paramedics arrived and loaded him onto a stretcher. Once the ambulance had taken the boy away, Megan escorted her back to the cruiser and offered her an entire package of liver treats. Brigit wouldn't have believed it before, but maybe you could get too much of a good thing. Rather than risk horking the treats back up in the car, she stopped herself at a dozen.

"Good girl!" Megan gave Brigit a kiss on the snout and ruffled her ears before leaning down to whisper in her ear. "You're the best partner ever!"

SIXTY-THREE
YOU *CAN* GO HOME AGAIN

Dub

Two days later, Dub sat in his bed in the hospital. The doctors had put a cold pack on his black eye and stitched up the cuts on his face and head. They said his organs hadn't been permanently damaged, but his abdomen still felt bruised from the kick Andro had delivered a few nights ago. He'd suffered a concussion, too, and they'd monitored him for signs of a brain bleed. Luckily, there'd been none.

You're not as tough as you thought, Andro.

So many people had been in and out of his hospital room in the last twenty-four hours it was crazy. A bunch of nurses and doctors. A detective Officer Luz had been working with on the burglary cases. A social worker. An attorney who worked juvenile cases.

The bimbo reporter with the big boobs had come to the hospital to interview him, but the doctors had turned her away. She made a report from the parking lot anyway. Dub saw it on the six o'clock news. She called him a hero.

He didn't feel like a hero, though.

He just felt like someone who wanted the world to suck less.

He had no idea where he'd be going when he was let out of the hospital, and nobody seemed to be able to tell him for sure. The social worker and attorney told him things were still being worked out and not to worry.

How could he not worry? This was *his life*. He felt like a stray dog in a pound, stuck in a cage, waiting to see whether someone would come along and adopt him or whether he'd be stuck there forever.

Officer Luz spoke with his teachers and the administrators at Paschal High. It wasn't clear yet if he'd go back to the school, or that he'd get full credit for his courses since he'd missed so many classes, but she'd rounded up the homework he'd missed and brought it to him at the hospital. She'd plunked his laptop computer down on the bedside table, along with the backpack and history book she'd found in his mother's apartment when she'd gone there with the crime scene team to look for evidence against Leandro Silva.

"Are you kidding me?" Dub said. "You expect me to work on homework in the hospital?"

"Yes," she'd said firmly. "I do."

She was pushing him. *He kind of liked her for that.*

"There's something else you and I need to discuss," she said.

"What is it?"

"You and Jenna."

He felt his face heat up. Megan looked a little embarrassed, too.

"You've been through enough already," she said. "I know what happened between you two. Be careful, okay? Don't screw up your life and hers, too."

"I won't," he promised. And he meant it.

It was ten in the morning on his third day in the hospital when a knock sounded at the open door of his room. He looked up to see his mother standing in the doorway.

"Hi, Wade." She walked slowly up to his bed. "You . . . um . . . you look like you're healing up real good."

It was true. He was doing well with the physical injuries. His emotional injuries, though? He'd need way more time to deal with those.

"How about you?" he asked.

"I'm . . . okay." She sat down on the end of his bed and looked down at the covers. "I never should have gotten back with Andro."

Ya think? He didn't say the words out loud. He wanted to lash out at his mother for what she'd done, but what good would that do? If he'd figured anything out over the last few days, it was that his mother was one hot mess. His feelings had been all over the place. He'd gone from wanting to protect her, to hating her, and now, to pitying her. Whatever connection he'd had to her, whatever obligation he'd felt, whatever hopes he'd had that one day she'd act like a real mother, all of that was gone now. In an odd way, it was a relief to finally accept that reality, to break the chains that had bound him.

Katrina took the edge of the sheet in her hand and worked it nervously between her fingers. "I'm going to rehab. I leave this afternoon."

"Good luck. I hope it works this time." He meant it. For her sake.

She looked at him with eyes full of pain and sorrow and shame and regret. "I'm sorry, Wade. I really am."

You know what? He believed her.

She stood and walked to the head of his bed, bending down to give him a soft kiss on the forehead. "I love you, Wade."

He offered her a soft smile. "Back at ya, Mom."

His mother had been gone only a few minutes when Officer Luz and Brigit came to the room. "Knock-knock."

Dub raised a hand to wave them inside. "Come on in."

Megan stepped up beside the bed. "I was just on the phone with your defense attorney and the prosecutor. Looks like things are finally sorted out. You won't be facing any charges."

He exhaled a long breath. "Good to know."

"And as far as where you go from here," she hiked a thumb toward the door, where Trent and Wes now stood. "These two gluttons for punishment say they'd be happy to take you back so long as you're fitted with a tracking device."

Dub's laugh made his ribs twinge. As much as he'd wanted a mother, these two men weren't a bad substitute. Besides, Wes had man boobs. That kind of made him a mom, right?

Trent came into the room first, a bag in his hands. "Hey, there, Dub."

"Hey."

"Surprise!" Wes seesawed the plastic food container in his hands. "I made your favorite lasagna."

"Great," Dub lied. The only good thing about running away was that he hadn't had to eat that horrible lasagna.

Wes set the food container down on the table next to Dub's laptop and leaned both ways, looked at Dub's bandages and bruises and stitches. He opened his mouth several times as if wanting to say something, but closed it each time as if he couldn't find the right words. Finally, he just reached out, took Dub's hand in his, and gave it a squeeze.

Trent stepped up to put a reassuring hand on Wes's shoulder. When he let go, he pulled a small foam basketball and a plastic over-the-door hoop from the bag in his hands. "You up for shooting some hoops, Dub?"

SIXTY-FOUR
PUPPY LOVE

Megan

It was a busy week.

While Dub recovered from his injuries, Leandro Silva was treated for fractures in both his radius and ulna, as well as several broken fingers, and taken to jail.

The remnant of chain on Silva's wallet was found to match the section extracted from the neck of Brian Keith Samuelson. Multiple individually bagged hits of meth were found in Silva's Subaru, which was discovered parked down the street from Meemaw's Day Care. Fingerprint analysis indicated that Samuelson had touched each of the bags in Silva's possession. This evidence told us that Silva had killed Samuelson for his meth stash.

After days in ICU, Mr. Prentiss rallied and was released from the hospital, expected to eventually make a full recovery from his gunshot wounds. He and his wife positively identified Leandro Silva in a lineup. When I learned that Silva had worked as a baggage handler at DFW airport, I passed this information on to Mr. and Mrs. Prentiss. Turns out they'd loaned their pricey Moncler suitcase to their daughter, who hadn't removed their address label from the bag before checking it for her flight. Silva had evidently picked his burglary victims based on both the location of their homes and the quality of their luggage. Of course he hadn't realized when he'd ripped the address label from the bag that it wasn't Mr. and Mrs. Prentiss who'd boarded the flight, but their daughter. Moreover, the gun Silva had used in both the Prentiss burglary and the invasion at Meemaw's Day Care was identified by the Harringtons as one of the firearms stolen from their garage. With so much evidence against him, Leandro Silva was looking at a life sentence and then some.

The fourth looter was located and brought in after his girlfriend, who lived at the same apartment complex as Gallegos and Duong, placed a call to police. That would teach Marquise Polk to step out on his woman.

All in all, it was a good week for law enforcement.

Late Saturday morning, Seth, Blast, Brigit, and I set off for Wes and Trent's house in Fairmount with a surprise for Dub. That surprise currently stood in the backseat of Seth's Nova, her tail wagging tentatively as she looked out the window, her furry brow furrowed, trying to figure out where she was being taken.

"It's okay, girl," I reassured her, adding a scratch under the chin as well. "We've got a surprise for you."

I'd gone to the animal shelter earlier in the week to see if they had adoption records for Velvet, the dog who'd been seized years ago when Dub had been arrested for buying meth for Andro. The staff had provided me with the name, address, and phone number of the man who'd adopted her. Though I'd merely hoped the new owner would allow Dub a visit with the dog, the man had hinted that he'd be willing to hand over the dog if Dub could take her.

"I have a new job and travel extensively," the man

said. "It's not fair for Velvet to spend so much time at the kennel."

I'd checked with Trent and Wes, who were thrilled with the idea of reuniting Dub with his beloved pet.

Trent, Wes, and Dub were shooting baskets in their driveway when we pulled up. I was glad Dub felt up to having some fun. He deserved to enjoy what was left of his childhood.

Jenna sat on the front steps with a book. Looked like her parents had relented and let her date Dub now that he'd proved himself a hero.

Dub glanced over at the car, a quizzical look on his face. Amazing how much younger he looked with a clean-shaven face and the weight of the world lifted from his shoulders.

I climbed out of the passenger seat, opened the back door, and took Velvet's leash in my hand. She hopped down to the curb.

Dub took a few slow steps toward the car, his eyes wide as if he couldn't believe what he was seeing. "Velvet?" When he realized that, *no*, his eyes were not playing tricks on him, he tossed the basketball aside and ran all-out toward the dog, dropping to his knees in front of her. "Velvet! It's you!"

Recognizing the boy she'd once called her own, Velvet pounced on him, licking his face from ear to ear, her body wriggling with unfettered glee.

Wes scurried up and fluttered his hands. "Careful, Dub! Careful! You're not all healed yet!"

The laughter coming from Dub's mouth said his injuries were no longer an issue.

Once Wes was convinced the dog's rambunctious affection posed no risk to Dub, he turned his attention to me and Seth. "Would you two like to stay for lunch?"

The bladed hands Trent waved side to side behind Wes

told us that the best course of action would be to decline. If the smell of the lasagna Wes had brought to the hospital was any indication, he wasn't in line to be America's next Top Chef.

"Thanks," I said, "but we've already made other plans."

When Dub and the dog concluded their raucous reunion, Dub stood and looked me in the eye. "Thanks," he said. "For . . . everything."

"Anytime," I reached out and ruffled his curls, "kid."

Seth and I took the dogs for playtime at the dog park. They tussled with their usual buddies, introduced themselves to a few dogs they hadn't met before, and played a dozen games of fetch with a tennis ball. Once they'd burned off their excess energy, we loaded them back into the car and returned to my new home.

Inside, I stuck my head into the hallway. The door to Frankie's room stood open. Dressed in her Fort Worth Whoop-Ass uniform, she scurried around inside, rounding up her skates, helmet, and pads, and packing them into a bag. Zoe attempted to climb into the bag, too, and Frankie had to shoo her out of it. "Scram, cat."

As much as I'd wanted a place to myself, I had to admit that having a roommate had its benefits. Frankie left the porch light on for me. She vacuumed the fur off the futon. She'd even done our grocery shopping after her shift ended early Friday morning. Making lunch was the least I could do in return.

"Hey," I called to my roommate. "Want something to eat before you h-head off to your bout?"

"Depends." Her nose scrunched. "Is it going to have tofu or quinoa or flaxseed in it?"

Those were items I'd put on our list. Her contributions had included Zingers, potato chips, and Dr. Pepper.

"Eating a vegetable won't kill you."

She unscrunched her nose and chuckled. "Count me in. The only thing I hate more than health food is cooking. *Ugh.*"

Seth and I went to the kitchen. While he unleashed the dogs, refilled Brigit's water bowl, and poured drinks, I grabbed a loaf of French bread from the pantry, cut it in half lengthwise, and loaded it with fresh veggies and deli mustard. I cut the oversized veggie sub into thirds and put each piece on a plate, adding a handful of potato chips on the side. *Uh-oh.* Looked like Frankie's bad habits were rubbing off on me.

While the three of us ate together at the dinette, Frankie filled us in on the rules of roller derby. "You ever want to give it a try," she told me, "just say the word."

"I might take you up on that." After all, I'd taken down a cold-blooded killer. Roller derby would be a cinch compared to that, right?

We finished lunch and Frankie grabbed her things to go. I wasn't sure what the appropriate terminology was for wishing her and her team success. *Break a leg? Break a wheel? Bust a kneecap?* I settled for "Good luck," hoping it didn't jinx her.

Once she'd gone, Seth and I went out back. The dogs lay down side by side to nap on the sun-warmed patio, while Seth and I climbed into the hammock together. He wrapped his arm around my back and I settled my head on his strong, firm shoulder. We lay there for a long time in silence, the hammock swaying softly, the shadows of the clouds playing over us.

As relieved as I was that Leandro Silva was behind bars and Dub was in a safe, nurturing home, I would've been much happier had the tragedies of the past few days never occurred at all. But the battle of good versus evil had been going on since the dawn of time, and it wasn't going to stop anytime soon. I could only hope that I'd continue to play some small part in making the world a better place.

Seth toyed with my hair. "You okay?" he asked softly.

After everything he'd been through himself, both as an explosives specialist in Afghanistan and a fireman here, he must have sensed my emotional turmoil. I might not understand why people felt compelled to do the bad things they did, but if I'd taken anything away from this investigation it was that we should appreciate those who care for us and treat them with love and respect and kindness. We should seize the moments of happiness we are offered, hang on to them with all our might, squeeze every last bit of joy we can from life. Given these epiphanies, there was no sense in postponing the chance to share some pleasure with the man I was falling for, right?

"I *will* be okay," I told Seth. "As soon as you kiss me."

"Is that an order, officer?"

"Yes," I said. "If you don't obey I'll have to cuff you."

His green eyes flashed and a grin tugged at his lips. "That could be fun."

He gave me a deep, warm kiss, leaving me wanting more when he pulled away.

"Let's go inside." I slid off the hammock and took his hand. "It's time for that sleepover."